Darkest Abandon

THE NETWORK SERIES
BOOK ELEVEN

KATIE CROSS

Chapter One

Flecks of gold filled Merrick's eyes. He smiled at me, drawing my gaze to the crinkles along his smile. Lines looped the edges of his full lips in familiar pathways, and adoration infused every hint of him. I memorized him again.

The feel of his hands in mine.

The reverence in his gaze.

Sniffles abounded through the crowd. Northern winter pinched their cheeks, reddened their noses. Somewhere behind us, Jacqueline calmed her streaming tears enough to quiet her hiccuping sobs. Breath billowed like steam, winding into the open mountain sky. The serrated rocks, imposing and reassuring, surrounded our hand-fasting in the meadow outside his childhood home.

The sensation of Merrick's hands holding mine, the way he whispered the words, "I give my heart to you, Bianca Marie Monroe, for as long as our love shall last," in a perfect mimicry of the High Witch of Balmberg Castle, swept my feet from beneath me.

With what felt like all of Alkarra watching us below an extravagant arbor of blooming winter flowers, and next to the High Witch of Balmberg Castle, I leaned closer. My heart pattered as I breathed the same.

"I give my heart to you, Merrick Hughes, for as long as our love shall last."

"Which is forever," he whispered in a definitive break from our pre-planned script—the only part of the ceremony over which Jacqueline had no control.

Grinning, I asked, "What?"

"The words I believe you're looking for," Merrick said in a comedically loud whisper all could hear, "are *as long as the love lasts, which is forever.* You can do it again, if you need to. I'd like this point very understood."

A ripple of laughter rolled through the sea of loving faces. Amidst it, and from the front, came Papa's low rumble, and Grandfather's wheezy delight.

My lips bunched into a poorly-suppressed smile. I whispered, "Which is forever," and the struggle to stop him from jerking me against his chest and dipping me into a kiss warred in his eyes. I smirked.

He smoldered.

We locked in a timeless and loving stare while the High Witch of Balmberg Castle spoke over us.

"I bless this handfasting between Merrick and Bianca for as long as their love shall last." He gave a wry smile, "Which, I mean to say, is forever."

Merrick laughed as he wrapped a hand around my waist and finally yanked me into his arms. I went willingly, ignoring the roar of his cheering family, the catcalls from the attending Masters, and the growing fervor behind Jacqueline's delighted sobs.

Melting in his arms, I set my fingertips on his stubbled jaw, his mouth a breath from mine.

"Forever," I reasserted.

He sealed our handfasting with a kiss.

Chapter Two

T he real torture began twenty minutes later.

Jacqueline slid into handfasting-priestess-mode, and the rapid fire demands started. "Get to your position!" she hissed under her breath, shooing us away from the arbor. Merrick rolled his eyes, set a hand on the small of my back, and led me away.

"She's a nuisance," he muttered.

I didn't argue.

The entirety of our family, friends, and neighbors shifted from the outside arbor area to inside a warmed, temporary tent that peaked at three places in the middle. A piping hot fire kept the interior and the food warm. Dishes burdened half a dozen tables atop stylish, ironed sapphire tablecloths. A winter feast awaited the guests, buying Merrick and me a few minutes to breathe.

He guided me into his mother's cottage, which was empty. Inside, I drew in my first real breath since this day began. No more witches staring at my simple dress, my curled, loose hair I hadn't gone to elaborate or complicated lengths to style, and my comfortable fur-lined boots.

Your ensemble is too simple! Jacqueline had wailed last night.

I ignored her.

Firmly.

Alone in the cottage, I tipped my head against the wall, closed my eyes, and drew in the quiet. Hughes family dinners, events, traditions, and a morass of requirements so prodigious I could barely remember them filled the last several weeks. This final meal after the handfasting ceremony would close the celebrations. Our part was nearly done.

Merrick stayed close while loosening a button at his neck. He grimaced. "I'm sorry, B, but there's only this dinner and then we're done."

"Are you *certain*? Your mother once spoke about after-events. Like breakfasts, and a meal *I* was supposed to fix?"

"I said no."

"Really?"

"Really. It's too much."

There could be no greater handfasting gift than *that*. "Take my heart," I said.

He scoffed. "I already have it."

I peered outside around a curtain, inspecting the almost-empty grounds. Could I go barefoot across the grass? It called to me. Jacqueline enchanted the dead, yellowed grass a pillowy, fluffy emerald right before the ceremony began.

It looks less sad and beaten this way, she had said. *We can't have the word* ragged *applied to anything that my name touches!*

The ironed tablecloths, folded napkins, and silverware that served the food hardly began to encompass the depth of her detailed preparations. She'd be exhausted for a week after this.

This rare opportunity to think highlighted a sense of exhaustion that weighed inside. For days we skittered this way and that, shoved into and out of places and things until, finally, the words had been said.

Freedom should have followed, but staring at the amassed crowd through the tent slips, I understood the necessity of *some* socialization. All these witches came to celebrate our union. Besides, the distraction took the edge off a creeping depression and silenced a voice that said, *You took a life weeks ago, why should you get to enjoy prosperity?*

Tyrant, I called it. I silenced him with a moderate struggle.

For now.

"What happens after dinner?" I asked, eager to turn the direction of my thoughts.

Merrick removed his coat, tossing it on the back of a chair, and rolled up his sleeves. He eyed me, sent a wink. My belly ignited with butterflies and heat. "Exactly what you want to happen." Soberly, he added, "Silence, food, sleep, and not another soul in sight."

I laughed. He knew me too well.

"Promise?"

Chortling, he asked, "You think I'd rather be here than in a quiet room with you, tucked up against me, in bed?"

The idea had delicious merit.

"Fine." I sighed. "I can do one more hour."

"Ninety minutes."

He curled his arm around my waist again, pulling me close with a kiss and a growl that promised more—so much *more*. Merrick knew how to play this game, because he tantalized me breathless, his warm lips a vow. When he released me, I stumbled, struggling to control my watery knees. His arrogant grin didn't help. Nor the way his sleeves bunched around powerful and still-tanned forearms.

Anticipation warmed me through and through.

"Ninety minutes," I muttered, because amidst that chaos lurked my friends and family, too. Seeing them gave me a boon. I held up a finger. "But you have to feed me as part of those ninety minutes, and I'm taking my boots off in here. If Jacqueline makes one comment about my lack of shoes, I'm transporting away."

"Agreed," he said with a seriousness that honored my intensity.

With his hand in mine, and following a high-pitched whistle from Jacqueline that was our cue to join the feast, we stepped out of the house, crossed the yard, and returned to the party. A chorus of rising cheers and elevated wine glasses followed, and I braced myself for ninety more minutes.

After that?

Blissful oblivion.

* * *

Merrick stationed me in the middle of the tent instead of dragging me from table to table, as Jacqueline originally planned. Keeping me in one spot allowed witches to meander up on their own time. I stole bites in between conversations, grateful I didn't have to wander.

A squeal, a pair of freckled arms, and luscious strawberry locks preceded a rigorous embrace. When I found my balance, Priscilla pulled away, tears brightening her jade eyes. Laughing, she held me close again. "You are so beautiful."

"Thank you, Cilla."

Michelle stepped forward. Her daughters, Sanna and Isadora, remained at home with Nicolas, giving Michelle a much-deserved break away from her forester-life toil in Letum Wood. She pulled me into a warm hug. "Truly beautiful," Michelle asserted in her quiet way. "That arbor was really amazing."

"Stunning," Priscilla insisted, eyes wide. "Who made it? The winterflowers sparkled with silver, and some of the pearlescent ones opened and closed. Did you see the ivy? It never stopped moving! So lovely. The white ribbons and bows decorating the posts! I've never seen anything like it."

Ruefully, I admitted, "Jacqueline. All of this is her handiwork. She's truly something."

Merrick agreed with a, "She's *something* all right," under his breath.

"She's wonderful," Michelle agreed.

Leda's white-blonde hair appeared on Priscilla's right, followed by Hiddleston's towering figure and swinging black locks, bound into a wide ponytail that trailed down his back. They broke into our group with smiles and joyful exclamations. Leda's skinny arms engulfed me. She held on for a second longer than I expected.

"It's about time," she whispered.

I could only smile.

Is it time? Tyrant asked, invading my joyful reverie. *Do you deserve this?*

My heart shook as I stuffed him away. Again. Tyrant's voice had a slight pitch that sounded a little like Ricardo Gallo, the witch I had captured and . . . well . . . led to his death. His family, too.

Of their own accord, my fingers reached for Merrick. A natural response these days when life and Tyrant overwhelmed me. Merrick was the only steady retaliation to Tyrant's insistence that I didn't deserve happiness after what I'd done.

A child died, and you killed her father after, Tyrant reminded me. *Their entire family died.*

My soul shuddered.

The instant Merrick's fingers squeezed mine, Tyrant vanished. Merrick stood behind me, within reach as he jested with two Masters. Dressed up, and not covered in blood or weapons, they masqueraded as a normal group of friends. Aside from their raucous ribbing about tonight, I might not have known them.

Scarlett approached with Aurora at her side. My friends cleared away, seeking food, while I spoke with our High Priestess. After they left, Kalli, Merrick's mother, slid into place near my side to coordinate introductions to a broad group of distant cousins. Her presence mitigated awkward small talk until the dinner fervor simmered.

Sometime between my eyes expressing get-me-out-of-here-before-I-obliterate-this-handfasting and I-never-want-to-see-Jacqueline-again, Merrick wrapped my hand in his. No one approached with teary smiles or beaming questions, so I reached for a glass of water.

He asked out of the corner of his mouth, "Want to get out of here?"

"Yes."

"Follow me."

Setting the water aside, I trailed him through the tables. My eyes skimmed each one, seeking the only faces I hadn't spoken with yet. Where was Papa? Grandfather? Regina? Merrick pulled me behind a partition at the back of the tent, separating us from the crowd. Away from the anxious small talk and staring eyes, I breathed easier.

"Thank you."

He grinned. "There's more."

My face dropped. "What?"

"Ah," came a familiar voice from the shadows. "There she is."

Papa emerged from the other side of the partition, Grandfather and Regina at his side. Merrick squeezed my fingers.

"I thought you'd want to speak with them away from everyone else."

My heart melted. With meaning, I mouthed, "Thank you," and fell into Papa's waiting arms. He clutched me for a full minute, not saying a word, and I held fast. Here, Tyrant also dissipated.

When Papa loosened his hold, tears soaked his lashes. He tucked a strand of hair behind my ear. His husky voice broke. "You look just like Marie. I almost thought you *were* her for a second. The gods, I'm so happy for you. I love you."

His loaded emotion cut through my heart. I pressed a kiss to his cheek. The balm of so many friends and loved ones soothed the ache of Mama missing my handfasting day.

"I love you, Papa."

Papa relinquished me to Grandfather's grasp, swiping his cheeks with the back of his hand. Regina snuggled to his side, patting his shoulder, an arm around his back. A loving smile filled her face as she regarded me.

"Beautiful," she whispered.

Grandfather's steady grip and loving voice wobbled as he held me. "This is one of the most prized moments of my life. Thank you, my dear, for letting me be part of it. You are the greatest gift I've ever known."

"I love you," I whispered.

Releasing him with an extra squeeze, I turned to

Regina. She hooked an arm around me and jerked her chin toward Merrick, eyes sparkling. "Watch this one. He's a real problem to live with, but I think you can handle it."

Merrick's jaw dropped. "On my handfasting day, Regina! Really?"

She grinned.

He yanked me back, glowering. "Enough of that!"

Jacqueline called over the gentle pandemonium in the tent. "The dance floor is open outside!" I wrestled a groan. Papa's eyes laughed at me.

Merrick kept me tucked under his arm when he asked Papa. "Think you can help us make an escape? Between the former Head of Protectors and the former Head Master, I assume you two can come up with something?"

Papa stuck his hands in his pockets and rocked back on his heels. "If pressed, we could distract your guests . . . I *suppose.*"

"It's not the guests that concern me," he muttered. "It's my sister."

Regina laughed. "I'll handle Jacqueline. Since working with her in the castle, I've learned how to deal with her. You and Bianca go."

Before Regina strode away as my savior, I wrapped her in the tightest hug I'd ever managed.

"It's the best gift you could have given me."

Regina winked before she disappeared. Papa withdrew a hand from his pocket, elevated it. Pinched between two fingers was an ornate, wrought-iron key.

"For you."

Papa handed it to Merrick, who accepted with a silent question in his wrinkled brow.

"You know it."

Merrick's eyes widened. "Is it . . . The Underroot?"

"Yes, it is." To me, Papa said, "This key opens a quiet little place no one knows about, and where Merrick's sister can't find you. Here." He withdrew a paper, curled into a ball in his pocket. I opened it, smoothing between two fingers. The vague directions meant nothing to me, but Merrick beamed.

The Underroot? I longed to ask. Merrick pocketed the key.

"Thank you, Derek. She'll love it."

Papa nodded. "I know. You have it for a week. If I were you, I'd stay away for at least that long. Sounds like Jacqueline will need the recovery time."

Fireflies danced above an icy pond, winking in and out of existence like tiny, blinking eyes. I stared, riveted at their there-but-gone forms. Along the pond edge, frozen slivers jutted toward the still-liquid interior like lightning knives. At the center of this charming pond, darkness gathered in a circle, endlessly deep. Wrinkled lily pads floated on top, forming a trail to a thatched-roof cottage, where candle flames pirouetted in a windowpane.

"Charming," I whispered.

A wooden door filled the wall, swept by loose flowers framing the edge. A single vine, with a bloom clinging to the bottom, bobbed in the doorway. The cottage was cradled in the gargantuan roots of a giant Letum Wood tree. The pond blocked our way, offering no visible entry point except for a small stoop, decorated by a rectangular rug and surrounded by water.

The trees welcomed me.

She returns.

The joy is here.

You belong to us.

Eyes aglow with the fireflies, Merrick said, "We have to transport over," and held onto me as he issued the spell. We arrived in less than a blink. When my foot alighted on the rug, the door swung inward. Grasping me, Merrick swept me into his arms. I laughed, delighted. The easy grace in which he carried me across the doorway was as blood-warming as his smile.

The door shut behind us. All at once, every candle in the underroot cottage illuminated. Their sparkling persuasion took my breath away.

"What is this place?"

"We call it The Underroot." He waved a hand. "For obvious reasons."

"Very original."

"A Protector found it abandoned a while ago. We put spells on it to protect it from outside eyes, and other things. We use it in case a Brother needs a break."

While many Brotherhood secrets remained mysterious to me, I knew their slang *needs a break* was code for badly injured or profoundly affected with memories. An escape, in other words.

"I can see why," I murmured.

The cozy ambiance breathed safety. With the tree holding it in a secure claw, what could intrude? The roots formed a dome-like ceiling. The space between each branching surface smoothed over and glossed, without visible cracks. Only bitty fireflies within the cottage cast an iridescent glow.

Merrick's hand trailed across the small of my back as he perused a basket of food left on a table large enough for two. Beyond it, a canopied oak bed with four towering pillars occupied most of the wall. Burnt orange draperies, pulled aside, gathered behind velvet ropes.

Plump white blankets and stiff pillows adorned the interior.

My fingers ran along the fuzzy edge of a claw-footed divan, stuffed to the brim, near a low coffee table. They cluttered a hearth with stacked books. I advanced, breathless. Warmth radiated from jeweled tones and scenes painted directly on the tree surface.

Merrick pressed a kiss to the top of my shoulder, his arm curling around my stomach. He pulled me into his chest.

"It's beautiful," he murmured, tugging my sleeve down for better access. A featherlight kiss graced my collarbone. "But nothing is as beautiful as you, B."

The stress of the day melted in slow waves as the realization settled: all of it had ended. No plans. No preparations. No dinners, smiles, small talk, nor conversations. All that remained was me. Merrick.

Together.

I spun, wrapped my arms around his chest, and brought our lips together. Hands clutching my hips, he lifted me into his hold. I wrapped my legs around his waist, tore away from his kiss long enough to growl, "Take me to bed," and we retreated to the giant thing together.

He drew the draperies closed, and I forgot everything but me, Merrick, and the heat of our entwined bodies.

Chapter Three

The bliss of our recent handfasting extended for the blessed week. Silence. Crackling fires. Delicious food. Not a soul in sight. Nothing to focus on but Merrick's calloused touch, gentle as a dove, and the new world we forged together.

With Merrick never out of touch, Tyrant was utterly silent. My heart breathed again.

While we nestled into our retreat, the first big snow swept Letum Wood. The storm blew sideways through the trees. Ice solidified the pond. Eaves of giant snow piled on top, drifting over until the ice shone.

Michelle sent meals once a day. Fresh loaves of bread, pastries, more treats than we could both eat, and hot stews to stave off the stubborn chill. Firewood appeared from Papa every morning. Books from Grandfather. Notes from family who didn't get to say *merry part*.

We existed together.

Only us.

Until the real world called us back again.

* * *

The treehouse remained utterly unchanged when we reluctantly returned. Pewter clouds filled the space between trees, painting a leaden, sullen world, with more snow on the way. Ava, who watched Goat and Other Goat, left a note with updates about our animals, who fared without problem. Ice crackled as I touched the frosted window panes.

The trees anticipated our arrival that morning, and had swished snow off the porch with vines and branches. I put my palm to towering Amanthis and thought to it, *Thank you, my friend.*

A chorus of replies sang, one resonant note deeper than the rest. Heat blasted my cool cheeks when I opened the door. Papa fulfilled his promise to start a fire before we returned, chasing away the frigidity. The last basket of food from Michelle perched on the table.

"Well," Merrick said, thoroughly depressed. "Real life awaits." He dropped our bags on the floor. I tried not to frown.

"Does it ever," I muttered, eyeing two stacks of messages three paces high. Reluctant to return from our hazy and too-short bliss, I ignored those to plan a trip to the market. Together, we made short work of unpacking, laundry, and cleaning, which left me two options: answer messages or query Leda.

Sighing, I lowered in front of the fire.

Leda?

My tentative question into the communication magic resulted in an instant reply. *You're back?*

Unfortunately.

Have a good time?

Yes, I did. Want to hear the details?

Please, no, she hastily said, and I laughed. *I have several things that I would like to discuss with you at your first availability. Amongst them is tea with Council Member Clare, and a luncheon with Council Member Theo.*

My nose wrinkled.

Urg.

Amongst the last things on my mind was vying the Council to support the Sisterhood with currency and *legitimacy,* as Leda put it. The Eastern Network insurrection that I assisted to curb had settled mere weeks ago, but the aftermath felt lifetimes long. Journalists learned about my involvement, which dragged the Sisterhood into light. Articles and questions exploded into the *Chatham Chatterer* that I hid from behind handfasting preparations. I ignored their queries, and the fervor eventually subsided.

The untoward attention made me uncomfortable. The Sisterhood wasn't ready for publicity yet. Besides, overcoming former Council Member Greyson, and assisting Camila and Cristian with their insurrection, had painted a clear picture: the Council complicated the Sisterhood's work.

I didn't desire complications.

Leda's plan to enlist Council Member approval in order for us to receive currency was still underway. Only . . . delayed by a few weeks. Until we had the Council's backing, I didn't want news of the Sisterhood to spread. More to the point, I didn't want *any* news to spread, because the thought of being beholden to the Council made me squirm.

The Sisterhood had to be different. Versatile. Down the Council path lay control and structure, and my gut rebelled at every point.

Explaining that to Leda was another issue entirely.

Your silence doesn't get you out of the task, Leda said with evident long-suffering. *Council Member Theo isn't that bad. There are worse. I'd say he's probably against the Sisterhood, but I think you could sway him. He's very into history. He mentioned your Volare to me before while discussing whether magical portals existed in ancient Alkarra. Use* that *as a talking point.*

My nose wrinkled. Ancient Alkarra? Magical portals? I didn't like either. As one of my most prized possessions, I kept a close eye on the Volare and tried not to discuss it with anyone. The rarity of Volares made it only more popular to the common witch. Witches knew I had it, but it didn't appear all that often.

That reeks of small talk, I said.

You won't die, she muttered.

Frustrated, I rubbed a hand over my face, already longing to return to The Underroot again. *I'm . . . trying to wrap my mind around talking to Council Members again. It'll take me a bit.*

Clare isn't so bad, she said diplomatically. *She sought me out for the meeting, which shows a lot of promise. She's firmly against anything that interests Georgette, which puts her in support of the Sisterhood.*

Is that enough?

Support?

Shaking my head, I steepled my fingers. *No. Is it enough that Clare would support us out of spite?*

I'll take whatever we can get, at this point.

Spite support wasn't enough for me. Still, there was no getting around the obvious: I had to talk to Council Members again. At some point, real life intruded. Merrick and I had been living together for months, so the transition, once started, wouldn't be different than our usual.

Besides, Leda had very patiently waited for me. I

couldn't fathom how hard it must have been for her to not act for several weeks on Sisterhood business.

When are you available? I asked.

In one hour, she said like a sigh, relieved. *Meet me at the High Priestess' office. I'll have lunch with you and we can discuss particulars. I won't have talking points,* she added, before I could ask, *but I do have pointers. Before you ask, yes. There's a difference.*

My mouth snapped shut. I had been about to ask. Lunch with Leda would allow me to keep this last dinner basket and delay the market trip another day. I liked that arithmetic.

I'll be there in an hour.

Merrick stood behind a chair, hands braced on top, and stared out the frosty windows. His jaw cocked to the side, his distant gaze a certain indication that he spoke through the communication magic. Probably checking in with Rognvald again, and enduring endless teasing from other Protectors.

With Leda's conversation done, I glared at the message stacks. Memories of my time as an Ambassador's Assistant followed, drawing a reluctant smile. Really, working as Grandfather's Assistant hadn't been *too* egregious. Learning from him made up for all the useless correspondence.

I plucked the first envelope off the top. After I spoke with Leda, I'd visit Grandfather. A neat, thin handwriting with ice blue ink grabbed my attention. This came from one witch, and one witch alone: Alina, High Priestess of the Southern Network.

I broke the matching wax seal to open it.

Bianca,

I hear your handfasting was lovely. Congratulations.

When you return to work, please let me know. I would like to hire the Sisterhood for assistance with compounding issues. Your discretion around my request is appreciated. Send me a note when you plan to come, and I'll meet you in my gardens. You have my priority for time.

Yours,
Alina

You have my priority for time was a clear bid for quick action. As High Priestess, everything Alina touched was vitally important to her Network. To open her schedule to my ease meant something big awaited.

Intrigued, I responded on a separate paper, spelling it away, and sent the original message to Leda separately.

Sent you something.

I see it, she said.

I'm going to visit with her first. Another spell brought my fur-lined cloaks and boots to hand. *I'll send you a message before we're wrapping up.*

I know how this will go, she muttered. *I'll see you tomorrow?*

Grinning, I said, *See you then.*

* * *

Snowflakes twirled around me as I strode through Zamok Castle's ice-bound gardens, seeking Alina. Zamok had its own allure away from the busy servants and flashy gems gracing the interior. It was far more powerful outside.

Stone walls buffeted my back as I approached the outer stone fence, facing foamy clouds that blasted lacy snow. Circumstances aside, the chill didn't pierce as powerfully as expected. I found Alina standing near a stone wall, out of earshot. A fur-lined cloak billowed behind her in an occasional grumpy gust, her ankles sensibly covered with boots. She wore a silk dress, despite the wintry gale. A sash crossed her waist, accenting her silhouette. There were subtle silver accents on her skirt, and amber ones on her torso.

A familiar man, equally subdued but powerful, strode at her side. He wore a heavy coat of arctic baer fur, and thick boots. Soot stained his clothes. When the tips of his fingers touched her elbow, she lifted her chin. Their intimate gaze revealed all, so I stopped walking and dropped my gaze to afford them privacy.

Andrei, the swordmaker. He re-forged Viveet from mere shards when I had little hope in a feat of magic I would never forget. The normally solitary witch often visited Zamok Castle, but only for Alina. Their long and storied romance culminated in a mighty and secretive relationship. I'd seen them in these gardens before.

"Bianca," Alina called. "You're welcome."

When my eyes elevated again, they regarded me together. Before Andrei left, he nodded once. A flicker of a smile appeared on his lips. I replied in kind. With a whisper of magic, Andrei vanished. The famed swordmaker avoided losing his magic years ago, when the former High Priest, Mikhail, broke the Mansfeld Pact. Rumors swirled that the illustrious silk clans also lost their power, but I dismissed them as conjecture.

Alina's hooded eyes, slim and long against her flat cheeks, welcomed me to her side with a wry smile. Unbothered by restless clouds and flakes as big as my fingernail, we strolled along the outer fence together, giving her a chance to turn her mind from Andrei.

Her amusement revealed itself in a rare smile. "You look like a woman blessed with a good husband, Bianca Monroe."

"That I am."

"Is handfasted bliss everything you desired?"

"Until we had to return, yes."

"Good." Her voice clipped with the rigid tones of business. "You and I have much to speak about."

Snow ground under our heels as we meandered amongst stone fragments on the ground. The ravages of ice took a toll in this hazardous climate, wearing away at the wall. Moss froze between the cracks, preventing the seeping, whistling wind. A trail circled the perimeter, and we walked along it.

"How is Tipa?" I asked, referring to a female demigod assigned by Gelas, god of ice, to assist the magicless witches in the South. Tipa, friend of Baxter's and daughter to Gelas, acted as the main intermediary between the god and Alina.

Until the Southern Network's next generation grew up—witches born after Mikhail's treachery had magical ability—the Southern Network were helpless against the magic-driven Networks to the north. Without the demigods, the Southern Network had been subject to magical attacks from rogue witches, mostly out of the Eastern Network. With god magic assisting, particularly at the borders, Alina had finally created peace.

"Tipa is fine," she said.

"Do you see her much?"

"Once a week."

"That's . . . good?"

Alina sent me a sidelong glance. "As of late, Tipa has

been as eager as myself for the Southern Network to manage our own problems with some level of independence."

As eager as myself pointed toward Tipa tiring of her emissary job. Not surprising. Though once a week work didn't seem like a lot of time investment, what demigod wanted to manage magicless witches as helpless as her father's mortals? None. Baxter aside, perhaps, but he had his own position in Alkarra. He was the only demigod I knew with interest in, and affection for, witches.

Alina's assessing stare didn't go unnoticed. "Enough about demigods. My inquiry is for both Bianca Monroe and the Sisterhood."

Yet another trait of hers I cherished—efficiency.

"You read about the Sisterhood in *Chatterer* articles, I take it?"

"I hear many things." Her vague response didn't surprise me. Alina spoke very little. She revealed even less. "I need your help with a problem arising out of the Western Network."

My metaphorical hackles rose. Anything involving the West might potentially involve Lana, the Western Network High Priestess. She was amiable compared to their former leader, Mabel. But amiability didn't make Lana easy to work with or trustworthy. She had an undisputed wild side, and a temper to match.

Lana also had expansion in mind. Whether that *expansion* might one day include the Southern Network, no one knew for certain. Leda kept an eye on Lana's dealings, and Scarlett took extra pains to remain communicative and friendly. I doubted Alina extended the same care to her relationship with Lana.

Head tilted to survey a hedge wall, Alina continued.

"Through written messages, several clans have reported witch abductions over the last four months."

"Witch abductions?"

"Mmm, yes. At first, the reports were slow. Perhaps . . . one report per week. It's not uncommon for clannish witches to run away from home and never return. At first, we kept track of them, but had little cause to act. These . . . abductions . . . might have been disgruntled teenagers running away from home, so we waited."

High color appeared on her cheek, but I couldn't ascertain why. She sent me a quick peek from the corner of her eyes. Seeing no response, she continued.

"After a month, the reports escalated to two each week, with a pattern developing. The reporting witches wouldn't come forward for interviews, and most wrote without a signature. We had little understanding and no ability to follow up. Eventually, we found one of the witches and spoke with him. He was a clan elder. Two ice witches had been taken from his clan."

"*Ice* witches?"

"During the winter, ice witches cut ice blocks from freshwater lakes and pack them in sawdust to store for the summer, or to sell them to other Networks."

"Like the Western Network?"

Alina slipped her hands into a furry muff and inclined her head. "And the Central Network. Particularly Chatham Castle."

"Makes sense," I muttered. Chatham Castle consumed a lot of ice in the sweltering summer.

"Two months ago, the abductions stopped. Thinking the problem resolved, the clans went silent. We attempted to speak with them, but they ignored our help. The clans and I . . ." Her lips pressed to a flat line. "We are . . . *working on* . . . our relationship. When the abductions picked up again later, at three or more per week, they came to the castle for help again."

To the castle wasn't to Alina herself. Tension underlined every part of this story, and I couldn't help but wonder over the source.

"From what we can ascertain, and with what little information the clans allow us, nearly all the abductions are ice witches along the lakes. We've attempted to learn names, but they're resistant."

"Why?"

"Clannish witches are distrustful of the Network, even when it's run by a clannish woman and former shieldmaiden. There's no changing the past," she added drily.

Clannish witch was the colloquial term for any witch born into or sharing heritage with the silk clans hidden in the tundras. Not all clannish witches worked with the silk, or knew the magic, either. Magical silkworms ran the beloved and steadfast silk trade, which occupied much of the Southern Network economy. The silk clans held tight to their magic and secrets. Recorded history held no successful instance of the magic being stolen, though fools had tried.

"We believe that the Western Network tribal traders, who have been buying ice this winter, have something to do with the abductions. This week, an ice clan is moving their families to a freshwater lake named Zameroz in advance of cutting the ice. A Western Network tribe—we aren't sure of their name—is already lined up to buy. In itself, their purchase is no cause for concern. Ice is ice, and my witches require customers and currency. But we believe this tribe may be purchasing the ice and stealing our ice witches on delivery. At least, that's when we think most witches have gone missing."

"You've warned your ice witches?"

Her cheek twitched. "Yes."

"Are they concerned?"

"Some are. Most aren't."

"Why not?"

She shrugged. "Many aren't handfasted with families that concern them, and most are barely surviving the winter. Ice witches aren't always friendly to one another, and they don't hold a culture that gives much weight to what *could* happen. They deal with reality one brutal moment at a time."

Unfortunately, this made too much sense. "How many have been taken?" I asked.

"Near fifty."

My eyes widened. Jikes, but I hadn't expected that many. Connecting the points, I said, "You need someone to follow the Western tribe and see if they have your clannish witches."

"Yes."

"Has Tipa tried?"

Carefully, Alina said, "She's not yet aware of this trouble."

While the decisions of a High Priestess weren't my business, I couldn't help asking, "Why not?"

Her pause told me almost everything. With a sigh, she explained.

"Gelas and the demigods have done much for my witches, but I don't want to involve them in problems I cannot prove, or for which I have little information. Tipa, while helpful, is not . . . accustomed to . . . magicless witches. Her patience is short. Her limited awareness of the way we live and operate isn't ideal when it comes to problem solving."

The realization of Alina's troubles hit me hard.

Demigods and witches were so different. Merging the two was never going to be easy. Baxter would be better suited for this role, but he wasn't Gelas' child, and Tipa wouldn't relinquish an opportunity to please her father and make a name amongst demigods. The strange dynamics of gods and mortals, when applied to witches, resulted in odd ends.

"Not to mention," Alina added glibly, "that it would be better for the Southern Network in the long term if firm and decisive punishment came from us and not the demigods. Tipa and Gelas will leave when our children can carry our security. Our reputation for taking care of ourselves needs to happen now, not later."

An unfortunate truth, but not an easy one.

"Do you suspect demigod involvement?"

"No."

If a demigod created this situation—though they had no motivation to kidnap witches when they had mortals to deal with—Gelas would have to become involved. As a matter of course, I avoided god involvement in anything. Gelas helped us against his power-crazed brothers that wanted to destroy Alkarra, but I didn't enjoy him.

"And you don't want to prod the sleeping desert dragon while figuring this out," I added.

She understood my veiled meaning immediately. "High Priestess Lana is a problem I'd rather avoid. I knew you'd understand. Of course I will stand up for my witches, particularly if we are being taken advantage of. But it must be done wisely within all parameters. Before I can speak with Lana or make accusations, I need solid, irrefutable, and trusted information."

"I understand."

"You do," she whispered. Relief hummed in it.

As Bianca Monroe, my agreement sealed the moment

Alina asked for help. She was one witch whom it would be hard to deny anything. As the Head of the Sisterhood, the lines weren't so easily drawn. Not with the Council hovering as an unknown.

Did that matter to me? Not in the slightest.

"You have me, Alina."

My simple statement brought her swinging around, face-to-face. We halted. Rimy vines, glued to the ground by frost, created uneven footing where we stood. Her brow arched.

"Are you agreeing so quickly for the glory of it?"

I scoffed. "Amongst Western tribes? Glory is not a consequence."

"To convince your Council?"

This time, I laughed outright. "This is far more likely to turn them against me. With our Council, there is no respect without control."

Her stiff shoulders eased. Alina scoured my face, making it difficult to maintain eye contact. Such vulnerability swirled in their darkness. She was frightened. Somehow, bigger implications lingered behind this situation. Leda and I would discuss them later. She accepted my willingness with a nod.

Several seconds passed before she spoke with the rock-hard inflections of a leader. "Return in three days, when the Western Network tribes will bargain at Zameroz lake for their pricing. Cutting begins after that. You can follow the warriors from there."

"I'll be there."

"I'm sure I don't need to mention a requirement for utmost secrecy."

"Only Leda will know. Perhaps my grandfather, but only on the occasion for advice."

"Thank you. You didn't mention payment?"

I shrugged. "We can figure it out later."

"Zamok Castle holds vast wealth that I'm turning to my witches. Mikhail was a horrid ruler, hoarding like a dragon. The depths of his depravity are revealing now. My goal is to turn his riches into assets my witches can use. I'm happy to offer you as much as you want."

The depths of Zamok Castle would involve rare gems, gold, silver. Their mining history was extensive, particularly amongst the clan. Nothing in that castle appealed to me. Currency, perhaps. I'd need it eventually, but not yet.

A different idea occurred to me. I'd been to the Southern Network countless times, with Grandfather and Mikhail, or sneaking in to find Andrei, explore with Merrick, or talk to Alina or demigods.

The Southern Network held one possibility I cared about.

"Do you happen to know a shieldmaker?"

Chapter Four

Leda eyed me with consummate suspicion the next afternoon. She placed both hands on her desk, squared to my seeking face. "Well?" she bit out. "What did you agree to help Alina with? I can see in your eyes that you said *yes* to whatever she asked."

I sat in a chair across from her tidy-but-busy desk in Scarlett's office and faked shock. Arms spread wide, I cried, "Who says I agreed to anything?"

She tipped me a look.

I blew a raspberry. If she hadn't sat behind an Assistant's desk tucked into a corner, I might have mistaken her as the High Priestess already. She held such command and confidence in this room. Leda had never spoken beyond her goal to become a Council Member one day, but I couldn't imagine any version of Alkarra where Leda didn't vault directly to the top.

Sinking into the chair, my head tipped back, I closed my eyes. "Well, this *one time* you're correct. Alina did request help and I granted it. It's a wild story. Can't wait to tell you about it."

Scarlett's office doors whispered shut behind a lunch tray, no doubt sent from the kitchen on Leda's request. The rattling silverware settled between us, awakening my ravenous stomach. After a chilly morning jog to satisfy my trees—whom I ignored while honeymooning—my hunger had grown into a monster.

Leda lifted lids and shuffled plates. "Well? Are you going to tell me, or contemplate it further?"

While she doled out food, spelled silverware, and poured tea, I sketched a brief review of Alina's request. Once I'd satisfied Leda's rampant curiosity, I dove into the deeper analysis. She'd draw her own implications regarding Lana and the tribes and Alina's position with the demigods, and I wanted to hear her take on it. Inevitably, we uncovered something different.

She pursed her lips, her frown deepening until I finished. A glower shadowed her face, cast into sharp relief by the gloomy weather. Hail flicked at the window with uneasy staccatos that resembled drumming nails, intensified by gusts of wind.

Leda straightened. "Alina's request was . . ."

"Unexpected?"

"Not entirely. But it is concerning. I see why you accepted it without my permission, and I'm not angry about it."

The phrase *without my permission* reverberated. In some regard, the assessment was fair. In others, infuriating. Should I require her permission? No. Also, yes. Yet another reason publicity around the Sisterhood worried me. We hadn't truly determined the most basic internal structure, though we chipped away at it every day.

"This sort of mission is far outside the purview of the Central Network," Leda continued, thoughts cogitating.

"Then again, that offers the expansion you desire for the Sisterhood."

"Exactly."

Her voice turned musing as she lifted a teacup. "And we aren't under Council control *now*, so Georgette doesn't have to know what you're doing. Nor the Council."

I snapped two fingers.

"That's why I took it. Because we can, and it's needed."

Leda rolled her eyes. "You'll never convince me that you thought about *that* reason before you accepted. Knowing that it came from Alina, I'd be a fool to presume that you didn't accept it without hearing what she said."

Leda flirted so close to the truth I almost choked. Somehow, I kept myself from blubbering through a damning response. Instead, I let her quirky genius flow and stir up new ideas.

After another full minute of ponderance, she declared, "I think it's a wise mission to take. Not only does it offer opportunities to learn and grow, but to aid witches in dire need of assistance. I stand behind it."

I shot upright.

"Really?"

Leda scrawled on a notepad. "Really. On a separate-but-related note, Aurora came into Scarlett's office for a meeting today because Lana has requested that Aurora visit the Arck."

I laughed. "I bet *that* request went well."

Leda glared at me through her pale eyelashes. "Aurora accepted, and happily. Despite your preconceptions around our Ambassador, she has phenomenal interactions with other Networks and draws firm boundaries, like Marten."

Surrendering with two hands in the air, I reached for a piece of toast to satisfy my hunger. Aurora was a cutting woman with an air of superiority I'd never been able to mimic. She also had an eye for diplomatic detail that I never *hoped* to mimic.

We had a tempestuous relationship. Between her need to prove herself a competent Ambassador in the wake of Grandfather's impressive legacy, and a general dislike for her arrogant attitude, I found myself avoiding her more often than not.

However, Aurora had proven a powerful ally for the Sisterhood during the Eastern Network insurrection, and worthy of her position. Her adeptness for political assessment made her stand above others. I found myself more inclined to trust her, though I didn't seek out her company unless I desired a verbal lashing.

"What does Aurora's meeting with Lana have to do with this?" I asked.

"Nothing, probably," Leda admitted. "But it's hard to tell when it comes to Lana and the Western Network. Her control over the tribes is tenuous; problems and riots expand daily. I want to keep our eyes open on everything."

Understanding flowed. With it, amusement. "*You* want to keep an eye on Lana, and you want me to do it for you."

Sipping primly at her tea, she said, "Maybe I do."

"You don't trust Lana?"

"No."

"Does Scarlett?"

"Mostly. Lana hasn't done anything overtly wrong, which is why I'm concerned. Since I can't command the Brotherhood, Scarlett isn't likely to agree with me, and as there's no specific mission in mind, the Sisterhood is the perfect response."

Ah, Leda's silent motivations lay manifest. Her loyalty to the Sisterhood had always been absolute for varied, and often unknown, reasons. The ability to deploy her own resources to underestimated situations must be at the top. Thus far, she hadn't tried it.

"Keep in mind that the Council wouldn't have approved of such a thing." I lifted my toast-filled hands. "Yet *another* reason the Sisterhood should operate outside Council approval."

The usual storm appeared in her expression at my words. Leda hated to agree, but she couldn't disagree, either. Not with our plan for Council approval still in motion. I wanted to withdraw it fully after the events in the Eastern Network, but she held on. Pivoting wasn't her strong suit.

She sank her teeth into her bottom lip, but recovered her haughtiness within moments. Her chiding, arch tone would have burned a lesser witch. "I'm more aware of that than you think, and I'm pondering the ramifications of removing our request for Council support."

"Really?"

"Pondering," she snapped. "That's not a promise. Take the mission with Alina with my blessing and let me think. We can't just withdraw our request. We have to have a plan. In the meantime, we need to discuss this."

A *Chatham Chatterer* newsscroll appeared in front of me. The bolded headline made my heart catch.

New Sisterhood In The Works?

By a hasty skim of the first three sentences, the biting tone revolted me. Disgust welled up, and I sent it back without reading.

"I don't care."

She batted it onto her desk. "You *have* to care. This is not the first. They've been quietly publishing since news broke that the Sisterhood had a hand in the Eastern Network. This is the most . . . bold."

"There are others?"

"Yes, but not as scathing. I can't prove it, but I think Georgette is influencing their inception." She waved to the article. "It's written by a reporter named Dorothee, but I think it's really Georgette."

Council Member Georgette had made no secret of her dislike for me, nor the Sisterhood. While embroiled in the mess with the Eastern Network, she cornered me after I interrogated former Council Member Greyson, and promised to speak against the Sisterhood as readily as I sought support.

In the aftermath of the Sisterhood's publicity with the Eastern Network, her irritation with the Sisterhood multiplied. I'd ignored her because of my handfasting, and bullies required little else. Leda, however, couldn't disengage with the articles as simply.

"Why do you think it's Georgette?" I asked.

"A hunch. The words they use included phrases I've heard Georgette say before. I'm working on proving it."

"To what end? You can't stop her."

Leda rolled her eyes. "To *know*, Bianca. In this political game, information is absolutely power. Listen, I won't bore you with every detail, but suffice it to say that the Sisterhood currently has one big problem: Council Member Georgette."

I scoffed. "That's nothing new."

Leda tapped the scroll. "No, but yes. She may not have liked us before, but now I see hints of her actively working against the Sisterhood. Georgette didn't take kindly to how well the Sisterhood was thought of in political circles after the Eastern Network debacle."

And why not? came Tyrant's droll voice. *You did rid Alkarra of many lives from the East. Rebellious lives. Lives that you took into your hands and squashed.*

The unwelcome reminder dampened my spirits. Swallowing hard, I forced myself to ignore his irritating presence and focus on the morsel of good news Leda imparted.

"Witches think well of us?"

Her lips pursed. "They're certainly listening. Hope for funding is higher than it's ever been—whether that's good or bad," she quickly tacked on. "I believe these articles are Georgette's attempts to counter our increased reputation. I can't say her concerns about the Sisterhood are unfounded, but they are taken to extremes. Regardless of the truth, I suspect she's going to launch a campaign against you and discredit the Sisterhood before our meeting with the Council."

"Which is when?"

"In four weeks. We had to shift it around because of Network business."

"Great," I muttered. How did time quicken and also slow at the same time?

"There's good news," she added with a little cheer. "We have one safeguard that is far more powerful than our enemy."

"Oh?"

"Marten."

My voice pitched higher. "Grandfather? How does he figure into this?"

"The High Priest is the only thing that's keeping Georgette from going full tilt against the Sisterhood. Articles like that?" She gestured to the scroll. "They're mostly to create awareness, but they're not an attack. She's holding back, and it's because of Marten. Scarlett *and* Marten support the Sisterhood, so Georgette has to tread carefully. The Council might agree the Sisterhood isn't necessary, but with the High Priest and High Priestess in support, there's not much the Council can do about it."

"If Grandfather didn't support it?"

"Georgette would push harder on the issue and appeal to Scarlett's supposed *favoritism* for you." She rolled her eyes. "Marten's reputation is too powerful for Georgette to contend with. Alone, Georgette can prove favoritism with Scarlett as your former teacher, but not with Marten agreeing to the Sisterhood. Your position as his former Assistant would bolster his reputation around your professional capabilities, and the Network loves him. If she attacks Marten's opinion, she sounds desperate."

Sighing, I ran a hand through my hair.

Jikes.

"Which puts us in an uncomfortably uncertain situation." Leda lifted her hands in a helpless gesture, bottom lip clamped between her teeth. "We're campaigning for the Sisterhood, Georgette is against it, and it's only going to worsen. Probably to an impasse."

"Thanks for the warning."

Leda grabbed a quill. "Sure. At least you know what you're up against. Forgive me, but I have missives to answer. Can I help you with anything else?"

Recognizing a dismissal when I received one, I stood.

"No, thank you Leda."

She waved me out.

* * *

Merrick stood in the middle of the treehouse, hands on his hips. His wet hair lay in clumps around his face as he frowned at the floor. I ran my fingertips across his bare back as I slipped behind him, toward the table.

"Bored?"

"Not bored. Just . . . uncertain. Rognvald doesn't have a mission for me or two other Brothers today."

"And so?"

"I'll have to train," he muttered, lips pushed to one side of his face. If he hadn't looked so irritated, I might have laughed.

"Is training a bad thing?"

"No." He spun, yanking his fresh shirt off the back of a chair. "There are a few things Rognvald wants me to test. A blanket that heats through the night on its own, and a new charm that, reportedly, repels blighters. Tysen and I volunteered to do it in the bailey, but Rognvald wants us to test them overnight in the cold. His preference is the Northern Network mountains."

Disappointment dropped my tone. "You'll be gone all night?" It would be a miserable sleep without him. Not just for cold and loneliness, but Tyrant muttered particularly loud in the late hours when sleep eluded me.

He brushed a kiss over my forehead. "Yes, but I'll return for breakfast. Hopefully, with a new blanket to keep us warm."

"I can think of something better."

His chortle accompanied him to the armoire.

I brushed aside the irritation of resuming life. My meeting with Alina yesterday still occupied my thoughts. This would give me enough time to iron it out. Accepting Alina's request guaranteed my plunge into responsibilities again.

Merrick sought his shoes, muttering about something, while I sorted through messages on the table. A new envelope arrived, hovering patiently a handspan to my right. Seeing the writing, I smiled.

Grandfather.

I lifted the flap as Merrick swiped the hair off of my neck and pressed a kiss to the sensitive skin along my spine.

"I love you, little troublemaker. See you in the morning."

A lingering kiss on my lips later, he departed and I returned to the message. Grandfather's thin, scratchy handwriting awaited.

My dear,

Would you join me for dinner tonight? Merrick is welcome, of course, though I overheard Rognvald speak about him and Tysen testing a few things through the night.

Without a moment's hesitation, I sent a reply along the bottom.

It would be my greatest pleasure. See you this evening, if not sooner.

* * *

After a full day transporting around the Southern Network lakes, getting a feel for the ice trade and the clannish witches who ran it, the smell of spearmint welcomed me into the High Priest's apartments. Winter twilight crept like a blanket over Chatham Castle, sweeping bitter frost and cold into the eaves and corners.

Reeves, bustling in his usual symphonic ministrations, opened the door with his scratchy clothes and quiet shoes. A wrinkle marred his brow as he admitted me. A hesitant part of his lips, and then a head shake, lent an air of uncertainty.

Odd.

"Come in, Miss Bianca. Is it Mrs. Hughes, now?"

My nose wrinkled. "Not sure yet. Still deciding where I land, but leaning toward keeping the Monroe. Mrs. Hughes sounds like a schoolmarm."

His lip twitched as he cleared the way for me to enter. Grandfather perched on a divan, hands folded on top of his thighs. He illuminated, but his full smile couldn't hide a blatant paleness.

Since when did Grandfather appeal frail?

I lowered at his side. His warm hand clasped mine, as strong as ever. The grasp dismissed my fears. Tyrant, too. Like Merrick and Papa, Tyrant's irreverent voice faded entirely in Grandfather's presence.

"How are you, my dear?"

I beckoned a chair with a spell. "Better now." Heat shed onto my boots from the fire. I peeled them off, placing them on the stones to dry the wet bottoms.

"Is handfasted life everything you wanted?"

"Almost exactly the same as before, but yes. Wonderful."

"I envy you." He squeezed my fingers before releasing them. "Mildred and I were all *but* handfasted. Officially, anyway. She crept to my quarters almost every night, or I came to hers. Her butler always knew. Still, there's something in that extra step. The promise, stated aloud . . ."

I lost him to deeper ruminations.

When he blinked free, I welcomed him with a smile that he returned, albeit half-heartedly.

"Leda and I had an interesting conversation today. Can I tell you about it?"

He eagerly swept a hand forward. "Please do, my dear. You know I always love to hear about you."

Grateful to air the situation out, I told him first about Alina, then Leda, then Georgette. Without his sage and subtle wisdom, the Sisterhood would have withered months ago, and he'd know what to do with the froth around my reputation. He'd loved Mildred all his life, and she stirred up witches daily.

The story flowed into his wise and capable hands, relieving me of an insecure burden. Reeves served dinner while I spoke; we ate at the fire. Grandfather sipped tea and picked at a piece of bread, listening with rapt attention.

I finished with an unsteady, "So that's where we're at." Grandfather tapped a finger against his chin. Taking the chance I had, I finished off the rest of my dinner, half-eaten in between sentences.

He leaned against the chair, an elbow propped on the armrest. The subtle clinks of assembling tea pots and tea cups whispered through the closed kitchen door, where Reeves puttered.

"Georgette's role has me particularly interested."

"Do you think Leda is correct? That you and Scarlett protect the Sisterhood?"

"To a degree."

Unsure of what to say, I opted for a sigh.

"Life is what we perceive, my dear. While there's truth in the idea that Scarlett and I protect the Sisterhood from Georgette's full wrath, that doesn't make it *all* true. What

I don't like about that sentiment is the idea that you need us. *That* is entirely not true."

Rebuttals arose instantly. Of course it was true. Grandfather provided advice, structure, insight. Without such, how would I know the best paths?

"Grandfather—"

He tapped a hand on my arm. "You don't give yourself enough credit, Bianca. You're stronger than you think, with more wisdom in between those ears than most your age. Consider it."

Spelling my dinner tray to the table for Reeves to gather later, I pulled a knee into my chest and contemplated the fire. Tyrant tried to whisper to life, but I didn't entertain him. The temptation to tell Grandfather of the intrusive thoughts whispered through my mind, but I dismissed it.

Some demons weren't worth sharing.

"Georgette hates me," I whispered instead.

He lifted a finger in the air. "Hate is a strong word. Georgette strongly opposes your stance, indisputably. From her view, she's a woman doing her best to protect a Network she loves. There is probably some truth in her observations, though her approach needs refinement."

"You're kinder to her than I would be."

Grandfather laughed, eyes twinkling. The full sound comforted me. "I have a fair bit more life experience than you, my dear. After a while, you learn how to read witches. Georgette is zealous, we agree on that. Sometimes, zealous witches become lost in their fervor. When boundaries blur, it can be hard to reorient and find north again, so to speak."

His more charitable observation wasn't entirely unfounded. Georgette's protectiveness around the Network was admirable, in some regard. Inspecting her motivations through Grandfather's eyes, however, roused difficult questions. Was Georgette wrong? Could two witches look at the same thing, see it differently, and both be right?

Grandfather tapped my chair with the side of his shoe. "Her concern isn't wrong, you know."

"What?"

He laughed again. "Her concerns are founded in some historical precedent. You weren't here for the Dark Days, where favoritism abounded. High Priest Donovan held regard only for his friends, such as Council Member Rand. He appointed witches without regard to ability, desire, or experience. There were leaders in positions that had no reason to be there."

Hand pressed to my heart, I cried, "What more can I do to prove my value to her, Grandfather? I've shown myself capable! This isn't favoritism. I'm able."

"Correct, but by an unestablished process. Based on the recent articles—which I have read—Georgette seems to dispute the way you came into the position, not your lack of qualification. At least," he added, "not entirely. She does seem opposed to your young age, which I believe is an emotional response on her part."

"So she's trying to prevent my *process* from happening again?"

"That's what I'd wager."

I rubbed a hand over my face. "This is why Leda is the political mastermind behind the Sisterhood. I'd rather spy on desert tribes than try to ascertain Council Member motivations, thank you very much."

"How is your anger?"

The question startled me. For a very brief moment, I'd almost forgotten Tyrant. Unlike my friends, I couldn't stave Grandfather off. A barren whisper answered. "There."

"What is it telling you?"

Those words wouldn't cross my lips. I could only shake my head, horrified at Tyrant's strength. He resurrected with glee in the wake of Grandfather's pointed question, providing ample choices to share.

You sent a man to his death.

His family, too.

Here you live your life with blood on your hands, acting as if all is well.

Understanding flooded Grandfather's kind eyes. He leaned closer. "Whatever the anger is telling you, it's not real. You are not to blame for what happened in the Eastern Network. There are bad witches in the world, Bianca. You are not one of them."

Unassailed adoration poured out of him. My eyes watered. If my heart had a bullseye, he found it.

"Thank you," I choked out.

"Honor your anger. Let it speak, then ask it to leave, for it has done its job. Anger is not the worst thing, but the actions that stem from it are. You know this already after your experiences with Mabel."

I nodded, letting the advice sink deeper. For another day. Not this one.

Grandfather chuckled weakly as he slumped against the chair. Lines carved his eyes. He'd tired himself out. His hand found mine again, tightening over the top of it. He regarded me with deepest love and warmth.

"The only concern I have over the Georgette situation, as you called it in your retelling, is your belief that you rely on anyone but yourself to be successful. The Council, Georgette, Leda, myself? None of us matter. You don't need the Council to be who you want to be."

His wrinkled hand lifted, tapped my heart. "Everything you need is right here, my dear. It is within you."

Before approaching the Eastern Network for the attempted overthrow of Magnolia Castle, Papa advised me something similar. *It's not about achieving, B. It's about being. You will never do enough. There's always more. More missions, more witches in pain, more struggles to resolve. But if you can be the witch you want to be—a witch that changes the world for someone else in some small way—then it's enough. It's always enough.*

Those words followed me, attached to my heels like a shadow. Every decision cast the questions, *who am I here? Who am I there?*

It felt particularly applicable at this moment, but I didn't see how. With the recollection came haunting remembrances. A dying girl, a broken father. Bodies petaling off a grand, curving staircase and blood shivering down marble stairs. I'd seen battle before. War wasn't new, but something about the Eastern Network insurrection struck me differently. It awoke a nerve I didn't know existed.

I didn't know why Tyrant haunted me. Why *those* deaths were any different than demigods in Letum Wood, or Southern Network Guardians invading the Southern Covens, or Mabel.

Frantic, I closed those questions off. They didn't belong in Grandfather's pure presence. Those were night-time reminisces. Things not suited for the light of day. Tyrant didn't deserve the time that I gave him, particularly not here.

Grandfather yawned. "I'm rather tired, my dear. The last couple of days, I've found that I sleep better out here, by the fire. My heart beats a little slower when I'm sitting upright." Grimacing, he rubbed his left shoulder. "My body is sore and ready to sleep."

Reeves, hurrying out of the kitchen with a tea tray, paused. I waved him off. "Thank you, Reeves, but no more tea tonight. Grandfather is sleepy. We're going to sleep out here."

Grandfather protested. "Oh, no! Please, take your—"

"I'd rather be with you."

He smiled his response, eyes at half mast. Born on a spell from Reeves, pillows and blankets hurried from the hallway. Behind the window, the sparkling lights of Chatham Castle glinted. Torches over the bailey, candles from chambers above and below. A glow perfused the apartment as Reeves soused candles. Sleepy, comforting darkness descended.

I perched on the edge of the divan, my hands tucked between my thighs, and studied Grandfather. His paleness hadn't resolved. He'd eaten like a bird, too.

"Are you all right, Grandfather?"

He chuckled, eyes closed. "Yes, yes, fine. Just tired." Another yawn accompanied his admittance, which I didn't believe. Reeves frowned over him. I caught Reeve's eye. He tilted an eyebrow, his closest approximation to a shrug. If Reeves didn't know what to make of it, and I couldn't put my finger on anything, then paranoia was the likely culprit.

The fire crackled and Reeves retired. I watched Grandfather gradually relax, comforted by his familiar presence. Firelight limned his peaceful face. Before he nodded into a deep sleep, I whispered, "Grandfather?"

He replied without opening his eyes.

"Hmmm?"

"I'm going to make it happen. The Sisterhood, I mean. Whatever it takes, and with or without the Council. Witches need me. That's who I want to be. Like you. And . . . Mildred."

A fleeting smile appeared between wispy, sleep-stained breaths.

"Remember, my dear," he murmured. "There is more to you than the Sisterhood. There is more to you than Merrick. There is more to you than what the Council deems worthy of acclaim. Choose what makes all the parts of you happiest, and you can never go astray."

His words sang me to sleep, banishing the terrors of before. While I dreamed of swirling, loose light, and Mother and Mildred and Camille and Stella, the reassuring cadence of his words whispered again.

Choose what makes all the parts of you happiest, and you can never go astray.

Chapter Five

Morning broke with Reeves shuffling around in the room, his busy steps pulling me from uneasy dreams. My eyes fluttered open to muted light, chilly air. No fire crackled in the hearth yet. Based on the aquamarine hue glittering from outside, snow clouds occluded the sun.

Something was wrong.

I felt it.

A downy blanket fell off me as I sat up, my body sore. My eyes skated around the room, stopping on Grandfather. I tensed, still too sleepy to understand why. His color was . . . off. A slight smile crossed his lips, frozen. Ten unblinking seconds passed before I registered that his chest didn't move, nor his limbs stir.

"Grandfather?" I cried.

I shoved off the cushion and dropped to my knees at his side, but I already knew what I'd find. His hand, cool. His features were calm, peaceful. He might have been sleeping. Stunned, I could only stare as I lowered.

A barren whisper wrenched from my throat.

"Grandfather?"

No response. Because Grandfather was gone.

A musky scent flowed around me, followed by a heavy hand on my shoulder. "In the night, dear girl," Reeves whispered. Something altered his usual lachrymose tone. "He enjoyed a peaceful passage. I've called for an Apothecary, your father, and your husband. They'll arrive any second."

The pressure left my shoulder. I wished it back. Wished for anything but . . . this empty disbelief. Grandfather . . . gone?

He couldn't be. He sat right there. Any moment and he'd open his eyes, give a warm smile. He'd whisper, "My dear," and unfold his arms to hold me again.

Grandfather didn't.

A blessed numbness stole over me with the shock. Reeves shuffled toward the door. My lips parted to call him back. *Please, don't leave,* I'd plead, but I couldn't make my throat work. Because being alone with Grandfather was also what I wanted.

My hand spread across Grandfather's and squeezed. Tears blurred the sight of his peaceful, happy slumber. Like a gash rending me in half, grief descended during my darkest abandon. Mourning, that old companion.

"Don't go," I whispered.

The door opened and Papa rushed inside and I was in his arms and questions for Reeves raced out of him. Regina followed and then Merrick and I lost myself in their warmth and the blur of tragedy over Grandfather's passage to where I could not follow.

That evening, Merrick stood behind me on Grandfather's balcony. My back pressed into his chest, stealing warmth and stability. His breathing was a steady cadence to follow. Night shadows roared to life minutes before, revealing twinkling torches, sconces, and the candlelight of Chatham Castle. A second sky at our feet.

I listened to the weaving bustle of voices inside Grandfather's apartment, which I refused to leave. Papa spoke quietly with Scarlett and others. Arrangements, mostly. After the funeral, Reeves would pack Grandfather's few belongings and give them to Papa and myself. Grandfather didn't have much.

Scarlett bore the greatest responsibilities after Grandfather's death, as it meant a new High Priest, addressing the Network, coordinating potential leaders, and working with the Council.

Raw heartache, abrasive and heavy, accompanied me through the day. Every breath shook. Every heartbeat rattled. My mind insisted Grandfather would wake up. How couldn't he? He had been *right there.*

Inside.

And yet, not.

My heart knew what my head did not, so I let them war. Eventually, I'd figure it out. The truth would settle, as it had before. Seeing Grandfather so altered, so peaceful, made it easier to believe. I'd spoken to him hours ago, but . . . now we wouldn't speak again. The slicing impossibility was difficult to comprehend.

How?

Had he known? He'd been pale, tired, too. Exhausted. His last words had been so full of love . . . Those thoughts led to another, and another, until I blurted out, "I should have called an Apothecary."

With tender patience, Merrick asked, "Why?"

"Grandfather was pale."

"Lots of witches are pale in the winter, and him more than most."

"Tired, too."

"He was an old man. No one calls an Apothecary because an old man is pale and tired. You had been speaking with him, yes?"

"Yes."

"Did he have any complaints of pain or difficult breathing?"

"No."

Merrick brought his arms closer, ensconcing me. His chin rested on top of my head. I closed my eyes and retreated to his safety, far from Tyrant's chilling voice and unforgiving reminders. Merrick didn't say another word, and didn't need to. Logic, of course. There had been no reason to call an Apothecary.

But still . . .

I opened my mouth, closed it again. There was so much to say, but when the thoughts formed in my throat, they dissipated from my head. I'd been in this disparate emotional miasma before. Too many times. I'd learned enough to know that grief was easier when I didn't try to shorten it, fight it. Some things I had to live with.

Leda called from behind us, banishing the ghouls.

"Bianca?"

Merrick half-spun. He'd been a shield all morning, not leaving my side. Checking on me, stopping witches from offering condolences unless I wanted to speak with them. He stepped away when I turned. With a quick squeeze of my shoulder, he slipped inside.

Leda's cloak framed her face in black fur, a striking contrast to her creamy skin and white-blonde hair. She peered out with teary concern.

"I'm so sorry," she whispered, and threw her arms around me. I soaked up her care. Until her warmth cloaked me, I didn't realize the polar cold. Snow, like swan down, feathered the balcony and railing, stirring up in puffs when she stepped away.

"I'm sorry I didn't come sooner."

"You did." I tipped my head to the doors. "I saw you. You've been in and out all day."

Leda wiped a trickling tear from her cheek. "Yes, I was in there, but I didn't speak with you until now. I wanted to give you space, and I needed to help Scarlett."

I smiled, grateful to see her.

"I understand. Are things chaotic?"

"Of course, but not in a bad way. In a witches-want-all-the-news-and-they-want-it-now way. Thankfully, most have been respectful. Including the journalists."

Respectful meant the editors hadn't jumped to the *Chatterer* to make educated guesses over who Scarlett would appoint as the next High Priest. All of the Network lay at her feet, but tradition usually pulled from within the castle itself. Experience lent great trust, typically.

Leda added quietly, "I sent a message to Alina, to explain."

My breath caught.

I'd forgotten.

Leda touched my arm. "It's fine, Bianca. She says to take your time, and let her know when you're ready. They're tracking the situation, and she said there's still plenty of opportunity. They finished initial price negotiations, today, so the ice witches won't be cutting for a few more days."

I whispered, "Thank you," and dismissed those responsibilities from my mind.

The forest beckoned. Night-bound thickets at the

edge of the Chatham Castle gardens paved the dark path to Letum Wood. They led to my home. *My trees*, who crooned for me. Their song reached my heart across the distance.

She holds sorrow.
We hold it with her.
You belong to us.

Night hid their gigantic trunks, as tall as the castle itself. Staring into their prodigious size often took my breath away. Not the magic teeming within, nor the soothing balm of the trees. The sheer enormity of the wood, the call of home from deep in my soul . . .

With a measured, searching tone, Leda asked, "How are your powers?"

I couldn't help a rangy laugh. Years ago, when Mama died, my magic had been nearly out of control. The gift of space and time helped me understand why. I'd been an emotional ball of stress most of my teenage years. Fighting the curse. Failing to win. Losing Grandmother, then Mama at Mabel's hand.

This felt . . . different.

Emotions flowed in waves, ebbing and retreating with equal unpredictability. Frustration. Anger. Disbelief. Relief. Tension, too. Beneath it all, a deep weariness to face this prospect again, and a fear that Papa or Merrick might meet the same, unexpected fate.

Thankfully, Grandfather wasn't taken from me in the same way as Mama. He experienced a lovely slide into the arms of the lands and lives beyond. Painful, but not traumatizing. My powers, vibrant and real, gave no insistent or unsteady clues.

"My powers are all right. This isn't like when Mama died. It's different." Quietly, I tacked on, "*I'm* different."

And a murderer, came Tyrant's unwanted voice,

bringing a flash of dying bodies, suffering witches. I blinked them away.

"How is your father holding up in your estimation?" Leda asked. She glanced over her shoulder. "Thus far, he seems . . . fine."

"Shocked, like me. But hanging in there. As far as deaths go, it was ideal. Quiet, peaceful. Grandfather slipped away in his sleep with family at his side. If he suffered, there's no indication, and I didn't hear a peep."

"You're a light sleeper."

"It's odd, isn't it?" I murmured. "He wanted me to stay the night. Merrick was testing things with Tysen and wasn't home . . . it worked out so perfectly."

"Fate has goodness, too."

A stirring sigh, a whispering sough, swirled in my chest, returning me to the vague-and-distant experience when I stood at the In-between, nearly dead because of the gods' treachery. The area between this world and the lands and lives beyond. Too clearly, I recalled Mama. Mildred. Camille. Their ethereal but very real presence.

Grandfather had been at the In-between last night. Did Mildred greet him? I couldn't fathom a world in which she wouldn't. The thought gave me great comfort. Jealousy, too. What I wouldn't give to embrace each of them.

The door opened. Leda spun. "Bianca?" Priscilla asked. Michelle strode onto the balcony at her side, woolen cloaks pulled tight around their necks. Tears surfaced for the first time in hours.

"You came," I whispered.

Priscilla threw her arms around me. "As soon as we could." When she pulled away, Michelle wrapped me in her strong arms. Worry lined her face, wrinkling the space between her eyes.

"I'm so sorry, Bianca."

"Me, too."

"Merrick caught us up on the details inside." Priscilla jabbed a thumb over her shoulder. "He told us as much as you know, I think. So fast and unexpected. And you were here! Oh, B. I'm so sorry."

Another breathy hug from Priscilla led to Leda joining, and then Michelle. The four of us stood in a circle, arms and bodies bundled close. My friends held me tight, allowing the raging, bundled, hot knot in my chest to dissipate.

In their circle of love, Tyrant retreated.

Smoky breath trailed in front of me while I stood in Letum Wood late that night. Merrick held my hand. Papa, on my left, stared into the cloistered trees with a dazed expression. For all his strength in coordinating, accepting condolences, and speaking with witches, he had his own shock to deal with. Regina stood at his side, an arm around his back, and a sturdy presence on which to lean.

A rectangular hole gaped in the ground. Grandfather's mahogany coffin sat at the bottom, a few steps away from Mildred's grave. Something in my chest settled, seeing him there. Finality. So, it *was* real.

Rognvald, Scarlett, Leda, and Reeves framed the other edge of the grave. A single torch illuminated between us, the only light at the midnight hour. We spoke in whispers, though we had nothing to hide. The trees sent me a steadying gift. A reminder of their love, their presence, in a looped refrain.

You belong to us.
Her sorrow is ours.

All will be well.

"I'd like to start," Papa said into the fragile air, "by thanking you, Scarlett. Your accommodations around our requests for his private burial are most appreciated. He would prefer this—to be buried quietly next to Mildred, with his closest friends and family, instead of a grand affair with the Network."

Scarlett gave a wan smile and a nod. "I agree. The Network will be pleased to honor him tomorrow at a banquet in his honor. His wishes, and yours, are most important."

She met my gaze.

I gave her a trying smile, which she returned.

Papa reached for a shovel and handed it to me. His serious hazel eyes captured mine. "You first." His voice caught ever-so-slightly. "He loved you the most."

I gently pushed the shovel into his chest. "He loved *you* most, Papa. I'll go next."

After a long thought, he nodded once, speared the shovel into the half-frozen loam, and dribbled it into the hole. It thudded dully. A sense of closure swept through me as I picked up my own shovel and did the same.

"I love you," I whispered, and the soil dribbled into eternity with him.

Chapter Six

Merrick swept me home, stripped me out of my dress, slid a nightgown over my head, wrapped me in his strong arms, and curled around me in the bed. We fell asleep in moments. The trees sang to me all night while Merrick held me. We woke at noon.

Sleep restored clarity. Clarity gave me energy. Thank the goddess for it, because the banquet began hours later.

Far too quickly, I stood in front of the ballroom, gazing dumbly around. All the Network leadership, including Coven Leaders, Council Members, and High Witches, turned out to honor Grandfather. A painting of him stood at the top of the room, set up on a stand surrounded by enchanted winterflowers. Castle staff bustled back and forth, sweeping the floor, replacing appetizers, offering hot drinks, and quietly keeping the room flowing.

"Just an hour," Merrick promised.

I nodded.

For Grandfather.

Ten steps into the room, a Coven Leader waved. Behind him, two others saw me and hurried forward. My chest tightened. As I steeled myself for the onslaught, something peculiar happened. A short arm slipped through mine and tugged me to the right. I only had time to glance over and see a head full of curls before momentum bore me away from the rapidly-approaching well-wishers.

Council Member Clare.

Merrick blinked in shock as I glanced at him over my shoulder. He held up his hands in question. I shrugged, stumbling away.

Council Member Clare's short legs pattered fast, slipping along with her prim voice calling ahead, clearing the way. We angled toward a far window, behind a circle of unoccupied divans. Few witches cluttered this area, away from the burning fireplace. The chilly windows shed boreal air like coats.

She shooed away a young couple with a sweep of her fingers, and released me at the window. Angled so she could see over my shoulder, she sent a spell around us, shielding our conversation from listening ears. This woman meant business.

I couldn't help a smile. "Council Member Clare."

"Clare, please. I'm not sure if you noticed, but Head Witch Mazzano was on his way to speak with you, and with him, his local Head Witch acolytes. Had he arrived, you wouldn't have escaped for at least twenty minutes. No one has time for that."

"Thanks."

"I'm sorry about Marten," she said crisply, "I know how much you meant to each other. But you're going to hear a lot of that today, and I want to discuss something else with you before you're worn out."

Intrigued, and grateful to talk about anything else, I asked, "What is it?"

"Georgette."

"Georgette?"

Clare smiled with a ferocity that surprised me. "You've seen the articles?"

"The ones against the Sisterhood?"

"Yes."

"Of course. Who hasn't? She's been posting one a week since the Eastern Network rebellion. They haven't ranked very high on the *Chatterer* scroll but . . ."

She shook her head. "Not *those*. These."

With a spell, she summoned an open envelope. Several cut papers stacked inside. Clare had sliced the stories out of several *Chatterer* scrolls to keep the article accessible. Cutting the scroll destroyed the magic, so she sacrificed many scrolls to keep these records.

Quickly, I thumbed through the headlines, unable to see the smaller script.

Favoritism Amongst The Elite?
Donovan's Reign Resumes
The Sisterhood Will Break the Brotherhood

My breath caught, recalling Grandfather's discussion of the former High Priest, Donovan. Leda hadn't shown me *these*. "I had no idea."

"They're much, much farther down the page, and appeared only the last week or so." Clare spoke with a voice of steel, though she wrung her hands together.

"But—"

"Not since Marten died," she added, as if reluctant to assign any goodness to Georgette, "but that's part of the problem. With the High Priest gone, your support for the Sisterhood might plummet."

"I know."

Clare's eyes snapped to mine. "You do?" I nodded, enjoying the affirmation of Leda's prowess. "Georgette's going to unleash her *real* attack now," she muttered. "These articles might have missed your notice, but what she does next won't. Mark my words."

"We've already anticipated this."

Clare's posture shifted a little. "I'm happy to hear you're tracking the situation."

Almost as surprising was Clare's unexpected warning. She'd proven to be kind and helpful, if not distant, but she hadn't extended such support in the past when the Sisterhood could have used it.

"Georgette is going to go on a rampage against the Sisterhood. She'll try to discredit you before your Council meeting," she said quickly. Her eyes darted over my shoulder, then back. There wasn't desperation in her words, but fervency.

"What do you see as her motivation?" I asked. As a Council Member, she'd have a completely different impression of Georgette than me.

Clare was too eager to comply. "Georgette is trying to prove herself a sort of . . . guardian . . . for the Network. It's a slow bid to position herself as the next High Priestess, if you ask me. If she does so now, before Scarlett firmly establishes a new High Priest, she can impress whoever is coming in."

"Whomever Scarlett appoints," I said under my breath, "is who would appoint the High Priestess that takes her place."

"Precisely."

A reality I hadn't considered, but one that made sense. "But Scarlett will likely reign for decades more," I pointed out.

"We hope so, certainly. Scarlett is wonderful, but things happen unexpectedly all the time. Illness, for one. Disasters, for another. As much as you'd like to assign security to anyone, it's a lie. Georgette's attempts to draw power into the Council through Scarlett have met with lackluster success. Scarlett has made concessions, but nothing that doesn't have historical precedent. Georgette remains . . . unsatisfied."

Silently, I congratulated Scarlett and Leda's wise-but-cautious approach.

Several witches strolled by, regarding us with odd stares. Georgette might see us in discussion, also. Would Clare care? Unlikely. Clare and Georgette had been at odds since Georgette arrived.

"Thank you, Council Member. Your view is helpful."

"I felt you deserved some warning. If I were you, I'd anticipate bolder articles as early as tomorrow morning. Politics and motivation rarely wait, and neither do Council Members. The Council tends to think Scarlett will appoint a new High Priest quickly. There are a few candidates most Council Members agree would be ready and willing to take the position."

Despite my loathing of all political machinations and the subterranean intrigue that accompanied them, I couldn't help asking, "Who?"

Clare opened her mouth to reply, but paused. Her head tilted to the side, prompting me to glance over my shoulder. Georgette stood a few paces away, her surprised brow raised high. Elegant shoes peeked out from the bottom of her silken dress, glimmering a pale cerulean.

She wore cream and white in honor of Grandfather's passing.

"Jikes," I muttered.

Leda, where are you?

By the fireplace.

Clare lifted a hand and waved to Georgette, but spoke to me through her teeth. "I'll handle this, if you like." Her smile had a saccharine, feral slant, which prompted the question of whether Clare cared about the Sisterhood, or seeing Georgette lose?

Go invisible and come to the far wall, I said to Leda. *Near the windows. Come up behind me. I'll explain in a minute.*

All right.

Clare's arm lowered. "I don't mind if she sees me with you, mind you. Hopefully you feel the same."

"I don't care about anything Georgette thinks."

Clare barked a low laugh. "Goodness knows, she's not leaving. I think she wants to speak with you."

"I won't speak with her today."

"Who could blame you? She's a nightmare." This solidified my hunch that Clare's motivation wasn't as much about the Sisterhood as . . . something else. Political rivalry at its finest, perhaps. The Sisterhood would not be anyone's weapon, but Clare's indignation provided an escape opportunity I couldn't ignore.

While Clare muttered about how to get rid of Georgette, eyes darting here and there, I turned my attention to sensing magic. Familiar spells blazed in a room full of witches. The sensation of their collective presence flowed in and out of my awareness as I gazed around. Transformation spells, summoning, cleaning, etc. My study revealed a familiar signature approaching my back. I knew that magic, had sensed it many times.

Leda.

She brushed my arm. An intentional, informative touch. *I'm behind you,* she said.

Thank you. When I go invisible, I want you to transport away so Georgette thinks I'm leaving. If she senses that spell, hopefully she'll believe I'm gone. Go anywhere. You can return right after.

After a beat, she said, *I understand. I'm ready.*

Bless her beautiful mind.

Georgette stood with her hands folded in front of her, ten paces away, an expectant look on her face. Clare had been correct. The stubborn set of Georgette's jaw made it clear she had no intention of leaving. To Clare, I said, "I'm going to leave you to deal with her. Is that all right?"

Clare's savage smile widened, honed on Georgette.

"My pleasure."

Going invisible.

I'm ready.

I vanished at the same moment that Leda transported from the room. Based on Georgette's widening eyes, which narrowed in outrage after I vanished, she didn't bother to sense what spell I used. If she had, she'd only sense transportation. My invisibility came from one of Grandfather's cached, unknown spells.

The ruse worked.

Clare trilled her fingers in Georgette's direction and removed the privacy incantation. Ballroom sounds flooded my ears. Clare advanced, her conservative skirt swaying.

"Georgette," she said.

"Clare."

"A pleasure to see you here."

"You as well."

Georgette's bland aloofness opposed Clare's blatant

ferocity. The two of them regarded each other like poised swords. After a moment, Georgette asked, "Where did Miss Monroe—forgive me, is it Mrs. Hughes now?—go?"

"She required a minute alone. She has safety with me, of course, which is why we spoke so extensively just now."

I rolled my eyes. Jikes, but Clare laid it on thick. Her intentional jab sharpened Georgette's antagonistic stare.

"Does she?"

Clare's smile widened.

Georgette's tight smile shared my irritated opinion. "How lovely for both of you. I shall have to find her another day."

As she spun to go, Clare called to her back. "Leave her alone, Georgette. She's lost a beloved mentor and handfasted within days of each other. The woman has enough on her plate as it is."

Beloved mentor gave me instant reassurance. Most of the Network didn't realize how deep my tie with Grandfather went. While I called him Grandfather in private, sometimes in public, Papa only referred to him as Marten. Most assumed he was a mentor and adopted paternal figure, not family. I preferred their ignorance.

Georgette paused. She spun with eyes like a hissing cat. "You're telling me that the Head of the Sisterhood, the entity you so closely support, must be guarded and protected?"

My stomach ached. Another spell glided into my awareness. Leda had returned, but invisibly. She slipped close. I touched her as the two Council Members postured.

"She's a witch, Georgette!" Clare exclaimed under her breath. "Even the Sisterhood requires a few days to grieve. Allow her space."

"She's the Head of the Sisterhood, and if she cannot

handle running the Sisterhood and dealing with the loss of a beloved, but old, mentor, then she's hardly in a position to take on the Network's challenges. This is something I'd rather know sooner than later, thank you very much. You have helped to confirm one of my more alarming concerns."

Clare's mouth bobbed open, then closed. Whatever her thoughts, she seemed to understand that nothing she said would improve her position. Nor mine. Georgette had cornered her, and by extension, me. Clare effectively made everything worse.

Recognizing her win, Georgette smiled.

"Merry part, Clare. Have a lovely day."

Georgette dissolved into the crowd at the same moment Merrick asked, *What are you doing, B? I can sense your magic at the window with Leda.*

I'll explain in a minute.

Clare smoothed a hand over her hair, smiled at a passing trio, and cleared her throat. Color darkened the tops of her cheeks. To Leda, I said, *We need to talk, but now isn't the time. Tomorrow?*

Exhaustion perfused her voice. *Yes, please.*

* * *

The next morning, I stood in front of my bookshelf, lovingly created by the forest and sculpted into the tree for greater grimoire protection. Most of the titles cluttering it once belonged to Grandfather. He bequeathed them to me months before.

Like he knew.

Did he? Perhaps, on some subterranean level. The thought struck a discordant note in my chest that I attempted to ignore. I stroked the edge of a most beloved tome. His journal. A diary of his life throughout the years, from before he met Mildred until a few weeks ago.

I couldn't read it. Not yet. Having it filled my heart full up, though. A promise for later, when his memory called to me.

A letter appeared on the table. The ice-blue text caught my attention. Alina. With a spell, I commanded it to open. It sped over, unfolding.

Sending my regards and comfort. Inform me of your availability, as the request is still yours if you desire it.

Heart in my throat, I scribbled a reply. *I'll come tomorrow.* A sense of footing followed. With something to do on the horizon, my internal flailing calmed. Leda interrupted my final sip of coffee with a message through the communication magic.

Transport to the Council Member hall invisibly. You have two minutes to enter the room before I close the doors in advance of the meeting beginning.

Intrigued, I obeyed immediately, bare feet notwithstanding. Something must be happening that Leda desired me to witness. We were supposed to meet for brunch in an hour to discuss Georgette and Clare's face-off at Grandfather's memorial.

Transporting invisibly had become second-nature, something I appreciated more and more. I landed outside of the Council Member room. Many Council Members kept offices in this hallway. Busy witches hustled through the corridor, underneath garlands celebrating the upcoming Yule holiday. Red berries sprouted at the peak of each swoop, scattered with silvery winterflowers. The smell of pine needles and cinnamon graced the air.

To my right stood the Council Member Hall's open door. Clare stood within the doorway, speaking in hushed tones to her Assistant. I couldn't hear the words. Leda stood across from her. I breezed by, touching her arm as I hurried inside ahead of another Assistant.

Leda pulled the door shut behind me.

I slipped to the far corner where I could observe from behind a sculpture of Esmelda, the first High Priestess in the Central Network. She stood erect, chin tilted up, eyes assessing, arms at her side. A powerful pose for an enduring legacy. The spot behind her sculpture promised a strong vantage point for the room. Most importantly, it allowed me to see Georgette and Clare's expressions.

Scarlett began the meeting with a simple, "Eloise, please give us the invocation of blessings before we begin."

A plump witch gifted the Council Members with a steady, lyrical chant. When she finished and returned to her seat, Scarlett spread one hand in an open gesture.

"While I have several points of discussion surrounding the passing of our High Priest and my plans for the next one, I would like to open the meeting with Council Member talking points. Is there something anyone would like to say?"

Georgette immediately stood.

I rolled my eyes.

No surprise there, I muttered to Leda, who stood behind Scarlett. A slight smile elevated the corner of her mouth as she shuffled through agendas, then flowed around the outside of the gigantic table, distributing one to each Council Member. Her focus remained attentively on the room at large.

Meanwhile, I devoured every facet of Georgette's unwavering expression.

"Thank you, High Priestess. As Speaker for the

Council and acquaintance of our former High Priest, I believe it's fair to say that I join everyone here in mourning his unexpected departure. We grieve with you."

Scarlett accepted the gracious words with a nod. I avoided staring directly at the empty chair to her side, which gathered all the power in the room. The desire to scoff nearly overwhelmed me. *And acquaintance of our former High Priest.*

Irritating gnat of a witch.

Georgette folded her hands in front of her, skimming the table with her stare. "It seems crass to bring up my concerns in light of recent events, but no time is more important than now, considering previous history." She turned her entire body to face Scarlett. "High Priestess, I would like to voice concerns about Bianca Monroe."

My stomach jerked. At the sound of my name, Scarlett's widening eyes mimicked a few confused stares.

"Bianca Monroe?" Council Member Eloise muttered to her Assistant. "Does that make sense to you?"

Clare piped up before Scarlett could respond. "She handfasted," she sniped. "Her name is now Hughes."

Wrong, I muttered to Leda. *I haven't decided yet.*

Leda bit her bottom lip. *It's her attempt to stand up for you. No matter what Georgette says about Bianca Monroe, Clare is going to counter it somehow.*

Is she standing up for me, or making Georgette angry? Who can tell?

Leda's eternal wisdom proved itself out moments later. After Georgette said, "It's common knowledge amongst the Council that Bianca and our High Priest were rather close. His mentorship of her was suspiciously deep."

"They weren't just close," Clare sniped. "They were like family."

Scarlett set Clare a warning glare, and she shrank into her seat. With a martyric huff, Georgette straightened her sapphire corset, neck elongating.

"We've seen Miss *Monroe* face grief in the past. She was raw and wild then, as many of us remember. There's some wisdom in deciding if the same remains today, considering her grief over her," Georgette cut Clare a snide sneer, "*family-like* mentor."

Sparse nods littered the room, relegated to the few Council Members firmly on Georgette's side. An air of tense anticipation followed her pause, giving everyone a chance to soak in her words. Scarlett revealed no change in her curious expression. Leda stood at her side, features arranged into polite interest.

"I hardly think it under the purview of this Council to decide anything about the emotional status of a witch not directly involved with the Council affairs," Scarlett parried lightly.

"Forgive me, High Priestess, but Miss Monroe *is* directly involved with our affairs. Or, rather, she'd like to be. Considering Miss Monroe's increasing desire to make the Sisterhood a part of the Central Network's defense system, we need to decide now whether we hold off on our decision to value the Sisterhood or not. I would like to advocate for caution around Miss Monroe until we ascertain whether she has issues with her powers."

"What issues do you anticipate?" Scarlett inquired.

"Control, Your Highness. Council Member Clare herself has voiced concerns over Bianca being emotionally capable of handling outside stress during a time of loss. In less than three weeks, Bianca plans to meet with the Council to determine if we will give her currency. Shall we postpone it? Now isn't an ideal time for her to focus on the Sisterhood. Surely, a mourning period must be observed."

Leda swallowed, but her lips didn't budge. She kept her disinterested eyes on Georgette, though her thoughts appeared far away.

Only a few witches in the Network understand that Marten is your grandfather, Leda said, *so this* 'mourning period' *is a* really *big reach on her part. She's attempting to get in our way through any approach she can.*

Clare thinks Georgette is trying to position herself as a guardian for the Network.

Maybe.

What do you think she wants?

Control, she stated clearly. So clearly it rang through my mind. *Georgette wants greater control to make specific things happen. Clare's assessment of Georgette's motivations wasn't wrong.*

Georgette continued her extrapolation on my faults with, "Bianca Monroe has been explosive and irrational in the past. She asserts herself as the Head of the Sisterhood —yet another point I feel the Council should be prepared to contest—at an emotional time in her life. Through her wild ways, she may discredit the Sisterhood. By extension, the Council *if* we approve of giving her currency."

Clare, near apoplectic, gripped her armrests with white knuckles and lips pressed bloodless.

Scarlett pondered her observation. "I hear you. Before we proceed, I must know: what has Bianca had to say about your concerns when you approached her with them directly?"

When Georgette fumbled to reply, dumbstruck, I silently cackled. Scarlett, the mild-mannered winner of all debates. Georgette's former sturdiness faltered. "Well . . . Your Highness . . . I-I haven't spoken with her."

Scarlett affected surprise. "You haven't?"

"Due to recent events, I felt it imprudent."

"You thought it more befitting to discuss concerns about her with the Council instead, while she is not present to respond?"

"This is a matter of Network security."

Scarlett looked to the Council. "Do any of you understand Bianca Monroe to be dangerous?"

None replied, though Council Member Winifired, over the Bickers Mill covens, appeared ready to raise her hand. Without regarding Georgette, Scarlett asked, "Are any of you aware that the Sisterhood has become a bonafide entity that we pay, and thus, have any say over their emotional state?"

Silence flowed.

Scarlett returned her attention to Georgette. "I see that none from the Council share your concern. It's my understanding that the official date for that decision is in less than three weeks."

With a tone that seethed with rage, Georgette nodded once. Her entire neck flexed with the motion.

"Yes, Your Highness."

"That doesn't mean anything," said Winifred, though meekly. "Whether or not Bianca is fit to run the Sisterhood while grieving Marten isn't the problem. Her impetuousness *is* the problem. There's more here than just the passing of a mentor."

"That is not the concern Georgette posed today," Scarlett replied, "nor is it within the scope of our weekly meeting. You may table that concern for our meeting three weeks from now."

Winifred nodded.

My eyes skirted around to catalog the other responses. Council Member reactions were far from what I expected.

Instead of agreement or irritation, most appeared down-right bored. One yawned. Another scribbled a design on a notepad.

Shock held me in place.

Boredom?

Georgette's inflammatory accusations hardly stirred Council Members out of their stupor. Only Council Member Henry over the Tate Covens, whom I once walked with through Letum Wood, and Clare showed concern.

The Sisterhood wouldn't struggle because of Georgette. We'd flounder by sheer indifference.

What a powerful tool I'd never anticipated.

Scarlett faced Georgette. "Thank you for your concern, Council Member. The record has noted it. Any of you with concerns over Miss Monroe's grief or behavior, please take it up with Miss Monroe. After several interactions with her, I have observed no change in her demeanor. Except," she added, "for the same sadness we all share, but from deeper wells. Now, to the next order of business."

Former Bianca—the one that Georgette called out minutes ago—might have exploded. The force of my rage would have bubbled and swelled my magic, creating its own problematic response.

Not today.

I was an entirely different witch. *Undeserving for other reasons,* Tyrant said brightly. *But not for lack of control. This time. You certainly had enough control to layer spell after spell on Ricardo and lead him—and his children—to their demise.*

Leave me, I replied.

He cackled and cackled and sang a song. *Murderer. Murderer. Murderer.*

My throat thickened. Hanging threads tied me together at that moment. I stared at the wall, seeing clearly for the first time what the Council thought of the Sisterhood as a whole. One loathed me. One supported me to irritate her opponent, and the rest? They'd prefer teatime to Sisterhood business.

My thoughts, spreading mist over a field on fire, cooled and settled.

I understood.

Oh, *how* I understood.

The irony hurt like a stab. Georgette wasn't entirely wrong about my emotions: I felt my grief, pain, and shock deeply. Lashed rage, tempered and present, bubbled. But I wasn't a wild teenager, nor unprepared. Mourning and I had become old friends, in a way. No, there was more to me than what the Council acknowledged.

Grandfather said the same.

Scratching chairs and shifting bodies drew me out of my long ruminations behind Esmelda. I blinked, startled to find the entire Council standing. The clock confirmed that more than an hour had passed while I floundered, lost in thought. In its passage, I'd come to the obvious conclusion.

I knew what to do.

Leda's voice broke my reverie as the last Council Member cleared. *Scarlett would like to speak with you. She was aware that I invited you after I heard whispers amongst the Assistants of Georgette's intent to bring you in as a discussion point. We'll wait for you in Scarlett's office.*

I'll see you there.

* * *

Scarlett kept a weathered eye on me. "That couldn't have been fun, Bianca."

Leda settled three scrolls on Scarlett's desk while simultaneously batting away darting messages that whirled in and out. The closed doors ensured our privacy, so I gratefully removed the invisibility spell.

"Revealing," I said. "Very revealing."

"Georgette saw an opportunity and she took it," Leda replied. "While her deductions were a desperate reach, we learned a lot."

"How so?" Scarlett asked.

I replied first, "We know exactly where the Council stands in regards to the Sisterhood. They'll kill us with their indifference."

Leda met my eyes for the first time. "That surprised me, too."

Scarlett put a hand to her temple and pressed, as if she had a headache. Observing the action, Leda summoned a quill and paper. She jotted a message, folded it, and pitched it across the room. The slim paper slid under the doorway. A request for a headache potion from the Apothecary, I'd wager.

"Georgette certainly has a vendetta," Scarlett agreed, "and so does Clare. Only Georgette is focused on you, and Clare is focused on Georgette."

"We can hardly consider Clare an ally with that motivation," I said.

Scarlett dipped her head. "I agree."

"Alina called me to the Southern Network, Your Highness. She requested me—and the Sisterhood—to help her."

Scarlett brightened. "Did she? She didn't mention it to me."

"Outside of the Council, no one associates the Sisterhood with you yet, Your Highness," Leda offered as she shifted through papers that Hiddleston sent into the room through a slot in the middle of the door. "Alina may not know. Besides, Alina likes to work directly with Bianca." Leda caught my gaze. "They have a friendship. Of sorts."

"I accepted, Your Highness."

"Naturally, I expected nothing else. It will have to stay outside the understanding of the Council for now." She frowned. "What *is* the mission exactly?"

"I'm sorry, but I won't tell you."

Scarlett straightened. "Forgive me?"

The rightness of my plan clicked into place as I closed in. "Not only did I promise Alina utmost secrecy for the time being, but the Council made it clear what they want today. The Sisterhood is going to give it to them."

Leda's head snapped up. She set the paperwork down and slowly asked, "What do you mean?"

Swirling to face her, I said, "You know this path with approval from the Council is over. It has been for a while. Can you accept that we won't get votes on the Council because they don't *care*? Anyone who does care, Georgette has already poisoned. She said today that she plans to challenge my *assertion* as the leader. We have Henry, and perhaps Clare. That's it."

Puzzled, she frowned. Withdrawing from her thoughts, Leda slowly said, "I see why you think this, Bianca. But . . . without approval . . . what is the Sisterhood?"

"Whatever it wants to be," I breathed, laughing. Burdens soared off of me at the thought. "Whatever we *need* it to be. Don't you see? Our path doesn't involve the Council. Tomorrow, I plan to stand before the Council and withdraw the Sisterhood's appeal. We're not going to fight for funding. We'll find a better way. A different way. They don't legitimize the Sisterhood. *We* legitimize the Sisterhood."

Leda's jaw split open. She stared in open astonishment. Scarlett couldn't summon a single word.

With a saucy grin, I declared, "The Sisterhood is going rogue."

Chapter Seven

Morning brought dawn, frigid breath, and icy branches. I lay in bed, curled around Merrick's steadily rising and falling chest, and commanded a fire in the distant stone hearth. Flames flickered with a slow growing light moments later.

Several minutes passed before warmth crept across the floor. While waiting for the gelid air to soften, I watched the falling snowflakes. Merrick stirred, felt me in his arms, and brought me closer. Tucked into his neck, his arms wrapped me, the world slipped away again.

"I don't want to go out there," I murmured.

He rumbled something unintelligible. Unable to help myself, I laughed. He cleared his throat and tried again. A trail of featherlight kisses began at my temple, trailing across my ear, my cheek, my neck.

"Then don't," he growled.

With a sigh, I let his lowering kisses distract me.

* * *

An hour later, Merrick frowned. Propped on his elbows, he hovered above me. His hair dangled in sandy strands around his furrowed brow. Charming, in a way. One might *also* call it a glower.

"You're what?" he whispered.

Reaching up to tuck a stray hair behind his ear, I murmured, "In an hour, the Sisterhood will officially withdraw our request for Council support."

"You're jesting."

I shook my head, lips pressed. Hand held out to the side, I summoned a *Chatterer* scroll from the other side of the room. As expected, a new article graced the middle of the scroll, right hand corner.

Can The Sisterhood Survive Turmoil?

I didn't bother reading the article. Leda probably scoured it on publication. A thrill zipped through me at the thought that Georgette played into my new plan. She gave me *exactly* what I wanted.

Evaporation.

Dissolution.

If the Sisterhood didn't exist, all the better for us to hide in the shadows and serve those who needed us the most—without the restricting control of the Council. Merrick skimmed the article, from which the words *Council Member Georgette* flashed several times.

"It's a load of drivel," he muttered darkly.

I braced my hands around his neck, curling my fingers into his silky hair. He studied me, his breath a caress.

"The Sisterhood will never serve this Council, Merrick. They're too indifferent, and some are actively hostile. I don't want to work in those circumstances. Fighting Greyson in Carcere taught me that I have power of my own, and so much capability. That's when I realized that the Sisterhood couldn't look like the Brotherhood, because the Network needed something different, right?"

"Right."

"Then, with the Eastern Network rebellion, I learned that we couldn't have our focus be *just* on Scarlett. Even though it was our most likely path to approval, it narrowed us too much to make a difference. There are other witches who need our help. We have to be trusted, fluid, and offer more protection."

"And?" he drawled.

Grinning, I said, "And, as always, Grandfather had the answer. The night before he died? He said to me, *There is more to you than what the Council deems worthy of acclaim. Choose what makes all the parts of you happiest, and you can never go astray.*"

Merrick's weight softened, just like his eyes. I pulled his lips softly to mine, enjoying their pillowy warmth, his comforting hold.

"You don't want the Council deciding what the Sisterhood does," he whispered against my cheek. "It's understandable. Admirable."

"Or who we *are*," I breathed. "Yesterday, I saw that they would never understand. There's too much indifference, antagonism, politics. Even Clare supports me through the angle of defeating Georgette. For the Sisterhood to truly thrive and do what we do best—"

"You need to go rogue."

Hearing him say it, accompanied by a wicked smile, brought bubbling laughter from within. I curled around him, chuckling, and we rolled onto our sides together. His hand weighed heavy and delightful on my neck. I held his wrist, his bare legs scissoring over mine until he trapped me.

"Whatever you do, B." He rubbed his thumb over my bottom lip. "I'm here every step of the way. Whether you're rogue, mercenary, or Council-approved, you have me."

Wryly, I said, "I believe the words you're looking for are: *which is forever.*"

We melted into the sacred space between ultimatums and adoration, which filled me with the courage to meet my destiny.

Chapter Eight

While striding down the Council Member hallway, I drew in three cleansing breaths. Air swilled at the bottom of my lungs, cold-tinted from a brisk, rousing jog. Dawn sparkled across the windowpanes in fragile aquamarine fractals. Not a hint of movement graced Letum Wood, visible in snatches through the windows. Frost coated the kingdom.

You're sure? I asked Leda.

Resigned, she said, *After thinking about it all night, yes. This is the best path. It could be political suicide for a future Sisterhood, but it won't be as bad as what you're probably going to face.* She paused, adding, *Georgette will shred you for removing it, call you weak, say you knew you couldn't hack it.*

I know.

Then get it done. As discussed, I'll remain with Scarlett, although I'd rather be with you.

This is mine, I said. *Mine to start, mine to steer. It's politically safer for you to be visibly disconnected.*

I stopped in front of the closed double doors. Leda

made certain they weren't locked after the Council gathered twenty minutes before. Her final words rang with bell-like reverberations. *Go well, and goddess bless you. I'll be waiting to hear more.*

Grandfather told me to honor my anger, but he wasn't the only witch with that advice. Years ago, Mabel taught me that anger had power. If I gave into it, it controlled me. If I controlled it, it gave back. Not forever, because then I became the monster, like Mabel. Because of that lesson, I'd learned that a fine line existed between acknowledging the monsters that fed my rage, and entertaining them.

Today, I would do neither.

I would banish them.

In full control of my magic, and with Tyrant tucked into a distant mind recess, I called on all that power at this moment.

Courage ballooned through my chest like crawling fire, born from memories, the grief over Grandfather, the certainty of instinct, the terrors that fed on painful recollections, the attacks on the Sisterhood, and the emptiness of death. With that power in my metaphorical hands, I shoved the doors open. They blew wide without resistance. I strolled inside, one hand on Viveet. The Volare strapped to my back, as always.

Immediately, Aurora's inquisitive eyes caught me. She sat on the far right corner, hands in her laps. Amongst the ten Council Members, Aurora had an honorary, Council-Member-like position. Almost, but not quite there. They tolerated her presence because Network borders touched almost half the covens, and they required her input.

Georgette stood on the other side of the room, where Scarlett usually sat. On seeing me, her jaw slackened and eyes widened.

"Council," I called affably, "please forgive me. I realize how crass this must appear." I met Georgette's astonished stare with a blithe smile. "What would you call it, Council Member? Right. *Wild*. This will only take a moment."

Three Council Members straightened out of dozy slumps. Several of their expressions twisted, but whether annoyed at the interruption or my presence, it didn't matter.

I spoke to Georgette. "I'm here to officially withdraw the Sisterhood's request to meet with the Council in three weeks, as well as my intention to request Network currency and legitimacy. The Sisterhood is no longer interested in being a bonafide Network entity."

Georgette pulled in a low breath, cycling through excitement and suspicion within a heartbeat. Her lips slackened. She stared in unfettered shock. Inclining my head to the room at large, I backed toward the door.

"Have a lovely day."

Clare shot to her feet. "Miss Monroe," she exclaimed, wide-eyed. "But . . . why?"

Leda anticipated this question, so I came prepared and said nothing. Their discomfort grew while her query hung like a coat on a peg for a solid ten seconds. The words reverberated in their residual stillness.

Georgette's shoulders expanded as she pulled in a deep breath, recovering her composure. "Well, Miss . . . Monroe. This is a surprise."

Inclining my head, I turned to go. Winifred's voice piped up from the far corner, preventing my retreat.

"What are your plans for the Sisterhood then, Miss Monroe?"

"That information isn't the interest of this room."

A ripple of surprise followed. "It certainly is," Winifred retorted. "We can't have a rogue mercenary force in the Central Network, thinking you can do whatever you want."

My brow elevated, but I said nothing.

Georgette's elation swiftly faded, becoming something else entirely. A sinister, livid tone edged her voice. "Miss Monroe, do we need to discuss the safety of the Central Network and the parameters under which you are allowed to operate?"

"No." I met her gaze. "The Sisterhood is disbanded."

Gasps followed. Georgette's chest rose and fell with greater force as she fumbled for a response. Clare appeared ready to cry. In the corner, Council Member Theodore covered his mouth with his hand, but it didn't hide his pleased smile. He ran the Southern Covens, where Michelle grew up.

Only Council Member Henry looked truly distressed, his focus bouncing between me, Georgette, and Winifred. The others gaped.

"I will take my leave now, Council. Thank you."

I whirled on my feet. Council Member Frederick's rolling voice escorted me out the door.

"You may not agree with Bianca Monroe, Georgette, but you've created a right mess. That girl isn't going to disband. She's Derek Black's daughter! The last thing you want is Bianca Monroe operating a Sisterhood firmly outside of our collective awareness. You just drove her into the shadows, and good luck getting her to return to the light."

The doors closed behind me.

Chapter Nine

Leda and I planned to meet at the Great Library of Burke, where we converged on the main atrium, that afternoon.

Birds fluttered from branches growing inside the walls. Ivy peeled to the left and right, their strands shivering each time a bird landed. Fluttering wings gave the room a feeling of movement.

The aviary was a new facet for winter in the Great Library of Burke. Reputedly meant to help witches study mating habits, and encourage low populations of specific species to recover. Magical spells protected the floor from falling projectiles. Their dropping poop evaporated halfway down from the high ceiling, then swept outside.

When I slipped through the main doors, Leda spoke to a quiet male Librarian with long salt-and-pepper streaks in his curly black hair. They stood across the room, heads bent close. Guilt swept through me at the sight of her. Bags hung low under her eyes. She fought a yawn every other breath. In addition to the stress of Grandfather's death, she now dealt with navigating the Sisterhood. I felt for her.

Her eyes connected to mine. She beckoned me with a wave. The man she spoke with nodded in greeting, but departed before I'd crossed halfway. She met me near the middle, underneath a flurry of blue-tailed doves.

Leda gestured down a long hall disappearing into black as I fell in stride. "I reserved a room down this hallway."

"Any reason you wanted to meet here?"

"I need a break from the castle, and we need secrecy. The first of many articles about your withdrawal just released in the *Chatterer*, and both of us are about to have correspondence up to our ears. Besides, I had a few favors to ask."

"Of that witch?"

"Yes."

While a glut of correspondences would normally have inspired deepest fear, her prediction failed to scare me. Papa and I gathered just enough celebrity through the years that witches sent me their opinions about my life often enough. Georgette's articles wouldn't change established patterns.

With that ominous statement hovering in my mind, however, I followed Leda through a corridor. We walked in silence, lost to our own thoughts. It felt good to stroll side-by-side again. Through the thick and thin of change, we always had our friendship. We'd weathered much together; I cherished our bond. All the more so after the bitter sting of Grandfather's loss.

We entered a quiet room with moving tomes. Books shuffled into towering piles that framed every wall of the rectangular room. More joined through windows every ten seconds. Each slap and slam of opening and closing windows emitted chilly air gusts. I watched in fascination.

As a book lowered, it settled on a thin counter that ran the length of the room. The front cover opened, a paper was removed, the cover closed, and it slipped to a different pile. At least ten piles occupied the room; I had no idea their organization structure. At any moment, any given book would soar out of the room through a hole in the wall on the far side. If they were issued from the middle of a pile, the tomes on top would lower carefully, and nothing fell out of place.

"Fascinating," I murmured.

In the middle of this gentle chaos stood two high-back chairs with velvet covers, the edges rubbed bare. Limp pillows struggled to stand against the tall, winged backs. The table in between them granted a cozy picture, considering the bold black-lined tea set that steamed and huffed, waiting with an impatient, rattling lid.

"Acquisitions," Leda said primly. "Books come to this room when they first arrive at the library, hence the holes in the walls."

The more I studied the room, the more holes I found. The constant flow should have created chaos, but the shuffling lent comfort instead of calamity. I unwound.

"It's oddly . . ."

"Calming?"

"Yes."

Leda smiled, her plan obvious. "I think so, too, as strange as it seems. Anyway, no one will bother us here. If you hadn't wanted to meet, I think Hiddleston would have demanded I leave. If not Scarlett herself. According to them, I'm tense."

I hid a laugh.

We sat, and the tea tray scuttled closer to her. She

spoke clearly to it. "One cup of coffee and one cup of tea, please. Cream and sugar for both."

While items on the tea tray summoned each drink at her command, she folded her hands in her lap and stared at me. Her acutely powerful focus threatened to consume me, like a phoenix rising from ashes. She already recovered some of her alacritous energy.

"Have you seen the headlines?" she asked.

"No."

"Do you want to?"

My hands curled around the ratty armchair. "Not yet."

"Fine. I'll keep records of what I receive. From preliminary reports, only a few witches have sent me letters. Council Member Assistants, mostly, inquiring what I know. Keep whatever letters you receive. I'll organize them, then you can access them whenever you're ready." Her chin elevated. "Tell me what happened. The resulting chaos has been significant. My Underassistants have tracked every scrap of gossip they've heard, and most of it is not flattering to you."

Shrugging it off, I relayed the story. It required minutes, at most, because I hadn't dallied. By the end, her resigned sigh had a hint of amusement.

"Well, that's that."

Nodding, I said, "That's that."

"Then . . . enough of Georgette and Network business! Don't you have a Sisterhood mission we need to discuss? I assume you're returning shortly?"

With a sly smile, I said, "Why yes, we do. I'm heading to Alina's after this—she wrote to me yesterday, right before you called me to the Council room. Are you interested in reviewing the mission together?"

Tea cup pinched between her thumb and pointer

finger, Leda said, "It would be my delight to continue our Sisterhood adventure with greatest secrecy." With a gleam in her eye, she added, "It would be a *shame* to disappoint Council Member Frederick and his hopes for Derek Black's daughter."

* * *

The thrill of a new adventure infused me when I entered the Southern Network, welcomed by the smell of pine. Filling my lungs with the bitter cold air sent a shiver cascading down my spine. At my side, Alina peered into the trees, her grimace fading. After losing her magic, any magical use near her caused pain. Transporting could be downright painful, though often necessary.

"This is the lake," she said.

Thank the goddess I hadn't put Alina through that discomfort for nothing. Before finding Alina, I sought Zameroz Lake. Having never been there, I'd transported to a nearby gem mine I visited years ago, then transported out from there about ten times, attempting to find it. Once relatively certain I'd found the spot, I brought her with me.

Needle-tipped pine trees surrounded us with spiny branches, stuck outright in growing layers like trailing skirt bottoms. Snow-drifted-fields stretched to tundra behind us. My fingertips trailed over a sappy trunk as I strode past. A barren, low-toned whisper replied.

We know you.

A new development. I'd been in the lower forests of the Southern Network many times, whether for diplomatic reasons, or when Merrick and I visited in an attempt to find Andrei, the swordmaker. In all those visits, the trees here had never spoken. I wondered what it meant.

My hand pressed against the trunk.

I belong to you.

The boughs stirred, but no more words came.

After twenty minutes of brisk walking, during which Alina's cheeks pinked along the top, she paused. We stood at the top of a ridge, hidden behind bushes, overlooking a lake.

Snow dusted the lake with white powder, hiding occasional glossy hints to deeper waters. Witches moved across the glassy surface, opaque and clear in varying spots. Gigantic metal saws, as tall as the witches wielding them, bit into the ice. Large tongs, lifted with pulleys, ropes, and witches, extracted each piece.

They had recently begun working this lake based on the equipment positioning and newly established footpaths. Serrated chunks floated down a canal toward the edge of the lake, where witches with long poles awaited. A donkey stood in the frigid air, lashed to a sled. I pulled my fur-lined coat around my neck.

Such cold.

"You see?" Alina quietly retracted a spiny branch. "With their magic gone, ice witches have resorted to tools and donkeys to move the ice. It's good. The work is welcome, as well as the acquisition of new skills. There are witches caring for the donkey, and others learning the blacksmith trade to make the tools."

"They make enough currency?"

"Not while apprenticing, but eventually."

"Then how—"

"The gems that I distribute have helped witches with apprenticeships," she said blithely. "They receive support until they know enough to work on their own."

"I see," I whispered. Incredible, the depths she plunged to create independence amongst her witches.

"The ice trade has given these witches purpose and independence," she continued, removing any opportunity for pity, should it arise.

"At the expense of their safety," I added in a grumble.

Her shoulders drew wide when she pulled in a breath. "Yes. For some witches, it's considered a worthy trade. If they lose a witch to someone else, there are more to fill their position. They feed their families, and believe life is risk."

"Macabre."

"Real," she countered. "Figuring out this problem is how I can serve them, Bianca. By caring about problems they cannot fix, and fixing them for them. It will . . . build trust. If I can prove to *any* clan that the Network cares, it will make inroads to the silk clans."

The Southern mindset was hard to appreciate, coming from a life of magical ability and stable resources. Alina's witches endured scrabbling determination in one of the most hostile climates in Alkarra, and they found their path. The loss of one or two witches paled in comparison to entire villages decimated by lack of work or trade. A small inconvenience. Unless you were the lost witch, of course.

I understood.

I hated it.

"No wonder your witches aren't reporting the losses."

Alina hummed. "In context, it makes sense," she admitted. "Though I'm still not pleased with it. Our estimation of over fifty abductions may be conservative, but it could also be less."

"Could be more."

"I hope not."

Two witches hauled ice blocks onto the sled to inspect. Like a puzzle, the chunk slid into an available corner spot. With a tap on the haunches, the donkey drew it away from the lake and up a slippery embankment. When the donkey arrived at the top, a female clan witch appeared alongside the animal. Her breath billowed in front of her as she settled the donkey. During her work, another witch appeared.

Alina lifted a mittened hand. "There," she murmured. "A tribal witch has arrived. My shieldmaidens believe they sometimes transform their appearance to blend into the tribes, and wear stolen clannish clothes from abducted witches. We have observed these tribal witches attempt to learn more about ice witches, but we have circumvented their attempts. We can easily tell them apart from us, however. Their magic radiates."

Shieldmaidens didn't go unnoticed. Traditionally, the Southern Network High Priestesses used the shield-maidens as their personal protective force, but I couldn't fathom Alina held the same fastidious tradition, having been a shieldmaiden herself. Undoubtedly, she had far more . . . creative . . . ideas for their skills, such as scouting issues amongst the populace. A sort of Sisterhood in itself, really.

"How often do the tribal witches arrive?"

"Whenever new ice is ready. With that sled prepared, it will be soon. The work at this lake began yesterday, and is supposed to last through the next several days. You see?"

As she gestured with her other hand, the tribal witch, the donkey, and the ice vanished. "Oh," I breathed. "They take the whole thing."

The clannish witch who inspected the donkey had retreated, a bag swinging from one hand. Currency, undoubtedly. She toddled through the snow and toward a hastily-made shack with another donkey. Meanwhile, the clannish witches on the ice never stopped sawing.

"Sometimes," Alina whispered, "the tribal witch takes our clannish witches with the ice, and they do not come back."

"The donkey?"

"The donkey, the supplies, the sled return. Always. We'll wait so you can see the process. Thus far, it has been the same across all the lakes this specific clan cuts. You see, they set a grid in the ice?"

Hints of slash marks were visible, hastily cut. Snow covered the rest of the lake, but this section had been groomed clear.

"They mark the cleanest, flattest section as far as they think is safe. They cut a channel to float the ice to the edge of the lake so the donkey doesn't slip on the ice and break a leg—which happens. But they can't cut the whole lake —the surrounding ice grows brittle, thin, slushy. They have to rotate lakes, positions, etc."

"I see."

A hint of steel—perhaps pride—tightened her voice. "It's a nomadic life and fraught with danger, but that's the clan way."

Twenty minutes later, the donkey and the sled returned. The witch did not. Alina rubbed her arms, her breaths punctuated with frustration. "I cannot follow these tribal witches to wherever they transport, and neither could the demigods. I have tried to speak with the buyers, but they refuse to speak with me. If they see me near an ice block operation, they leave and don't return."

I winced. "I'm sure that hasn't helped your relation-ship with your witches."

"No."

"Can't they stop selling ice to them?"

"Who else would buy it?"

"Lana at the Arck?"

She shrugged. "If so, she hasn't come forward with that desire. This Western tribe requires ice and has currency." Alina pressed a hand to her chest. "I cannot stop my witches from selling it. Compared to what clannish witches might earn in various positions, the West pays them a lot of currency. In the depths of winter, there are few jobs. My witches would be scrounging off wildlife and barely avoiding starvation. If not succumbing," she added.

The details formed a broad picture. A difficult one, too. Alina fought an unknown enemy and prosperity couched in danger.

"Are both men and women taken?"

"Yes."

"You don't know why?"

"No one does."

Fifty something witches abducted with no certain lead on who took them, nor their motivations.

"Any chance these witches wanted to leave?" I asked carefully. "Would they prefer life elsewhere if it were offered?"

Alina considered my question for a long time. "I have wondered that myself, but I don't know. We asked spouses, children, and the friends who remained behind, and they weren't sure. Life isn't easy here, but the ice is part of us. Clannish witches understand cold, not heat." She pressed her fist to her breastbone, then into her chest. "We would never abandon the ice."

I understood the sentiment, as I felt the same about the forest. Glacial air assaulted my nose with eye-watering stings when I pulled in a deep breath. "I'll walk down and hide behind that shed. When the next tribal witch comes, I'll follow their spell and let you know what I find."

Alina slid her eyes to mine. "Thank you. I would like to ask . . . I read the articles and heard—"

"It's true."

"The Sisterhood has collapsed from the inside out because of weak leadership structure and internal drama amongst its members?"

Tipping my head back, I laughed. "Is that what Georgette wrote? Hilarious."

"Is it true?"

"No! Leda helped me plan a few approaches to this mission before I arrived."

"You want them to think you're done?"

"Yes."

Alina smiled with a spark of rebellion embedded within. "Good for you. You'll be better off on your own."

Her support meant more than I expected.

* * *

While waiting behind the donkey shack for the tribal witches to return, a message popped into the air in front of me. I frowned. How had I forgotten to set the repellent spell? Grandfather's death scattered my normal attention to detail. A specific type of magic diverted messages away from a witch, sending them to a preferred spot, to avoid this very thing.

The handwriting caught my eye, distracting my irritation. I didn't recognize the near-perfect script on the outer envelope. Had I ever seen such perfect loops and swirls? Curious, I pulled the wax seal free and unfolded it. Annoyance streaked through me in instant response.

Georgette.

Lovely.

Dear Miss Monroe,

Shall I address you as Mrs. Bianca Hughes? I hear you plan to keep your former last name. Please, do let me know.

I'm writing to discuss the current Sisterhood situation. In light of your recent declaration to remove your request for Council support, several Council Members and I are wondering if you wouldn't mind signing an agreement? Just to ensure the Network remains safe, a goal I believe we mutually share.

Enclosed.

Feel free to sign and return upon receipt, or as soon as possible thereafter.

Regards,

Council Member Georgette

Bemused, I peeked into the paper behind it. A contract. With the distraction of a mission occupying half my mind, I only skimmed the contents, plucking sentences here and there. *Promise not to act as leader of an entity similar to the Sisterhood* and *will not take 'missions' or 'activities' or 'responsibilities' on behalf of another witch . . .*

More drivel spilled down the page. I stacked them together and spelled it to Leda.

Take a look at this.

Then I shoved Georgette firmly out of my mind. I had witches to save.

Chapter Ten

The tribal witches returned for more ice when the next donkey crested the hill. In between the time when I sent Georgette's contract away, cast the repellant spell to prevent messages from arriving again, and this moment, I'd watched the Southern Network witches. Manual labor on icy lakes in a world where sunshine barely graced the slopes.

Brutal.

The light of day crawled away, diminishing their work time. The ice-cutters slip-slid off the ice, toting their long axes and saws, while the floaters used the long poles to send ice blocks toward the lake edge. A gaping, black hole filled the white lakebed. Water slurped along the fresh cuts, where a new skin hadn't yet hardened. As the day closed, a sense of rest and relief permeated the air. In the distance, small huts piped smoke.

I'd positioned myself at the top of the bluff where they'd met before, not far from the donkey shed. Cleared trees made a road for the donkey to plod through. I hunched under an invisibility spell near the trees and tried to keep my teeth from chattering.

The tribal witch that arrived wore a heavy clannish cloak, undoubtedly appropriated from one of their abducted witches. She was a female witch with voluminous hair and matching brown-black eyes. Her skin matched the reddish-brown desert sand, and her eyes slanted a little like those of the Southern Network clans. But she was distinctly different in a way I couldn't quite identify.

She spoke to a female clannish witch in Yazikan, the Southern Network language. I picked up a word or two here and there. *Water* and *ice* and numbers between two and several hundred. It confirmed my vague idea that they haggled over a price when the tribal witch summoned a bag of coins and tossed it to the clan witch.

The female clannish witch opened the drawstring, dumped the contents out. Coins tumbled to her hand. As she examined them, her eyes flickered to the tribal witch, and back to the heap. Nose wrinkled, she asked, "Too much?" in Yazikan.

The tribal witch smiled, infectious and attractive. She exuded an undeniable aura of authority and power. The clannish witch tipped her palm, pouring the coins into the bag. Uneasy, she plucked five or six coins free and extended them.

"Too much," she insisted, more firmly. She edged a step back, legs braced. Her eyes watched the tribal witch uneasily. The two women chattered back and forth. While distracted, I used a summoning spell to grab one of the coins off the top. At the same moment the clannish witch wrapped her fingers around them. She didn't notice the shifting weight in her palm, however subtle.

The tribal witch tipped her head to the side and

laughed, a waterfall of straight, ebony hair flowing from her hood. The clan witch didn't share her amusement. The tribal witch brushed one arm toward the donkey, and then her other arm on the opposite side.

To the west.

I tucked the coin into my pocket.

"No," the clannish witch insisted. She shifted another step away, eyes darting to the ice, where other clannish witches congregated. The tribal witch assessed her, eyes narrowing.

"Are you certain?" she purred in Yazikan. A string of words followed I couldn't decipher. She said something similar to *life is grand* or *there is more*.

Dodging several steps back, the clannish witch pitched the extra coins to her. "Go. No. Go." Panic spit the words from her lips. She tripped over her own feet, dropping to the snow.

The tribal witch sighed. "You have decided." She put a hand on the donkey and vanished. I had the time to grasp the clannish witch's inevitable surprise, then teary relief, before I pounced on the magical trail.

* * *

Heat swamped me.

Sweltering air billowed in surges, hitting like punches. From the right, then the left. Last, it rained with a surge and sticky, prickly power. By the goddess, the desert was torturous. Switching from obliterating cold to obliterating heat sent shockwaves through my body. I suppressed a gasp.

Shifting sand granules beneath my winter boots, the bray of a donkey, and a guttural shout, brought my head up. No one stood nearby, nor gave indication they noticed I arrived, which was a relief.

The desert awaited.

Sweat popped along my skin as I stared, flabbergasted, at my surroundings. While I had expected to arrive in the desert, I hadn't expected a *thriving* desert.

Greenery abounded in tall, thick trees that sprouted fibrous leaves as long as my body and as wide as my arm span. These leaves stacked in layers, providing a shaded canopy thirty paces overhead. A line of these towering trees marched in a row, wide enough for two carriages side by side, and led to a sparkling . . . something.

Ahead, the donkey lurched toward a ramshackle building surrounded by a dense thicket of the trees. Magic emanated from the structure. Didn't take a genius like Leda to deduce it must be a powerful ice shed.

Raw ice wouldn't last more than minutes in this miasma, so the female tribal witch hurried the beast into the building made of sand and magic. Several witches waited inside darkness. A rush of cool air dissolved seconds after a broad wooden door shut behind the donkey.

I shucked off my boots and cape, spelling them home. A summoning spell brought my sandals. While I longed to follow the witch into that ice shed, preparations were required. Swapping my footwear and removing my outer dress—I'd planned for this inevitability—decreased the oppressive heat. My bare arms and shoulders breathed with only my slip and sandals as barriers.

Sweet relief.

By the time I finished changing, the original female witch hadn't returned from within. She might stay inside, but she might also transport. Sufficient magic radiated from within that I could have missed any other spell.

My attention drew beyond, to the sparkle at the end of the desert trees. Witches milled around the edges. On second thought, this area looked like the outskirts of a thriving area. Not far away lurked endless sand. The reddened hills swelled in undulating vistas that ended near the horizon. An oasis.

My attention extended around the oasis, hungry for any information. The trees shot from the sand at every available spot, providing cover from the unbearing sun. These also emanated power. Spells, then. Interesting. They formed a square grid. Every five paces, another three. Five paces over, another. Not far into the trees, a crowd of witches milled. They surrounded a structure protected by warriors.

Ah. *That* had my attention.

At least five of thirty witches standing stalwart and intimidating around a glistening structure held giant machetes. They surrounded the glass, protecting water. A captured fountain, perhaps?

Ah, how interesting.

Hired warriors guarded it in a circle. Or were they part of the tribe that ran this oasis? It must be a tribe. The only rogues in a place like this were fools with a death wish. One didn't survive the desert alone.

A hunch told me I'd probably find Southern Network ice within the enclosed fountain. Western Network witches had always been clever, surviving the ravages of sun, sand, and time. But this glass water dome was a surprise. A complication, too.

If any witches here bothered to sense magical use as a security measure, I'd draw attention by shifting around, so I stayed near the shed, observing. Back in the Southern Network, clannish witches ended their work day, so there wouldn't be more shipments to observe . . .

but staying in one spot meant I couldn't scope out the oasis . . .

Better risk it.

I crept to the ice shed and pasted my back against the wall. A carving twirled along the outside, filling the two doors and top corners. A swirling sun with eight rays zagging out in lightning streaks. In the center lay a heart nestled within a bigger heart. Tribal sign, which wasn't uncommon. I committed it to memory, hurried along the exterior, and updated Leda.

I followed a witch from the Southern Network to the Western Network.

Where in the West?

An oasis of some sort, but not sure yet. I'll send you iden-tifying characteristics, just in case.

Ready anytime.

My update with sparse details finished by the time I circled the ice shed. They built the shed near the middle of the oasis, not far from the main structure at the center, where a tree-lined desert road stopped.

Any sign of clannish witches? she asked.

Not yet, but I just arrived. There's a symbol on one sand structure. I'll draw it for you later. A spiral sun with eight lightning streaks for light and nested hearts.

I've never seen anything like your description.

No distinguishing signs, witches, or hints of language revealed as I padded through the tree grid. Few tribes bothered with the common language, because they rarely left the desert or sought outside education. Motivated tribal witches who wanted currency would travel from tribe to tribe, collecting dialects, and offering services as a translator for Networks or traveling witches. They tended to congregate at oases, where other witches sought help.

Instead of tents, bedrolls and small sacks appeared

here and there. Desert camals, horse-like creatures with narrow heads, wide eyes, and a heavier girth, did most of the travel work. They clustered along a long stable-like area, eyes lidded. If witches couldn't or didn't transport, they rode a camal. The wide hooves and thick, sun resistant hides were all but desert proof.

After twenty minutes winding along the edge of the oasis in a haphazard circle, I found the other edge. The same sandy road stretched into the interior, ending at the water fountain. Set slightly within the sand, and banded below, the road had a hardened appearance. Someone cut the track leading to the middle and firmed it with a spell. A caravan lurked on the horizon, drawing closer. No one moved quickly in the desert. Too much work.

I circled inside the oasis, passing sleeping witches, packs. Most rested on top of their packs or curled around them, a light blanket pulled over their face for a hint of privacy. Definitely a spot for the weary to rest.

I sent Leda descriptions of coins, clothing, but it varied. The amalgamation was consistent with an oasis that brought all travelers to its refreshment.

But who *ran* it?

Where were the clannish witches, and the woman who brought the donkey? Transporting herself, a donkey, and a shed of ice was no small feat. She had her own cache of magical ability, and wasn't someone I planned to underestimate.

When I approached the water, my heart beat faster. No one had called me out, and no magic seemed all that active, but I still felt concern.

The structure in the middle is a water holding storage, I said to Leda. *It's a dome, with water running inside.*

She replied, *To prevent water loss, certainly, but also to prove they have it?*

Looks like it.

More than twice my height, the rounded glass structure resembled a turtle shell. Water and mist curled inside, condensing along the panes. A pond with water clear all the way to the bottom awaited. Fountains spurted from the bottom, arcing high in erratic displays. Witches made soft sounds as they watched. Stones lined the bottom of the dome, sealed with a hard resin to prevent leaking. Not a single droplet of water visibly leaked. Beads trickled down the left and right of the glass, kept safe within.

Two tribal warriors, marked by red slashes across their cheeks, glowered near a spigot and a bucket. The sunburst symbol I observed on the ice shed tattooed their burly necks on the left side. A sign stood behind them, marking the cost per bucket of water in ten different languages. The common language lay at the bottom, below tribal dialects, presumably.

A female witch approached. She wore a pale cream dress, and a shawl over her light blonde hair. Five leather sandskins hung from her forearm, dry as bones.

She spoke to the first guard, gaze cast to her feet, and handed him a bag that clanked. He glanced with, hefted it, jerked his chin toward the spigot. The middle guard lifted the bucket, opened the spigot, and water gushed out. He let every drip settle in the full bucket before setting it on the ground.

The woman filled her sandskins right there. A little remained at the bottom, which she drank herself, then dumped the rest on her head. Laughing, she turned and called out something I didn't understand. Chuckles floated from the crowd.

Based on her response, I wagered it was ice water from the Southern Network.

It's so brilliantly simple, I said to Leda. *They're*

running an oasis that offers ice water in the hottest environment in Alkarra.

Who are they?

No idea.

How do you run *an oasis?*

You create shade, provide water that's protected, and take trades for access to both. This is a business.

Was there anything inherently wrong with it? Not at first glace. A shout behind me ripped me out of those questions. Instinct had me ducking. The edge of something hard brushed my arm, like a searching hand. A weapon, more likely.

Had someone sensed me?

I transported away on the spot. A long breath hold and the agony of squeezing through space and time later, I landed invisibly near a waterfall in the Northern Network. The slightest tug on my magic told me all I needed to know: a witch followed my spell.

Luckily, they didn't maintain invisibility. A broad shouldered male with full lips and a pouting scowl crouched a few paces away, eyes darting. His brilliant white hair, braided into a bun atop his head, gave way to a fierce scowl, strong arms, and a protective snarl. He had the palest of skin. I couldn't fathom a witch I would be less likely to find in the desert.

"Where are you?" he hissed.

I departed and the telltale tug occurred again, at the last possible second. He followed, which meant he'd sensed my signature as I left. A witch versed with spell recognition, then. If the next stop didn't work, I'd have to get sneaky.

Transportation swept me away again. Water yanked me from this torturous spell and brought me into the ocean. I landed ten paces below the waves at a tempestuous spot ages from a beach and swirling with currents. Sanako, a worker at the Great Library of Burke and my sandal maker, lived not far away.

Without surfacing, I left for a frigid tundra in the South.

The verdant jungle of the East.

This one I touched so briefly I barely saw the wet leaves. Yet, I felt the burden he placed on my spell. Canny witch. How had he kept with me? One place remained as a guaranteed spot to lose him: the dark heart of Letum Wood, a place I rarely ventured.

I landed amongst shadows and gigantic tree roots. Darkness swarmed it, palpably heavy. Hand pressed to a branch, I gasped, "Don't let him come. Send him away."

Was it possible?

Could Letum Wood divert a witch mid-transportation?

I'd never asked, nor tried. The plea must have worked, because no sensation of his arrival came. He'd tagged me at every turn, so he was skilled. Very skilled. Practiced. But he was no match for my trees. When he failed to arrive, I whispered, "Thank you."

A low, symphonic chorus replied.

Are you all right? Leda asked.

Collapsing against the roots, I shuddered. Sea water ran from my hair in rivulets, and the quick Southern Network chill hadn't warmed. Exposed to the snow, I trembled.

Fine, I gasped. *Just . . . back in the forest. Someone noticed me. He followed.*

I pictured her stunned silence and slow blinks. *How did he know you were there?*

Must have sensed my magic.

Something very careful entered her voice. *Are you . . . on your way home?*

Eventually.

When you arrive, let me know?

Why?

Oh, she said daintily. *No reason. Just . . .*

She didn't finish the sentence.

Exhausted, not sure if I should be sweating from the West, frigid from the frozen Southern plains while sopping wet from the sea, or just exhausted from maintaining magic for hours and hours on end, I slumped against the trunk.

How does it feel, Tyrant sang, melodious and chuckling, *to be chased? How does it feel to be overpowered? To fear for your life? How does it feel knowing you did the same to others, and then they died?*

Vines crawled toward me, borne on whispers that not even the dark heart of the forest could suppress. Their voice dimmed Tyrant's constant questions, the barrage of intrusive memories into a moment I didn't request them.

You belong to us, the trees crooned.

The darkness cannot touch you here.

You return.

We belong to you.

Chapter Eleven

Cold notwithstanding, I couldn't deny my curiosity. Rumors about the dark heart of Letum Wood swirled through the Central Network. Whispered terrors about living shadows and stories of strange creatures. Why hadn't I spent more time here?

For minutes, I sought the supposed monsters, but found only poignant, soul deep stillness. Under its power, my thoughts settled and realigned. When I extricated myself from the snowy roots, saplings surrounded me by pulling through the dirt with their roots. Their leaves extended, reaching.

When my scalp prickled from the cold and my teeth chattered, I whispered my farewells. The saplings would drift to their corners like children returning home while I departed for the treehouse.

On arrival, an envelope careened toward me the moment my feet touched the floor. Ducking, I managed to avoid getting sliced by it's . . . energetic . . . search. Several envelopes followed in a swarm.

Anarchy awaited.

Batting one away from my ear, I cried, "What is this?"

"You tell me," Merrick shouted, slapping one particularly aggressive scroll against the table, then chortling when it shriveled like a dying bird. He plucked it from the top. "Finally got you, you little bugger. They've been pouring for the last hour. Look!"

He gestured to the other side of the room, where a bulging net strained against the press of letters. Oh, no. This boded nothing good. I pulled several arrivals from the air. As soon as they touched my fingertips, their frenetic energy died. It came from spells that created persistence and guaranteed receipt of the letter.

In a word?

Journalists.

Five minutes of dodging missives and herding scrolls passed before Merrick and I could approach each other. The plucking movements warmed my frozen fingers and toes. While he cast another net to restrain the latest messages, I sank into a chair near the fire.

Merrick hissed, shoving hair out of his flushed face, when a paper cut appeared on his cheek. "Jikes!" Blood dabbed onto his fingertips when he probed the wound. "I feel like I've wrestled an arctic baer."

"The paper equivalent."

Of all receptions I desired when returning home, this was not one of them. A *Chatham Chatterer* scroll soared across the room. Merrick caught the scroll, flipped it, and held it out. His sandy hair fell across his shoulders, and a black, long-sleeved shirt stretched down his torso, highlighting his verdant eyes. I'd prefer to gobble him up instead of reading.

"Have you looked at the articles, B?"

"No. I've been in the Western Network."

He surveyed me for the first time. Dripping wet clothes, sand granules . . . everywhere. A hint of jungle flora wafted from me, but I hadn't been there long enough to reek. "What happened?"

"The Alina mission. I'll explain later. What's going on here?"

Merrick nudged me again.

"Take a look."

With trepidation, I unfurled it. The headline spanning the top bracket caught my eye. All my compounding dread nose dived, taking my heart with it.

The Sisterhood Quits

"Quits?" I muttered.

Merrick grimaced. He pushed a hand through his hair, blowing out a long breath through his lips. "It gets worse."

"Do I want to read it?"

"No."

"Should I?"

"Yes. But not yet. I thought you'd at least want to see why they're coming in. It was just published. Maybe two hours ago?"

With a sweep of my hand, I cried, "All of *these*? In less than two hours?" He nodded. I plucked an incoming envelope from the air.

Dear Miss Monroe,

Regarding the article in the Chatterer today, we were wondering if you would be open to interview with us as well? We're a smaller publication out of the Brant Coven in the Middle Covens.

Regards,

Stewart

"Interview?" I cried. "Regarding what? I told the Council the Sisterhood was dissolved. To common knowledge, there isn't one anymore." I grasped a missive that followed me to the bedroom, recently birthed from the window.

Bianca,

We're a women's rights organization out of Ashleigh Covens, and we'd like to discuss your decision to withdraw the Sisterhood. We stand ready to support you if you feel you have a lack of representation in a Network structure largely afraid of women taking up spots previously occupied by men.

Yours in support,

The Ashleigh Sisters

Kind, but not exactly what I needed. I stopped in the doorway and spun on my heels. Merrick dodged and ducked six envelopes marked with red *urgent* writing. "I expected witches to send their opinion, but no idea *this* would happen."

"You're better known than you think." He crouched, avoiding a long, rectangular paper folded in thirds, and stomped it with a foot when it zoomed low. "Ha! Got you."

"This is . . . I mean . . ."

Merrick jumped to catch a message inching toward me along a seam in the wall. "Because of your father, your name goes farther than most."

I crumbled the previous letter and tossed it into the flames with a spell. "Well, I'm making my own waves now."

A third message unfolded in front of my face. Audacious, but effective. I wondered what spell managed to send a message, open it in front of a specific witch, and hover at the same time. The note sent me into a separate tizzy.

Dear Miss Monroe,

Since you're not employed by the Network, might we hire you to help find our son? He has been missing for several weeks, and we have very few hints as to how or where. We would pay you whatever you require to see him returned.

Please, reply soon.

I tucked that one under my arm. Comments about going *mercenary* and *rogue* flittered darkly through my head. I wasn't a mercenary for hire, but . . . what was I now? A witch who used my unique skills to help others. Definitely. So this plea for help wasn't all that surprising, was it?

I'd answer it . . . later.

Merrick tossed me a small scroll the length of my pinky finger. "It's from an old lady in the Northern Covens who wants to introduce you to her granddaughter. She seems to think you'd get along."

An incredulous laugh stopped him in his tracks when I suggested, "We could set the letters on fire. Not in *here*, of course. But outside."

He conjured flames in his hand.

"Say when."

I held up a staying hand. "No, don't. I was teasing you. Some of these are very heartfelt."

"Like this one?"

He dug one out of a pocket, sending it with a spell. Reading it, I scowled.

Dear Miss Monroe,

Glad to see you finally saw sense. We don't need a Sisterhood. Kindly return to the classroom or the kitchen.

Unsigned, the hateful little devil. "And some aren't so heartfelt." I tossed it into the fire and spoke to Leda through the communication magic.

There are hundreds of letters at my house.

I assumed so.

Are you receiving any?

No. You're the face of it. Georgette only included you in her article. Probably a concession for Scarlett, since involving me would involve the High Priestess, and Georgette isn't looking to get booted out.

I rolled my eyes. *Scarlett would never.*

You might be surprised. Georgette is more savvy than I expected in some of her methods. She published this one in the evening edition, too, which gets far more readers than the morning. I can't fathom what else Georgette has planned.

I shook my head, still stunned. This scenario reeked of impending disaster. *I suggested we burn all of them,* I said. Merrick found it funny.

Don't!

What am I going to do with them?

Give them to me. They're valuable insight into the Network and our witches. I want to know what they're saying, and so will Scarlett. Bianca, this information could be pivotal to our future success.

But there's so many.

I'll bring Hiddleston to help. Plan on us descending tomorrow, since it's not a work day, to sort them.

Sighing, I agreed. *Sounds like a plan.*

Merrick dodged four incoming messages. The escalating sound of so many papers rustling around, fighting to break through a magic-reinforced net that he cast, required me to shout over the din.

"Do you need help?"

"I have this under control. Get dressed and dry off," he called. Another envelope zoomed in, but I caught it before it smacked my face. "Now that we have some of the chaos under control, I'll put more complicated incanta-tions out to gather the rest." He added in a growl. "I have a feeling we'll need a lot of nets."

* * *

Five nets bulged with messages the next afternoon. The *Chatham Chatterer* published a second article early in the morning, which led to another surge of envelopes arriving in the wee hours. They rained on our floor.

Do Women Belong In The Guardians?

This wave of feedback was something I wanted nothing to do with. These irate responses had far less to do with the Sisterhood, but fury directed at the subject in general. Georgette hadn't masked the fact that I spurred the topic, however, by mentioning my failed Sisterhood in the first paragraph.

The second article brought Papa and Regina to check on me. Convincing them to stay wasn't hard. Merrick sent them to work sorting through the mail. The two of them quietly flirted, laughed intermittently, and used spells to tear into each net.

Leda and Hiddleston followed, fresh snacks and accoutrements in hand. Coffee steaming from their fresh mugs, they settled at the table, decided on a system, and tore into each scroll and message.

Michelle arrived shortly after, with Nicolas, children, and lunch in tow. I set Sanna and Isadora to work scrib-bling on the hateful notes and pitching them into a pile near the fire, while Michelle worked in the kitchen to feed everyone. Within thirty minutes of her arrival, the delicious smell of meat pie and a baking crust wafted through the treehouse.

Tomasso and Priscilla arrived shortly after. Miss Celia slept in the rocking chair at the school. Priscilla dove into the positive messages with glee, organizing them by size and subject for Leda and I to review later.

Within an hour, Leda sat at the top of the table, commanding the entire room like a High Priestess. Messages trickled in, but she funneled them into a specific basket, making it unnecessary to chase dozens at a time, or avoid them as they darted inside. All of us deferred to her guidance around organizing. She reviewed each request and supportive remark. Granted, there were far fewer of them than opinionated, written rants.

"There are definitely themes," Leda called to the room at large, consulting a sheet tracking the general flow. "Most witches hadn't heard of the Sisterhood and were confused. Which isn't too surprising."

"Not sure if I'm happy or sad about that," I replied.

"I'm happy about it. Georgette has done us a favor. She's brought the name farther than we ever did." Leda tapped a finger on a box marked *Indifferent*. "Most witches land here. They don't care either way, as long as their taxes don't go up."

Yet again, the power of indifference.

"Georgette has sent three letters to you, all of them including the contract." Her nose wrinkled. "Ghastly piece of work, if you ask me. As far as contracts go, I've rarely seen one so one-sided and horrid."

Hiddleston murmured, "I agree."

"I'm glad all of us have consensus on that point. I won't be signing it anytime soon."

Leda brushed a quill along the underside of her jaw,

musing. "You've frightened Georgette, I think. That's the only conclusion I can draw."

I leaned my palms on the table, studying the other data points in a bid to ignore Georgette and her contract. Amongst the columns, *Supportive* had a low tally, right next to *Confused,* which had the highest. *Not Worth Recording* hit a lesser midline that impressed me by sheer amount. On the far right, with only six slash marks, was the *Legitimate Need* category.

"What does it all mean?" I asked.

She rubbed two fingers along her hairline, lips pursed in thought. "Well . . . it's simply a view into the general consciousness of the Network. This is giving us real-time feedback about what people think of the Sisterhood." She reached over and tapped on a handful of collected parchments and one small scroll. "And *these* are very intriguing leads."

"I'm dealing with Alina."

"I know." She primly slid a few requests into her pocket. "I'll follow up on them, thank you."

No new messages had come in for almost fifteen minutes. I found myself relaxing and hopeful. I couldn't wait for the sound of shuffling paper to leave my treehouse.

Leda leaned back, regarding me. "In the end. Georgette has achieved what she wanted. She put a death stab in the reputation of the Sisterhood, and ensured that if we were to try to raise it again, we'd be unlikely to garner popular support."

Her conclusion failed to concern me. The exact opposite occurred—relief. "I don't care about resurrection," I admitted.

She quirked an eyebrow. "Maybe not yet, but sometime in the future, you might. She's banking on that, I think. Georgette is playing a long game, something I doubt she expects you to consider. She thinks you're impetuous and not detailed oriented. In fact, I'd wager she's banking on it."

In truth, I wasn't thinking about *a long game*. Did I know or care what the Sisterhood would be doing in ten years? Maybe. But maybe not. The future seemed too far away to control it here.

Leda continued, oblivious to my thoughts. "Georgette may have assumed that you made a spur-of-the-moment, passionate decision that you might regret later, so she's trying to make it so you can't take it back."

"Effective."

"Efficient, too." Leda made a squeaky noise with her teeth and lips. "There's not much else to be said, Bianca. The Sisterhood, as we once knew it, is dead."

Chapter Twelve

S now blasted the windows of a small coven library along the outskirts of the Western Covens, not far from the Borderlands. Such a tiny coven.

Such a sprawling collection on Western Network tribal literature.

The wintry gale hit the glass panes with occasional plinks and hisses. The sound soothed me while I perused a book, lazily turning the pages. A librarian hummed a ditty, unbothered by the cloak and hood I kept over my face. The library was lukewarm, at best, but it suited my needs better than the gargantuan Great Library of Burke and its hoards.

With gentle but quick fingers, I perused through a directory of known Western Network tribe names, seeking drawings similar to the symbol of a spiraling sun with lightning designs and nested hearts. Ten pages out of thirty, I had not found it.

Alina's advice followed me here after speaking with her over breakfast that morning.

"Find the symbol, find the tribe. If the clannish

witches aren't at the oasis, they must be somewhere else, with the tribe. Those warriors have to live somewhere, and they won't take up room at the oasis that could harbor paying customers."

Logic followed, but not a path. It would be unwise to ask the witches at the oasis the name of their tribe because some tribes held their name sacred. Others shared their name liberally. Most knew each other as much by symbol as name. I could poke ask witches who used the oasis and left, but that was a last-ditch-scenario. First, I'd exhaust other options, difficult as they might be.

Simple research posed several blatant challenges. For one, a lack of trustworthy records outside the West. Their oral tradition meant most writings were told by other witches *not* their own. Or original writings that no one had—or could—translate. Access to the sparse literature, for another. The Central Network wasn't a trove of Western Network lore.

After slipping through the final twenty pages and finding nothing, I re-shelved the last book that showed promise. Terminating these resources required a trip to the Arck library.

Incoming, Leda said.

What?

No further answer came. I spun to leave, but came to a dead stop. A familiar-looking witch strode across the cozy library, gaze trained on me. I'd seen her before, but couldn't put my finger on where.

Before I could ask, she'd already spoken. "Miss Monroe—or do you go by Hughes now?"

The reminder of my decision wasn't lost. I kept putting it off, unsure of how I desired to represent myself in the world these days.

"Call me Bianca, please. May I help you?"

"My name is Abby." She lifted an arm, which I briefly clasped in mine. "We've met before, but not officially. I work for Council Member Clare. She sent me in search of you, and Leda told me you were here. I hope that's all right?"

She had an easy cadence and bright tone. Nothing about her gave me pause. Plus, she explained Leda's hasty warning. If Leda sent her, I likely had nothing to fear.

"That's fine. How can I help you?"

"Clare would like to speak with you somewhere private. Not here, nor the castle. Would you accept an invitation to her personal residence?"

"She doesn't want to be seen with me?"

Who would? Tyrant quipped.

I ignored him.

Abby smiled. "Quite the opposite, actually. Clare desires nothing more than a good relationship with you. She's concerned for your safety."

Despite the odd situation, Abby impressed me. She held herself confidently, spoke with ease, but firmly. She was Leda's total opposite in every physical regard—broad, tall, powerfully built, with dark skin and hair cut close to her scalp—but resembled Leda in personality and presence.

"I'd be happy to meet with Clare."

Abby smiled, revealing white teeth. "She'll be pleased. Are you available right now? She's opened her schedule for you today."

Planning my foray into the Western Network castle library to get more information on tribes would require finesse, and probably Aurora, which meant I'd need a little time to think through my approach. Lunch with Clare would be a worthy distraction.

"Now is fine."

Abby's smile widened. "If you'll follow my transportation, I'll take you right to her."

* * *

Clare lived in a thin, tall, dominating townhouse with as much space as my treehouse.

Perched on the edge of Pem, the largest city in the Western Covens, it looked as if it had been folded in half between two other buildings. An afterthought. Or a plug. Pem was a bustling intersection between Chatham City and the low-population farms that filled most of this Coven. Somehow, Clare fit the mold perfectly. A little old school country, a little bit magical city.

Abby escorted me inside the front door. No butler awaited, nor maid hurried from room to room. Stillness echoed through the foyer where I stood. I'd wrongly assumed there'd be an elegance and richness to Clare's personal life. All first impressions pointed to simplicity and functionality.

Boots stacked in neat lines near the door. A coat rack with two different options—light linen and heavy wool. The doors were shut, the floor worn and clean. If anything set the townhouse apart, a love of art would be it. Paintings adorned all available wall space, each of them gilded.

Abby led me through a thin hallway and into a widening room along the back. Sunshine spilled through windows, illuminating snowy flakes that collected along the sills. The sparkling panes occupied most of the back room, giving way to comfy divans, a snapping fire, and more art. In fact, I saw little else *but* art. Not a book in sight. No desk, parchment, quill, or other paraphernalia that bespoke the preeminence of a Council Member.

Clare stood near the fireplace as we entered. A genuine smile wreathed her face, brushed with relief. I forced my tension to abate. While I couldn't assume we'd exit this conversation as allies, we didn't have to be enemies.

I started with my warmest smile. "Council Member. Thank you for having me, and for making allowances for the current situation."

"Welcome, Miss Monroe." Clare gestured to a pair of chairs drawn closer to the fire, no doubt in preparation for our conversation. "Please, have a seat."

Abby, with a dip of her head, bowed away, leaving the two of us alone. Clare settled next to me, and something in her short, prim movements spoke to nerves. What had the past several days been like for the Council? The withdrawal of the Sisterhood could hardly have much impact in the shadow of Grandfather's death. Most of the attention would eventually settle on Scarlett and her choice for the next High Priest.

"Abby will bring us refreshments." Clare motioned to the hallway and cleared her throat. She crossed her ankles. "I'm grateful to have you with me, Miss Monroe. If you don't mind, I'd like to dive right into the reason I invited you."

Wordless, I motioned for her to continue, though a dozen questions occurred to me. What was the Council's reaction after I left? Had Georgette spoken to Clare about the Sisterhood? These queries would only complicate my stance. Better to act as if I didn't care. I did, but that hardly mattered.

Clare stared at the fire as she spoke, the crackling, reaching arms of the flames extending up the bricked chimney. She studied me from the side of her eyes, without facing me.

"To be forthright, Miss Monroe, I feel as if I should apologize on behalf of the Council. The way that Georgette and others have treated you is shocking and deplorable."

Mildly amused, I asked, "Is it shocking?"

A hint of a smile appeared on her face. "Perhaps not. On some accounts," she added.

"There are a lot of opinionated and well-respected witches in that room. I imagine nothing is all that simple."

"All the same, I'm sorry it pushed you to a point where you felt you must withdraw the upcoming request on behalf of the Sisterhood. This is what I want to discuss."

She paused, and I sensed searching in her words. Though she asked no question, one lingered. *Is this real?* With gaining awkwardness, I waited her out. Around the time the air became so burdensome I wanted to clear my throat to dispel the weight, Clare broke it.

"Is it true, Miss Monroe? Is the Sisterhood truly over?"

Ah.

There was the real question. She sought confirmation. For herself, for the Council? Did she want to request a job from me, or did she seek closure? Solace? Could I trust *any* Council Member who asked for Sisterhood assistance?

"Why do you ask, Council Member?"

"There is an assumption amongst . . . several of us . . . that the Sisterhood means to continue without Network approval."

"There was little indication of that when I left the meeting. I made it clear that the Sisterhood has dissolved."

She nodded. "Yes, but I'm curious if this is true." She hastily added. "Not that I would call you a liar, but, having been backed into your decision by domineering leadership, I see why you must *act* as if it ended. For my part, I'm hoping not. There were many reasons to believe in and support the Sisterhood. The greatest of which revolves around a possible Network need for you."

My mind raced to try to understand her motivations. Clare, while supportive, had been distant and more often singularly focused on Georgette than actual support. The Sisterhood came to Clare's attention when it had a reason to benefit her. With the Sisterhood, she could oppose Georgette and establish her own political standing. For the life of me, though, I couldn't see any clear motivation here.

Why did she ask?

Thankfully, Abby bustled in with a tray, breaking the commanding quiet. Clare shrank into her chair to wait while Abby set the refreshments out. During the lull, through which Abby pasted on a professional smile, I spoke to Leda.

What do you think of Clare's motivations to help the Sisterhood?

Only a moment paused before she replied. *It's difficult to tell. She's not unlike myself, in that she saw an opening for a future or current alliance that might help her move positive projects forward in the Network.*

But?

But I cannot say that her behaviors to date have entirely supported an approach that speaks to sincerity.

Leda had political drivel down to an art.

Can I trust her?

If I were you, I'd trust no one until this dies down. I can't fathom that Clare would report anything you told her to Georgette, but she would use it for her benefit. Play it carefully, Bianca.

Fair.

Abby withdrew as quickly as she came. Clare reached for an already poured teacup, clearly arranged to her preference, while mine remained empty. Out of a sense of decorum, I tipped the teapot into my tea. Coffee was my preference, but I could handle a gentle chamomile. Knotted cookies petaled a plate, piling high. They were saccharine confections, meant to dissolve in the hot water and add a different flavor to the tea.

As Abby's footsteps vanished, Clare resumed. "I asked you here to learn the true fate of the Sisterhood, and what you plan to do next. My aim isn't to report your responses to anyone else. Certainly, I've never been a lapdog for another witch."

"I wondered."

She scoffed with a tint of bitterness, and I realized how close I'd come to offending her. Would it matter? In the long run, perhaps not. But Papa's lesson about *being* who I wanted to be lent me caution. Did I want to run a Sisterhood that offended witches without regard? No.

Drawing in a breath, and having a required sip of tea, I said, "I appreciate your curiosity and concern, Council Member. I apologize if I offended you."

She smiled with a stiffness reminiscent of a decorum lesson. "No offense taken. This situation is delicate. You may call me Clare."

"Clare," I amended. "Certainly, anyone that once believed in the idea of the Sisterhood is a welcome ally. But the Sisterhood as you know it is done."

"Truly?"

A haunted tone echoed in her voice. Regret? The death of the Sisterhood on a collective Council conscious? Not collective, perhaps her own. Utterly unable to read the room on it, I assumed that Clare's uncertain motivations weren't worth courting. Until Clare showed more of her cards, I wouldn't trust her.

Besides, the Sisterhood didn't need the Central Network Council in order to find work. The pile of requests at the treehouse, and Alina's current mission, made my freedom an obvious point. In fact, it would be far better for the Sisterhood if we steered clear of any Council Member.

Very clear.

Using Leda's advice, I didn't mince words.

"I will not serve the Central Network Council, Clare. I'm sorry."

If she read between the lines of my narrow promise, I saw no sign. She said a barren, "Oh," and stared into the fire. She cut a morose figure, her teacup in her lap, her expression glazed and distant.

For the first time, I wondered if Clare wasn't . . . lonely. The empty house, so quiet. Cluttered walls, heavy with portraits and landscapes. Not a speck of dust nor hint of life to be found in the walls.

Did she spend much time here? The utter stillness made me wonder.

"I can't say that I'm not disappointed," Clare said slowly, blinking out of her stupor. "A little surprised."

"Surprised?"

She elevated her cup, focused firmly on the fire. "I didn't expect the Sisterhood to give up so quickly. Was your success really that tied into the High Priest?"

A rush of rage followed. I tightened my fingers, then forced them to relax. If Clare couldn't see the truth about the Council, Georgette, and our hopeless efforts to gain support, this conversation had nowhere to go.

Careful with that rage, Tyrant sang, *last time, you murdered witches with it.*

I breathed out, doubly vexed. Tyrant hadn't flexed his annoying persistence in several hours, and I hadn't missed his reminders. He cast a dim glow on every situation he entered, and he wormed his way into most.

"The success of the Sisterhood wasn't tied into the High Priest at all, Council Member."

When I didn't use her name, her lips bunched.

Standing, I said, "Thank you for the tea, and your time. Should the Sisterhood resurrect with interest to grow and expand anytime soon, I will let you know."

Clare didn't meet my gaze. As she made to stand, I held up a hand. "Don't go to the trouble, please. I'll see myself out."

Abby materialized in the hallway with her expected smile. An undeniable strain undercut her friendliness as she escorted me to the door, and nodded me out. The city of Pem swallowed me as I drifted into it, grateful to escape.

Chapter Thirteen

Ambassador Aurora peered at me over the top of an ostentatious pair of glasses with wings sweeping to the side. The painted colors—silver, umber, white, and black—reminded distinctly of an owl. As always, they had no glass within.

Her inscrutable study took me in. "Well, you look better than ever. Imagine. Getting the Council off your back improved your life."

Her wry tone brought a smile out of me. "Good to see you, Ambassador."

"You too."

Aurora didn't invite me to sit, because she offered no chairs. The once-tidy and well-maintained Ambassador's turret—the only office in this high tower—had belonged to Grandfather. Being here made my heart hurt. Aurora altered it so drastically that almost nothing of his memory remained.

Perhaps that's why it ached.

"How are you?" Aurora asked. Her hands curled around a parchment once floating at her side.

"Fine."

"With Marten passing, and you revoking a request for Council recognition, I imagine you're not fine. But if you prefer, I'm willing to feed your delusion."

"Thank you, Ambassador."

"Believe it or not, this is for you."

She extended the scroll. It floated between us, stopping in front of me. No wax seal accompanied the petite slip. Most political witches had signature wax seals. Many Council Members selected a specific color of wax as well. A visual signature, but none showed. My suspicion ratcheted.

Aurora's cat-like smile simultaneously set me at ease and made me nervous. Steady Aurora rarely changed, but that didn't mean I could predict what came next. Before I unfurled it, Aurora said, "Council Member Georgette asked me to give it to you."

My fingers froze.

She elevated her brow. "Odd, no? Believe me, I have been sorely tempted to peel it open and read it, but I haven't. Perhaps a better Ambassador would have given into the temptation. It must be important if she's going through me. Which I *don't* appreciate," she added snidely. "The last thing I need on my list is to be your messenger."

The scroll continued to hover. While curiosity swept me, I could only stare.

"Is there poisoned powder inside?"

Aurora barked a laugh. Deciding not to torture myself, I opened it, perused the brief writing, and rolled my eyes. When I sent it into her fire, Aurora's silent question filled the room.

"Well?"

"She sent me a contract and wants me to sign it. This is a reminder."

"You haven't signed?"

I scoffed.

"You won't?"

"No."

Her pursed lips relaxed. "Good. Has she been sending messages to your house?"

"Yes."

"Ignoring those too?"

Sighing, I said, "As best we can. She sends them daily. Merrick burns them."

Intrigue glittered in her stare. "Does she message Leda?"

Did I trust Aurora? Oddly enough, yes. While I didn't long to be in her presence at any given time—her wild mood swings often had an irascible undertone and weren't easy to deal with—I had a feeling I needed her.

No, the *Sisterhood* needed her.

Shrugging, I said, "I don't know. If Leda receives anything from Georgette, she hasn't mentioned it. Would I be surprised? Not at all."

"Hmm."

"Council Member Clare asked me to her townhouse this morning," I said, side-cutting into a more interesting conversation. Aurora's lips twitched, as if she were about to protest, but she said nothing. "She asked me if I'd truly stopped the Sisterhood. I had a feeling she was trying to assess whether or not I was working under their noses."

"She was."

"You know that?"

Aurora rolled her eyes. "Don't be a troll, Bianca. Of *course* she wants to know. If she puts herself into your confidences, it elevates her position amongst those that may one day want to resurrect the Sisterhood. It also leverages a position of power over Georgette. If there's anything you did in that Council meeting the other day, it's stirred them up."

Sensing what might be my only opportunity with Leda so busy helping Scarlett uncover a new High Priest, I decided to trust my instinct.

"Will you tell me your thoughts on the Council meeting the other day?"

Aurora's eyes gleamed, her smile turned coy. "What are you asking, Miss Monroe? You want me to inform you about the Council's response to your withdrawal?"

"Yes."

"That indicates you care."

I elevated my chin. "I'm not a troll, Ambassador. Of course I care. While I may act indifferent, the Sisterhood is still very much under my care. Our organization will thrive best outside their watchful eyes."

Aurora sobered unexpectedly. The rapid change in her expression felt like missing a step. "You're obviously continuing to work, then? The whole presentation was a lie?"

"Not entirely. The Sisterhood as they knew it is gone."

"What did you tell Clare at your meeting with her?"

"The same."

"Why?"

"Because I don't want her to know."

"She's a possible ally."

I countered as quickly, "Is she?"

Aurora huffed an aggressive laugh. "She thinks she is, but she isn't."

The niggling discomfort I felt since leaving Clare's townhouse finally eased. As simple as it sounded, *She thinks she is, but she isn't*, perfectly encapsulated my own instincts.

"You, me, Leda, and Scarlett are the only ones in

Chatham Castle who know that the Sisterhood plans to continue. For now," I added softly. Eventually, I'd tell the Brotherhood. Rognvald. They deserved to know the truth. "And Alina," I added, but frowned. "Though she's not part of our castle."

Aurora withdrew her hideous glasses, which made her face appear much smaller. She kept her hair cropped close along her head, the wiry curls forming a stylish afro. Gray and white spiraled intermittently within. She tapped her teeth together, voice curling like steam.

"Alina knows about the Sisterhood, you say?"

"Alina."

"Interesting," she murmured. "Why are you allowing me to know?"

"I know who I can trust," I said evenly.

A flush of surprise swept her, altering the calm calculation. Aurora's disapproval of the Council, her general distaste for politics in general, and her focus on inter-Network relationships made her an ideal ally.

A true one.

Although Leda might have a differing opinion about bringing Aurora into our confidences, I felt firm on this point. Besides I had a very targeted reason to ask for her help with Alina and the Southern Network.

Aurora nodded once. "I'm glad to hear it, Miss Monroe. You're a real pain in my side most of the time, but I accept what you're saying. *This* is why I will not be your messenger." She tossed a hand toward the clock. "You've occupied entirely too much of my time."

"I would like to ask for one minute more."

Peering at a pocket watch that she summoned from the other side of the room, she said, "You have sixty seconds."

"I need to get into the Arck library to research

archives and history on Western Network tribal witches and their symbology. What do you know about it?"

Her brow rose, curving the hairline of her eyebrow so faint it nearly vanished. "I know that it's well-guarded, but open to all Western Network witches. They enter by providing proof of residence through letters from teachers, tribal leaders, or high citizens, like Council Members. Council Member Assistants can also prove heritage. Those papers are easy enough to forge."

"Good. That was my next question."

"This is tied to Alina?"

I nodded. She eyed her pocket watch, and shot me a warning. I almost laughed. She meant to hold me to that minute.

"Do you have much experience with Lana?" I asked.

Aurora shrugged. "Not personally. Before becoming Ambassador, I worked with several witches from the Western Network when Lana took over. The Western Network High Priestess and I know each other in cordial terms."

"I know her vaguely."

"You don't need Lana to enter the library."

"No, but I'd like to know if Lana has any qualms about punishing tribal witches for abducting Southern Network witches from their home, in order to exploit the ice trade and profit off the clannish witches' magicless state. Depending on your answer, this might *also* be your arena."

Aurora's eyes widened. She closed the face of the pocket watch, our time restriction dismissed. She leaned closer to drawl, "Tell me more."

* * *

Why did you tell Aurora? Leda screeched through my mind that evening, jostling me out of my current task: attempting to parse together a Western Network robe and pants with a transformation spell. Based on the picture in the book I tried to mimic, my lackluster results wouldn't fool anyone.

I winced. *Why are you so shrill?*

Because I'm upset!

I'm sorry.

You could have told me.

Rolling my eyes, I abandoned the transformation spell. Priscilla would help me later. *I tried to tell you. You told me three times today that you were too busy to talk.*

I reached into my armoire for a different dress. Merrick, bustling around the treehouse, cursed under his breath. Every attempt to iron out his nicest pants resulted in burns that he reversed with a spell.

A pause, then, *You're right. I'm sorry. I'm on edge. We've been finalizing the candidates for High Priest and have finally selected.*

Perking up, I asked, *Oh?*

No, I won't tell you. You can wait and hear the announcement like the rest of the Network. I can't wait for this to be done. Before Yule, too! There's so much to coordinate . . . that stupid ball . . .

Stress deepened her voice, and I felt a glimmer of regret that she found out about Aurora without me telling her. Aurora herself, probably. The feeling faded with Leda's final snap.

And this isn't helpful!

Sighing, I reached for my best dress. A deep emerald with long sleeves, a fitted waist, and braids along the side. The skirt swept just above the ground, hiding my bare feet. The Brotherhood decided to throw a Yule dinner with all the Brothers and, if applicable, their family. There weren't many Protectors that chose to have a relationship or children, because it used to negate a future appointment to Head of Protectors if they desired it. Some rare exceptions existed in history.

It would be an interesting evening.

I'm sorry, Leda. When will you be ready to talk about Aurora?

After the announcement in two days.

Let's talk then.

Will you be there?

I almost said, *Yes,* but stopped at the last second. *Is Scarlett hosting a celebratory ball that evening?*

Yes.

Is she inviting the other Networks?

Yes. The Highest Witch of each Network has confirmed that they'll attend. A few of them will be at the Empowering.

Who?

Alina and Lana. Not sure about Cristian or Camila from the Eastern Network yet, nor Nadira in the North. She paused. *Why do you ask?*

No reason, I said, eyeing the half combobulated Western Network garb a few steps away. Perhaps it would be wise to ask for Priscilla's help *before* I went to the Brotherhood Yule celebration tonight. If Lana were away from the Network all day, Arck security would be lower. Yet, I didn't want to wait an extra day.

Just thinking . . . I said.

Leda sighed, or so I imagined, through the magic. *Bianca . . .* No scolding came. Instead, a hasty, *I need to go! Yet another disaster to deal with from the kitchens.*

Which was ideal. I had a Western Network mission to plan, and budding ideas for how to do it.

* * *

Festive garlands, glittering candles, and the distant song of a violin filled the Gatehouse. Witches milled within while snow cascaded past the window. A merry fire brightened the room, fragrant with the smell of cranberry and cinnamon, thanks to a bubbling cauldron releasing the heady scents. A Yule potpourri. The number of witches crowded into this place surprised me.

"So many witches?" I whispered to Merrick.

"I guess so."

"Haven't you met all of the Brothers?"

He slanted me a sarcastic stare, and I grinned. Nothing delighted me more than drawing such a response. He curled a hand around my waist and pulled me into his side. His warm breath brushed along the shell of my ear.

"Are you going to make wisecracks all night?"

Breathless from his forceful heat, I cut him a smile. "Noooo, I would *never*."

He pressed a kiss to my cheek, a delighted and rolling laugh low. "Then it'll be a good night. It's boring without them."

When he released me, I couldn't glide far. He kept a tight hold on my hand, tugging me to the right. This gathering was far less daunting than the celebratory ball would be tomorrow, which I would easily dodge. Whoever Scarlett chose as High Priest didn't worry me. I trusted her and Leda. Besides, there would be too many Council Members present, half drunk on wine, to tempt me to attend.

Merrick introduced me to a few other women. Some of them wives, others romantic interests. Only a handful of children scampered around, and I thought I saw echoes of my own childhood in them.

Had Papa attended these before? Unlikely. Only recent Head of Brotherhoods had shown willingness to bring the Brotherhood together in very un-mission-focused terms. Rognvald would be the first Head of Protectors I knew to publicly gather in a mutual celebration. If it happened before, history didn't easily note it.

A pair of bright eyes caught mine, and I smiled.

"Merry meet, Papa."

He crossed the room with his boundless smile. Regina remained in the corner, speaking to Chi.

"My favorite daughter," he said, wrapping me in his arms. I breathed out, comforted by his smell. Though I'd seen him days ago, all this business losing Grandfather made me want to keep Papa close. Mortality only had so many strikes; I felt unduly anxious that Papa would use up all of his.

He pulled away to inspect me. "How are you, B?"

"Fine."

Words wanted to bubble out of my throat. The mission with Alina, Aurora's willingness to help, and my ideas for getting into the Western Network library to identify the tribal symbol. I kept them back. This certainly wasn't the place, nor the time.

Papa would be interested in anything I had to say, but this mission was an ideal opportunity to stand on my own. For the Sisterhood to make her decisions and survive her failures. He squeezed my shoulder. "I'm glad to see you here."

"Have you ever attended one of these before?"

Papa laughed. "Definitely not."

"You never threw a Yule celebration as Head of Protectors?" I feigned shock, a hand sprawled across my chest. "No!"

More seriously, he added. "Mildred wouldn't have allowed it."

Ah, yes. The crux. It made more sense than ever that the party happened now. Scarlett might have had something to do with this . . . softening . . . of established traditions. About time, too. Merrick returned, two mugs in his hands and one floating nearby.

"I thought you might like to try it."

Sniffing, I peered inside. "What is it?"

"Wassail. Better than tea, if you ask me." He floated Papa a cup. "Here's one for you, old man."

Papa sent him a challenging eyebrow lift, and Merrick laughed. I ventured a tentative sip. The warm concoction puckered my tongue with the pleasant sweetness of apple juice and the comfort of cloves. Lovely, and definitely better than tea.

Breathing deep, I wrapped my cold fingers around the mug. The burgeoning strains of a melancholy song rose up from the other side of the room, altering the festive air with something more somber. Jacque, a burly brother with a heavy gait and low brow, lumbered over.

"I heard about this Sisterhood mess," he declared. He stopped a pace away to loom over me with his long, braided beard. He looked adorably out of place in a clean shirt, freshly combed hair, weaponless, surrounded by his team of Brothers, and not a speck of business to be found.

"I assume few haven't heard," I replied.

He glowered, as if I'd dealt the death blow to the Sisterhood. "I don't support it."

"What?"

"The removal."

"It was my choice, Jacque. Are we enemies now?"

He leaned closer. Tobacco and an intoxicating swirl of wine lingered on his breath. "The Brotherhood and the Sisterhood will never be enemies. The Central Network Council may not recognize you, but they've never had knowledge of—or approval over—those we choose to involve in our missions."

A flutter of surprise and delight swept me. I managed to smile without infusing a gigantic shriek.

"Thank you, Jacque."

He clapped me so hard on the shoulder I stumbled into Papa, who caught me with a laugh. Hot wassail sloshed to my fingers. "The best approval you could ask for," Papa said under his breath. Merrick watched Jacque fade, bemusement in his half smile.

"I'm grateful for the support," I replied. "As unexpected as it is."

Papa hid behind a sip of wassail when he murmured, "I think you'll find a similar sentiment of frustration amongst most of the Brothers."

"Really?"

"The Brotherhood isn't too pleased with the way the Council has treated the Sisterhood," Merrick said, "and Rognvald hasn't hidden his displeasure. They turn on one entity, they could turn on another."

Inspiration struck.

Was *this* why Clare reached out?

"That wouldn't explain Council Members attempting to court me in response? They're attempting to stave off a Brotherhood revolt and removal also?"

Papa grinned as he shrugged. "They did it to themselves."

Tysen materialized next to Merrick with a big smile. "Merry meet." He nodded to me and Papa. His gaze honed in on me. The same consternation from Jacque appeared in Tysen's intense expression, and I marveled at the silent support. His eyes darkened with a fury that took me by surprise. "I heard about the Council Meeting."

I almost laughed. Such lividness on my behalf? I'd expected mild irritation, but not frothing ire. So *this* would be the gossip of the night.

"Are you also reading Georgette's nasty articles?"

Tysen rolled his eyes. "No one gives that old bat any credence. No, Chi was in the Council room at the time."

"Was he?"

"He's everywhere. He told the Brothers about it. You were right to separate yourself from the Council. They're wretches."

"Apathy is a real motivation killer," I quipped, skimming the tops of the crowd. "Where *is* Chi?" He had that rare and innate ability to vanish into any situation.

A silky voice came behind me.

"Here."

I almost jumped out of my skin, whirling on Chi with a glare. His mild-mannered smile calmed my racing heart. Merrick and Papa dissolved into laughs.

"Not funny, Chi," I cried.

He merely nodded. As always, he stood with his hands behind his back, wearing clothes as engaging as a pile of rocks. Hardly surprising that he'd eavesdropped on the Council Meeting, but it *was* indicative of Rognvald's concerns. I itched to ask the Head of Protectors why he sent Chi. Georgette would have had paroxysms.

"You listened to the meeting, eh?" I asked.

"You presented well." His bland tone slipped into analytical Protector mode. "The most interesting part was after you left."

"Ooooh, do tell. I've been dying to hear, but didn't want to ask. What happened?"

"Very little. Georgette sent attention off of your removal and onto the next thing immediately. Others protested. Many wanted to debate. The meeting fell to shambles. They had to split and meet again later."

Hardly surprising.

"What they didn't say about the Sisterhood was the most interesting," he added.

"What didn't they say?"

"They didn't say anything, and that was the loudest part of all."

Before I could summon a reply, a heavy hand touched my shoulder. I twisted to see Rognvald standing back there. His beady eyes met mine.

"Can you talk?"

By Alkarra, they were a chatty group tonight.

He stepped away, gestured a hand toward a lesser-trafficked corner of the room. Handing my wassail to Merrick, who watched with burgeoning interest, I followed Rognvald across the room. Separate from the hubbub, he stood as still as a witch with ants running down his spine. His occasional jaw tightening, lips pinching, darting gaze, made it difficult to know if he was nervous, stressed, or irritated.

For him, the emotions weren't all that far apart to begin with.

We stood near an open window that dispelled the stuffy heat and the scent of congregating bodies. The Yuletide perfumes made it almost oppressive, and standing in the cool breeze was an unexpected boon. I enjoyed the air slipping over my heated skin.

Rognvald swallowed, his throat working. "So." He lifted his eyebrows. "Council Member Georgette."

"So."

My repetitive intonation yielded no encouraging explanation. Rognvald sucked on his front teeth, stared into the distance, and brought himself from the thought haze by the shaking of his shaggy head. When he spoke, it came out all at once. Fierce. Stressed. Battle-hardened.

"If she would do it to the Sisterhood, she'd do it to the Brotherhood. We're paying attention."

Blinking, I attempted to process both his fraught words and his doomsday tone. While lost in his thoughts, Rognvald seemed to forget that I didn't share his brain.

"By *it*, you mean seek to destroy?"

"Yes."

A fair point I hadn't considered until this evening. I acknowledged the vague awareness that something bigger stirred, but I didn't have my finger on it yet.

Rognvald's heightened and unexpected response cast Jacque and Tysen's anger toward Georgette in a new light. Tysen and I had worked together in the Eastern Network, so some allegiance made sense, but *this* was something *else*.

"You're worried Georgette is going to do to the Brotherhood what she's doing to the Sisterhood?"

Rognvald laughed outright. "Nothing about Georgette worries me. She's as consequential to my life as a bug. But when someone shows me who they are, I believe them. We're paying attention. That's all that I'm trying to say. Prepare for the worst—"

"—hope for the best," I finished for him. A common saying amongst Protectors. Papa repeated it often when I trained as a young girl.

"The Brotherhood has had enemies on the Council before, but nothing as extensive as what you've faced with the Sisterhood. I'm sorry she's slandering your name, and wanted you to know you have the support of the Brotherhood at your back. I keep my enemies up front, and she's on my list."

"Thank you, Rognvald."

"Are you shutting it down?"

"In the eyes of Alkarra? Yes. Are we *actually* stopping? Not even a little. I have an active mission as we speak."

He grinned. "You're not telling anyone?"

"Just the few that need to know. Scarlett is aware, as are Aurora, Leda, and Hiddleston. You and the Brotherhood can know, and obviously Papa and Regina and Merrick. I want . . . *things* . . . to settle down before I decide what the work will look like."

He grinned, clapping me on the shoulder. "Thought not. Glad to hear it. We might need your help."

"I'm ready."

Seeing Rognvald's shoulders relax and his gaze uplift, two other Protectors closed in. After greeting them, I left them to stroll and look for Merrick. Papa and Regina spoke with Gregary, a steady Brother embroiled in the drama of a recent handfasting separation. His wife of five years left with his two small children and stopped all contact. According to Merrick, Gregary tracked his family to their new location, but his former wife hadn't realized it. He didn't dare intrude, but she refused to explain.

A horrible impasse.

Unlike many Yule parties—several happening in various places in Chatham Castle at this moment—none of the Brothers became sloppy drunk or forgot themselves. A respectful, milling conversation hung in the air.

My heart quickened as Tyrant's grating singsong filled my head, replacing Rognvald's warm support. *Moments after a child died in her parents' arms, you stole her father away.* I balled my hands into fists.

Go. Away.

You bound her father with spells moments after her death, dragged him to Magnolia Castle. There were other children there, you know?

Despite my best effort to keep the memories at bay, I flashed to the Gallo house. The antiseptic in the halls, the murky swamp outside. Sweat popped out on the back of my neck. My chest lifted; I couldn't control it. Attempts to withdraw from the tunneled vision failed. Tyrant carried me along, reliving every horrid moment.

What of their mother? Oh, yes. She's dead too. Because you dragged her father to the castle and the High Priest slaughtered all of them. All of them!

I tried to slow my elevating shoulders, curling into a defensive growl. My body protected itself as the memories rose in terrible images. Mangled bodies. Ricardo weeping. The feeling of hastening death on the air.

Feeling as if I drowned, I cast my eyes about.

Merrick.

Where was Merrick?

Deny it, Tyrant sang. *I dare you. You see the blood on your hands.*

No, I said firmly. *Not here. Not now. Some of that is true—*

All of it is true, he snarled.

Jikes, when had it become so warm in here? Tears clouded my eyes. The good gods, Tyrant's foul whisperings shouldn't have such an emotional punch. Not tonight, under this calm atmosphere.

You don't deserve a blessed handfasting, a beloved life, Tyrant hissed. *Murderer.*

The room began to whirl when Merrick captured my gaze. He sent me a silent question, instantly concerned. I shook my head, reaching a hand. He moved into fast, instant strides, not tearing his eyes from me.

The moment our fingers collided, Tyrant dissipated. Merrick reeled me in, holding me to his hard chest. The images scattered, Tyrant curled away. Merrick gently walked me toward the wall, his lips pressed to my temple. I could feel his false smile as my spine hit the wall, reassuring someone who walked by. After they passed, he ducked his head to my ear.

"You all right?"

"Fine," I whispered. "Just . . . need a moment."

He pressed our foreheads together, hiding me in a lover's embrace no one would question. Tears bubbled to my eyes again, hot and stinging. I wanted to gasp them out, tell him everything, but the words stuck.

It's my fault.

I'm a murderer.

"Take your time, B." His soothing touch slipped down the side of my face. "No one can see you. Deep breaths. I've got you. You're safe."

Steadiness resumed at rapid speed with his heat, the power of his protection surrounding me. I breathed free and easy. Swallowing the rest, I whispered, "Sorry."

He tucked a strand of hair behind my ear. "No. Not that. Never sorry. Shall we take your mind off of it?"

I nodded.

"What did Rognvald want?"

"Support," I said, my voice gaining clarity with each word. "As you likely already knew."

"It's good to hear the words from Rognvald, though," Merrick murmured. My ribs pressed into his when he whispered in my ear, "Any chance you want to steal out of here? Have our own . . . celebration?"

I breathed out my relief. "Please."

When I glanced up to offer to transport myself, Papa and Merrick stared hard at each other, but their lips didn't move. They spoke through the communication magic, then. About me, undoubtedly.

Merrick drew up, gathering me with him. "Let's go, little troublemaker. I'll transport us. Your father will give our merry part's to everyone else. I want to hold you in my arms in front of the fire. "

Chapter Fourteen

The Arck library fulfilled my expectations, and then some.

The gargantuan space took up nearly four floors, rising out of the red stone cliffs like a sandstone behemoth. On the northern wall, chiseled windows spilled sunshine across several floors. No art, books, floors, or shelves cluttered the area, only glasspanes in the formation of a spiraling sun, with a circular window as sprawling as a dragon and decorated with stained yellow glass. The open area between the walls could have swallowed entire wings of Chatham Castle.

Rustles and murmurs and drawers shuffling and silence filled the room. A single scroll drop from the other side rippled through the expanse. It smelled faintly of paper and sand, like the rising heat near the Borderlands. Witches glided around, mostly silent, others whispering.

I stood at the entrance, awed. I had three hours before I needed to return and meet with Scarlett. I'd make excellent use of every minute.

A short witch at a rectangular desk beckoned me.

Resisting the urge to straighten the fake nose ring Priscilla helped me create, I obeyed the command. As I approached, he apprised me. He spoke in the common language, correctly guessing that I wasn't a local.

"What do you want?" he barked.

I tipped a scroll onto his desk. Priscilla's alterations of my appearance had been minimal and should last most of the three hours. My hair remained dark, braided out of my face. My eyes were mocha brown instead of gray. I wore a sleeveless, slit-side skirt common in the West. It swung around my knees instead of my ankles. The utter lack of sleeves delighted me. They had fashion right in the West.

"I'm here in pursuit of my ancestry." I tilted my head toward the scroll. "My mother is from here, and I seek her tribe. They're nomadic."

I rattled off a few details gleaned from my perusal of the Western Covens library. The sparse information was enough to give him an idea that I knew whom I sought, but not how to find them. Information that a father might impart to his daughter. Though a bald lie, truth laced the story.

"My mother died years ago, and I'm seeking to find my family. We lived in the Central Network, with my father's family."

He eyed the pedigree I set before him, a carefully-curated piece that I'd used Leda's connections to create. An Underlibrarian at the Great Library of Burke, eager to talk about common Western Network pedigrees, had been too happy to help. Apparently, not many witches requested information about Western Tribal symbology and the impact of the ice trade on oasis cultivation and development.

The document was a curated list of names, details, and places. A gift handed from one generation to the next.

I planned to write my own and age the parchment with spells, but Leda cautioned against it with a roll of her eyes. "Do you *want* to be caught?" she'd growled. "Of course they check for that kind of fraud!"

Instead, the Underlibrarian offered us an old, genuine pedigree abandoned years ago. With only a few base modifications to reflect my assumed name, Rotu, it worked well. Mostly tribal, aligning with the *Rota* goddess of stars many tribes worshipped.

For several breathless moments, the Western witch scrutinized every ink slash and pen mark. With a sharp exhale, he closed the scroll, picked it up, and handed it back. He studied the glinting circle in my nostril and my bare feet. There, his gaze lingered.

"No sandals?" he asked.

"Do you require them?"

"No."

"Is it a problem?"

Obviously irritated though I couldn't fathom why—the Western Network was known for going without footwear just about anywhere, but especially in the Arck —he simply rolled his eyes and gestured to the side.

"Proceed."

Gathering up the scroll, I said, "When do you close?"

"We don't."

"You're open all night?"

"I said as much, didn't I?"

I nodded and said, "*Lak yon jayid,*" a common tribal saying that translated directly to, *may your sun and stars align.* Or a different form of *merry part.* He ignored me, his attention attached to a parchment and quill.

Unmoored, I drifted into the library. The sandstone bathed everything in reddish-yellow jewels. Striations raced through the floor, which they'd coated with a shiny lacquer. No sand granules clogged in between my toes or dusted my feet as I slipped into the main area, where a maze of bookshelves awaited.

Around the edge, scroll cubbies stacked twenty paces overhead, where ladders rolled back and forth to accommodate patrons, though most summoned higher scrolls with spells. Each cubby had a letter and number marking below it. Easy to organize and identify.

A steady bustle of life beckoned me farther into the annals. I didn't know exactly what I searched for, but I had a feeling I'd find it here.

If I didn't get lost first.

* * *

An hour later, and no closer to my goal of tribal symbology identification. Most of these books were written in tribal languages, which left me stranded. I'd armed myself with a few translation spells, but each attempt I made sputtered out unsuccessful death throes. These tribal languages were too nuanced for a non-native speaker to successfully use spellwork.

Like the Southern Network where the clans had been altering the Yazikan language for years, too many dialects from different origin points existed for Central Network magic to be useful here.

I almost returned to my scowling friend at the front desk to ask for help, but the words, *I need to find a wandering tribe in the desert*, stuck on my tongue like glue. Requesting aid from someone who showed a deep irritation at my bare feet was a step in the wrong direction, considering I'd only met one other witch *with* shoes.

Obviously, I needed assistance. But where to find it? Librarians were difficult to locate, and most patrons actively avoided each other. More than once, when I turned into a new row to study what it offered, other patrons had turned the other way.

The answer materialized around the next corner. Another row of books awaited, their stuffy shelves lined with tomes. A male witch knelt on the ground, twiggy legs crooked out to either side of his aged body. He mumbled, pulling books from a shelf, inspecting their cover, returning them or setting them to either side. At first, I planned to creep past him, but he stopped me.

"You are lost, are you not?"

I froze.

He spoke in the common language, for one. A mild Southern Network accent pervaded, but not heavily. Before I could form a reply, he lazily turned an introductory page in his book and continued to speak.

"This is a vast library with fathoms of wealth in terms of knowledge. There is much to learn. Which is a problem."

Light amusement accompanied his last words.

"This is my first time here."

He chuckled, turned to another page. "Yes, that is obvious."

"Do you work here?"

"Not really."

"A patron?"

He gestured to the books with a sweeping hand. "Do you think I'm doing this for fun? Search for a single spell amidst all of this." He made a low sound in his throat, something between a growl and a chuckle. I'd heard it before—a Western Network habit. Similar to a curse word without vowels.

I lowered onto the ground next to him, on my knees. My feet were tucked underneath me, though not awkwardly splayed to the side in mimicry of his position. How an older gentleman could handle such a position, I couldn't fathom. He peered at me with laughing eyes.

"Who are you, *zizi*?"

"What does zizi mean?"

"An endearment. Similar to *my dear*."

"Oh."

"You're younger than me." He ran a hand along his beard, the fingers tangling in several curls. "That makes you a *zizi*." Shutting his tome, he said, "You have been wandering without selecting a single title for an hour. What do you require?"

Aside from wondering why he cared, or why he tracked me, I voiced my greater need at the moment. While I repeated the same story I told the witch at the front desk, he pushed off the ground. Books trailed him in a long line as he motioned for me to follow. I chased him down the aisle. With those long, skinny legs, he took one stride for every two of mine.

"Ah, yes. A tribal locator. Easy enough."

Easy? I almost cried, but better sense schooled me into quiet. Books didn't follow anyone else, and a golden badge glinted from his chest. A worker, of some sort, though he'd said *not really*. Volunteer, I wagered. As we walked, books peeled away from the long tail and shelved themselves.

He led me to the southern wall, which faced away from the windows. Behind it lay most of the Arck Castle, or maybe more of the same striated red rock. Who knew how many fathoms of caves, grottos, and caverns lingered out of sight? Somewhere near here lurked Faleen Borg, a hideous monstrosity of magic, darkness, and caves. Legendary in its own strange way.

"What's your name?" I asked as I trotted behind him,

weaving through two final shelves before we stood at the gigantic wall.

"Akmar." Impatient with the question, he lifted his spindly fingers overhead. "You see what this is?"

My breath caught. From a distance, I *hadn't* seen it. In fact, from the power that emanated off the wall, I wasn't sure I could have. A spell hid this massive map of the Western Network unfolding across the wall. Paintings brought the area to life, embedded with tribal names and areas painted black. The name repeated in different languages beneath the first, with the common language at the bottom of each stack.

There were *hundreds* of tribes.

At first, I could only take it in. Akmar gave me a few moments, studying the beautiful edifice with his own appreciation. Then the map shifted. Out of the reddish-sands appeared another tribe. A symbol shimmered out of the sandy wall, near a painting of red rock cliffs forming a canyon. A black raven, wings spread, with words in a half circle beneath it. It stood on top of the name, which tripled into different rows beneath.

"Ah." Akmar smiled. "The Dalae tribe has finally settled for a short time. They've been wandering for awhile, you see, seeking new grounds. Those cliffs will be beneficial. Very nice. They are busy. They wander a lot."

"Wow."

Akmar chuckled. "Very powerful magic," he said as an aside. "The librarians maintain it here. It only changes twice a day—too much work to update it constantly. There's only so much they can do."

"It's impressive."

Akmar folded his arms over his chest. "Now, to the point." One hand rose to his chin in thought. "Where is your mother's tribe?" He clicked with a tsking noise as he dove into thought. I tried, unsuccessfully, to peel my eyes off the map. "Your pedigree doesn't quite make sense with the information you've provided."

A cold shot of concern slid into my blood. I'd considered this possibility while speaking with Leda's friend at the Great Library of Burke, of course, but I hadn't expected to encounter it so soon. Part of the reason I hesitated to ask for help had been details. The tribe I sought was likely not the tribe on the pedigree.

Akmar tapped his teeth together. "Not surprising," he murmured, eyes skating higher, "considering second-hand information. Tribes are notoriously hard to track. Details, all that."

His murmurs weren't lost on me, but I paid more attention to the expression on his face as his eyes drifted higher. A cluttered knot of tribes formed around a symbol that most Alkarrans—at least anyone who'd attempted to travel to the Western Network—would know. A droplet of water with smaller ones surrounding it like sun rays. His focus stopped there.

An oasis.

"The pedigree is from a tribe in the southwest," he said, without peeling his eyes off the oasis, "the Alnasajun tribe."

Alnasajun tribe ran through my mind. Never heard of that one before.

He blinked, as if coming out of his thoughts, and swept his gaze to mine. "Did your mother ever mention the name Changan?"

"No."

"That's for the better, probably. They're quite violent. Did she wear a tassel?"

I paused, as if sweeping my memory.

"No," I drawled. Should I make up details, or act as if I wasn't certain?

"Was she ever stolen?"

"Stolen?"

"Taken captive by another tribe, forced into servitude or marriage? These are common issues in the West. But less likely from the Jelani tribe, you know. Changan?" He blew a raspberry. "Now *those* witches are used to hardship."

"Oh, I'm not certain. She handfasted my father and had me." With a shrug, I said, "There's not much I know about her childhood. She died years ago, and I don't think she told my father much."

He blinked again, fluttering with thought. "Hmm . . . there's a disparity, for sure. I'm inclined to lean toward your pedigree, which is the Sahuren tribe. Small tribe, often preyed on. I'll show you where they roam these days. But what you described is indicative of a tribe that's usually on the other side of the Network, the Kavari. Wider. Greater population, with less movement. You may want to research both."

A line of light issued from his fingertips and sped toward a low corner of the map, too high on the wall to reach with his hands.

"However, the symbol you described belongs here, to the *Thabit* tribe. They're one of the longest-running nomadic tribes. They used to be quite powerful. For the last decade or so, they've been quiet, living their lives without much ransacking or many issues. We believe that water scarcity has been difficult for them."

My eyes lingered on the oasis, making a note of it as if I truly cared, but drifted higher when his line did also.

"The Thabit tribe?" I repeated.

Uneasily, he nodded. "Yes. They're one of the oldest

tribes in the Western Network history, enduring over a thousand years, perhaps more. The oral tradition isn't precise. The tribes didn't care much about recording history when the mortals first left. Regardless," he cleared his throat, as if annoyed with ancient witches, "you have likely heard of them before."

"I don't think so."

"They're known in the common tongue as the Weavers of Magic."

My breath arrested. I could barely lock my thoughts into place. *The Weavers of Magic.*

Memories swept me to a surprising day, several years ago, when the Volare first appeared at my side. The former Eastern Network High Priestess, Isobel, had once loaned it to me. The magical, flying carpet had been a worthy companion to rescue a friend. After Isobel died, the carpet chose me as its next owner.

My Volare.

A note had come to me with the Volare, mentioning a witch named Tuffer, the Weaver of Magic. I had it somewhere at the treehouse. Licking my lips, I gathered my thoughts together.

"Yes, I have heard of them under that name before."

If possible, his troubled expression deepened. "Well, if they *are* your tribe, you're lucky."

"How so?"

"You won't be an enemy of them, if you can prove your pedigrees. You are young, which means your mother would still be known. They are . . . gaining more attention these days."

"How so?"

"Water."

His line of light swirled the oasis symbol at the top of

the map. Based on the number of tribes sprawled there, it had to be the same place I had just visited.

"They've found a way to harness water in the desert and their oasis expands. Because of their deep roots in magicks and magic systems, be wary."

"Are they dangerous?"

"Proud."

"Isn't that the same thing?"

Shaking his head, he said, "Not at all."

* * *

Curiosity compelled me to visit the Thabit tribe oasis, but prudence held me back. Though I wanted to explore again, I withheld. A meeting with Scarlett approached, and I needed to return.

I asked Akmar several questions that fit my story of someone seeking her mother's tribe, confirmed a few hunches as best I could, and followed him to stacks that gave more information. History on the pedigree was abundant, along with written stories, maps, and grimoires associated with the tribe. I noted their location, but followed Akmar more eagerly toward the section of the library that covered the Thabit tribe.

Shelves awaited.

"They have a history of trouble," Akmar admitted, running the tops of his fingers along the book spines. "As you can see. They dabbled often in different magicks. Their witches like power, but they're also very wise. Intelligent. More than the average witch, it's said."

"And that gets them into trouble?"

"In a world of survival instead of society? Yes. Cleverness turns from mathematical formulas and into power struggles. When magic bears the brunt of an intelligent witch's attention, problems always arise. Particularly when water is the currency. If you decide to approach them, be very cautious, and take an offering."

"What kind of offering?"

Head tilted, he said, "A grimoire. If it's one they've never seen before, they'll welcome you. If they already have it, they'll turn you away."

This advice only increased my dread.

Eventually, Akmar drifted away, dozens of books at his back. He loped along until he turned at a twist in the stacks and left me alone. For minutes, I stood in the same spot and stared at all the books, absorbing what he revealed. On purpose, I'd left the Volare and Viveet at home. Most libraries didn't allow weapons, and only an idiot strolled into the Arck Castle with visible defense. Most witches didn't know what the case on my back contained, but once they found out, the Volare tended to draw attention.

Now, I wish I *had* brought it.

Perhaps it held clues.

Careful not to think too much about it—I might summon the beloved thing—I turned my focus to the stacks again. After twenty minutes perusing each shelf, it became clear that the books weren't listed in alphabetical order by title, nor by author, but by the supposed time-line. On the far left were the books most ancient in origin. To the right, those most recent.

I finally stumbled on what had me the most curious.

The Weavers.

My finger touched the top of a book and pulled it out. The title *The Weavers of Magic.* sprawled along the spine and across the front, which was a flimsy leather clearly sewn together. I pulled it off the shelf and fanned the pages. Gently, because time had clearly wreaked her havoc here.

Do you ever consider, Tyrant inquired with his terrible melody, *that you stopped an entire pedigree from existing?*

I rolled my eyes. Jikes, but he followed me everywhere, in every situation, with unrelenting prejudice. No small task escaped his notice.

Leda?

Two breaths later, she asked, *Yes?*

Can you find out if the Great Library of Burke has a book titled, The Weavers of Magic?

In twenty minutes, I can.

Thanks.

I slipped past the first few pages, gliding through each one at rapid speed, not surprised to eventually see the name I expected. My heart double-beat at the sight of it.

Tuffer.

Embedded within the words came other familiar ones. Volare. Rug. Magic. History existed within these pages, but I didn't have the time to absorb it now. I had the tribe name, information on how to approach. I didn't want to return and draw more attention to myself, but I couldn't take this book with me, either. Enchantments on this building didn't allow any artifact to leave. If a witch tried, they lost their hand.

While I perused a journal that looked fairly recently written—at least within the last ten years—by a young woman taken captive by the Thabit tribe who had finally found her way to freedom, Leda responded.

The Great Library of Burke doesn't have it, nor any copies or abridgments.

Do you think anywhere else would?

Based on that title alone, it seems unlikely. The Academy in the East might have before the insurrection damaged their archives. Though their restoration efforts have been largely successful, much is still tucked away. The next best place to inquire is in the Northern Network.

Disappointed, I said, *Thanks.* Going that far to read this book wasn't worth it with Alina's mission to fulfill. There was work to do, and reading more about the Volare was a luxury, not required. I settled several books onto a nearby, low-slung table formed from sandstone and held together with magic. A giant pillow on the floor beckoned, but I had to ignore the temptation to stay and read.

Did you find what you need? Leda asked.

And then some.

Are you returning in time for our meeting?

On my way.

After reshelving the title, I headed out of the aisle and into the working area. The broiling temperature of the Western Network left the place utterly devoid of fire-places, replacing them with spells that moved the stiff heat. As the sun crept higher in the sky, and the slanting sunlight altered its angle through the dusty air, the calefaction increased.

Time to return. In the end, I'd received exactly what I wanted. Now, I had to make sense of it.

Chapter Fifteen

Scarlett stood on the other side of her office, framed by snowflakes and flurries, with a weary expression. She wore a cardinal dress that highlighted the burgundy tones of her hair, which she'd pulled, as usual, into a bun. The strict lines had ebbed, lessening the tension. Her hair gleamed.

When I entered her office, she smiled.

"Thank you for coming, Bianca."

"Anything for you, Scarlett."

Leda entered at my side, bearing scrolls, her copy of Scarlett's schedule book—which was linked to Scarlett's by a spell, so both could make changes in their copy and share the update—and an expression of utter relief. Hiddleston closed the door, taking his usual defensive position in front of Scarlett's office.

"I understand you've chosen the new High Priest?" I inquired lightly.

As hoped, a surprised smile alighted on her features, removing some of the fatigue. "I have, and it is likely a greater relief to Leda than myself. In fact, that is part of the reason that I've asked you here. Only part of it," she added gently. "We're going to announce the High Priest tomorrow morning. We're hoping the weather will be more cooperative. I plan to stand on the balcony, as Mildred did when she announced Derek. That will allow witches from all over to witness."

Unable to resist, I asked, "Who is it?"

"Who do you think?"

This question had gone back and forth for days in the *Chatterer* and throughout Chatham City. Merrick and I had debated long into the night, but I hadn't settled on a good candidate.

"I know who I *don't* want it to be," I said, thinking of several male witches on the Council I'd rather avoid in greater power. Some of them, like Henry, I didn't mind. With a little more time, I could come around to D'artagnan, but I wasn't sure yet. He was still too new. Then again, Papa called Scarlett up from the Head of Education . . .

"Talmund," Scarlett stated. "I've asked Talmund to be the High Priest, and he's just agreed this morning."

My entire body eased at the news. Talmund, the current Head of Guardians, was an even-keeled man with a steady head. He wasn't reactive, and tended to think more than he spoke. As a supportive High Priest, he would be almost ideal.

"Won't Talmund be bored?" I asked.

She laughed, as if she'd shared the same thought. "He assures me that the promotion is appealing. He watched the process for Derek, has injuries troubling him since the Battle for Letum Wood, and appears eager. We spoke extensively. I think Talmund makes far more sense than Rognvald."

I laughed outright at the thought. "But why not someone on the Council?"

Scarlett cast her gaze to Leda, who smiled in her quiet way, which would have been an outright beam for anyone else. "Leda had very sage and wise advice, as she often does. Sometimes, going outside the Council is a better option. For . . . diversification of thought. Talmund thinks like the Head of Guardians, not a Council Member. Bringing in a variety of experiences is prudent. Your father certainly stirred things up for the better."

"I like Talmund," I said. "I think the choice is a wise one."

"Thank you." She softened. "Though I wish, perhaps like you, that I didn't have to make this choice at all."

A little tremor moved through me. This time, I managed a smile when I thought of Grandfather.

"Me too."

A knock came at the door, which opened enough to admit a silver dinner tray. Scarlett ignored the entrance, clasped her hands as the dinner tray settled, and turned to face me fully. With the crackling fire and snowy night, she cut a cozy figure.

"I brought you to ask if you'd act as my protection during the announcement tomorrow? While I don't expect the furor that your father received over his empowerment, it seems wise to anticipate trouble."

"You have me, Your Highness."

"The Brotherhood will be out in full force, as expected. Hidden in the crowd and at various points in the castle as well, but I would appreciate someone at my side. I'll allow you to strategize whatever protections you want to put into place, and when."

A dozen ideas already trickled through my mind. Shield spells big enough to expand above and beyond the balcony, like an invisible half bubble. Tracking incantations, put into place immediately, that allowed me to know if anyone tried to set enchantments on her balcony.

"I'm honored, Your Highness."

"Thank you." Scarlett peered into my soul, as only she could, when she asked, "And how are you?"

"Fine."

"Truly?"

Rage bubbled in a constant flow under my thoughts, but it didn't control me as it used to. *I hear a voice in my head named Tyrant, and I dream about little girls dying and their family sobbing,* I thought of admitting, but I couldn't. Not here. Not to Scarlett, who bore the weight of a Network.

The memories themselves were difficult enough, but Tyrant made them worse. His constant nattering resulted in introspection I wasn't ready for. Questions arose constantly. Could I live with the decisions I'd have to make?

Maybe it was foolish for me to press forward into this mission with Alina, and helping Scarlett, without answering those questions first. But I couldn't deny these witches the help they sought. The Head of the Sisterhood is who I wanted to be.

At least . . . I thought I did before blood spilled across my hands in buckets. What I didn't want to admit was my own uncertainty.

With a dismissive smile, I said, "Yes, Your Highness. I'm doing well enough after Grandfather's death. There was a time when I couldn't control my emotions or my powers as I do now, but that time has passed. Losing Grandfather, while sad, is also happy. He's back with Mildred, and that's where he wanted to be most."

I hadn't entirely convinced her. My voice lacked fervor, and her eyes lacked trust.

Of course, Tyrant drawled. *Who could trust you? You're lying to everyone, including yourself. Murderer.*

"Thank you, Bianca. I'm happy to hear that. Regardless, he's left a Marten-sized hole in our lives that no one, not even Talmund, can fill. He will always be missed, even as life, by necessity, moves on."

I wanted to ask her about Georgette and Rognvald. Wanted to see what she thought of the articles that continued to yarn out, yammering about ridiculous rumors and stirring up unnecessary drama, but something held me back. Acknowledging it only brought more attention.

Did it matter what Georgette said?

Not really.

Despite her flailing against the Sisterhood, we continued to exist in the world the way that felt best for now. She didn't impede my mission. Her frothing against me had no real impact into my mission, my important relationships, and my handfasting, aside from feeding Tyrant's horrible voice in my soul.

So did Georgette matter?

Not enough. Georgette wasn't worth mentioning. Eventually, the hullabaloo would settle. Hadn't it with Papa? Witches still thought poorly or highly of him, but he lived happily with Regina and her Apa in the forest, and was quite pleased with his life.

Scarlett lowered to her chair, glancing askance at the dinner tray, but with little interest. Despite the day drawing to a gradual and snowy close, a hot cup of coffee would have hit just right.

"Thank you for agreeing. We'll see you in the morning, Bianca. Seven o'clock should do it."

Sensing the gracious dismissal for what it was, I turned to Leda. "I'll plan out my precautions and be in touch within the hour. When is the announcement?"

"Tomorrow morning at nine o'clock."

* * *

The next morning dawned with a bluebird sky, whipped clouds on the horizon, and crackling, fresh powder.

Merrick and I awoke at the same time, sleepy-eyed as we dressed in our warmest winter boots. I yanked on pants instead of a dress, armed myself with Viveet and the Volare, and kissed him before departing for the castle. He, for the Gatehouse.

Invisible on Scarlett's balcony, reassured that protective magic remained unmolested and in place, I watched the ministrations and building anticipation below.

Snow lined all gables and eaves of Chatham Castle. Servants shoveled it off the Wall, brooming it from handrails and steps. Spells blew it from the lower and upper Baileys, clearing an advance path for witches milling outside the closed portcullis. They had red-tipped noses and bright voices, with several crooning Yule songs.

A crowd stretched from the portcullis down Chatham Road, through the clearing on either side of the road, and to the gates of Chatham City. Bodies packed all available standing space, and there were still two hours before the announcement. Letum Wood loomed close by, like bold shepherds.

The door opened and closed behind me. Papa spoke, though I saw no one. "Scarlett said I'd find you out here."

"Preparing."

"I'm glad to hear it."

His arm brushed mine as he stood at the railing,

which Scarlett's butler, Marjorie, had cleared before I arrived. Not a hint of snow remained on the wrought-iron gabling. The pinching cold restored me. A fresh day. New start. I missed Grandfather, but sunshine chased away the grieving shadows.

"How are you, B?"

"Fine."

"I, uh . . . had something interesting happen."

"Oh?"

A laugh lived in his voice. "Council Member Georgette approached me."

My surprise was so great I almost released the invisibility spell. Instead, I gaped, then realizing he couldn't see me, asked, "What?"

He laughed, and the rich sound was a delight. For some reason, it made Grandfather not seem so far away.

"Last night."

"Where?"

"At the Gatehouse. I was speaking with Rognvald about today and asking if he required help. Regina plans to attend and we thought we could be of service."

"Naturally."

"As Rognvald and I were talking, Georgette walked in."

Astonishment slowed my response, but not by much. "To the Gatehouse?"

"Mm hmm."

"What did she want?"

"To speak to you."

I rolled my eyes. "Jikes. She keeps sending me the same message."

"Have you read them?"

"I skim them. It's the same request each time. *Sign this contract.*"

"Will you?"

"No!"

Another laugh. "That's my girl."

Curiosity compelled me to ask, "What did you say to Georgette?"

"If she wanted to talk to you, she could find you herself."

"Ha!"

"Her response was . . . not pleased."

"What do you mean?"

"Her cheeks reddened for a moment. She wasn't sure what to say."

Hopefully, that meant she'd attempted to find me, but couldn't. Good. I hadn't tried that hard to avoid her, but it had still been easy. Few knew where I lived. With Letum Wood protecting me, Georgette would never find the treehouse.

Sighing, I shoved away from the railing. The grind and squeak of the rising portcullis bled witches into the upper and lower baileys. Scarlett had the castle staff place gigantic, round bowls through the baileys. Fire sprang to life in each one, providing heat while witches waited.

"Georgette asked Aurora to speak to me on her behalf, too," I said.

He chuckled. "She's determined, that's for sure." After a minute or two of quiet, he added. "I'm sorry, B."

"About Georgette?"

"And your grandfather."

Selfishly, I hadn't focused much on Papa since Grandfather died. Reaching out, I blindly searched for his shoulder. His magic was a surprisingly low register, not bold and obvious, even when standing so close.

"How are you, Papa?"

"Fine."

"Really?"

Without seeing his expression, I wasn't sure how to gauge his reply. It must be *somewhat* true, certainly. He functioned. This wasn't the first parent that he'd lost, though he was arguably closer to Marten than to Mildred. Regardless, I couldn't imagine losing Papa, my final link to my own heritage.

"How is living with Regina and her father?"

A smile filled his voice. "Wonderful. The noise and laughter and . . . life . . . in the house again."

"You don't plan to go on a walkabout alone again?"

"No," he said softly. "I much prefer this."

We remained in the companionable silence while witches filtered into the Baileys. The crowd from Chatham City thinned as they shuffled through the wide doors and under the portcullis. High Witches, Coven Leaders, and others transported to predetermined spots on the Wall. Guardians kept track of their individual assigned areas to make sure no one uninvited attempted to transport in to steal a better position. In that mess, Merrick and other Protectors lurked.

"Do you have an assignment, then?" I asked.

He drawled a vague, "Not officially."

The muffled rap on Scarlett's main apartment door drew my attention inside. Leda and Scarlett welcomed Talmund. He ventured in alone, having no spouse, nor an Assistant as of yet.

"I better focus on Scarlett and my spells again. Thanks for coming out, Papa."

His hand found my arm, squeezed it. "Love you, B. Good talk."

Chuckling to myself, I stepped inside. Papa left by climbing over the railing, dropping off the balcony, and transporting with a burst of magic.

* * *

The exultant roar of the crowd after Scarlett announced Talmund as the newest High Priest position was a welcome relief. I crouched on the Volare, invisible, but hovering next to Scarlett for the duration of her announcement, and then after. No one attempted to harm her.

From that point, it was a matter of carefully navigating the castle events with Scarlett in my field of vision, though no obvious threats presented themselves. While she trusted the populace, instigators might make themselves known amongst the hordes.

None showed.

Hours blurred into a series of meticulously planned and careful events. Talmund's public welcome, a luncheon with Council Members, and a meet-and-greet with High Witches. All led to a ball at the end of the day. His Empowerment, which would officially bring him into the position, would occur later in the week.

Sometime around ten o'clock that evening, Scarlett said through the magic, *Thank you, Bianca. I believe that's sufficient.*

The crowds outside had calmed. Fewer witches congregated in the halls, though platters of food remained. The celebratory ball would last well into the wee hours of the morning, as some witches had just arrived. The band was bright, and the ballroom candles were blazing hot.

I asked, *Are you sure?*

Yes, thank you. You may leave anytime. Leda will issue your currency tomorrow.

Your Highness, I —

I insist.

Understanding when I would lose, I snapped my mouth shut and forced myself to say, *Thank you*. Technically, Scarlett could have asked for any member of the Brotherhood to watch her and not paid a sacran. Since she asked me, she'd pay from her own coffers.

Enjoy yourself, if you can, she said drily.

Laughing, I twirled to leave, but a familiar visage held my attention. Alina. She stood across the room, near the edge. Though Tipa wouldn't be visible—what demigod would want to be found amongst so many witches?—I suspected she must be close by and also protecting Alina. Alina's indifferent stare circled the room. Meanwhile, an equally familiar face stood at her side.

Georgette.

Something in Alina's stiff features, flat lips, and oddly still hands caught my attention. Alina had never been a warm figure. She rarely smiled, and her approval was as likely as raining rocks. Yet, she still appeared . . . off. Then again, when didn't Georgette's presence inspire such an emotion?

I crept along the outer wall, closing in.

Alina's unreadable expression wasn't the strange part, but how Georgette stared at Alina with such high expectations. Alina had sipped a drink, appeared bored, and murmured a reply. This set Georgette's lips to speaking again with greater fervor.

Before long, I'd closed the distance. I doubted Georgette would seek magical signatures in a crowd this heavy, perhaps not at all. My focus on detecting what magic worked around me was a result of my work. Few witches cared all that much.

"It is interesting," Georgette said in her usual business-like tone, "that Miss Monroe has attempted to vanish nearly completely from Chatham Castle, don't you think?"

The back of my neck prickled.

She *had* to be jesting.

Are you busy? I asked Leda.

Surprisingly, no.

Leda had been haunting Scarlett's side all day, until Scarlett released her to relax when the ball began. I suspected Leda would retire soon. It wasn't often she left work before Scarlett, but lately she'd been more inclined to duck away. A good sign, I thought.

Georgette paused, allowing Alina space to reply to her strange observation about me. Alina blinked, her jaw lowering slightly, as if she suppressed a yawn. During the awkward beat of silence, I replied to Leda.

Can you fathom any reason why Georgette would be fishing for information about me from Alina?

I presumed Leda's silence was a moment of shock and comprehension, because when she spoke again, her voice mirrored my expectation.

What?

Strange, right?

Are you eavesdropping?

Naturally.

Georgette smiled at a passing witch, allowing Alina's unnaturally long silence to continue. Too many more beats of it and Alina would be blatantly ignoring Georgette's question. Georgette held on for another fifteen seconds, nearly drawing a giggle from me.

What is she saying? Leda asked.

Alina refuses to reply.

Oh.

Georgette pulled in a breath through her nose, but didn't speak again. The demure way she folded her hands in front of her and planted her feet spoke to determination. She had something she wanted to learn, and she wouldn't leave until she learned it.

Alina's head cocked ever-so-slightly to the right, though her bland expression didn't alter. A lock of hair around her ear shuffled, disrupted, as if a breath stirred it. A breath from Tipa, perhaps?

Georgette continued, "Miss Monroe has been a known confidante of yours since you took power, has she not?"

To my surprise, Alina asked, "What is your definition of a confidante, Council Member?"

A flare of shock registered in Georgette's wide eyes. Probably that Alina had responded. She maintained a cool response. "A confidante is a trusted person. Perhaps a friend, in some regards. Bianca has been known to flitter around the Southern Network. As such, rumors that she's friends with you have resulted."

Alina's resulting chuckle nearly swept the breath out of me. *Georgette* had amused her? Alina's head straightened again, her eyes sweeping sideways to glance at Georgette from the thin corners.

"Many descriptions have been applied to Bianca Monroe," Alina said, "but *flittering* is not one I've heard before. I'm sure she'd be delighted to know you feel that way."

Georgette faltered in reply.

I smiled.

Alina drew in a breath, gathering part of her full skirts in one hand. She had a regal mien, with a full, rose-colored skirt, a creamy lace shawl, and her hair swept high off her thin neck. Her bare shoulders, despite the cold, retained the muscular testament to her former Shieldmaiden days.

"Thank you for the riveting discussion, Council Member. From it, I've gathered that you have a personal issue with Bianca Monroe that, instead of talking directly to her about, you're attempting to learn more about by speaking with other witches. Most revealing."

Georgette sucked in a breath through her nose. "You speak as if I haven't tried," she hissed. "She's proven to be . . ."

"Elusive?" Alina smiled, her glacial stare meeting Georgette judgment for judgment. Her position as High Priestess gave her ultimate advantage over this battleground. "How audacious of Bianca, with her name smeared in the *Chatterer* and your rallying against a cause she seemed very suited for. I can't imagine the fool that would want to be seen with you under such circumstances. My regards."

Like a closing door, Georgette locked down. Her formerly affable exterior melted into austerity. She said nothing. A concession.

"Whatever you think of Bianca Monroe," Alina concluded, "I can guarantee you don't see her *flitting* around this ballroom talking about you in less than flattering terms with anyone who will listen."

Alina whirled, skirt pirouetting around her, and sought the exit. After a short pause, she turned her body toward my hidden position, and I caught myself the fool. She knew I'd been listening. Of *course* she knew. After losing her magic, Alina had been more attuned to power than ever. Exposure to any amount of magic caused her physical pain. She'd gradually gotten used to being in the presence of other witches, but I doubted it was comfortable.

She grazed by me. I followed, grateful to leave a

fuming Georgette behind. Out in the hallways, alone, Alina said, "Tomorrow. Meet in my personal quarters."

I peeled to the side without a word.

Chapter Sixteen

Alina sat behind a tray of hearty offerings. A thin gravy, clotted with onions, black bread flecked by white oatmeal flakes, and a poached egg propped on a tiny plate off to the side. Coffee steamed from a pot, filling the air.

She ignored the food to focus on me as I crossed the floor. A pair of woolen pants kept my legs warm beneath my long-sleeved dress, a deep blue without decoration. My hair, braided out of the way, hung almost to my elbows.

Light slanted through windows and onto the wooden floor, softened with wide rugs. Sparkling blue skies topped the landscape, where snow glimmered so brightly I had to squint. Her cool room smelled like lavender. Alina waved her hand to an open chair across from her. I lowered into it.

"I appreciate your support last night."

An arch smile replied. Alina lifted her coffee cup from the tray, but didn't sip. She held it in her hands. "Council Member Georgette has a real vendetta against you. What have you done?"

"Shown the audacity to create change."

Alina scoffed. "What a terror." She lifted a delicate, sugar-spun spoon off the tray and dunked it into the coffee. As she stirred, it dissolved, breaking beneath her touch until it crumbled into the muddy liquid and dissolved. She rubbed her finger and thumb together to clear the granules.

"Let's not waste our precious time discussing Georgette," she said.

Heartily, I agreed. "I have updates about the Western Network tribe."

She peered at me. "What are they?"

Quickly, I recounted the initial visit to the oasis, my thoughts, the visit with Aurora, and finally my experience in the Arck Library. Details about the Thabit tribe, the oasis, and an extensive Network history of abductions didn't register much surprise. Her serene expression only altered to surprise when Aurora's name surfaced. By the end, she appeared contemplative.

"I read what I could of the Thabit tribe, but much of it was historical." I finished with my hands resting on my knees, my mind far away. The sprawling interior of the Arck library whipped through my memory as I attempted to recall *The Weavers of Magic* book. Though the information had been interesting, and the peek into the deserts fascinating, it held little pertinence. I almost didn't mention it to her, but decided to tell her everything instead.

When I shared the sentiments, Alina frowned. "I think you're wrong about *The Weavers of Magic* not mattering to your mission," she pronounced.

"Why?"

She set aside the coffee and reached for a basket at the side of her chair. Several books filled it, most of them tattered and old. The one she withdrew might have been the oldest.

"This is a hand-written account of the clans. My clan, for the South has many," she amended carefully, thumbing through the pages with utmost care. From where I sat, the language didn't remind me of Yazikan, though I couldn't see each word very well. Her reverence held a sacredness to it. Out of respect, I kept my eyes off the interior.

Alina continued. "The Western tribes aren't dissimilar to the clans. They're rooted in pride, tradition, and respect. Whatever the *Weavers of Magic* book said about the Thabit tribe, it's probably a bigger insight than you're giving it credit for."

"It was written hundreds of years ago."

"But the insights are unparalleled. Look *beneath* the time. What drives this tribe? What do they want? Could it be traits and motivations they share with *this* one? The desires and delights of my clan, though generations apart, resembles our forefathers to a shocking degree."

"Survival," I immediately countered. "All of them are focused on survival."

"Yes, but how? *How* have they survived this long? The answer is in the details, and I think still relevant to this day."

Frowning, I asked, "The magic, you mean? The grimoires that triggered the Volare?"

"Magic *systems*. The man at the Arck Library stated that they invest in grimoires, didn't he?"

"Yes."

"Why?"

"To survive." So I didn't sound lazy, I quickly added, "From what little I read, they'd find rare magic systems and create. Those creations, like the Volare, enabled them to have an advantage over other tribes."

She returned her clan book to the basket, bent an elbow, and leaned it onto her knee. Her fervent stare bore into me as she put her weight forward, investing her whole body into our conversation.

"Yes, that's it. Do you see the pattern?"

Feeling like an idiot for not seeing the parallel on my own, I said, "Yes. I do now."

"Good. If you want to take charge of the Sisterhood, you must dive deeper than most witches. How does the Thabit complete the same pattern today as their forefathers did then? The tribe has lasted on these basic core principles. Find a rare magic system, exploit it for their benefit, and thrive."

"With water, they've done the same, but . . . different."

"They found *us,* have exploited our witches and water, and elevated themselves to a higher status in the desert with an oasis."

"The question is how to take that information and find your witches?"

Alina rolled her eyes. "Yes. That's what *you* are here to answer, Bianca." I hated the slight chiding in her tone, if only because she shouldn't have had to say it. The reminder that I was still very much learning knocked my vaulted self-importance down a notch. Alina defended me against Council Member Georgette at a time when few might dare, but that didn't mean I could get comfortable. Respect had to be earned, and I tucked the reminder into my pocket.

"This isn't just about water." Alina straightened, her gaze distant. "They could steal fresh water from many lakes. There's some other reason. Perhaps another magic they're exploiting, to make this oasis."

"Your witches make it easier to exploit," I said. "They're practically defenseless out there, in the forgotten lakes."

"A facet, certainly."

"You think there's more?"

She nodded.

Questions flooded me with her observations. Despite not having gone to the oasis herself, she wasn't wrong. Her assumptions built a bigger picture, but the sense of something missing, the idea that more lay beneath the surface, made me restless. So they traded for water . . . then why abduct the witches?

Our short conversation felt like a punch to the gut. My head pounded from the quick implications it created, and all the sprouting avenues in my mind, like reaching roots. I had a lot to answer. A lot to observe. There was work to do.

"I'll return with updates," I promised.

The corners of her lips lifted with a smile.

Bringing the Volare to the Thabit Oasis might have been a stupid idea. Then again, it may have been brilliant. A test, and an option, in case an opportunity to use the Volare to my advantage presented itself. Besides, I didn't plan on getting caught. There wasn't time for distractions with clannish witches to find and answers to seek.

I transported to a less populated area, near the outer ring of sand. The temptation to practice invisibility, trans-porting, *and* hovering at the same time was a powerful one, but I forwent it. Magical stacking could come later, under less demanding circumstances.

An hour of observing, intermittent creeping around, and attempting to translate the myriad of languages gleaned little. There weren't any spots where I sensed magic, but didn't know the source. Nothing obliquely unexpected or unexplained that fit Alina's suspicion of deeper motivations. Little true information gleaning would happen while invisible, and I'd been discovered last time, anyway.

Though I loathed it, I had to be seen.

Quick transformation spells, a change of wardrobe, and a twenty step jog down the main road, away from the oasis put me in the clear. Once fully transformed, I spun, faced the oasis again, and removed the invisibility spell. Few witches paid me any attention as I strolled down the road, relieved to glide under the canopy of magical trees and out of direct sunlight.

At the water's edge, I paused. Two guards stared at me. Witches ringed the glass-domed area, but no one came forward to drink. Recalling my last departure from this oasis—chased by a very pale witch with white hair—I kept a wary eye out. No sign of him right now.

Heeding Akmar's advice from the Arck library, I summoned an old grimoire on household incantations I'd long ago memorized. A common household book in the Central Network, but unlikely to be so popular in a transient population.

I held it up.

The guard studied it, plucked it from my hands, reviewed the title, fanned the pages, and tossed it to another guard. They barked a few words back and forth. Finally, the one before he said in the common language, "Water?"

Nodding, I reached for an empty pouch. He gestured to the other guard, who already spelled the grimoire away, and reached for the bucket. Their eyes focused on me when I submerged my leather pouch, let water glide within, and pulled it out. Bodies stirred along the edges while I tipped the bucket into my open mouth, drained the rest, and handed it back. Cold and crisp and clean. Very refreshing.

They're going to see right through your lying facade, Tyrant purred.

"Thanks," I said to the guard.

He watched me as I ducked away, heading for the trees. I settled out of sight toward the edge of the oasis, ignoring Tyrant's continual drivel.

Are you going to kill that witch?

Ooh, there's a mother. Will you slay her, too? It hasn't stopped you before.

Minutes passed before I felt the eyes on my back slide away. A quick glance convinced me no one, not even the Guards, regarded me anymore. I withdrew a map of Alkarra from my pocket. In the middle of the Western Network appeared a pinprick of light.

I'd set a tracking spell on the bottom edge of the hand-sewn grimoire binding. Minuscule, almost impossible to sense unless one looked for it. Wherever the guard had spelled the book would be revealed on this particular map.

Whispering the tracking spell, the edges of Alkarra dissipated like water. New ones formed, bringing me closer to the grimoire's location. The Western Network took up the entire page, and the pinprick of light moved with the shifting structure. The light focused near the top, not far from where the Thabit oasis had been on the Arck library map.

I frowned.

Wait.

That was almost *exactly* the same spot.

Another command blurred the edges again, zooming us closer to the light point. I stared at a bigger picture of the Thabit Oasis. The pinprick of light was due north. Far enough to be out of sight from the oasis, but close enough to reach without much effort.

Did they live there?

Why? Tyrant inquired casually. *Are you going to kill them, too?*

Eyes rolling, I mentally growled, *Go away!*

A touch on my back sent me leaping to my feet. The map folded together and slid into my pocket. Viveet leaped out of her sheath and into my waiting hand as I whirled around. In a second, I faced a male witch with massive eyes, hands in the air, black hair flowing over scrawny shoulders.

He squeaked, *"Paina!"* but I had no idea what it meant.

Breathing hard, I attempted to control the rising heat in my chest. Magic flared with it, bubbling and filled with the ire I thought I'd locked down. Ire that Tyrant, and his irritating presence, unlocked. If Tyrant hadn't filled my head, I would have heard this witch.

My shoulders and chest heaved while we stared at each other. His wide orbs roved from me, to Viveet, and back again. His fear calmed my instant response. When death and blue fire didn't befall the stranger, he slowly lowered one hand, and then the other. Tension baked the sweltering air until I lowered Viveet. Her flames zipped into a smolder.

The witch and I regarded each other for one more tense moment. "Don't ever touch me again," I hissed.

Understanding lit his gaze. "Common tongue?"

Wary, I nodded.

A hand splayed across his chest. "Me too! My name is Hasan."

"Zolta."

"Yes, yes. Zolta. Very nice." He waved impatiently, then gestured to my shoulder with a pointed finger. "Where did you get it?"

I risked a glance over my shoulder, but saw nothing back there. Did he mean the Volare? Impossible. It coiled in a case and I hadn't brought it out. Gesturing to Viveet, I said, "Andrei."

Hasan rolled his eyes. "Not *that*." Another eager jab. "*That!*"

"What are you talking about?"

He scoffed. "I am Thabit! I know our magic when I sense it."

Blinking, I asked, "Sense what?"

"A Volare!" Eyes alight, he danced from foot to foot. "You have one! It calls to me!" Grinning, he asked, "Who *couldn't* feel it? It is so powerful! Please, may I see it? In all my years . . . I never!"

My heart raced. I stepped back. "The Volare is mine."

He laughed outright. I didn't appreciate the hilarity, because it took too long for him to calm. Hand on his stomach, he shook his head and hands at the same time, giggling. Dramatic witch, but not unpleasant. I began to unwind, realizing he hadn't come to harm me or take the Volare.

"Stop," he pleaded, swiping tears from his eyes. "Stop, this is too funny. You think I would take a Volare from you? You think that I *could*?"

Another round of laughter.

Gritting my teeth, I muttered, "I'd love an explanation."

He sobered with surprising speed. Rearranging his features into surprise instead of hilarity, he asked, "You don't know?"

"Know what?"

"The rules of the Volare."

"How could I?"

He waved to me. "You are an owner! You must know everything."

I opened my mouth, closed it again. Truthfully, I hadn't done any research on the Volare. All these years, and it hadn't seemed necessary. The Volare and I figured out the most important things through trial and error. It accepted silent commands, anticipated my needs. What more was there?

All amusement drained from his expression. His jaw slackened. In a stunned whisper, he asked, "You really don't know?"

"The Volare chose me years ago."

"As they do."

"I've . . . I've just used it."

Thoughtful now, he tapped his chin with a finger and dropped into deeper thought. "You are from the Central Network?"

"Is it that obvious?"

A wide grin showed white teeth. "Your voice, yes. Certainly. But this is not a problem. There isn't much literature about Volares in the Central Network?"

"I'm not sure."

His hands broadened across his torso. "There is a big library, no?"

"Yes."

Head tilted, he exclaimed, "You didn't search?"

"Ah . . . no."

His lips quivered, as if he held back another laugh.

This, he swallowed and said in a strangled voice, "Of course, of course. You must be a forest witch. Anyway, there are rules and capacities and magic for the Volare. Can I see it?"

My eyes darted around, although we remained alone. While I didn't necessarily fear the Volare leaving me—he made it clear that it wasn't likely—I wasn't sure this was a bright idea to maintain a low profile for reconnaissance.

Then again, I needed to find the clannish witches, and they weren't *here*. Which necessitated me locating the Thabit tribe outside of the oasis. If I played this just right, the Volare might be my ticket inside the tribe.

Calculating a hasty plan, I leaned away from my hesitation.

"Sure. You can see the Volare."

Excitement brightened his endlessly black eyes. "Thank you!" he cried, clapping. "Oh, thank you. There is much I can tell you about the Volare just by seeing the intricate weave and pattern. There are only five, you know? Five originals, assuming this *is* an original. There were others, of course, but not so powerful . . ."

He trailed off, gazing with greater anticipation over my shoulder. For better or for worse, I pulled the case around. Commanding it gently, the lid popped off as the Volare slid free. Slowly. A breath at a time. The tassels, the edges, the underside revealed.

Hasan gasped. His hands waved, feet dancing. A high squeal that pierced my ears issued from his throat. The Volare hesitated, likely responding to me, before it calmly unfolded in the air at my hip.

Very still, Hasan whispered, "By Sarena," and fainted dead away.

Chapter Seventeen

Hasan's strong pulse and steady breaths reassured me that he would be fine. In the meantime, I studied the Volare with new eyes. The corner of it uplifted, reminding me of a quirked eyebrow. It lowered, the whole thing rippling as if wind stirred it.

"Rules," I whispered. "You have rules? Really?"

The Volare whipped overhead, disappearing into the leaves. The moment it hid, a voice came from not far away.

"Hasan?"

A woman padded through the sand wearing a pale linen dress, bare feet, hair wild around her shoulders. Her tawny skin, lighter than Hasan's but darker than mine, had sun-worn wrinkles along her lips and eyes. A desert witch, through-and-through.

She glanced at me, then to Hasan.

Before I could comprehend what to say, she stopped walking. Hands on her hips, she cried with an unmistakable Chatham City accent, "Not again!" Snapping two fingers, she pointed and asked, "How long has he been like this?"

"Uh . . . thirty seconds?"

She eyed me, recognizing my accent. Eyes rolling, she closed the distance, crouched down, and slapped him across the mouth. I jolted back, stunned by the violence. Hasan's cheeks bunched as he moaned. His hands rolled, feet twitched. Color leaked into his cheeks as he roused, gazing at her with blunted eyes.

"What'd you do?" she shouted. "Did you make trouble and scare yourself again?"

I edged a step away, but the woman threw a hand up, finger pointed at me, and shouted, "Don't you dare, unknown woman! I'll tackle you the moment you toe away from me. If he doesn't explain himself, you demmed well better explain *for* him."

Frozen to the spot, I obeyed. Curiosity, more than fear, trapped me. A Chatham City witch at the Thabit oasis? *Why?* She kept a wary eye on me, in between Hasan's incoherent mumbles. With each interjection, he gained clarity.

"Leave her alone, Stef." He rolled onto his side, a hand on his head.

"It's not her I'm angry with," Stef shouted. "It's *you*. What are you doing on the ground? I gotta come over here and clean you up too? Like the tent isn't enough, you faint all over the place?"

I sidled a step to the side. She whirled on me.

"I said not a step!"

My hands zipped up, but I kept an unknown invisibility spell on the tip of my tongue. I had a feeling this witch could decipher those, too. Hasan pushed to his feet, swaying, and caught himself. His eyes latched onto me with quiet but intense fervor.

"Where is it?" he rasped.

I jerked my chin higher in a quick motion. His gaze skirted up, latched on the Volare's underbelly, and he whispered a curse word under his breath. "To Alfea," he cried.

By some miracle, Stef quieted.

"Alfea?" she whispered. Stef tilted her head, peering into the leaves. "What are you looking at?"

I asked, "Who is Alfea?"

"I cannot say," he breathed. "We take her to Alfea."

"Are you mad, Hasan?" Stef cried. "You can't take a traveler to Alfea! She'll laugh you off the oasis. We just secured employment. If you lose your job, I'll kick you out of the tent. I swear I will! You can faint on someone else's time!"

Tucking aside my questions regarding their *employment* and *Alfea*, I kept my eyes on Hasan. He hadn't torn his gaze off the Volare. Stef leaned to the side, studying the leaves. She paused, blinked, and gasped, hand to her mouth.

"A Volare?"

Throat bobbing, he asked me, "Will it come down?"

"If I tell it to."

"Will you?"

"Depends. Tell me more about Alfea."

Stef opened her mouth, but Hasan held up a hand. She silenced, but she didn't look happy about it.

"Alfea is the Commandant."

"What's that?"

He swooped an arm around, encompassing the oasis. His eyes never stopped devouring my rug. "As the Commandant, Alfea makes decisions for the oasis. She's not the leader of the tribe—that's Haruto. But she answers only to him."

The tribe. *The* oasis. The ringing difference remained with me.

"I apologize," I said, striving for some humility. "I didn't know. Why do you want to take me to Alfea?"

"Because everything in the oasis goes to Alfea and *she* ascribes its value," Stef snapped. She shot me a dirty scowl. "Don't you know anything? You came to the oasis, therefore, you have to offer something." More calmly, she added, "That Volare would be a pretty offer."

Hasan ignored her.

Returning her defensive energy, I firmly stated, "There's no offer available," and wasn't surprised to see a hint of respect amongst her deep irritation. For now, Commandant was the title of someone in charge. Thus, someone I wanted to meet.

Sighing, Hasan tore his eyes away from the branches, downright morose. "Let's go." His shoulders slumped. "I'll take you to her."

Before I could ask why he looked as if I'd kicked his cat, Stef slammed a fist into his shoulder. "Stop being glum! Alfea will reward you for bringing a Volare for her to see, you fool. Besides, you don't have time to sit around and inspect a rug. We have *work* to do, remember?"

Hasan muttered to himself as he trudged through the sand, returning the way they'd both come. At my command, the Volare slipped out of the leaves, curled up, and raced into its case. Hasan glanced back a moment too late, and his depression amplified.

I followed behind, aware that I had to stay one step ahead if I wanted to find the clannish witches, or the motivations the Thabit tribe sought to answer. Now, I had to add *protect my rug* to my growing list.

* * *

The witch Alfea stood under a thick canopy of trees. She wore a dazzling yellow dress that glimmered garishly in the white-hot desert sun. Her short-cropped hair revealed a rounded head and appealing eyes. She had a wide smile made brighter by the lack of accoutrements. Of all desert witches in the oasis, she was the least adorned that I'd encountered.

When Stef and Hasan dropped to a knee in front of Alfea, heads bowed, I stopped. Ten paces separated us, which gave me plenty of time to transport if someone rushed me. As Commandant, Alfea might be the exact witch to answer all my questions. If approached very carefully, this might provide a big advantage.

I sketched a quick glance around, but my hasty perusal was pointless. Only the vast desert lingered behind this thickly shaded area. No sign of clannish witches here. Nor hidden magic, nor unknown magic. If the clannish witches didn't serve or stay by Alfea, I could almost confirm they weren't here at all. With no one behind me, and no discernible magical presence detectable, I would let the situation unfold.

"Wise Alfea." Hasan's low intonation altered him entirely. He braided both hands together, palms touching. "We bring you a treasure."

She all but ignored them, her eyes latched on mine. With a flick of her fingers, she dismissed them. Hasan shoved to his feet and grabbed Stef by the arm. They departed quickly.

Alfea and I regarded each other. "You're no ordinary witch," she said.

"How can you tell?"

"No ordinary witch holds herself the way you do.

Given the opportunity to fight you or a belua, I'd choose the belua."

"Depending on what you're fighting for," I replied, "I commend you."

She laughed. A quick sound, more gasp than hilarity. A harsh wind danced with her skirt, drifting far enough to reveal long, skinny thighs. Her snapping eyes, well-spoken voice, and lack of insecurity were a confident combination. She probably mentioned a belua as a test because beluas lived exclusively in Letum Wood. My accent would give me away as a Central Network witch immediately, so I couldn't fathom why she bothered.

Alfea regarded me with deepening suspicion, lips pursing, as if she sensed something she couldn't put her finger on. When she spoke, her tone elongated.

"Why did Hasan bring you?"

"I'm sure he's disappointed not to share it himself."

A flicker of uncaring didn't surprise me. "Hasan is eager about many things. Fortunately, he doesn't mind dirty work. It keeps him valuable."

I commanded the Volare. It slipped free, unrolling at my side, and hovered by my neck. The wind, pressing in bursts, sent it rippling like a banner.

Alfea breathed, "By Sarena." She stared, lips parted, hands balled into fists. She stepped forward twice, jerked herself to a stop. "Who are you?" she demanded.

No one special, Tyrant insisted.

With a thought, I returned the Volare to the case. My anxiety eased significantly. "My identity doesn't matter all that much."

"Lies."

"I came for water."

Her arms spread. "Have all the water you want."

"I already paid."

She drew up. "You can't pay again. I may ask nothing of you, a Blessed Witch. There are so few of you. Two, maybe? We haven't met any in . . . generations."

Blessed Witch would require getting used to. "I didn't mean for Hasan to see the Volare," I admitted. "He sensed it."

"We all can," she said quickly.

"Right. I didn't bring the Volare here to ask anything of your tribe, either, though I am in the desert to learn more."

"About the Volare, you mean?"

With a nod, I said, "Yes."

"Naturally," she breathed, as if this was the most normal response in the world. "The magic called you to us, did it not?"

"I think so?"

"Yes, yes." Her snippy insistence reminded me of Hasan. "Of course it did."

"You are the Thabit tribe of legend? The Weavers of Magic?"

Something flickered in her eyes. "You have found the right place, Blessed Witch. It is my greatest honor to attend you. May I see it again?"

With a nod, I beckoned it to return. The Volare retracted from the case and unrolled, giving her a full glimpse of the design. Alfea drew in a shuddering gasp, dropped to her knees, planted her hands on the sand. Ten seconds later, she stood. Her proud chin elevated.

"Blessed Witch, it's my duty to help you understand my loyalty. You do not have *only* a cherished Volare." She paused, indrawing a breath through her nose. "You have the Volare woven by Tuffer, our forefather. The witch who received the grimoire and enacted the magic and firmly established the Thabit tribe within the graces of our goddess, Sarena. Blessed Witch, you have more than a simple rug. You have the original and most powerful magical rug. *This* is the Reigning Volare."

* * *

That evening, I sat on the Volare as it glided through Letum Wood and re-read the letter that came with it.

Dear Witch Who Finds This Note,

This rug is a Volare.

It was formed in the hot sands of the Western Network during the Time of the Weaver. Its roots lie deep in my heart. Creating it was no easy process. The magic the Volare works by is deep, born of love and sacrifice and my own blood. As its original weaver, I've enchanted this note to appear to the new owner of the Volare, should it find itself without an heir to pass on to. In such a case as this, the Volare chooses its next owner.

The magic is loyal; it will serve you well. Do not take this gift lightly. Be good to it, and it shall be good to you. In this way my legacy shall live on.

Wishing you many happy flights under the stars,

Tuffer, the Weaver of Magic

Snow-painted tree trunks passed in and out of my awareness, alternately calling for me, sending their usual adulations, and whispering.

You belong to us.
We belong to you.

Their beckoning voices centered me. With their guidance, I returned fully to the Central Network, mentally sweeping away the Western Network sand to focus on what these puzzle pieces meant.

The Volare.

Tuffer.

Weaver of Magic.

None of this was wildly unbelievable, but it was . . . odd. I should have given more thought to the strangely skilled and powerful rug that obeyed my silent will with loyalty and fearless skill. Thinking of all that the Volare and I experienced together only drove home my confusion.

How *hadn't* I considered it more?

Leda had been researching Volares since I informed her of these developments. We'd speak the next day about her findings. I had a hunch that she had taken some time off of work and didn't want to discuss it tonight.

Shaking that off, I considered my next plan. Today, I found confirmation that the clannish witches didn't serve the leader of the oasis—or Commandant. The warriors accepted the tracking grimoire and sent it somewhere north, which gave me reason to believe the Thabit tribe lived to the north of the oasis. My magical rug drew Thabit tribe member's attention, and happened to be the most powerful Volare in Alkarra.

A productive day.

Not only did I need Leda's help on how to proceed with the Volare, but I needed to transport to the desert and find the location where the grimoire had been sent. Having never been there, it could take several attempts.

At least I had a plan, and updates for Alina, and a potential asset to leverage with the Thabit tribe.

Albeit *carefully.*

In the following quiet, I found the capacity to wish Grandfather to my side with his constant and fervent desire to help me unwind the complicated puzzles life provided. I closed my eyes, allowing the murmuring trees to take me to a different place. A calmer space where Tyrant couldn't follow and memories of Grandfather abounded.

What do I do? I asked.

Leverage this connection to your advantage, Grandfather would say. I could *almost* hear the soft tones of his voice. The undulations. My eyes opened again, and my thoughts drifted. Was Grandfather with Mildred?

Mama?

Camille?

I hoped so. If they didn't gather together, what good were the lands and lives beyond?

Sighing, I murmured, "Let's go home," to the Volare. While it quietly turned, easing through the forest again and toward the heart center where home awaited, I sensed it respond to my low mood by keeping the pace simple, quiet.

My deepening gratitude was no surprise. The Volare and I had been through many scrapes together. Like Viveet, I couldn't imagine living without it.

"I'm sorry." I ran my palm along the woven designs. The bright stars, brilliant colors. "I didn't seek a deeper understanding of you. You and I . . . we've always been so easy. You and me. We've accomplished so much together. I trust our bond, which is as real as your magical ability. Thank you for all you've done for me."

The rug twisted its edges around me, tenderly twirled

me, and righted us. My bond with the Volare tightened. "I promise," I whispered. "I promise that you are mine, and I will always honor you. Even if I don't do it correctly," I added.

The Volare shivered.

I knew it understood.

Chapter Eighteen

The smell of muddy soil breathed through my nostrils, filling my head with earthy scents when I stepped through an open fence and onto an expansive property. Snow crunched beneath my fur-lined boots as I crossed a fenced yard, chickens clucking and scattering in all directions. Buildings dotted the perimeter, ending in a house on the left. Sheds, another house, though smaller. Very quaint, this habitation that testified to a massive family.

Two figures crouched along the ground, trowels in hand. I recognized Leda's heavy sweater—knitted by her mother's patient hand—and the woolen skirt beneath it. Her thin fingers dug into chilly earth as I approached, stopping a few paces away.

"What are you doing?"

Without looking up, she said, "Planting winter bulbs."

Hiddleston's wide shoulders toiled at her side. He'd abandoned his heavy coat to wear a long sleeved gray shirt with old sweat stains, both made from thickest wool. The trousers had leather-reinforced knees and his boots laced up all the way to his mid-calf, which was significant on a man of his size. Discarded gloves petaled off to the side. Like Leda, he worked barehanded.

"My grandmother had a spell that enchanted spring bulbs," he explained, breath frosting. "If we plant them around the solstice, when the sun is at its lowest energy, it engages the enchantment. They will produce better the next year."

"Flowers?"

"Very special flowers."

Intrigue almost led me to inquire, but Leda sent me a discouraging glance.

What are they for? I asked.

His sister is an advanced potionmaker. She uses them for love potions, but the recipe is extremely secret, and this ingredient is very rare.

Leda left it at that, so I did, too.

"Is this a bad time?"

"No," Leda retorted primly. "This is the time I requested to meet with you."

"Let me guess: you called me here to help while we talk?"

She nodded without apology, as usual. Not that I'd complain about working outside with growing things, even in the cold. Grandmother had extensive gardens that I assisted with while she ran the Tea and Herb Pantry in Bickers Mill. We didn't work in the winter, but she would have loved enchantments that required winter planting and produced robust results.

Leda nodded to a standing shovel near a plot squared off by boot prints. "That's next. You and I are going to work on it while we talk. Those plants are root vegetables with the enchantment."

"Better cabbage," Hiddleston said, as an aside.

"Naturally."

Ten minutes later, Leda knelt on a wood plank while I bit into the slushy snow with a shovel, scooping piles away until I struck the earth. Once mud revealed, I moved a step over and continued the shallow trench. She dribbled seeds in my wake.

"Tell me about what you found," Leda said.

While working, I updated her aloud so Hiddleston could hear about the Volare, the lack of clannish witches, and the Commandant, Alfea. Grateful to air my findings, I spoke until we dug to the end of the rectangular section. Once Leda caught up, she pointed to the next line.

I continued digging

"Sounds . . . interesting," Leda said in her non-committal, I'm-still-thinking-about-this-problem way. "I'm not surprised that there are no visible clannish witches, nor that the Thabit tribe employs witches from outside their tribe, but I am surprised that they could sense the Volare."

"I feel like a fool for not looking into the Volare sooner."

The Volare waited on my back, safely ensconced in its round case. A leather strap secured it around my chest, as comfortable as Viveet at my side. Having it closer reassured me, though no danger to either of us approached.

Leda's high brow and silence were all the suggestions I required to know she felt the same. Leda researched *everything*, including the source of ground peppercorns the castle kitchen used on her favorite pasta dish. Fina hadn't appreciated the intrusion.

Instead of a chastisement on my lack of thoroughness, Leda sighed. Sometimes, I wondered if she'd accepted my lack of detailed ways and decided not to complain.

"I have been curious enough about your rug since it found you to look into it a little," Leda admitted, "but there are very few mentions of it in any texts."

"Nothing?"

She paused the seed distribution to glance at me. A cold blush dusted her cheeks with circles of rose at the top, heightening her color. Against the snow, her porcelain skin nearly blended in.

"Not *nothing*, but not much."

"Anything helpful?"

"Well, in a way, what I didn't find is helpful. Certainly, there wasn't a list of rules discussing how to use a Volare. As far as enchanted objects go, they're very . . . unknown. Part of their reverence stems from their rarity."

Sighing, I used my heel to coerce the shovel past a layer of ice. It broke through, pierced the ground, and I deposited the load to the side. Leda scooped the dirt and snow mixture back into the holes after she planted.

"That makes sense."

"Did you read *The Weavers of Magic* at the Arck Library?"

"I skimmed it. It was too long to read word for word in the little time that I had. Considering I lied my way into the library, I'm not sure it would be wise to return."

Leda shrugged, as if espionage wasn't a big deal. "Was it helpful?"

"Maybe?"

A perturbed raspberry blasted her lips. "If you didn't read *all* of it, how can you make a judgment either way?" She stabbed her trowel in my direction, "Completion matters. Regardless, what I found out was fairly basic, but might help clarify the picture."

Hiddleston arose, patting snow and earth back into position with his boot. Behind him, smoke unwound from a chimney, set into a cozy wooden house. Window-panes gleamed, revealing a bustling woman and two middle-aged men huddled around a table, studying parchments. Unlike Hiddleston, they didn't have long locks. Their hair was nappy, sheared into manicured afros. The stern woman moved slowly, but steady, carrying teapots, cups.

Hiddleston quietly said, "I'll do the next section, Leda, and then we're done."

Leda nodded, attention riveted on the ground. She curled both hands together, breathing on them, before she reached into her pocket, withdrew pinched fingers, and sprinkled seeds into a hole. While she smoothed snow and dirt back over the top, she continued her explanation.

"There are five well-known Volares, called the Originals. Others existed after the initial exploration of the Weavers of Magic grimoire, but the others didn't have as much power or loyalty as the five. The Weavers of Magic created a bustling trade with magical rugs, and all the ones that followed were woven in the image of the Originals. The lesser Volares disappeared over time, because they didn't have magic preventing their destruction. But the original five were so powerful they shouldn't *ever* disappear. Well," she added blithely, "or so rumor says. The original grimoire has never been found, nor three of the originals. Of those five, there's a sort of . . . magical hierarchy."

"What does that mean?" I tossed aside another shovelful.

"Each of them has one thing it does very well. No one knows the exact characteristics or talents, either. Of the five, one is the greatest. It possesses all the magical skills of the other four. The most powerful Volare is the masterpiece forged by the original Weaver."

"Tuffer."

Leda eyed me askance as she patted a snow mound. "Yes. Tuffer is the witch who discovered the magic and set things into motion that would change the Thabit tribe forever."

"What does that mean?"

She shrugged. "That's all I know. History is barren on those details. Tribal witches were too busy talking about rugs to discuss their historical culture."

Her vexed huff bestowed deep judgment.

"What I know are rumors collected from a review of literature I derived out of the Great Library of Burke and what I gleaned from a contact in the Northern Network." She paused, head canted, and added as an aside, "You wouldn't believe what resources the North has regarding the Western Tribes. When you consider the geographical ramifications of how closely related the two Networks are, it makes sense that—"

"Leda . . ."

"Right, sorry." She sniffled, crouched on her heels to shuffle her board to the side. "There's a distinguishing characteristic on the *Reigning Volare*, as they called it. Apparently, in their world, color was also hierarchical and meant a great deal."

Anticipating what she would say, I asked, "Is it the color plum?"

Her gaze met mine with surprise.

"It is."

Deranged hilarity and awe washed over me. Of course I hadn't disbelieved Alfea, but to hear confirmation from Leda drove the reality home in a new way. How could the most powerful Volare have found and chosen me? I paused to lean on the shovel and take that in. The confirmation had a stunning and humbling effect.

For the first time in days, Tyrant had little to proffer.

"I would urge you to caution," Leda said in her I'm-going-to-be-prudent voice. "At least in pulling the Volare out when you're anywhere near the Thabit tribe. I saw nothing regarding their feelings toward the rugs, but I imagine some would feel possessive."

"They were more respectful."

"*Those* witches were respectful," she countered. "There's no telling what other Thabit leaders would think of a Central Network witch in possession of their most prized historical work. Tuffer put his tribe into a very powerful position for decades—perhaps centuries—because of his work and his life. Traditions in the Western Network highly favor ancestry." She sent me a cutting look. "Don't play with fire."

I nodded to appease her, and she resumed her work. For several minutes, we dug in silence, only the shuffle of Leda's sweater, her woolen skirt, and the slide of wood on snow could be heard. I stepped toward the third and final line in the rectangle, while Hiddleston did the same work on another plot. Dishabille graced the ground in several places. Leda's water-stained knee spots and messy braid made me think they'd been here for a while.

"I hear your call for caution, but the Volare is an asset in this mission, don't you think?" I asked. "I'd be a fool not to use it."

Leda snorted, the indelicate sound as odd as seeing her do physical work outside the office. Not that it didn't suit her; she seemed fairly happy with the change.

"You'd be a fool *to* use it."

"Sometimes," I murmured, "a little foolishness can be productive."

If I were a Thabit tribesman, the last thing I would expect is a foreign witch to descend on my tribe with the most prized possession in our history, particularly to use it in a bid against us.

Taken that way, I saw Leda's point.

And yet . . .

Hiddleston speared his shovel into a snowbank and trudged over, color spreading through the top of his cheeks from steady work.

"You're fast."

Nodding to his plot, I replied, "Not as fast as you."

A quick flash of white teeth accompanied his reply. "Been digging lines for Mama for years. Leda?"

"Almost done!" she chirped.

Patting the final scoop into place, Leda stood. Outdoor work highlighted her differently-colored eyes and a lingering pleasantness I rarely saw in the castle. Hiddleston had been a blessing for Leda in all kinds of ways, but certainly diversifying the way she lived. She thrived in utterly new fashions.

Faint eyebrows high, she asked, "What's your plan?"

I'd cogitated over the question for long enough. Laying it out to them helped me see a path. Perhaps not the *best* path, but one I could tweak and adapt as it required.

"At this point, I've done enough observation of the oasis. I plan to find and focus on the clannish witches to the north of the camp."

"Without the Volare?"

I laughed. "Not a chance. It goes with me everywhere."

Did I imagine a little tremor of agreement from the Volare's case? Hiddleston took my shovel, then leaned against it. A *Chatham Chatterer* scroll appeared in the air between us. Without a word, he nodded to it. I accepted, using my teeth to tug my hands out of my gloves, and skimmed the top.

Beneath a headline about a potential escalation of tension between the Southern Network and the Western Network—I'd ask Aurora about it later—stood another one.

An ugly one.

Sisterhood Leader Deserts Her Ideas

"As much as I loathe Georgette personally," Leda said with a breathy sigh, "I can't fault her attack strategy. There's a touch of brilliance in her incessant game. She's still not letting up, and we already have a new High Priest."

Brilliance?

I had *other* words for it.

As I skimmed the article, nearly all of which was conjecture, heat rose through my chest. With it, the return of Tyrant's delighted, wrathful voice. *Earned,* he stated confidently. *Every bit of this is earned. You desert more than just ideas, don't you?*

I shoved aside his visual reminders of dying Eastern Network witches to continue reading. The phrases *Miss Monroe continues to avoid interviews* and *despite a warm reception from the Council, the Head of the Sisterhood refused to discuss strategy,* didn't bother me. I'd long ago learned that one couldn't control anyone, nevertheless popular opinion.

But to say it to the Network?

Hiddleston asked, "Are you going to respond?"

Before I finished reading the drivel, I returned it to him. "No."

"Why not?"

"Bullies only get bigger with acknowledgement."

He sent the same inquisitive stare to Leda, who considered my response. "Maybe that's the right plan? I don't know. Sometimes, I think it would be easier to hear Georgette out just to quiet her."

"It won't work."

"I know."

"She was clear enough in her first letter."

"You don't have to agree with her, Bianca. Simply hear her."

"I hear her loud enough through the articles."

Leda stared at the scroll. Thoughts moved behind her eyes like a play, and I only caught a hint of what she might be thinking based on the occasional flare of darkness.

"I stand by my point," she said firmly. "I think you should meet with Georgette, but I'm not foolish enough to think my opinion alone will sway you on this issue." Leda met my stare. "In regards to the Thabit tribe, you're right. It's time to find the clannish witches, and I'd wager you'll find them through both the planted grimoire *and* Alfea."

Merrick, hands on his hips, fumed at a letter when I returned from talking to Hiddleston and Leda. I strolled up behind him, grateful to return to the treehouse, and wrapped my arms around his waist. I read around his bent arm.

He held a message from Jacqueline. Her loopy but beautiful scrawl was short and to the point, although she left no signature.

*Do you think it would be weird if I wrote a message
to Tysen?*

I tugged on Merrick's elbow. He spun, lowering the letter to his side. An unabashed scowl darkened his features. Storm clouds built in his eyes, and I rued the day he released such brewing power.

"Why do you look like someone stole your cookie?" I drawled.

He shook the letter. "Can you believe this?"

"The audacity."

Merrick crumpled into a brotherly grimace. "Why does she have to ask? I don't want Tysen to talk to my sister. It's . . . it's weird."

"She's a little sweet on him. It's not a big deal." I shrugged. "He's cute and he's really nice and he's definitely not chasing trolls."

My reference to Jacqueline's other love interest, Finan, went unheeded. Probably better. Everytime someone mentioned Finan, Merrick's scowl darkened to the point of pain.

"Not a big deal?" he cried. "It *is* a big deal. I won't have my little sister gallivanting around with a . . . a Protector! And not Tysen, at that."

"She's an expert gallivanter."

"Protectors are trouble," he continued, outright ignoring me now. "And no," he quickly added, "it's not unfair of me to say it! I *am* a Protector. Therefore, I can make the call. She deserves better."

I rolled my eyes. "Are you saying that I settled for you?"

"Definitely."

"We're speaking about the same witch, aren't we?

Calm, steady, sometimes-emotional-but-mostly-stable Tysen?"

His fury gained ballast.

Arms spread, I asked, "Who is better than *Tysen*? He's sweet and kind and not out hunting trolls and breaking her heart." My emphasis drowned in the sea of his hearty disapproval.

"He's too young."

I tugged on his shirt, attempting to kiss him, but he didn't get the hint.

"He's almost the same age," I countered.

"The two of them together wouldn't work."

"*We* work."

"That's different."

"How?"

"I don't know," he snapped. "It just . . . it just is. I'm going to write to her, and I'm going to tell her that Tysen is dating someone else."

"Excellent plan. Lying to your sister has never gone awry before. She'll gallivant her way to a different witch of whom you entirely approve. Do I need to say *Finan* again? Digging in your heels definitely won't cause the opposite of your desired action."

Finally picking up my sarcasm, his eyes lowered to mine and tapered to slits. Delighted by the sharpened senses in that stare, I beckoned him to a better mood with my warm smile. He lifted a hand, running it through my hair. His shrewdness morphed into affection.

"What are you doing, little troublemaker?"

"Attempting to seduce you." Winking dramatically, I shifted in my arms so he had to dip me. One of my legs popped into the air with equally awkward gusto. Unable to hold the terrible performance, I burst into a giggle.

He rolled his eyes.

"You don't have to work that hard," he muttered.

"Glad to hear it." Plucking the discarded letter from the floor, I waved it while he straightened me. "How about I respond to her instead of you? You'll just make her more likely to fall into his arms."

He snatched it from me. "That's equally as bad."

"Why?"

"Then it's . . . it looks . . ."

"Lest you forget," I muttered, snatching it back, "Tysen and I have also worked on missions together. I know him as well as you do."

Glowering, he said, "Fine. It wouldn't be *that* weird for you to write her . . . but still!"

I sent the letter to the table for later, wrapped my hands around his neck, and tilted his head so he had to look at me. Blinking, I stared into his eyes with a grim seriousness that I hoped calmed his fears.

"Merrick?"

"Hmph."

"It's going to be fine. Jacqueline and Tysen are curious, not handfasting. Let her have her . . . gallivanting, as you called it . . . and then see what happens. As far as witches go, she could pick far, far worse than Tysen."

He closed his eyes. "She's going to be the death of me."

"You're the only one that's stressed, Merrick. If you die because of your sister, it will be entirely your fault."

He silenced my correct observation with a kiss that turned my knees to water. The heat of his lips slanting over mine, and the promise of our welcoming bed, drew me into his arms. He lifted me, carrying me across the way, when a most unwelcome intrusion burst into my head.

Rognvald.

Come to the Gatehouse. Transport in the common area, far right corner. It'll allow you to land if you're careful— I've let you into the restrictive magic. Land invisibly and shut your mouth.

He cut off.

What's wrong?

Georgette.

Growling, I tore away from Merrick. Confused, hands clasped around my back, he whispered, "What's wrong?"

"Your boss just summoned me."

Fire flared in his passion-hazy eyes. "What? Right *now?*"

I relayed the message and finished with, "Georgette. Had he said anything else, I would have ignored him."

His flare of rage ebbed into puzzlement. "What's she got to do with anything?"

"No idea."

"Could be interesting."

"It guarantees to be interesting."

Dropping out of his arms, I attempted to pull my hair into something of order. Realizing it would be fruitless, I paused before my transportation spell.

"Are you coming?"

Eyes rolling, he straightened his shirt and muttered, "Fine, but only because I'm curious."

"Can we both transport to the same Gatehouse corner? I know he has designated spots, and the rest is blocked."

"There are other ways," he said cryptically, and vanished first. Drawing a breath, I cast the invisibility spell and prepared myself for the worst.

* * *

What I saw was exactly what I expected.

Georgette and Rognvald stood opposite each other. Rognvald near the entrance to the Head of Protectors office, and Georgette in the middle of the room. Slushy snow littered the window panes outside, hinting at an occasionally bright blue sky. Sunlight peeked in and out of bulky clouds, built thick as cotton balls with slate under-bellies. Whirlwinds blasted in snowy funnels, hitting the window panes with puffs of white.

Rognvald leaned against the doorway to his office, one meaty eyebrow elevated while Georgette spoke. Merrick's signature slipped surreptitiously into the room from the Head of Guardian's office, where a new witch would soon take up residence.

Georgette spoke.

"The past several decades have been very stable between the Brotherhood and the Council. I'd hate for that to change."

My neck rankled at her slightly condescending tone. In some weird way, it made sense for Georgette to speak down to *me*. Young, still proving myself, and daughter of a High Priest who managed to wiggle his way out of a large responsibility and now live free. That, I almost understood.

But Rognvald?

Head of one of the most powerful organizations in Alkarra?

Nothing made sense about the implied threat in her tone. Astonishment kept me rooted to the spot, though I was vaguely tempted to roll my eyes and leave. Commentary to Rognvald or Merrick through the magic would only distract Rognvald, so I kept my lips sealed.

Rognvald laughed in response to her audacious

words. A punchy, breathy thing as much a scoff as amusement.

"Would you now?"

Georgette took his response in stride. "A firm relationship with the Brotherhood is a pivotal building block to a stable Network. We're invested."

"Of course you are!" he cried. "Invested Council Members come in here all the time to deliver understated warnings about our relationships, instead of a general *thanks* when we keep them safe. This is routine."

She pressed on, dogged. Her rote words had a note of memorization to them, but Georgette always had an air of having practiced everything she said.

"There are . . . other . . . witches in the Central Network who find it their duty to take the safety of our Network into their hands with no formal training, authority, or approval. Renegades have no place in a stable society. I came seeking your reassurance that the Brotherhood will have no part in these ploys."

A crawl stole up my spine. Ignoring Georgette had been largely beneficial for my mental state. I couldn't loathe her as easily if I didn't know what she was saying. But this was something else. She brought the fight to Rognvald and crossed into *my* territory. She must know it. That's why she came alone, no Assistant, at a low hour of the day to avoid other Brothers intruding.

Her argument sounded logical, perhaps somewhat reasonable. Of course the Central Network didn't want renegades, but the Sisterhood hadn't been a renegade, and I certainly didn't lack training or experience.

For a helpless moment, I attempted to think what Grandfather would make of this development. Would he laugh? Frown? Doubtless, he'd draw some wise conclusion that I hadn't yet considered.

Rognvald drew me out of the spiral before I descended too far. He lifted a hand, one finger pointed up. "Let me get this straight: You want me to report to you about what the Brotherhood is doing?"

His careful intonation, layered with a glaze of ice so slick she threatened to slip on it, coated the words with frost. Georgette paused, carefully considering his words. Unable to restrain myself, I smiled.

"No," she said slowly.

"I didn't think so."

"I seek reassurances that you don't plan to work with renegade groups who take matters into their own hands."

"So you're asking me to divulge my partnership sources?"

"I didn't say that, either."

"Neither did you specify the renegade group, forcing me to draw my own conclusions. Renegades have their places, to be sure, but we use them wisely."

Georgette's dark eye fans batted. "You do?"

He smiled. He discomfited her, and I couldn't blame her uneasiness. Rognvald grinning was as natural as a smiling cat. Georgette cast for something to say. Whether he'd surprised her with the admission that the Brotherhood had used renegades in the past, or his ghoulish grin, didn't matter.

What happens if you agree to her request? I asked Rognvald while waiting for her response.

Not good things.

Council control?

Yes.

Jikes, but I hated politics.

Seeming to decide on a different tact, Georgette gave the appearance of backing down by lowering her chin. "I appreciate your position, Rognvald. There is more common ground between us than I think you believe. The Brotherhood hasn't been held accountable to the Council for their actions in many years, and I'm not saying that should be the case yet. But I *am* advocating for the safety of our Network, and I think that's something you can appreciate. Can we approach this issue from our common stance?"

The word *yet* lingered in the back of my mouth like a bad taste. The lines around Rognvald's eyes tightened, but he didn't reveal it in his voice.

"Say the renegade you're worried about and I'll consider."

She spoke confidently, except for the slightest tremor. "The Sisterhood. Or, more commonly, Miss Monroe. You and Bianca have . . . a warm enough history."

"Do we?"

"On the surface, it would appear so."

"Sounds like an assumption." Rognvald kicked his leg out, straightening his stance. Instead of slouching against the doorframe, he filled the entire space. A bit more daunting, taking up so much air.

Georgette moderated her response with a breath. "Regardless, I would appreciate some reassurance that the Brotherhood won't encourage the Sisterhood down this dangerous path."

Rognvald tossed his eyes left, right, left again. He shrugged. "What Sisterhood? I don't see one. Last I heard, it dissolved."

Goddess love Rognvald, I didn't know whether to hiss at him or hug him. Making this conversation more difficult for Georgette was delightful, on some level. Terrifying, on others. Her viewpoint on Alkarra, the things she said, might put a target on the Brotherhood down the line. But wasn't that what Georgette desired?

Power through fear? Through control? Well, she'd kicked the wrong beehive.

Georgette's lips pressed. "Destruction was never the goal. Protection, on the other hand, has always been. Miss Monroe has a long and storied history that wasn't considered before her rise to the Head of the Sisterhood, an organization she wanted to support with Network funds."

Rognvald laughed outright. "Long and storied history? She turns twenty five this year!"

"Exactly. A witch of her youth shouldn't have so many obvious concerns. The idea of elevating such a witch to a position with so much freedom and power should be thoroughly examined, and without bias."

He rolled his eyes, then his hand, in an impatient gesture. "You're threatened by a young woman, you want to get rid of her, and you want my reassurance that I'll dance on the Sisterhood's grave. I hear your position, Council Member. Very valiant. Now, let me have a chance to explain."

Rognvald's eyes turned terrible. Low slung, jaw tight, his words as powerful as a mountain slide. His words gained power and punctuation with each syllable.

"You overreach yourself coming to the Brotherhood, Council Member. You put your fingers into an organization that doesn't involve you, then you personally set out an onslaught against the members of that organization. That isn't Network protection. That is control. As Head of Protectors, I'm not interested in entities with such an attack strategy, as it's not *safe* for our Brothers. You have created problems, not solved them. Who is the most dangerous one here?"

His tone eased slightly as he regarded her, tutting. "You're thirty-five years old. Imagine a young Council

Member such as yourself, with a long and storied history that hasn't been considered in your rise to Council Member over the most arguably powerful Coven in our Network, which uses Network funds to support you."

He left the jab in the air, tensing it like a blow about to strike. Georgette paused so thoroughly she stopped breathing. For several moments, they stared at each other. When she spoke, her measured tone carried all the veracity she refused to reveal otherwise.

"I hear you, Rognvald."

He tilted his head to the door. "You may see yourself out, Council Member."

She opened her mouth to speak, but Rognvald shuffled forward a step. Scuttling back, Georgette hurried toward the door and grasped the handle. Frigid air blasted into the room as she hesitated, door half open, blowing her perfect ringlets off her shoulders. I couldn't read the tone in her final words.

"Enemies are made every day, Rognvald. I hope you know what you're doing."

Slamming the door shut behind her, Georgette strode five steps into the storm before disappearing. I stayed invisible, soaking in the quiet room. Rognvald stared out the window.

"She's gone," he muttered. "Her spell went into the castle, and there are no signatures outside."

I didn't reveal myself. My thoughts wound through the complicated maze Rognvald managed. Somehow, despite the heat of his fervor, he'd blessedly kept my name entirely out of his response. He protected the Brotherhood, not me.

But also me.

Though sometimes awkward and bumbling in real

life, I hadn't given Rognvald enough credit for sheer mental brawn.

And yet . . . the power in her stare. The challenge in her voice. The expert way she'd woven an argument against me, speaking to *renegades* and *Network protection* instead of my faults as a leader. Perfect. Near flawless. Spoken to the right witches, under a situation where they didn't know me personally, it created the exact scenario that descended across Alkarra right now.

Utter slaying of my reputation.

Thank you, I said through the magic, unable to gather any other response. I couldn't fathom revealing my face right then.

He nodded once.

"Never," he promised.

I kept it close to my heart.

$$Chapter\ Nineteen$$

Heat, dust, and sand swamped me the next morning. With it came Tyrant's rampant insistence around my insecurities, spoken in a tone as brutal as Georgette's accusations.

You'll figure this out, and what? Leave a trail of bodies in your wake?

You're going to kill again?

Leave me alone, I muttered in my head.

Retreating to the Thabit oasis felt like a form of escape, so I left early in the morning, before sunrise, swapping the scouring snowflakes of the Central Network for the blazing desert. I lost myself in the differences, ignoring the *Chatham Chatterer* scroll that Merrick hid on the top shelf of our bookcase, ignoring the horrible things Georgette said, ignoring Rognvald's very kind treatment of my reputation, ignoring the urge to request help of Grandfather, and ignoring Tyrant.

I banished all of it. I wanted to be here, at this moment. Part of this mission and nothing else. Alina and the clannish witches deserved my full attention.

Invisible and quiet, I slinked along the oasis, alert for all faces. Locating Alfea took almost an hour, but when I saw her, my gut clenched with anticipation.

Finally.

Instead of transporting to random parts of the scalding desert, I planned to observe Alfea and follow her —Volare free. The rug would draw their attention, and I didn't want that.

Odds were good that Alfea might eventually transport to the Thabit tribe camp, though I didn't expect that right away. In the meantime, I could gather information on the oasis, her position in it, and other warriors. In this situation, I had to be constantly alert. If Alfea faded into thin air, I had to follow her transportation spell, which meant I had to tail her.

Very closely.

It would be an exercise in stealth as much as attention. I kept the clannish witches at the forefront of my mind, and left all the rest in the Central Network. Once Alfea began to stroll along the sand, waving to oasis witches, I moved into place behind her.

The day had only just begun.

* * *

By the time the sun sank toward the horizon that evening, my throat burned with thirst, my eyes with sand, and my ears with the constant, irritating sound of desert camals, those gigantic, brutish creatures that spit like viper snakes.

Alfea spent most of her time checking warriors at the water, around the oasis edges, patrolling the trees, or near the ice shed, which she never entered. The nondescript building still emanated magic, making it unlikely to host clannish witches.

Only once during the day did I glimpse two witches near the ice, both tribal, covered in sawdust. Alfea greeted each by name. They stood outside the shed, smoking cheroots. Each one shared sun-tanned faces and the rough expressions of witches who lived too long outside. Eye, hair, and skin color varied widely between tribes, making it impossible to tell them apart by appearance, except for a brightly colored sash the oasis workers tied to their waists to distinguish them.

Alfea closed her final round for the day, waving farewell to several caravan leaders who would move on once the sun sank—few witches traveled the Western sands during the day—before she stopped at the ice shed. Not far behind her, I crept along, eager for the day to be over with. Tailing her had been revealing, but rote.

She rapped on the door. A witch appeared, eyes bloodshot. Cooler air slipped out, but the other witch closed the door too quickly for me to see inside as she stepped into the sweltering heat.

If Alfea didn't go somewhere that led to clannish witches, I'd break inside the ice shed to rule out their presence there. Alfea and the witches spoke in a tribal tongue that led to several nods, gesticulations to the sand, and finally, Alfea disappeared.

For a blink, I hardly comprehended it. Having waited all day for this exact moment, it seemed incomprehensible she'd *finally* left. Her vestiges of magic had almost dissipated by the time I pulled my mind together and stumbled into action.

Inevitable, yet unexpected.

Thankfully, I landed without problems, and not far from her spot. The transportation magic required little more than a breath before it deposited me—thankfully still invisible—on more sand. This occurred a little less gracefully than in the past.

Scrambling to my feet, I stood upright. Alfea strode six or seven paces away, heading toward a familiar witch: the male with white hair and a cutting glare who followed me after my first visit.

He opened his bare arms and welcomed her into a lover's embrace. He wore a pair of leather pants, and nothing else. They sealed my hunch with a passionate kiss, a silent promise for more later, and finally parted. The way he curled her into his side, beckoning for her to sit, made me think she'd come to his tent. Or campfire, rather. I viewed only a ring of sandstones and low flames, no canvas or belongings nearby to speak of.

Their exchange occurred in murmurs in a tribal dialect, so I padded to the first safety I could find—a tree trunk. I needed to put something between Alfea and myself. It would be better to be *up* the tree, but with Alfea and the other witch this close, I didn't want to jostle the branches. A quick touch confirmed these weren't real trees. No life stirred within. Magic, only.

Back pressed to it, I gained my bearings. A hearty and bustling camp sprawled to the left and right, filled with tents of various kinds. Smaller, lighter canvas canopies stretched in a triangular set up around a single rope, while more elaborate sprawling tents had fluttering, sheer drapes and candlelight and giggling children. A healthy, thriving desert community.

Forcing my eyes to skim over the western delights— clay pots formed out of sand and painted with black figurines, beads strung on a wire in an X, and skins from old lizards that drifted like talismans in a breeze—I drank in the number of observable witches.

Considering how far the camp stretched, there would

be hundreds of occupants. Many times bigger than the oasis, for certain. Was this the Thabit tribe? It must be. A stamp of the lightning sun with nested hearts symbol graced every tree.

Confident no one spotted me, I headed around a pathway formed in the sand, eager to get away from the male witch while Alfea distracted him. He nearly caught me last time.

I cut down the path, across a low dune, and attempted to move without dribbling granules. Once I had a better idea of the camp, I'd use hovering magic. For now, I wouldn't draw attention through more than a lesser-known invisibility spell. The path led me through various tent communities, probably clumped by family.

Fifteen meandering minutes later, I found an outer edge. With the setting sun conspiring against me, it was impossible to decipher the exact camp shape, but the rounded edges hinted at a circle. I crept along the far side, ear attuned. No obvious group of imprisoned clannish witches to be seen. No witches in irons, tied up, fenced in. Not obliquely, anyway. Most tents wouldn't host more than a small family.

Then, a hint.

Black hair, fine as a paint brush, disappeared between the trees. I cut after them, locating the clannish witch I sought in mere seconds. Through the firelight, I made out their final steps as they lowered to their knees in the sand, clustered around a tribal family. Further inspection revealed that I'd been a narrow-focused fool.

Clannish witches existed in many places, but I'd sought them as a group. Prisoners locked together. But the three I spotted moved freely. They strode from place to place, carrying items, water. Another held rags.

My chest locked as a warrior that I recognized from

the oasis strode closer to my hiding spot, eyes set ahead. I backed against a tree as he passed by, closing in on the sprawling tent the first clannish witch approached. A woman exclaimed and children rushed him.

The clannish witch retreated to the fire as the warrior returned, eyes lowered. The clannish witches wore no medallions to keep them confined to a specific area. They had no magic to escape with, so what should the tribe fear? Who would run into the vast desert? A death wish. A horrendous, burning suicide.

I lowered, set a group of three sand clumps at the foot of a specific tree, and paused. No sign of being watched thus far. Jogging through the loose sand outside the camp, I kept my eyes locked on the interior and counted each step. I swept all the way around the camp in three thousand steps, which gave me a vague approximation for size. Big, but not big enough to accommodate all the clannish witches.

I circled the camp again, this time within, and found ten clannish witches. The effort cycled me to my first entry pointy. Alfea and her lover sat near a fire, knees together. While she spoke, one hand gesticulating, he gave her his total attention. The quietude and lack of interruptions gave me an opportunity to study him.

He looked up.

Right at me.

Resisting the urge to duck, I stood still. It wouldn't matter. He couldn't see my movement with the invisibility spell, but I didn't like the idea of being taken off guard. My breath locked, but I didn't have to look to confirm my invisibility incantation remained.

A second later, his gaze slid away. He spoke quietly as before, nothing out of place. My breath whooshed out of me in relief. *Coincidence,* I told myself. *Nothing more.*

Unless, of course, he sensed my spell. Highly unlikely. This ancient spell wasn't well known, and wasn't the same as my first visit. If he had sensed me, wouldn't he have acted?

Movement to my right caught my gaze. I crouched. A girl sat on the edge of Alfea's firelight circle, hands bound, on a bench of molded sandstone. Other such structures littered the camp, created by incantations to form temporary furniture from sand. The structure faded after a week, leaving remnants of a civilization to persist for days after a tribe departed.

The girl gazed overhead, contemplative. A hint of a nearby burning torch cast illumination on her features. Thin, pointed eyes. Wide cheeks, petite nose.

Clannish.

Hedging my bets, I slipped over. She had use of her feet, but not her hands, and the rope didn't cut into her skin. She seemed to be waiting, but under no guard save for Alfea and her lover's proximity. Of course not. Why would they? Clannish witches couldn't do magic and save themselves. If they left the camp, footprints would be simple enough to follow.

Easy prey.

My nose twitched at the thought. Pausing to assess my surroundings, and taking another beat to ensure no magic systems activated nearby, I crept to the clannish witch's side. Crouching, I whispered, "Are you clannish?" in Yazikan.

She gasped.

"Shhh." A hasty glance confirmed neither Alfea nor her lover noticed. In fact, they'd deserted the fire to speak with witches a few paces away. All the better. Continuing with Yazikan, I said, "I'm a friend. What's your name?"

"Anya," she breathed. Her jaw trembled, ready to lose a sob.

"Are you harmed?"

She shook her head, head wobbling a tear free. Desperate, she asked, "Who are you?"

A laugh drew our attention higher. Voices drew close. Three men and a woman approached. Alfea, the male, and two others.

"Help me!" she squeaked, tugging at her ropes.

I set a hand on her wrists, issuing a spell to undo the complicated knots. "Calm. Quiet." Casting for the right word, I said, "Two minutes."

"Who are you?"

Hesitating only a beat, I said the name she'd recognize. "Bianca."

Elation bled through her features. *Don't kill her too,* Tyrant muttered, but her hope shut him up. The quartet of witches approached, so I said only, "Common tongue?"

She switched to it. "Yes."

"Good. Have them speak in the common tongue. I'm behind you."

I backed into the desert when the four witches arrived. Distance would make it harder to detect my low magic, but I didn't go far. They half circled Anya, who managed to look terrified. Undoubtedly, she must be. She might have heard my promise, but promises didn't translate to freedom.

"Common tongue?" the blond male asked in the common language. He gestured to Alfea. "She can speak Yazikan."

Alfea said, "A little," in Yazikan.

Anya said, "Common."

He braced his legs wide, hands folded in front of him.

Despite his angular features and a multitude of scars slashing his arms and shoulders, his voice softened. Utterly transformed from the fierce man that sought me.

"We do not desire to harm you. My name is Haruto."

Haruto, the leader of the Thabit tribe. My interest deepened.

Anya lashed out. "You took me!"

With long-suffering patience, Haruto said, "We brought you to a better situation. Not a cold, barren ice land where you eke out a miserable existence and eat only fish. We have more magic and families ready to receive you. This is an improvement, with enough food, less hard labor. A better life."

Anya blinked, as if dazed. "I don't want this life."

"You will." His arrogant assurance made my fists tighten. "Give yourself a few weeks. Maybe less. You'll see how much our tribe offers. No more cold. No more suffering. We'll find you a family to assist, and there you can belong."

Panic welled up in Anya's young eyes. She couldn't be more than fifteen, her arms and legs slender, face thin but rounded. Tears splashed down her cheeks. "Take me home! I want to go *home*. I don't want to be here, in the heat. I want the cold."

Haruto said, "Give it time, Anya. This is your new home. You're needed. *Very* needed. We're happy to provide for you. As long as you don't cause any trouble and serve one of our families with honor, you shall live a full and promising life."

Alfea smiled warmly over the girl, and I saw the twisted, nefarious plot for what it was. Enslavement couched behind pretty words. A front. They brought clannish witches from their homes to work for warriors and tribesmen so the tribesmen could labor over the oasis.

The connection, so clear, infuriated me. Shackles were shackles no matter how they dressed it up. Anya, nearly in a full panic, resisted when a warrior grabbed her wrist. Flailing as they hauled her to her feet, she cried out, "Please! Help me!"

Haruto called over her shouts in a commanding voice. "Take her to our guest mat until her assignment in the morning. A good night's sleep, a full meal, and appropriate clothes will help Anya settle in."

The warriors took the struggling girl between them, dragging her flailing body through the sand. I tailed close, but kept an eye on Alfea and Haruto. They faded, walking the opposite direction. The moment they were out of earshot, I sent two paralyzing spells on the warriors from behind.

Collapsing in the sand, I grabbed Anya by the arms and rolled her free.

"Hold your breath. I'm taking you home."

Anya spoke in between bites of food, while she chewed, before sips, after sips, and every other opportunity, in her attempts to keep the words flowing. If she could have, she would have spoken as she swallowed.

Relief kept her chatter high and fast, sometimes indecipherable. Alina, endlessly patient and serene, didn't interrupt. Two young women flanked Anya on either side. They sat back several paces, worked frantically with scrolls and pencils, their transcription speed relentless. They attempted to record every word out of Anya's mouth, which was no small feat.

Still invisible, I stood at the window, staring out. Telling Anya my name had been a risk. Probably a big one.

If she told others, word of Bianca's involvement in the Southern Network would spread. Georgette's strategy to discredit me to the Network replayed through my mind, and I hated the paranoia that it inspired.

At the time, though, telling Anya had been the right move. She had relaxed, sank into what my name meant, and helped me learn more. *That* is what stuck with me. My name meant something to witches who needed help, despite Georgette's best attempts at slander. A powerful reputation preceded me. Georgette painted me one shade, when I offered an entire palette of colors.

I had a lot to give, and *that* was who I wanted to be.

Settling more firmly in my own feet, I glanced at the reflection in the window as Alina approached. An Assistant stood to help Anya, who stuffed one last bite of food in her mouth and waved to Alina. They escorted her into another room to await her family.

"I don't know where you are, Miss Bianca," Anya called from the hallway, "but thank you!"

Alina paused a few steps away. "I wouldn't reveal yourself yet. Someone might come in."

"Thank you."

We waited for both Assistants to clear the room, and then several moments longer. The snapping fire, the quiet hush of distant castle sound, was a soothing melody.

"Her family will be here within the hour," Alina said, and I enjoyed her predictable crispness. "Thank you for what you've done."

"I know more than I did before, but it's still not enough. There are lingering questions, and reconnaissance. I'm assuming that they want the clannish witches to work so tribal witches can run the oasis, but there might be more reasons."

"I assumed."

Thinking ahead was too much to ask after a day full of magical use and realizations, so I simply said, "I'll come up with a plan tomorrow and let you know. Can you start working from your side?"

"We're already sending clan representatives to speak with the ice witches again. This time, we're telling them everything Anya has revealed. It will . . . help."

But probably not stop the abductions. While there was currency to be made, and the desperate thralls of winter awaited, the clannish witches would put up with a little danger in order to survive. My anxiety lessened knowing they'd have more information. At the very least, a reason to be wary.

"Good."

Quietly, Alina admitted, "There's a chance that some of the clannish witches might be willing to stay in the desert."

The results of her statement tripled in horrifying ways through my head. Some clannish witches might not desire to return. They might prefer the desert life. I didn't want to contemplate that—not yet. Truly, I didn't have a whole picture. Perhaps the whole reason Haruto's plan had been working thus far is because he knew he *could* provide a better life for them. In some regards, at least.

Not all.

Enslavement wasn't the way.

"My Assistants have written down all Anya's responses," Alina continued, and I sensed an ending drawing closer. "I will have them copy a scroll for you to review when you have a little more . . . energy."

Exhausted, I rubbed a hand over my eyes. "Thank you. I'll be in touch. First, I need to sleep. Take care of Anya. I like her."

Chapter Twenty

Candlelight and laughter blazed from the treehouse when I landed on a branch. My thoughts were too sluggish to fathom why several voices laughed at the same time. I stood in the same spot and yanked the fragile strings of my mind together.

Using magic all day, comprehending the desert world into which I'd thrust myself, rescuing Anya, and ending in the Southern Network to review it with Alina had sapped my strength. Only understanding that the clannish witches—as far as I could tell—weren't actively starving or beaten gave me the reassurance I needed for food and sleep. I could pick this up again tomorrow.

You belong to us.

She returns.

Stumbling closer, I trailed my fingertips along the bark. *We belong together,* I said, and the chorus sighed with peaceful contentment. Meanwhile, voices continued to ring from inside. I recognized one voice in particular: Jacqueline. A more masculine voice followed, and I couldn't help a smile. Tysen.

Ha! Jacqueline had written Tysen. How droll. Goat and Other Goat bleated as I trailed past, running my hand over their rough hair, as I headed for the main door. Ava's manulele birds nested in the Eastern Network during the winter, and I missed their hasty wingbeats.

Inside, Jacqueline and Tysen laughed from the table. Merrick presided at the end with a perplexed expression, as if he wasn't quite sure how he came to be there. Remnants of dinner scattered the top with empty plates, utensils, a mug, and what appeared to be roasted meat with stewed bitter greens. Jacqueline and Tysen sat with their dinner shoved to the side, a deck of cards between them. They hastily set down and picked up cards in a pattern with some unfathomable purpose.

How long have they been here? I asked Merrick through the magic, a frivolous use I rarely employed. Both Leda and Rognvald could hear any of my conversations with Merrick if they had their attention open, so we kept it business-only.

Merrick's head shot up, snagged mine, and he wilted in relief. *Get them out of here, will you? They aren't listening to me.*

Jacqueline burst into a laugh when she set down a final card, declaring herself a winner with a trumpet-like sound. Admitting defeat, Tysen held up both hands and slumped in his chair.

"Conqueror," he said.

Jacqueline beamed. The urge to kick them out quickly scuttled. I'd known Jacqueline for years and I'd never seen her smile that bright. Her recent struggles with depression and gloominess had been a real issue. I didn't have the heart to ask her to leave. Not with such unadulterated joy in her expression.

The cold blast of wind I brought with me clued them in. Tysen stood when he noticed me slipping inside.

"Merry meet, Bianca."

"Lose, did you?"

He grinned and stated with an absurd amount of pride, "She's quick, Jacqueline."

Jacqueline shot to her feet. "You returned!" Her expression fell. "Oh, you look terrible. Is that . . . sand . . . on your clothes?"

"Thanks," I muttered. "And yes, it is."

Merrick planted his hands on the table and pushed to his feet. "Bianca's been on a mission all day, so the two of you get out of here. She needs food and a bath, and if you don't leave, I'll make you help with both."

Giggling quietly, Jacqueline followed Tysen out the front door, as if they couldn't get away fast enough. The shock of their joyful voices, and then the utter silence, was a stark plunge. Realizing they'd left quickly, Merrick snorted.

"If I had known that would work," he muttered, "I'd have sent a deception spell a long time ago. C'mere, little troublemaker. You do look worse for wear."

Despite a full schedule of sweating, sand, and stalking at my back, he embraced me without hesitation. In his arms, the day melted like ghosts. So did I. Leaning my weight into him, I forced him to hold me up. When the pressure on my feet relieved, I realized the extent of my exhaustion.

"Long day?"

"Very."

"Need a bath?"

"Can't you tell?"

He laughed. When he swept an arm under my knees

and lifted me into the air, I gave a little squeak. My arm braced the back of his shoulders.

"It's time for a bath, a massage, and dinner. No one wants to take a bath alone, do they? Allow me to assist you in your deep fatigue, little troublemaker. Then we can talk about your day. I can tell you're bursting with stories."

* * *

After a luxurious bath, where I steamed all my tense muscles, scrubbed sand out of my hair, and dirt from between my toes, Merrick warmed my dinner. I brushed through my tangles at the table while Merrick told me about his day, setting a fresh plate and fork in front of me. The juicy smell of roasted meat and bitter greens made my stomach simmer. I almost jumped onto the table when he poured thick gravy onto an equally thick slice of bread. My stomach gnawed on itself when he set it in front of me.

"Eat," he commanded.

Picking up the fork, I motioned to him with a stab. "Gladly. Thank you, my heart. It smells divine. While I chew, tell me why you look like you'd fight an arctic baer and win."

Scowling, he jerked a chair out, sat down hard, and scowled. His foot was gentle under the table when he sought mine out, and I comforted him by rubbing the side of my foot along the crackling hair of his calves.

"I don't like it," he muttered.

"Jacqueline courting?"

"Courting *Tysen*," he corrected. "But I also know that I have no leg to stand on, so to speak, which makes me more grumpy. For one, I'm her brother. That automatically makes her want to do the opposite of whatever I suggest."

"Whether asked or not."

He ignored the quiet interjection.

"And for another," he continued, "I'm a Protector myself. I just handfasted a woman, so it's not like *I* can say any different. Not to Tysen, nor to Jacqueline."

Swallowing a bite of gravy-saturated bread that sank all the way to my stomach like scrumptious, hot butter, I managed to hide my smile. Trust Merrick to be livid with his sister, then angry with himself about it. While I shoveled food into my mouth, he continued to speak, gaze locked on something in the distance.

"Tysen is . . . he's . . ."

"Wonderful?"

His expression darkened further, if possible. "Exactly."

Chortling, I reached for my knife to separate a chunk of gristle off the meat edge. "You have complained about many things with Jacqueline, but never because she dated someone *too* wonderful. Tysen has had heartbreak, just like her. They both had previous relationships, a little time to build life experience, and budding careers. Let them decide what happens."

He mumbled something distinctly indecipherable, and I didn't pry farther. Over half my plate lay in ruins and gravy, and my ravenous appetite slowed. While I popped the last piece of bread in my mouth, he motioned to a basket.

"I came up with that today."

"What is it?" I asked. At least ten envelopes stacked inside, running end to end.

"Georgette sent you four letters. Just today," he tacked on. "Every four hours, she's sending another one."

Fork halfway to my mouth, I straightened. A slippery onion dropped to the plate.

"Four?"

He gestured to the basket with a thumb. "I've enchanted any message from her to go in the basket." He eyed it. "I put a few others in there, but they look like legitimate requests for the non-existent Sisterhood."

Requests had trickled in since Georgette ramped up her exposition against the Sisterhood. For the most part, I passed them to Leda. From this vantage, Georgette's letters appeared similar. Same envelope size, writing, ink. A spell made them in batches, likely.

Merrick folded his arms, giving me his full attention.

"So? What happened?"

In between the final bites, I relayed my day, grateful when I ended the telling at Alina's. By the time I finished, his eyes returned to the right kind of puzzlement. A Protector working out a plan of attack instead of a livid brother. Good. *Someone* needed to think about the situation, because my mind was too far gone for processing. With a warm bath, my hair in a drying braid, and food heavy in my stomach, I fought off my third yawn.

Merrick asked only, "What's your plan?"

"Not sure. I'll figure it out in the morning, when I'm fresh, but I'm inclined to think I have a little more scouting to do, and then a meeting with Rognvald."

Merrick's lips twitched. "Are you going to ask for help?"

"You bet I am."

"Could you ask him tomorrow afternoon? I had an idea to go to our mountain cabin tomorrow morning and put some work in. I've gathered our supplies. We can clear things out, make sure the roof hasn't collapsed under the weight of snow. You want to come?"

Grinning, I said, "You bet I do."

Chapter Twenty-One

Our quaint cottage at the top of a mountain ridge held a surprising amount of heat for how rickety it looked. Given a study kick in the right spot, the entire shack might topple. Merrick's willpower and attachment kept it standing.

The smell of cleaning potions thickened the air inside. Sunlight streamed in, so vivid against the valleys of undulating snow that I couldn't look directly outside without squinting and blinking. Fire snapped in the hearth, sending heat into the bitterly cold air. For being so extraordinarily dazzling, little warmth came from the sunshine. The air felt as tight and cold as an ice bath.

More brilliant than the trillions of glimmering gems on the glazed snow was a thick line of unending froth. Cloud banks slammed into the mountainside below and extended to the horizon. Curled up in the valleys like a hibernating animal, they had a wispy, harmless appearance. Below their bulwarks, a massive blizzard lashed the snowy peaks. When we transported to a nearby village to purchase goat cheese, winds squalled against the panes, shrieking into corners. In the peaks, we found abandoned, pristine clarity.

On the other side of the room, Merrick made a sound in his throat between a grunt and growl. He had his hands on his hips, head cocked to the side. He'd left his hair wild today, and it dropped past his shoulders in handfuls of sandy blond. I wanted to wrap it in a fist and jerk him into a promising kiss.

I crouched near the fire, inspecting a dozen hearth-stones broken off of each other. Unable to piece the stones together again, I cast a spell, watched them flip, flop, and whirl, then settle into a new position. Not bad. A little jagged, but it worked.

Tapping a toe on the old bench the former occupant created, Merrick tipped the rickety thing over. The wooden amalgamation crashed on its side, then splintered into several pieces. "I don't think we can save the bench," he said.

"Unless you want to pick wooden shards out of your backside?"

He chortled, lifting the bench from the end. "We'll toss it in the fire and I'll make one at the treehouse."

Glancing at the table, which stood by hope instead of strength, I said, "Might want to make it two benches *and* a table."

The necessities would add to our ever-growing list of things required to finish before we could call this cabin a home. We prioritized protection and claimancy first. Merrick filed our ownership at the coven and let witches know. Unsurprisingly, no one protested. Most laughed.

After securing the structure with spells to make sure others didn't shack up after our efforts, we turned our attention inside. Winter made it difficult. We couldn't stay overnight because it grew too cold in these alpine heights.

The poorly-patched walls didn't trap enough heat during the day. Night would be downright deadly.

With the broken hearthstones no longer a hazard to toes and ankles, I swept up the remaining bits, tossed them in the hearth to crackle in the flames, and turned my attention to the next hazard: mouse holes. The critters had been eating through the interior, shredding books, tearing holes into the wall that led outside. If we left them alone much longer, there'd be nothing to fix.

Before I could inspect more thoroughly, Leda's voice distracted me.

I've been thinking about the Thabit tribe and the Volare.

Have you?

My jaw hardened as I crouched down. The wonderful thing about speaking to Leda through magic was privacy and the ability to keep working with my hands.

What are your thoughts?

They seem to revere that Volare, and they called you Blessed Witch. That seemed to give you an exalted position, due to her offering all the water you want.

I hadn't thought much about that.

Probably not something you'd want to take advantage of, as it would draw attention, but worth being aware. I've searched for more information on the Reigning Volare and found none. I'm tempted to send an Underassistant to the Arck Library to read The Weavers of Magic, *but we've been rather busy.*

Better not to involve someone else, I added. *With Georgette always frothing at the mouth over anything associated with me.*

True.

A nearby mouse hole, not very large, gave off the unique scent that only mice conjured. My nose wrinkled.

There were spells that drew mice away from their holes instead of killing them outright. Could I transport a mouse to the forest instead? Only if I could *find* them. The walls to the cottage were reinforced in some areas . . .

There's something else I want to discuss. Leda's slightly elongating tone is one she used to hide hesitation. My emotional guards crawled higher.

Yes?

I'll send it to you.

A *Chatham Chatterer* scroll appeared next to me. Dread filled my gut. Of course I didn't want to read it. Leda had been shielding me from the worst articles. No matter how terrible the report, she plowed through the news with a relentless zeal that frightened and annoyed me.

Georgette, she said with impressive resignation.

Another article?

Yes.

What's her angle this time?

Your history, combined with your father's.

Jikes. She really doesn't let up, does she?

There's more than just Georgette to consider from this particular article. On the right column, third down. It's interesting, though not implicit. You don't need to read the full article, just the title.

My finger traced ahead of my eyes, stopping near a headline that was, indeed, interesting yet not implicit.

Escalating Tensions Between the South and the West

Does this have to do with the clans and the tribes?

It's very vague, she said quickly. *I've messaged Aurora to ask her if she had greater access to details, considering your mission. She hasn't responded. Has Alina mentioned anything?*

No.

Scarlett isn't aware yet, but I want to track the situation in case she needs to be. Aurora is in a meeting, so I haven't heard. I'll let you know.

I skimmed the effusive article, plucking out phrases such as *riots in Custos* and *demands for independence*. The journalist said little of consequence, citing *perceived border issues* and *discussions over protective details* which meant absolutely nothing to any witch outside the Arck. Drivel, really.

The Sisterhood's article today is on the top left, Leda said. *I'd be surprised that they haven't featured you as the main headline yet, but I think the current editor, a woman named Hortense Bigelow, doesn't desire to be on your bad side. Or Derek's.*

My heart thudded heavily in my chest. The headline was difficult to miss, though not the worst.

Council Member Cites Security Concerns

Georgette needs a life, I said, skimming the words. Reading them too deeply pulled me into Georgette's fathomless hole, and the fury I kept stuffed there with her. Not to mention Tyrant, which attempted to resurrect but I strangled with forced indifference.

At the end of the article, I said, *Georgette doesn't mention Scarlett.*

She hasn't mentioned Scarlett in any of them, Leda countered. *Not yet. Drawing Scarlett into this would be a political death knell, and Georgette is skirting a fine line. The problem is, she's skirting it well.*

Or she has people supporting her.

That, too. Did you see the article toward the bottom of the scroll?

Sliding it farther down, I eventually caught an opinion piece in the middle. The journalist, a male witch I'd never heard of, received a finger span of space. The cramped writing was difficult to decipher at first, but the headline was simple enough, set next to an advertisement for goat milk soap.

What's the Fuss?

A frustrated extrapolation about Georgette's personal takedown of the Sisterhood followed. Little more than a tirade, it didn't come to the Sisterhood's defense as much as it complained about Georgette.

Odd, I said.

I thought so too. Hortense may be trying to hedge her bets with how she's handling all these articles in the Chatterer. *I'd also wager that Council Member Clare had something to do with the defense piece, though there's no correlation that I can see.*

Do you know that journalist?

No.

The final lines of Georgette's article snagged my eyes; I'd skimmed too fast to notice it the first time. For several breaths, I couldn't tear my gaze away. Not even when Merrick began to swear under his breath, and something thudded on the other side of the room. His explicative string reassured me that all was well enough.

Georgette's article read: *The question isn't whether the Sisterhood would have been successful as a protective entity. The question is why we're encouraging the creation of programs where witches have achieved their position based* on popularity with those in power. *Have we forgotten the Dark Days?*

The words attacked more than me. They attacked anyone associated with the Sisterhood. I sat on the floor near the mouse hole and spelled the *Chatterer* away, sick to my stomach. Georgette didn't say Scarlett's name, but I knew an attack when I saw one.

Georgette is building her premise around me finding my way to a position of power through others, I said. *She's discrediting* everything.

Softly, Leda said, *Yes.*

And there is *an argument for it. We can't refute that I have those social ties.*

Not strictly speaking, no. But this is a far more nuanced situation than a simple yes or no.

Another chilling reality descended. *My withdrawal, framed in this light, makes it look as if I knew I wouldn't have a chance in the Council. As if I knew that we weren't ready, or worthy. She's making it seem like I was running away.*

Yes, if you're not familiar with the intricacies of your story.

You're saying that witches who know me personally will understand my connections?

Yes.

And what percentage of witches in the Network is that?

In a small voice, she said, *Not worth calculating. To the witches who don't track the details of your life and the way you've served the Network, Georgette is making an argument that is damning for the Sisterhood. Not a strong argument,* she added, *but an argument most witches won't bother to refute.*

Enough to give her traction.

Yes.

In order to create a reputation that advances her own career.

Or, Leda said both quietly and with convincing belief, *she simply believes that she sees a potential for corruption that others don't. There have been other witches in history who have been convinced of far worse things, and with lesser arguments. Did you see the final line? It's why I brought this up, or I wouldn't have mentioned any of this.*

Rubbing my forehead, I said, *No.*

She's holding a rally.

What does that mean? I asked, although I'd attended rallies before. My brain couldn't skip away from the words *Georgette sees a potential for corruption that others don't.* Could that really account for her intended harassment?

I doubted it.

She's gathering other witches that feel similarly about the Network allowing witches jobs too easily, Leda countered. I eyed the line where location details had a bolder font than the rest. Downtown Chatham City. What a perfect rallying point.

Are you going? I asked.

Undecided. I don't think I need to ask if you are going.

You bet I'm going.

It's at the same square where Clive held the rally against your father.

I laughed outright. How perfect. The past raced forward to give me a second chance at a better future. Clive had personally attacked Papa during that rally. In my grieving rage, and after a few men attempted to hold me down, I'd lost control of my magic. Several witches were harmed in the aftermath of my powers, though they deserved it. Merrick appeared, taking me out of harm's way.

This time, I had control on my side, and I'd write a new story. A better one.

Thank you for showing me, Leda.

I'm sorry.

I'm not. I managed to mean it, though I grimaced. *Ugly as it is, Georgette is doing exactly what we want. The Sisterhood is thoroughly discredited. It doesn't exist, and it never will again, to the Network at large. If we're truly here to serve witches, Leda, it's the only way we can.*

I know. We shared her sad resignation. *I just wish it didn't have to be this way.* With a little more energy, she added, *You know, it can't be any worse than this. Might as well talk to her. Rumor says she has sent Assistants and other paid foresters to try to find you.*

Drily, I said, *I doubt that,* and pushed to my knees. The mouse hole caught my attention again, and I wanted to focus on anything *but* Georgette. Knowing the Sisterhood continued to thrive and serve gave me courage, but the constant rattling against my reputation irked me.

Georgette sends me two letters everyday, Leda continued, *requesting my help to speak with you. I imagine she's sending more to other witches, too. If you hear her out, maybe she'll shut up.*

With that, Leda closed the conversation, and I returned to the mouse hole.

* * *

Curiosity beat out better sense that evening. While Merrick visited a local lumber supply place and a black-smith seeking supplies for the new table and bench, I slipped into the castle through a lesser-known entrance once darkness had fallen.

Invisible, I sped through the long back hallways

Grandfather once preferred. Being here again made me think of him, and some of the shock of his departure ebbed. The two halves of my brain had, for the time being, ceased their war. He *was* gone, no matter how often I still expected to see him behind a door, or speaking quietly from a corner. As unreal as it felt once, time made it more real. I hated it, but I understood it.

I made my way to the Council Member hallway. Most Assistants and Council Members left with daylight, so only a few offices remained heated, lit, and occupied: those of Clare, Georgette, and Frederick, over the Middle Covens.

I hovered outside of Georgette's office. To my surprise, she left her door open and spoke to her Assistant in a not unkind tone, but a business-like one.

"Make sure we see those final tax forms submitted before the end of the evening," she said between shuffling papers and the whistle of a dying winter wind. It scuttled over her window panes, rattling them.

I pressed my spine to the wall and tilted my head back. My eyes remained open while the two of them discussed office coordination tidbits. Nothing happened in the hallway. There was something cathartic about the slow-moving castle. The place I normally avoided actually provided a layer of calm.

A moment before I nearly left out of boredom, her male Assistant said, "There's a letter from Hortense that needs addressing."

I tightened.

Bless Leda for mentioning the *Chatham Chatterer* editor, Hortense Bigelow, a witch I had no interest in keeping up with. A letter for Georgette from Hortense was worthy gossip.

"Is there?"

"You inquired about purchasing another article space for a second rally, but we haven't confirmed that we're going to hold a second rally yet. There are other interested witches in the space, and it needs to be decided immediately."

"Then we'll take it and hold another rally. At . . . Ashleigh House. The first must be in our home covens, then the second outside of it. We'll rally more support in Ashleigh. Depending on the response, we can plan for a third in the Middle Covens. Unfortunately, we'll need to avoid the Western Covens, though I think their population is worthy. Clare is not worth our energy."

She spoke with a harried rush, as if she made the decision out of pressure. His tone was calm, but withholding, when he replied.

"Is that wise?"

"Why wouldn't it be?" she snapped.

"We're behind in our Coven reviews."

"They were caught up to date last month. Being a week behind isn't all that concerning, if you ask me. There are other covens that haven't done them for a year. We're in a strong position, Peter."

He didn't say another word, and who could blame him? The dismissive tone, the authority, made it impossible to say anything else. A second rally at Ashleigh House. Did coven funds pay for these slots?

News from Georgette, I said to Leda.

Do tell.

After updating Leda on my eavesdropping, and she agreed to look into Georgette's rally funding, I shoved away from the wall.

Why had I come, anyway? There was nothing to be sought. A small—very small—part of me considered whether I *shouldn't* just talk to Georgette and have it over with. If I strolled in tonight, I'd take her by surprise. She'd have to grapple without being prepared and at the end of a day where she already juggled details. This was the most vulnerable position in which to confront her.

But then . . . what?

I sought nothing from Georgette. She might plaster my name as a fraud or lazy or privileged, but did it matter? The witches who I cared for knew otherwise, and others continued to send messages requesting help. While I didn't love being maligned, it wouldn't keep bread off of my table. Not with Merrick, Scarlett, Alina, Papa, Regina, and others at my side.

This bully didn't deserve the effort.

Feeling better, I left down the other side of the hall, and left Georgette to her exhausting machinations. Tyrant in my head was silent, and I wished I knew what shut him up. He was yet another bully not worth the effort.

Chapter Twenty-Two

The Thabit camp had moved.

I tracked the motions from far behind, not surprised to see strewn sand and discarded possessions. They headed north-northeast, and rather slowly. Like most desert witches, they began their trek at night, sleeping and resting through the hot hours of the day.

I trailed them, curious. Now that I'd located some clannish witches, several questions required answers before I could finalize my plan to pull them free. How many were there? Did the Thabit tribe have more than one location? They must have others. Alina's reported fifty missing witches, and I had counted ten. It wouldn't be unheard of for a Western Network tribe to spread apart and cover more ground.

Before I involved Rognvald, I needed solid information. It would be an embarrassing mistake to involve the Brotherhood before I knew every detail and contingency. Georgette, unknowingly, put pressure on my every move.

Besides, the Thabit tribe, in order to hold the position

as one of the most powerful tribes, had to have more witches than those I observed west of the oasis.

The witches exiting this camp walked in something like a semicircle. It must be on purpose. But why depart at all? Did movement provide greater security? How many camps did the Thabit tribe have?

These questions ran through my mind as I followed a hunch and returned to the treehouse. There, I flicked open the same map that showed where the grimoire had gone after I set a tracking spell on it. The grimoire, once north of the camp, had shifted southeast.

Like a moving circle.

Time to find that grimoire.

Transporting magic required a level of certainty to deposit a witch in the right spot. Unconscious transportation—throwing the spell to go *anywhere* while in a dangerous situation—was a real enough possibility. Plenty of witches had safely transported without a firm destination in mind, only the hope of escape. Most of the time, it sent them somewhere. Those witches for whom it didn't work were never heard from again. The danger of transporting to an unknown position in the sandy vistas was real enough.

For my part, I hadn't canvassed or scoured every portion of the desert. Even if I had, the sameness prevented certainty. How could anyone perfectly recall details or locations when horizon to horizon hardly varied? The risk of transporting to random spots didn't center around lack of experience, but the vast landscape.

As a child, Mama and Papa taught me that transportation was a risky and dangerous magical task, but adult

Bianca had seen worse. Besides, familiarity with the transportation magic gave me a certain level of confidence.

Risk loomed over the reward of locating another camp sooner than later, so I took my chance. Transporting to an approximation of where I desired to land left me ankle-deep in cooling sand, no hint of life, and moonlight casting shadow divots across the rolling hills.

I tried a second time.

A third.

Little altered. The vast vista awed me. So *much* nothing. This part of the desert—more sand than striated red rock without water support—was particularly stunning under star shine.

"Pointless," I muttered, hovering. There was no way to know where I had been in order to mark a radius. The tracking spell I used on the grimoire wouldn't hold onto sand granules, and the complicated magic required time. Still, I didn't want to yield my goal just yet, so I altered my plan.

Any chance you have a map of the Western Network that can track where I currently am and have been? I inquired of Leda.

No.

Her brusque reply left me curious, but I didn't ask.

Papa?

A laugh lived in his reply. *Yes, favorite daughter?*

You wouldn't have a map of the Western Network that would track where I currently stand, would you?

No. But I have one for Alkarra.

Can I borrow it?

I thought you'd never ask. Sending it now. Tap once to mark, twice to remove a mark. Holds up to twenty marks, and mine are all removed from my nomadic days. Each mark lasts a week, unless you tap three times, then the mark is permanent until total erasure of all marks.

A curled map arrived moments later, settling into my awaiting palm.

You're my favorite father, you know that?

Don't insult me.

With moonlight as my guide, I studied the inked lines. A glimmering amethyst marker glowed from the middle of the upper Western Network. Myself. All things considered, my current position hadn't been *too* far from my planned landing spot. Near my current position, the oasis appeared as a water drop.

To test it, I transported to the abandoned, previous Thabit camp. My dot glowed to the west of the oasis, as expected, but the faintest shadow remained at my former spot. I tapped once. The shadow solidified.

"Nice," I whispered.

My approximation of the first Thabit camp placement had been wrong by close to forty five degrees. They hadn't been due west, but northwest. My blind transportation location had been farther out from the oasis, too. *Much* farther.

Reissuing the spell, I tried a different spot in the same general area, and nearly landed on top of a disbanding Thabit camp so similar to the first that it could have been the same. My invisibility spell was the only thing that saved me from discovery.

I landed a pace away from a tent pole and a working witch. Skirting away with a hidden gasp, I hovered high above until I could gain my bearings. My heart thumped a hard, shocked beat.

Jikes!

I hadn't expected to find witches so quickly. The disbanding camp scuttled with sharp hustles, mumbled exclamations, and harried whistles. They flung items into wagons, or rugs pulled by ropes that they'd then tug over the sand. A group of witches lurched into the open desert, possessions in tow. Others trailed in a line, barely visible in the simmering night shadows.

But . . . why leave? Couldn't they stay in fixed positions?

A witch growled nearby, drawing my attention. I whirled around. A male witch pointed a meaty finger at a sand sled ten paces from his huge feet. He barked a command in the common language.

"Put the bundles in that sled!"

A clannish female witch, recognizable by her slim figure and ebony hair, dragged a tied cloth bundle away from a disbanding tent. The male witch cursed under his breath, propped four different bundles of a similar size on his shoulders, and followed.

Thank the goddess, I found another clannish witch. No chains. No visible injuries, nor signs of starvation. Only misery etched on her face. As I planned to approach her, another witch appeared from a tent, throwing a flap aside. She spoke and the clannish witch scuttled to obey.

Nausea rose in my throat. Miserable, tribal wretches. I couldn't wait to remove all the clannish witches from this hellhole. Other mysteries awaited, however. I had a hunch this *moving party* had something to do with Anya vanishing from their clutches two nights ago. I hadn't stayed around to figure out what Haruto thought.

Tonight, I'd try something a little different before rescuing her.

Nearby, another witch cursed in Ilese, the language of the Eastern Network. A physical shock ran through me at the sound. Ilese? Here? Eastern witches rarely visited the Western sands. The witch grumbled in Ilese.

"Why must we rotate again?"

"Fool," hissed a voice in the common language, but with a Northern brogue. "We keep our boundaries by constantly claiming them."

Tribal law, probably. Didn't sound like a rule Lana would enforce. Too messy, prone to fights. Lana kept a loose hand over the tribes by necessity. No Western Network leader had successfully held reins over the rare desert city, Custos, *and* the tribes. Coexistence was the rule between the Western Network and tribes in the sand. Such tolerance happened as long as wholesale or overt slaughter wasn't an issue.

Loose boundaries.

The two male witches scurried around their tent, which wasn't big. The single-roomed structure had an entire wall missing; they'd turned it open to the desert. They lacked the same panic as others. Spells collected their items, tossing them into baskets. Bedrolls spiraled together, blankets folded.

We, the Northern witch had said. Did the Thabit tribe accept outsiders? Stef had clearly lived in Chatham City, and she held anxiety around maintaining their position with Alfea. These two male witches weren't native Western tribesmen, for certain.

I backed away, settling into a position at the edge of the disemboweled camp. The ambiance was far more intense than the first, with radiating tension. The shape, the layout, the close proximity of witches, was similar, though.

I sent a message to Rognvald.

Any chance you have an available Protector fluent in Yazikan?

Yes. Why?

I need to speak with a clannish witch.

Which dialect?

Not sure. She's young. My age, I'd say. Perhaps a year or two younger.

Hold.

Witches scuttled by, legs swishing back and forth. This camp had three adult camals and two younger ones. The gigantic beasts groaned, laden with bundles and goods. Bells tinkled from their halters as they thumped by. Their owners jogged along their side in the moonlight. A shout rang from a distance. I waited, taking the pleasant scene in while counting clannish witches. Thus far, I noted eight.

Rognvald interrupted my thoughts. *Gregary is available and he's fluent in the dialect of your generation. You want him?*

Please.

Come get him.

* * *

Combined with Chi's aloofness and Merrick's assessing stare, Gregary's sternness reminded me of Papa.

Seeing him, I remembered briefly meeting him at the Brotherhood Yule party. He looked worse for wear since his former wife had obliterated their handfasting. Fatigue lines cut from his eyes, and a perpetual frown drooped his lips. If it wasn't for the curiosity in his stare, I might have considered an alternative.

A quick debrief and one plan later, Gregary followed my spell, landing invisibly at my side. I'd been gone for ten minutes.

Being in charge of other Brotherhood members during a mission was still a relatively new experience. With Gregary's daunting personality at my side, I felt a wash of gratitude that my first solo mission with a Protector had been mild-mannered and easygoing Tysen. A far easier barrier of entry.

Gregary and I stared at the disbanding camp while I finished my explanation through the communication magic.

I have several questions left to answer before the Brotherhood and I can plan a liberation of the clannish witches, and one of them is this: do the clannish witches want to come home? To know that answer, I need to speak to a clannish witch—if not most of them. The witch ahead of us, at two o'clock, is not well guarded. She's our best bet.

The family had almost gathered their belongings inside the tent while the clannish witch scrambled to contain a young, balking camal. The father barked orders while loosening ropes. Sand poofed in the moonlight behind their camp as magical trees evaporated. The wife shouted at her husband, one child wailed, and the family descended into a storm.

Is that all you want me to ask the clannish witch? Gregary inquired.

No. After you ask whether she wants to be liberated, ask her how many other clannish witches are here. Does she know if they want to go? Their names? I don't want to take her home, draw attention, and lose an opportunity to remove someone else tonight. The more we transport in and out, the more attention we might draw.

Understood.

I'll create a distraction while you speak to her. The father is ignoring her, but the mother keeps looking.

Understood.

When the clannish witch calmed the camal, I slid around a tree and sent a spell to the interior of the family tent where five empty baskets stood in a neat row, awaiting belongings. On my command, they overturned, rolling onto their side and into the dark. Folded blankets silently unfurled, sprawling along the ground. My spells unwound a bundle of clothes, scattered whittled toys.

In the shadows, the clannish witch crouched at a sled half-filled with bundles, not far from the camal. Her hands moved slow and deliberate. The tilt of her head indicated she listened to something, though her eyes remained downcast.

The wife spun, mouth half open to bark something, and stopped short. A mess scattered at her feet. Her lips closed, brow furrowed in confusion. She stared at the haphazard display of their belongings. A child snoozed in a bassinet, and a toddler hiccuped near a corner, no longer wailing.

The wife cried out in another language. The husband whirled, tossed his hands in the air, and chattered so quickly his anger radiated from each word. Kneeling in the sand, she hustled to replace the baskets. As she scrambled for the toys, I misaligned the baskets again.

She released a muted scream.

I rolled my lips to keep from laughing. With violent slams, she stacked one basket inside another until they towered unevenly at her side. She kept a hand on top and a stream of steady chatter.

Hands gesticulating to the baskets, the male growled and stalked into the night. My heart shrank, and I almost followed him. All he had to do was turn slightly to the side to see his clannish witch frozen, not moving, at the sled. But the dark swallowed him, and he glided past.

Shouting after him, both hands raised, the wife reached for the top basket. Thinking fast, I cast another spell. Normally cast to seal two items together—many librarians used it on book interiors and covers that had broken—prevented the baskets from pulling apart. Arms straining, she grunted and muttered mutinously under her breath.

Meanwhile, the clannish witch rose on shaky legs. Her lips barely moved, and she paused. I coordinated a spell that pulled each item off the hastily packed sled, sprawling them across the ground with levitating spells and utter silence.

Update? I asked.

She wants to return.

Are there others?

Yes.

Any that would want to stay?

Not clear.

Then go ahead and take her, I said. *Go to Zamok Castle in the Southern Network. Give the front guards my name, and ask for Alina.*

I paused my disaster-creation in the tent when the female whirled around, saw the destroyed sled, fisted her hands in her hair, and let out a piercing scream. She stalked to the tent. The clannish witch vanished.

I crept away as the male returned, trilling harsh words that earned him a fist to the chest. The female picked up the baskets, but I had already released the spell. They split apart, resulting in another irritated wail.

Other clannish witches remained elusive as I crept around. I sought others, but the moon had slipped behind a cloud, cloaking visibility. Most families and witches had dispersed.

Gregary said, *A maid is taking us to the High Priestess' personal chamber with the girl. What would you like me to do next?*

Escort her to Alina. Tell Alina we're going to try to bring others to her tonight, then return to the same spot. I'll wait for you there, because we have other camps we need to visit. If possible, we'll take a clannish witch from each one that we find. I'm not sure, but I think there might be more. I can confirm two, so far.

Understood.

I slipped into the night, watching further chaos unfold as the couple began to search for their clannish witch. They shouted a name. My hand wrapped around the map Papa sent me. There might be other Thabit camps. Based on the relative position of these two, which flanked the oasis on either side, I wagered there would be at least two more camps. If they constantly moved and patrolled a circle around the oasis, they protected their investment.

Ten minutes later, Gregary met me in the sands. When we left to search for another camp, I was too happy to say *merry part.*

* * *

Gregary worked with relentless ease and determination. He never once betrayed fatigue, hesitation, or concern. Together, we located not two, but three more camps in similar states of disarray. All together, five Thabit camps created a roving star, with the oasis at the center.

Near dawn, Gregary swept away a male clannish witch so eager to leave he stumbled over every word. I surveyed the settling camp alone. Witches yawned, rubbed their faces. Water canteens tossed back and forth. Rudimentary tents erected and witches ducked beneath them.

This final Thabit group had been more difficult to locate. Their old camp had been deserted for days, but low-wind left a faint trail. They settled at a dusty, sandy spot in between their old camp, and another camp ahead of them. An eternal, moving circle, that somehow satisfied tribal laws of ownership, protected their way of life, and allowed witches to . . . what? Be inconvenienced?

I eavesdropped on all the sloppy tents, searching for Alfea or Haruto. Throughout the night, I'd glimpsed no sign of her, nor her lover. Did they roam from camp to camp? As the leader of the entire tribe, it seemed strange to settle in one camp of five.

Someone interesting caught my attention at a sprawling canvas tent with a single witch inside. He wore a hat of carved wood as dark as ebony. Speckled green-and-white feathers sprouted from it like flower petals. He sat, hands on his bent knees, and glowered at the sand. "The clannish witches sent us a warning tonight."

His ominous words seemed at odds with the lightening sky, altering from black ink to blooming sapphire. Stars faded to blurs along the edge. His clear Western Network accent reminded me of Custos, the city containing the Arck Castle.

The Thabit tribe had no candles; they used low lamps stabilized by sand granules. Lamps surrounded this witch, but he illuminated none. Another body sat on the other side of the tent, in flickering shadows.

A familiar voice queried, "What do you mean, *the clannish witches sent us a warning tonight?*"

Alfea.

I smiled.

The growly male snapped, "Yes, the clannish witches. There were disappearances."

Alfea remained along the edge, clinging to shadow. "They couldn't," she insisted. "They have no magic."

"Then they've brought someone in. There will be a rebellion." He elevated a hand, skinny finger held high. "It won't be pretty. We have taken too many. I told you—it's too much!"

She laughed. An airy thing with teeth. Parchment winged into the tent, folded into the shape of a bird. Papered wings fluttered around the male's head until he snatched it. A voice spoke from within.

"Two clannish witches lost tonight," said a low, gravelly register. "One from the second camp." He set the paper on fire.

Alfea had gone very still. Another note followed the first, but this did not fly nor speak aloud. After reading it, the male crushed it in his fist, setting it to flame.

"Another from the fourth camp. That makes one clannish witch removed from each camp through the night. That is no accident."

There had been too many clannish witches for a full-scale removal with so many tribal witches awake and busy. The chaos of moving camps made extraction more complicated in some ways. But we'd taken enough to earn us more information, and a glimpse into every camp.

Gravely, Alfea asked, "Who do you think it is?"

A third voice spoke. Haruto. "Isn't it obvious? The Southern Network has recruited someone to find their witches," he declared.

"A demigod?" she asked.

Haruto snorted. "I doubt it. They're lazy mongrels."

Alfea's head turned to regard the other side of the tent, where Haruto crouched in the shadows. His ivory skin, so strangely transparent, glowed in the burgeoning daylight. By Haruto's lack of surprise, he'd clearly considered this before. A formidable distemper built in his shifting jaw, slotted glare. He didn't appreciate being bested on his own property.

Safe in the South, Gregary said.

Wait for me there, please.

Understood.

"What do you recommend, Haruto?" Alfea asked quietly, with grave concern. "We can't stop now. But if we return the clannish witches . . ."

His strange eyes lingered on the other male. "We wait," he murmured. "They'll reveal themselves again. I believe I have chased this . . . witch . . . before. Clever. Quick-witted, too. They escaped me in the Central Network forest."

Alfea blinked, registering surprise.

The tribal male extended his arms out and stood from the ground with muscular finesse. "We wait for rebellion, then. If you're wise, Haruto, you get rid of the clannish witches now. We have one that—"

"We have *nothing*," Haruto hissed. "Not yet. We need more of the right clannish witches. Thus far, there's only one."

Though I wanted to learn more what this *one* meant, instinct retracted me from near the tent. Haruto's stare unnerved me. Eternal. Deep. Filled with hatred. I raced for the fake trees, where their magical signature might obscure my own.

Haruto stalked out of the tent, casting a flap aside, and stood under the lessening stars. Hands on his hips, he lowered his eyes to half mast, drew in a deep breath. He switched to sensing magic. I left before his attention fell to me.

His words rang hollow through my mind. *We need more of the right clannish witches. Thus far, there's only one.*

* * *

Five clannish witches waited in Alina's personal apartment, four females and one male. The women clutched each other's hands and stared at a feast. Frozen fish with melted fat. Dried mushrooms simmered into a gravy. Onions—so many onions.

Maids appeared with clannish clothes made from silk draped over their arms. One woman wept, the others stared at their High Priestess in disbelief. The male kept his gaze on the ground, arms locked over his chest, fingers tucked under his arms.

Alina, voice soft, spoke to her clannish witches in Yazikan. I translated every fifth or sixth word, but Gregary filled in the rest. *The witches will speak with Alina after a full meal and time with their families. They'll stay here until she knows they'll be safe in their clan.*

Thanks, Gregary. You were a huge benefit and help tonight.

Softly, he said, *You're welcome.*

I whispered, *"Spashta,"* or *I'm grateful* in Yazikan. Alina, the only one close enough to hear, inclined her head. She gazed at the clannish group with a maternal warmth.

We can go, I said.

Gregary departed, but I lingered, chewing on Haruto's final words. *We need more of the right clannish witches. Thus far, there's only one.*

I sent a message to Leda. *Are you already up and working at the castle?*

I am.

Do you have a few minutes?

I do.

If you're interested, I have a night full of details to share, and a few things that require research before we can assemble the Brotherhood to make a plan. We rescued some clannish witches in the night. Alina is going to question them. With their responses, and what I learned, we can proceed into a plan with the Brotherhood.

With greater interest and energy, she said, *I'll have breakfast waiting for you.*

Bless you, I said eagerly. With a full night behind me, coffee and food sounded divine, but the opportunity to unburden my observations for Leda to study propelled me out of the Southern Network. Gregary and I made a dent and a statement tonight, but this wouldn't work again.

Leda could take all these details and cobble something together while I slept, and then I'd assemble my Brotherhood team.

The real planning started now.

Chapter Twenty-Three

Flurries filled the afternoon skies, thick as goose down, as they drifted through the stalwart, silent branches. Each snowflake took its time as it fluttered from spot to spot. I strode through the lovely storm, cutting a trail across the ground, while the saplings crooned to me.

You belong to us.

We belong to you.

She always comes back.

Papa's house appeared, welcoming me with the *thwack, thwack, thwack* of an ax. Unlike many foresters, Papa refused to use magic to split his firewood. "Keeps me young," he always said. "If you do it right, firewood warms you twice."

Others would flow to his home soon. Rognvald, Merrick, Chi, Tysen. Jacqueline, too, since Tysen planned to come. As if Rognvald heard my thoughts, his voice cut into my mind.

Anything you need us to bring to the planning meeting tonight?

Just yourself.

Gregary said you learned a lot.

He's correct. Alina questioned the witches we liberated and provided Leda the details while I slept. Leda's come up with a solid idea. We're ready to discuss.

Happy to hear it.

Smiling, I strode closer, my fur-lined emerald cloak billowing. Frigid air surged around my arms and legs, drawing me from the sleepy vestiges clinging to me since I woke. This late in the day, and along the low forest floor, the sun would set soon.

Papa reached for his split wood pieces, tossed them aside, and straightened. He slammed the ax into a flat stump and slung his forearm along the top.

"B."

"Papa."

Swiping his forehead with his shirt sleeve—he didn't even wear a coat—he asked, "Was my map helpful?"

"Very, thank you. Did you want it back?"

"No need."

I paused a few steps away, feeling a rush of . . . grief. A haunting question lingered on the tip of my tongue, meant for him. It was a topic I would have taken to Grandfather for advice. While Papa was as qualified—if not more so—to dispense wisdom, I couldn't help wishing Grandfather remained.

Papa softened. "How are you?"

"I'm not sure."

"I can tell. You look like you're in pain. Are you thinking?"

Rolling my eyes, and earning a laugh for it, he peeled his calfskin gloves off and tossed them onto the stump.

"What is it, B?"

"I'd like some advice, if you're open to it."

"Anytime."

"I guess . . ."

"You usually went to your grandfather for this."

Nodding, I tried to bite back the tears that welled up. The hollow ache ate at me again, and I hated it. Dealing with all these awful things with Georgette, the work in the Western Network, and Grandfather's death. Too much.

The emotions swamped me, and so unexpectedly. Tyrant's voice arose with a whispered, *you deserve this,* but vanished when Papa's arms embraced me with their perfect strength. I breathed deep the smell of pine and sweat. Comforting and steady. After I'd calmed my emotions, I swiped tears from my cheeks with the back of my hand.

"Thanks."

"Anytime."

Sniffling, and feeling marginally less hollowed out, I elevated the map. "Can we talk before the Brotherhood arrives? I have a theory I'd like to put in front of you."

He lifted a hand to stop me, gaze focused over my shoulder. After a split second, his features rearranged into a thunderous rage that took me by surprise. Something awful must have caught his attention to create *that* expression. I whirled.

Georgette stood there in a blood-red cloak lined with whitest rabbit fur. It highlighted her face and petite shoulders. Her elegant presence befitted a High Priestess, loathe as I was to admit it. Papa stepped forward, but I held out a hand.

"No, Papa. She's here for me."

He restrained himself, fists clenched, and spoke through the magic.

I'll be watching.

I sent him a wry, humorous look in place of a laugh.

She's not stupid enough to try to physically attack me, certainly not with you looming behind us.

Let's hope not.

Papa stalked inside the house, sending a final lour in Georgette's direction. Resigned, I turned to meet her halfway. She hadn't moved since we spotted her, which kept her clear from Papa's closest property boundaries. In the forest, no one drew hard lines, but there was an understanding of general space. Wise witches didn't proceed beyond a tree line surrounding a structure, and Georgette had already crossed almost half of Papa's.

"Bianca," she called. "Good day."

"Can I help you?"

"I'm sure you've received my correspondence?"

"I have."

Her brow arched. I left my comment sitting there. With a breath, she picked the flow up again.

"It's been hard to find you since our last discussion. I took a wild chance that you'd be at your father's place."

I hid a scoff. No one found Papa by a *wild chance*. "I'm only surprised that you knew where he lived," I countered, sending a sidelong glance toward the house. "Not many do."

She sealed *her* lips this time.

Continuing, I said, "If I were you, I'd expect a visit from him after this. He'll be wanting to know exactly how you knew where he lived."

To her credit, she didn't pale, but her lips thinned. "I assure you, I have no desire nor plans to return. Considering recent events, I think it would be beneficial if you and I had a civil discussion. A sort of . . . cease fire."

"Cease fires apply to war and battle, of which I have no current part. Are you conducting either?"

She blinked twice, then her eyes tapered. "No. Naturally, not. I suppose . . . that is . . ." Georgette recovered herself by clearing her throat, lifting her chin. "You and I have always had differing opinions on the Network's need for the Sisterhood. Now that you've resigned the position, I'm concerned that the real issue behind my concern for the Sisterhood will be lost."

"Remind me of the real issue?"

"Unproven witches gaining power in our Network government structure."

"Right. That one."

"For the betterment of the Network, I came to ask if you would sign the agreement that I sent you." Tersely, she added, "Several times. My mistake might have bene sending it to your home without an in-person explanation, though it certainly hasn't been without multiple attempts to speak to you."

Her musing tone had a cutting layer, comical in its underhanded sneakiness. Combined with the steely-stare and taut jaw, it helped me understand what Leda had been muttering about Georgette all along: Georgette might truly believe in the rightness of her position.

In the world she inhabited, Georgette sought to protect the Network from enemies that she perceived as dangerous. Because my approach to the Sisterhood didn't involve the path she felt qualified as safe, I had become her enemy. Did it make her wrong? It certainly didn't make either of us *right*.

Was there grace to be given for a witch that genuinely believed their path was the best, yet prevented the opportunity for others to be different?

Existential floundering nearly brought me out of the moment. Georgette sniped a mean, "I suppose all of us can look back and find mistakes on our paths. You as well, Miss Monroe," and kept me anchored here.

My former grace-extending dissipated in the face of her hardening stare. Coming to Papa's had been a risk that momentarily mollified her confidence, but her vinegar had returned. I liked her better this way. At least I knew what to do with her. Georgette routinely attempted to gain the upper hand in a conversation through words, which made silence a weapon. Again, I stared.

Wordless.

With a flutter of her eyes, she exhaled a heavy breath. "Are you mute, Miss Monroe?"

"No. I just haven't heard a question."

Exerting greater control, she gave a cold smile. "Miss Monroe, would you accompany me to my office where we can discuss this agreement to greater depth before you sign?"

She summoned a paper that dangled between us, half unrolled. It bobbed in the mammoth snowflakes.

Snatches of legalese bled from it, the same words that Leda had already reviewed and rolled her eyes over. The control Georgette desired to exert long passed the hope to better our Network. It landed concretely in *control Bianca Monroe.* In the end, I had a feeling the Sisterhood had little to do with this discussion.

"I have a better idea, Council Member. My father and Regina are inside. Merrick is on the way. Why don't you come in? We'd be happy to hear your side and discuss this agreement—as well as the impact it will exert over Alkarra. Your motivation to protect witches from the *unsavory types that threaten our peace with their confidence and gate-jumping,*" I quoted her own article with a welcoming smile, "is something all of us would love to discuss with you."

She bobbled a second time, caught in a crossfire.

Unable to move forward or retreat. When she gave no response, puzzlement on her features, I leaned closer.

"Are you mute, Council Member?"

Her cheeks flushed crimson.

"Here's the problem that I see," I continued. "You think I care about your opinion or the opinion of witches in the Network. I don't. You think I care that you're splashing my name in articles, destroying my reputation. You think this is in the name of safety. You don't seek safety, Council Member. You seek control. I will not have my name smeared with something so heinous."

Taking advantage of her dumbstruck stare, I closed the discussion with a swish of my hand and a firm voice. "There will be no signature."

"Say it," she hissed, eyes flaring. Snow collected along the rim of her hood, brightening the wild affect. "Say that the Sisterhood is gone."

"It's gone."

My immediate, toneless response squelched her ire. Licking her lips, she stuck out a hand. "Make a vow with me that you'll never resurrect it, never work within the bounds, and I will be satisfied. All of this will stop, and you can return to your hidden life in the forest, running these trails."

"No."

Did I imagine fatigue in her eyes? The flicker of . . . something . . . certainly wasn't rage. No, a step beyond. Something softer, yet infinitely more powerful.

"You've proven the kind of witch you are, Georgette, and I never make a bargain with someone controlling, nefarious, or overreaching. Have a good evening."

Snow swirled around me as I twirled.

"This isn't over!" she called. "You've chosen the hard path, Bianca! I gave you a chance to make this simple. To leave with grace and live your life. Whatever happens from here out, this is on you!"

Screaming shrew, Papa muttered.

You might want to follow that shrew after she leaves, I countered, glancing at him through the window as I strode closer. *She knows where you live.*

His lips puckered into a frown. *Excellent point. I'll return soon.*

I felt no joy, no sense of winning, when the monster stole her way through the woods and returned to her lair, where she plotted to unleash yet another round of pain. Regina opened the door as I reached for the handle and pulled me into her arms.

"She's a bully, Bianca."

I nodded against her, the snow on my cape melting. The reminder was one I desperately needed: no matter how much others might rail against me, I never stood alone.

Reddish curls spilled onto Regina's shoulders when she giggled. "The good gods bless her, but Derek's going to put a memory charm on that woman she won't soon break. She'll never find her way back to this place."

An hour later, Georgette remained little more than an unpleasant afterthought. Steaming hot pie piped in front of me, issuing heat into the air that smelled like beef, onions, and peas. The golden crust crumbled to buttery goodness. My mouth watered.

Jacqueline bustled around the table, setting out plates. She placed one in front of her empty spot, next to Tysen. Regina followed, scooping hearty spoonfuls of meat pie onto each. When Merrick reached to pinch a piece of crust, Jacqueline slapped his hand.

"Wait until all the plates are distributed, you bog monster."

At *bog monster,* Tysen hid a laugh behind a cough, which amplified Merrick's irritation. I reached a hand onto Merrick's knee and squeezed. He placed his hand on top, relaxing through the shoulders. Rognvald loomed at the end of the table, not far from Regina's father, who laughed so hard he wheezed. Rognvald's twisted expression, which meant he clearly didn't understand the joke, made my suppressed hilarity worse.

Regina called over the rising din, "Everyone settle in, please! Dinner is ready to eat, and then we can plan." She pointed at Papa, Merrick, Rognvald, and Tysen—but skipped Chi and Gregary. "I'll have no shenanigans tonight. We have a mission to plan. Each one of you better eat, and like it, so you're not cranky. *Then* we will get to work."

Papa pressed a hand to his chest, affronted. Her sparkling, coy smile held extra intensity for him. Twirling her finger toward him, she murmured, *"Especially* you, Derek Black. Eat." She waved to the food.

He winked.

Like obedient sons, they dove into their food. Papa slid Regina's father—a man we only knew as Apa—a glass of cold water. Tysen ribbed Rognvald about the missed joke, who didn't take it very well, while Chi watched with a pleasantly bemused expression, as if he'd never seen such a thing called *family dinner.* Tysen's quick attention, haste to get Jacqueline whatever she wanted before she could ask for it, made my lips twitch. She fluttered under the attention. Gregary ate and stared into the distance, looking preoccupied. Every swallow was strained, and I wondered if the family setting without his children pained him.

The pleasant laughter dissipated my tension in the wake of Georgette's visit. Leda finished up a few things at home with her parents and would arrive after we cleaned up dinner.

Chi's quiet voice cut through the other layers of sound when he said to me, "You had a visitor a little while ago, I hear."

All silenced. Their eyes shot to mine. I nodded, heaving a rueful sigh.

"Georgette."

Rognvald leaned his forearm on the table edge. "What did that prune have to say?" Affronted, he turned to Papa. "And how'd she know where you lived?"

Papa grinned. "I took care of it."

Gregary huffed a breath and set his fork aside. Rognvald pointed at him. "Don't you know Georgette personally, Gregary?"

He shrugged. "She's childhood friends with my . . . wife." He almost choked on the word before finishing in a dark mutter. "I don't know Georgette well."

The revelation surprised me.

His attempts to keep his handfasting together have failed, Merrick said. *His wife is not only requesting the obliteration, but trying to keep his children away from him by citing his job is dangerous. It's growing uglier everyday. He hasn't seen his children since she took them weeks ago. He tracked them, but he's too afraid to confront her in case she says he's stalking them and unsafe.*

My heart softened for Gregary. That explained why he tripped over the word *wife*, and carried a menacing energy at the reminder.

Undaunted, Rognvald pressed. "Has Georgette always been this determined and angry?"

Gregory replied with a single-shoulder shrug. Accepting his reluctance, Rognvald concluded with, "She's a problem, B. Watch her."

Rognvald's use of my family nickname had a stirring effect, but I wouldn't embarrass him by acknowledging it. I nodded, tucking the warning aside. A flash of white-blonde hair drew my gaze to the window, where Leda stood outside. Papa spelled the door open, and Leda hurried within, bringing snow and wind gusts.

She blushed seeing us gathered around mostly empty plates. "Sorry! I thought—"

Papa waved her in. "No problem. You're right on time. You'll want to hear this story anyway, Leda. Bianca has a new one."

She cast a curious look my way, and I nodded. Regina stood up to dish the last of the pie onto a plate, which Leda refused with a shake of her hand and a smile while she bustled in, unwinding a scarf. She kept herself busy laying her wet, snowy layers by the fire while I made quick work of recounting Georgette's confrontation. The retelling wiped out our happy environment.

"You did well, Bianca," Chi said. "Sometimes strength is standing still and holding ground."

Touched, I said, "Thank you, Chi."

Leda lowered into a chair Regina provided. Thoughts moved behind her eyes. Regina swirled a hand around the table. "Gentlemen, you're on dish duty, while the ladies prepare for Leda and Bianca's plan and the Brotherhood's involvement. Shouldn't take you long."

She waved them into action. Too many burly bodies stood at the same time to do her bidding, so they bashed into each other like balls turned loose. Leda suppressed a smile by rolling her lips. Jacqueline bustled to my side and threw her arms around me. "Thank you," she whispered.

"For what?"

"Talking to Merrick about me and Tysen. He's been . . . tolerable . . . instead of unbearable for the last several days. I imagine you had something to do with it."

"He loves you, in his own overbearing way."

Her eyes shone. "I really like Tysen," she whispered. My heart hiccuped, remembering the thrill of twitterpation with Merrick. The longing to see him, the excitement with every light touch. At the time, I wanted to clobber him over the head for making me sprint and haul water and cut firewood. Still . . . there had been an undercurrent of elation underpinning every touch. Handfasting had deepened the emotion.

I squeezed Jacqueline's hands. "Tysen is wonderful."

Ten minutes later, we reconverged around the table with Leda and I occupying opposite ends. Firelight flickered in a silvery glow while she distributed papers. She'd spent the last ten minutes duplicating the fact sheet for each person present, including Apa, who listened with great interest and a keen curiosity.

"These are the details we've gathered from High Priestess Alina, which adds details to Bianca and Gregary's sleuthing of the Thabit tribe." Leda stood tall, neck straight. "Including a roughly drawn map. In summary, the Thabit tribe inhabits the area around the oasis. They have five different camps that resemble a star. We suspect the Thabit tribe packs up their camps and moves every two weeks. This creates a rotational pattern that, according to tribal culture, enables them to keep hold on that oasis."

Her fine eyebrows elevated, both hands aloft. "My

initial and preliminary research into the subject revealed that an oasis is *claimed* if the tribe that runs it can protect all of its borders all the time. In addition, they must continue their nomadic life."

"If they don't?" Papa asked.

"They forfeit their claim to the land and lose tribal respect. Other tribes could descend en masse and slaughter without recrimination." She bit her bottom lip, gaze narrowed. "Brutal, and perhaps a little strange and off-putting, but there is a system."

Each witch skimmed the provided information. I watched them instead, mulling over my plan to piece the mission together. This would be my first time presenting a plan to a Brotherhood crowd greater than one and organized so far in advance. Other situations had been vastly different.

With Greyson, I'd plunged into Carcere on my own. With the Eastern Network insurrection, I had involved only Tysen. With the clannish witches, I needed a group with me as the centralized leader. The progressive stair stepping of each learning opportunity required more skill each time.

Once each witch met her eyes again, Leda silently turned the meeting to me. I stood up.

"I have a plan, and it requires all of you. I can't say when it'll happen, because it depends on when tribal security lowers again. Gregary and I made a bit of a stir in order to gain the information we have, but it was necessary. I'd assume a week will buy us enough lessening of guards, but it might be two."

Rognvald set his parchment down. "We've sat on missions for years in the past. A few days doesn't mean anything as long as expectations are firmly established."

I pressed my fingertips into the table and smiled.

"Happy to hear that. Because this one will be multi-faceted, complicated, and relies on quick magic and ready skill in order to save all the clannish witches."

Chapter Twenty-Four

The forest embraced Leda and me early the next morning. Our breaths trailed in stringy wisps and midwinter's kiss graced my cheeks. I thought of the Western Network and rolling sands and broiling heat and pulled my coat a little tighter around me, grateful for the trees' stalwart presence.

You belong to us.

We belong to you.

Leda daintily stepped over slushy puddles, leaping icy patches in between roots, hands out to the side for balance. Her nose wrinkled. She hated my preferred sort of "meeting", which meant walking through Letum Wood while we discussed necessities. As she had nowhere else that guaranteed our privacy quite like these woods, she tolerated my rare requests. The trees, on alert, watched for magic and witches.

So far, all remained winter silent.

We had a few minutes of walking before Michelle and Nicholas' house appeared, and we needed to finish our current topic before we arrived. Little Sanna and Isadora would squeal their way into our day with the most delightful distractions.

Leda's waning chatter showed signs of finalizing a minutes-long explanation about working with the Brotherhood in our current underground mode. She'd drifted into a side tangent about establishment of processes that made me sleepy. I tried to pick my energy up off the ground, and bring my thoughts into clarity.

"I think the mission is bound to succeed," she declared, landing on a rock.

"I'm glad to hear that."

Leda avoided a frozen, shriveled mushroom encased in ice and sent me a cutting glare. "Were you listening?"

"Yes. I'm also thinking."

"Don't think your way into unduly complicating this mission, please," she retorted. "Despite the intricacies, the mission is simple. Get in, find the witches, get out."

I understood her hesitation over me complicating a fairly simple goal, though simple wasn't the same as easy. Because the phrase the tribal leader uttered still haunted me days later, and with no clearer understanding, I hadn't settled on any sort of certainty.

We need more of the right clannish witches. Thus far, there's only one.

What did it mean? How could clannish witches be right, or wrong? It might mean a specific clan? A skillset? Or . . . something else.

Something foul moved in the background, and I hadn't found the true motive yet. The Thabit tribe enslaved the clannish witches without obvious compensation in order to free up warriors to work for the oasis. Clearly, ulterior motives existed.

"Your mission plan is sound, Bianca. You should be proud of it."

"Thanks."

Effusive praise from Leda came so rarely, I clutched the compliment. Having her at my side last night was a welcome boon. She filled in missing details, and I took action. Together, we made a dynamic, well-fitted pair.

A distant laugh, then scream, drew our attention ahead. Out of the forest depths, a pitched roof jutted between evergreen branches.

A voice called out, "Ho the trail!"

"Ho the house!" I shouted back. Nicholas laughed as we rounded a trail corner, opening their quaint foresters cottage to view. Michelle stepped onto a rickety porch, holding Isadora in her arms. Priscilla emerged with Tomasso clinging to her skirts. They waved, calling for us.

Tonight was the Alkarra-wide Yule celebration. Priscilla would host Camila at the school, as well as girls without families to return to, Ava included. Baxter would join them. Nicholas, Michelle, and her brothers would amass here when dark began to fall. Leda planned to spend Yule evening with her family, and the next day with Hiddleston's. Michelle had suggested a Yule lunch to be together during the holiday before families dissolved into their separate entities.

Strange, the constant roll of time, whirling ahead on self-propelled momentum, while taking us with it.

A chubby pair of legs bore down the trail. Leda opened her arms for Sanna to sprint into them with a jubilant shriek. Isadora toddled from the porch, her drooling grin welcoming us. Nicholas waved from a woodpile dusted with snow, ax slung over one shoulder.

When so many young bodies lay under the earth, why should you enjoy this happiness? Tyrant inquired.

A ball lodged in my throat. *Please,* I pled. *Not here. Not today. Happiness awaits.*

I would wager the Gallo family pleaded the same before their execution, Tyrant muttered heartlessly. He mocked me with his next words. *Please, not here. Not today. Happiness awaits.* When I conjured no response, he laughed.

I froze. Something in little Sanna's bouncing curls. Her jubilant smile. The innocence in her eyes swept me to Gallo house. There had been no very young children there, only beloved daughters. Sick daughters. Sanna's delightful giggle interposed over Ricardo Gallo's dying daughter, seeping into death before my eyes. I'd taken advantage of his weakened emotional state, and led him to slaughter.

A faltering beat became my heart. I didn't have the strength to fight Tyrant. While Leda spun Sanna through the air, and Isadora toddled her way to my arms, I attempted to recover myself. Extracting from the memories was difficult. Nigh impossible.

Desperate, I said only, *I hear you, Tyrant. I get it.*

Tyrant paused.

There were daughters there that night, I continued, remembering the smell of swamp, the quiet coughs. *It was awful. Their memory has never left. Certainly not his daughter as she drew her final breath. Her eyes. Her caving, sick chest. Weak coughs. The other women, trying to be brave and bright and cheerful, but I could hear the truth in their tones.*

Silence. Blessed silence. When had he ever silenced because of what I said? Normally, I had to wrangle him into submission. Ignore him.

I didn't like it, either. Had no idea what we'd be walking into at Magnolia Castle.

Does it matter? he sniped. *You did it anyway.*

My arms and legs stiffened, held fast by guilt. As if I'd thrown open a flood, I couldn't extract from the wash, the tide, the torrent of murkiness and misery. Tyrant gathered his strength again, plunging me into the dark place. Bodies discarded on the floor. Puddles of blood. Ricardo Gallo, immobile under my magic. Layer after layer, I infused the incantations that would claim his life. Without me, he might have lived. The entire Gallo *family* might have lived.

Oh, how those memories burned.

Replaying those horrible moments took something out of me. Formerly high energy shrank. Excitement for the luncheon waned, and I wanted to plunge into the forest and leave. Something tickled my ankle, grounding me. The desire to flee became curiosity, and I glanced down.

Letum ivy.

Sorrow, the trees crooned. *We feel your sorrow.*

Grandfather, I thought, helpless. My word, a plea. *Grandfather.*

Isadora, mere steps away, shrieked, arms held up to me. Her grasping, chubby firsts opened and closed their gummy, delightful fingers. Leda and Sanna's spinning motion slowed. I felt Leda's stare as powerfully as my rigid body. Isadora stumbled, grasping my dress to keep from falling. But I couldn't grab her.

My body wouldn't move.

Ricardo's house. His daughters. The gravestones, the tears. His wife. The witches. The eaves that held life no more.

Empty.

Black.

My skirt tugged as Isadora whined, babbling for me. From a great distance, Leda asked, "Bianca? What's wrong?"

Tyrant's chilling voice invaded my mind. *Why do you*

deserve life? Why should you laugh? Who are you to dole out life and death?

I blinked back tears. *His daughters didn't deserve it either. I never thought they deserved it.*

And yet . . . he hissed.

. . . their ghosts haven't left me, I snapped. *Not once. Hardly an hour has passed that I don't think of what I brought to the Gallo family, or hear you in my mind.*

He growled a barky, *You plan to continue, Sisterhood. You plan for* more *of this, and why? Do you like something in the power? Are you a murderer?*

Tyrant dissolved. My elbows and knees surged to liquid. I collapsed, masking weakness by wrapping my arms around little Isadora, burying my face in her neck, and sinking into her delighted giggle.

I stepped into the love she provided and tried to hide my trembling knees.

* * *

Merrick's and my first Yule log as a handfasted couple burned in the hearth that evening. The enchanted wood had been smoldering since after my friend's lunch, sending a light blue haze into the sky. A farewell to last year. In an hour, the color would morph to pale yellow. An invocation for blessings next year.

At the castle, festivities abounded. Parties, a dance, and several gift exchanges. Most witches would scatter to their individual homes afterward, tucked against the bitter chill. In the North, Kalli and Drogo nestled in their cottage, safe from blizzarding storms, and Papa, Regina, and Apa wrote their regrets to burn, strung popcorn on strings while counting their blessings to come, and laughed together.

I lay in Merrick's arms, fingertips trailing the bronzed firelight on his skin. The quiet cadence of a story he told me occupied my thoughts. When he stopped, a comforting silence fell. Here, I was safe. Here, Tyrant could not be.

Only Merrick.

Me.

Grandfather's memory.

There is more to you than the Sisterhood, he said, as one of the last things I'd heard from his voice. *There is more to you than Merrick. There is more to you than what the Council deems worthy of acclaim. Choose what makes all the parts of you happiest, and you can never go astray.*

This, I thought, relaxing against Merrick. *Grandfather, this is what makes me the happiest.*

Merrick gently flipped me onto my back, his hand in my hair. The pad of his thumb traced my lower lip.

"Where are you, B?"

Pressing my hand to his, I said, "With Grandfather."

He smiled. "It's a good place to be." His lips sealed over mine, beckoning and accepting. He asked nothing of the darkness that broiled inside, of the tempest I'd glimpsed today and saw in minute capacity. I could not state it. And though I knew he saw it, that Leda likely told him of my strange moment outside of Michelle's, he did not ask. His steady touch kept me from giving into Tyrant's storm, providing my refuge.

I curled into Merrick, and there I stayed.

Chapter Twenty-Five

Gregary spoke to my mind early the next morning.

Are you busy?

Merrick and another Protector—Erik, I thought—were off on a quick mission per Rognvald's request that morning, with plans to return tonight. To hear from Gregary jarred me out of my sip of hot coffee.

What's going on?

I have something I need you to see.

Where?

At the oasis.

What is it?

Council Member Georgette.

* * *

The Thabit oasis bustled with bawling camals, hissing water under enchanted glass, and witches gathered restlessly in queues. The normally calm, orderly oasis had an edge of tension, and greater warriors rimmed the outside than normal.

Bartered goods passed back and forth, with Thabit warriors scowling at approaching crowds. Most witches had enough sense to form a line, empty jugs held at their side, while Thabit warriors and women traded in exchange for precious water. Anything from currency to clay pots to clothes passed back and forth.

I skirted the edge, wearing a fabric hood, my skin transformed to a dark brown, my hair light yellow. Sandals protected my feet from the hot sand. For good measure, I flung empty water pouches over my shoulder.

Standing on tiptoe, I peered over the throng.

Where do you see Georgette? I asked. Various members of the team planned to take turns watching the oasis and Thabit camps over the next week, so Gregary's presence hadn't surprised me. His *finding* did.

She's standing by the far line, near the back, lurking around. Purple wrap around her neck and hair. Half-hides her, but not enough.

Georgette revealed herself through sheer presence. The way she held her shoulders—low, angled down—and her daring, distrustful eyes. Western witches were accustomed to this chaos and insecurity. A poorly hidden Central Network Council Member was clearly out of her depth.

She'd taken pains to slightly alter her appearance, darkening her hair color and donning a muted-yet-bright thick linen of desert witches—thick enough to dissuade the sun but not thick enough to contain heat. Simple transformative magic swept her face. The spell that female witches used the most. It thickened their eyelashes, smoothed wrinkles. It remained in place for an hour, at most. Sometimes longer, depending on concentration and repetition power. Nothing that hid her as Georgette, surely.

What is she doing? I muttered in exasperation.

Gregary didn't reply.

I angled to stride behind Georgette, turning before she saw me. Her head swung my direction after I left, as if she'd sensed my stare. As I slipped farther away, my thoughts raced to form a plan. By all rights, she could go anywhere in Alkarra she wanted. If she wanted to leave the Central Network during the Yule holiday and wander the West, who cared? But that couldn't be her intent. Not *here* of all places, and certainly not after she found me at Papa's and promised greater vengeance.

Any idea if Georgette has friends at this particular oasis? I asked Gregary, wondering where he stood.

No idea.

Could you find out?

He replied with a hard, *No.*

Fair enough. I didn't need inside information to understand that Georgette wasn't at the Thabit oasis by circumstance. She'd reveal herself soon enough, anyway. A little patience would go a long way. I ran my tongue over my teeth as I cut behind the magicked trees and flowed along existing trails.

Firmly behind Georgette now, I stopped to peer at the congregation near the warriors. For good measure, I spelled a bucket into my hands from home. The wooden circle, reinforced with metal bands, was a far cry from the pottery to which the West ascribed.

Pondering my options, I quickly realized that I had two. I liked neither of them. First, I could approach Georgette and demand to know why she was there. Foolish, for several reasons. I already knew why she was stalking the Thabit oasis—to find me, presumably, in the middle of a mission. Second, I could do nothing and observe. Other options existed in the middle, but staring at the edges gave me a glimpse of extremes.

Stewing on this, I leaned my shoulder against a tree. Jikes, but how did Georgette *know*? How had she dug her long fingers into the Thabit oasis?

How long ago did you spot her? I asked.

Twenty minutes.

Did you see her arrive?

No.

Hmm.

After several minutes, a barky question sharpened Gregary's voice. *You're not going to approach? Do something about this?*

What would I do?

He proffered no ideas.

Shoving off the tree, I added, *Only a fool would wait around for her to find me. I'm not her mother or her nanny.*

You think it's wise to leave her?

You want to approach Council Member Georgette and explain your presence? There's nothing here for her to find that creates a problem for the mission, nor for me. Who could she talk to that would know about me?

As I said the words, my mouth went dry. Georgette brightened when a woman appeared—a woman I would never forget. The loud-mouthed, angry Central Network witch from my last visit.

Stef.

Jikes.

My pride went before this rather ugly fall.

Georgette and Stef clasped hands and exchanged warm smiles. I couldn't read lips, nor hear what they said, but I didn't need to be that close to see their natural friendliness. New, or recent? Hasan lurked a few steps away, a scowl darkening his low brow. I resisted the urge to clutch my Volare, which I hadn't brought. Not since meeting Alfea.

I take that back, I said slowly.

Gregary asked, *Who is that?*

No friend of mine, I muttered.

Both women linked arms at the elbow. Stef tugged Georgette beyond the water lines and farther into the oasis. *Could there be a very, very,* very *distant chance that Stef and Georgette are . . . somehow related?* I asked weakly.

Not at all.

Switching tactics, I asked Leda, *Do you have a minute?*

She didn't respond right away, forcing me to slide into a loose tailing of the pair. Stef's hands arced overhead, fingers twisted, as she regaled a story. Georgette laughed. When Leda replied, several minutes had passed and the women had paused to talk under a shady spot.

Only a minute. What do you need?

Do you know much about Georgette's personal life?

There isn't much to know. Single. A few siblings, some nieces and nephews. Both parents are aged, but alive. Happy enough family, for the most part. No egregious records, or anything to set her apart.

Any sisters?

No idea.

Female cousins?

She snapped, *Why are you asking?*

Any reason for her to be at the Thabit oasis as we speak, meeting with a woman with a Chatham City accent that saw my face and my Volare?

Her irritation withered. *Ah . . . no.*

Didn't think so, I quipped.

To Gregary, I said, *Thank you. I'll clear out.*

Deadpan, he repeated, *You're leaving?*

Yes. There's nothing for me to do. If you want to listen to their conversation, please do. Let me know if they say anything interesting, but it won't make a difference. With our plan in place, I won't return to the oasis unless necessity dictates it, and only in the depths of night. If Georgette is here to sabotage something, and she focuses her time on the oasis, all the better for us. Besides, I reasoned, as much for myself as for him, *if she finds me, we're just making her life easier.*

Understood, Gregary replied, and hard disapproval lined his reply.

I returned to the Central Network.

Chapter Twenty-Six

The high-backed chairs outside of Scarlett's office couldn't contain me, so I paced in front of her office—invisibly—and waited for her to finish another meeting with our new High Priest. Since the announcement days ago, he'd been locked behind closed doors in sundry meetings.

Hiddleston sat at the desk directly in front of the double doors, ignoring the occasional scuffle of my foot on the ground. He planted himself in that spot ages ago, decreasing meeting interruptions to null. His broad shoulders and professional, flat affect encouraged no one closer. Except Leda.

With that thought, Leda approached Scarlett's office while speaking to a flock of Underassistants. She halted halfway to the door. She might sense me, but more likely her intimate knowledge of Scarlett's schedule reminded her that I was next.

And Scarlett was *late*.

Through the magic, Leda said, *Let me guess—*
She's late.

That's not uncommon with Talmund. He, understand-ably, has a lot of questions.

Moving again, she placed a pile of folders onto the desk near Hiddleston and slipped around to stand next to him. In front of Underassistants and castle workers, they displayed purely professional facades. *If I didn't know how deeply they cared about each other, I wouldn't have guessed.*

The left office door cracked open and drew inward. "Tomorrow," Scarlett said with a bolstering and familiar affection. "The Empowerment ceremony begins at noon. You'll have a few hours to . . . pull together again . . . and then we'll attend our first official dinner with the other Network leaders."

Talmund nodded as he widened the door. He seemed no worse for wear, though exhaustion ran through his features. His short-cropped hair, dusted with touches of gray, was a little rumpled, as if he'd run his hands through the strands. I could vaguely imagine the ruffling that his transition to High Priest had caused. Comportment was how I remembered him. Talmund, former Head of Guardians, held himself together well, and always.

"Thank you, High Priestess." He acknowledged Leda, Hiddleston, and the Underassistants with a professional nod. He spun, sharp stare honed in on Hiddleston.

"Are you available as we discussed?"

Hiddleston swallowed, nodded. "Yes, sir."

Talmund waited while Hiddleston stood, gathering his favorite quill made from a hawk feather and an old ink pot he swore prevented flaking. A confused expression crossed Leda's face. When she opened her mouth to speak, Scarlett silenced her with an upheld hand. The High Priestess and her Assistant stared at each other.

Leda paled.

Her chest began to rise and fall quickly. Scarlett tilted her head minutely, eyebrow lifting. I'd been on the receiving end of *that* silent command and it meant *don't say a word.* Leda clamped her lips together. In that strange moment, she resembled the frightened teenage girl at Miss Mabel's School for Girls, clutching to her textbooks and hiding behind the library.

Only the lightest touch of Hiddleston's hand on Leda's elbow as he slipped behind her gave away this odd moment. What it meant, I couldn't fathom, because Hiddleston didn't quite meet her eyes. Leda stared at Talmund and Hiddleston as they retreated down the hall, Talmund talking fast.

Her hands bunched into fists, nostrils flared, and jaw tightened. I almost reached out to touch her, but with an expression like that, she might bite.

Scarlett saved the day. "Leda, will you accompany me in my office?" Standing back, Scarlett swept a hand into the room. My cue to enter, so I slipped inside. "I'm sure the Underassistants can maintain the desk for Hiddleston's brief absence. Thank you."

Leda, what's going on?

I don't know! He's not responding to me, Leda hissed.

As I suspected long ago, she must have brought Hiddleston into the communication magic. Little vixen. She'd never outright confirmed, but I hadn't asked.

I'm sure everything is fine.

It's not!

Scarlett whirled around at her desk, waiting. I removed my invisibility spell after the door closed, and she smiled a greeting.

"As planned. Thank you for coming, Bianca. Please, forgive my delay. As you can imagine, Talmund has a lot of questions." Her astute gaze slid to Leda, who stared at the floor. If she clenched her jaw any harder, her teeth would crack. I could imagine her barrage of inquiries to Hiddleston.

"Good to see you, Your Highness," I said. My greeting went unnoticed. Scarlett kept her gaze on Leda until, finally, Leda lifted her eyes. She drew in a shoulder-expanding breath, pure stubbornness in her muted glare. Such a raw display of emotion was beyond unprecedented, but not beyond belief.

Gently, Scarlett said, "It's time for him to have his own opportunity, Leda."

"He hid it from me!"

"He didn't tell you because Talmund and I asked him *not* to tell you. Until we knew for certain that Hiddleston was a good fit and wanted the position, no one knew." Sighing, Scarlett added, "The Captain that Talmund brought with him from the Guardians has been ill-prepared for Chatham Castle. Talmund is already behind, struggling to understand the culture, and his Assistant was making it worse. Talmund *needs* Hiddleston. As you can imagine, there's no one more suited to the job than Hiddleston, though he will be missed amongst my own team. He deserves the growth, as you did."

Oh.

Oh.

Talmund planned to hire Hiddleston, and Hiddleston kept it from Leda. Talmund, especially, would require an Assistant he could trust. One outside of the Guardians, who understood the castle and the political game and the way it worked. Like Papa had chosen Baxter, someone skilled in Papa's weakest areas, Talmund needed someone like Hiddleston that understood the daily ebbs and flows, could manage witches, and aspired to make a difference.

Hiddleston would receive one of the most powerful positions in Chatham Castle.

Assistant to the High Priest.

Which took him away from Leda.

My instinct to soothe stirred to life, but I tamped it down. I couldn't fix this. All emotion cleared Leda's face. She lifted her chin. "Of course, Your Highness."

"You're upset."

"Not with you."

"Hiddleston doesn't deserve your wrath for doing what his High Priestess and High Priest commanded of him."

After all we'd endured together, I thought I'd seen all facets of Leda. Until this moment, I realized I'd never truly seen her enraged. If she turned that power to Georgette, our defamation would end.

"When?" Leda asked.

I didn't understand the lacking question, but Scarlett seemed to follow. She folded her hands in front of her as she responded. "Hiddleston is completing the final interview right now. Talmund told me he plans to extend the offer right after, and work would commence as quickly as Hiddleston can pack."

Her fists trembled. "I see," she whispered.

"Forgive me, Leda," Scarlett said gently, "but I don't think you do."

Leda wrenched herself together one breath at a time. Her fingers relaxed. Taut neck eased. She attempted a calm outward display, but the inner wrath had only grown. Without a hint of emotion in her voice, Leda said, "Hiddleston is well suited to work with Talmund, Your Highness. He'll make a strong Assistant to the High Priest."

Scarlett hid a sigh. "I'm glad we agree on that. If you need any help with the transition—"

"I can handle it."

"Thank you."

I attempted a pithy query through the magic.

Do you want to talk—

No.

Her immediate, quick snap burned like fire. I pulled my metaphorical hand away.

I understand. Let me know if you do.

She turned away. Tears sparkled in her eyes. I sent a message to Priscilla, who would inform Michelle. Something in Michelle's unruffled speech, her steady work cadence, soothed Leda. She opened more to Michelle than Priscilla or me.

Leda departed the office without another word.

Scarlett cleared her throat, pulling my attention again. "How are you, Bianca?"

"Busy, Your Highness."

"I'm happy to hear that. Leda spoke about an issue with Council Member Georgette that she felt ought to be reported to me tonight. What happened?"

"Georgette was in the Western Network, at the Thabit oasis, speaking to one of the only witches that can identify me through the Volare."

Scarlett's eyes darkened. "Georgette?"

"Yes, Your Highness. I kept this mission, and the details, from you before, but Leda and I agree that the time has come to tell you and get your counsel." *Because Grandfather isn't here*, I silently added, and my stomach twisted at the strangeness. I added to Scarlett, "I informed Alina, and she's given me permission to share with you."

She waved me to proceed.

While I filled her in on the details, including our rescue of the clannish witches and involvement with the Brotherhood, Scarlett stared out the window with her hands at her side. I'd never seen such stillness in a leader. Mildred would have snapped at me to fix my own problems. Stella would have frowned, moved items around her desk while she thought. Scarlett turned inward, pulling her thoughts to a center no one else accessed.

After a time, she said, "While her visit may not at all be related to Alina's mission, I can't fathom a world where it's not. She has an extensive family, but as far as I know, they're all in the Central Network."

I bit back the urge to say, *that doesn't discount cousins or distant family,* because I couldn't bring myself to interrupt her train of thought. Part of me didn't want to believe this development, because it made all the once-clear water very murky and far more difficult.

"Stef is from the Central Network." I sighed. "She could be related or connected to anybody."

"Maybe."

"We plan to execute my plan within the next few weeks, Your Highness, when the Thabit tribe has shown signs of relaxing their warrior patrols. Tension is still high. We're watching their behaviors to determine their least protected time. Merrick, Gregary, Chi, Tysen, and myself are studying each camp. We have our assignments and we feel confident. Alina says the clannish witches will begin ice cutting at their next lake when we're ready to start the mission. They're traveling there now."

Scarlett hummed before putting a hand to her chin. "Do you think Georgette is attempting to get in the way of your mission so that she can sabotage it?"

"I think she seeks proof that I'm working as a mercenary so she can blackmail me into signing a paper that says I won't."

"She can't hold you to rules that don't exist in the

Central Network. No one on the Council can tell you what you can or can't do."

"If I've signed the contract, she can."

Scarlett eyed me. "Will you?"

"No."

"Good."

"Georgette can also deepen the mistrust against me."

Scarlett conceded with a lift of her eyebrows. "Yes, which she's already doing with some gusto. I see both sides, Bianca, and agree with facets of both. Unfortunately. Georgette has proven to be a thorn in your side. She may be the first witchy obstacle the Sisterhood has had to face, but she will not be the last."

Her sage words rang of something Grandfather would say, and in them, I found a sense of stable ground. Without him, I still had many witches to trust. Tyrant ramped up to speak, but I prevented his wrathful reply by simply saying, *Not now, please.*

To my astonishment, it worked.

Oblivious to my internal realizations, Scarlett continued. "For my part, I will continue to remain on alert around her. My professional relationship with Council Member Georgette is unchanged, as she continues to be present for the necessities of her Coven."

"Good." I meant it. While I might struggle with Georgette, I didn't want the same to be true for Scarlett, or for Georgette's Coven.

A hint of a smile appeared on Scarlett's face. "I look forward to hearing how your approach works, Bianca. Like your beloved Grandfather, you always come up with the most creative ideas."

* * *

Sprinting through the forest in midwinter had less appeal than during the transition seasons—spring and autumn were mellow and delightful, beckoning me. Summer, thick and sultry with air thick enough to chew, was often miserable. Winter's gelid breath glided in every crevice, freezing each breath I sucked into my lungs.

Still, I ran.

Because my legs demanded it. My heart required it. The trail and trees kept Tyrant at bay. Glittering snow banks and frosty breaths couldn't keep me in. I *had* to be outside, under the canopy. Racing across packed trails created space for my thoughts. Breathing was easier when I asked my body for more, and thus, my thoughts raced with my feet.

My attention slid to Leda. I sent her a quiet, *I'm thinking of you if you need anything,* and received no response. Michelle had written a message to me yesterday evening that said only, *Give her space. She'll be okay.*

Unable to do anything for my best friend, I kept running.

Few witches attempted to find me while I vaulted through the trees and snow. Merrick often joined, and sometimes Papa. No one else. Not Leda, nor Scarlett. They left me to the woods. Which made my surprise all the greater when a looming figure caught my attention. I slowed, snow crunching beneath my boots, and came to a stop five paces from Ambassador Aurora.

She stood in the middle of the trail with a regal grace, gazing at me through narrowed eyes and full lips. She wore a hat, because her wound black curls coiled tight and close to her head provided little relief from the cold. Hints of shoes peeked out from beneath a sweeping wool hem.

Gasping, I asked, "Ambass . . . ador?"

"Miss Monroe."

Forcing myself to straighten, I propped my hands on my hips and stared at her. "What—"

"Am I doing here?" She gazed around, as if just realizing where she stood. "It's really lovely in the forest in the winter. Granted, I don't venture out here much, but I felt inclined to do so today."

Her tone hid something. Not concern, but disquiet.

"What's wrong?"

Aurora rolled her eyes without moving her head. "How do you always manage to ask the wrong question, Miss Monroe? It *is* Miss Monroe, isn't it? Or are you taking your husband's name?"

I swallowed, my breath calming. "I . . . I've had my mind on . . . other things . . ."

"Does he care?"

"No."

"I like Monroe."

"Thanks. I think."

Something must be very wrong for her to hunt me in the forest. I waited her out. Finally, she spread both hands and cried, "Well? Are you going to invite me to your house or not? We need to talk."

* * *

Coffee and tea luffed steam into the air twenty minutes later. Freshly dressed, washed up, and ready to talk, I lowered into a chair across from Aurora, near my snapping hearth.

Cold winter light diffused through the treehouse, coating the world in somber grays. Only the cackling fire imparted heat and color. Goat milk and coffee converged in a mug under my silent spell, buying me time to glaze over the shock of Aurora in my home. I'd never invited an acquaintance here, but I didn't dare refuse Aurora.

She sipped her tea, eyed what little decor we had—neither Merrick nor I desired artful decorations—and cast a general sense of disapproval over everything. The flow of woodgrains and creeping greenery winding inside brimmed my soul with the forest. I couldn't bring myself to cover it up.

Aurora had another sip, canvassing the room, muttering about *boredom* and *can't you find a painting?* in a pithy attempt to control the conversation.

"Utilitarian," she declared.

Over the rim of my coffee mug, I said, "Didn't ask, thanks." The hot brew zipped into my stomach, purling with a heated curl that settled me. I set the mug on the table and stared, hands clasped, elbows on my knees.

"So?"

Finally, she set down her tea. "Well, Miss Monroe, you plate a heartier spread than I expected." Her sarcasm over my less-than-bountiful offerings wasn't lost. "Don't you believe in snacks?"

"Not if I'm in charge of them."

"You *would* say something so obscene."

"Our definitions of obscene vary greatly."

"To my point. You have a problem."

"I have many."

"This particular problem is bigger than you think." Lifting a watch from her skirt pocket, she opened the cover, consulted the interior, and closed it again. "You have an hour before said problem commences."

"What problem is this?"

"Georgette and her first rally. Starts at ten in Chatham City."

My lips rounded. "Oh." I'd utterly forgotten. Leda

warned me days ago, before information gathering kicked off at the oasis. Plans to study the Thabit oasis all afternoon kept me from considering that something important might be happening in the Central Network.

I slurped coffee and strove for idle nonchalance. The last time a high-ranking member of the Central Network held a rally against Papa, terrible dominoes toppled. My magic, wild and untamed after Mama's murder at Mabel's hand, spiraled out like a storm.

Aurora's midnight eyebrow rose with a dramatic crescendo, and without affecting the other. "That's all you have to say? *Oh*? One of the most powerful Council Members in the Central Network is holding a rally against you in Chatham City, and you manage a mere syllable in response?"

I wanted to say, *It's a family thing.* "Georgette holds many events these days, Aurora. I lose track. Besides, it's not exactly the first time a witch in power maligned my family at a rally."

"I've heard all about that other time, but this is something different."

"It must be."

"Why do you say that?"

"For you to find me in the forest and come to my house implies a large problem, Aurora. Whatever you're deriving from my minimal response is not all that I feel. I appreciate the gravity of my situation. I'm not ignoring it, either. I'm . . . choosing my battles."

The first sign of caring appeared in Aurora's distant stare. Sighing like an exasperated parent, she clucked. "This could be more than a *large problem*, Bianca. Witches might become unsafe. I would advise you to stay in your treehouse while it's happening."

"But you know I won't," I said quietly, "and that's why you came."

"Yes."

"You want me to go with you?"

"Yes."

"Why?"

"I want you to attend safely, if you must attend at all."

"And you know I'll attend."

She inclined her head, neck stiff. "I would feel considerably less irritated and distracted if I knew you were safe."

My lips almost twitched into a smile. Aurora would vanish the moment I showed any humor. We played a careful game these days. She pretended not to care, and I pretended not to notice that she did.

"Thank you for the offer, Ambassador, but I will graciously decline."

Huffing, she asked, "You're going alone, then?"

Deciding not to answer her outright, I said, "I'm not that teenage girl anymore. I can handle my magic." I pressed a hand to my chest. "You would know if I couldn't. Witches around me could feel it after Mama died."

"Yes. Marten told me."

Something in her discomfort forced me to study her. "Why do you feel this could be violent and dangerous to me?"

Aurora scooted to the edge of her seat, her empty glasses tipped on her nose. "Because you don't know how deep her roots have grown. I do. Leda has a smaller scope of the real picture here, but neither of you understand everything."

"What are we missing?"

"Georgette's creating unrest amongst witches who were once adamantly against Derek as High Priest. She's given them a reason to emerge again and seek blood—yours. You can't appreciate their hunger to find and overcome an enemy. She's setting you up as the perfect outlet."

A deep chill glided through my veins. Avoiding Georgette had been a necessity, on some level, and a definite strategy on another. It created a blind spot. Aurora was kindly reminding me not to be an idiot. Just because I discounted Georgette and used her to achieve my purposes of making the Sisterhood invisible didn't make it a wise plan.

"Can I ask you a question?"

Aurora scoffed. "Like permission has ever stopped you."

"What do you think Georgette really wants?"

This gave her pause. She held the teacup half off the plate, tilted toward her. She set it down and leaned against the divan, head curled.

"Leda thinks it's political positioning," I continued.

"Maybe."

"Papa thinks Georgette is greedy and power hungry."

"Another possibility."

"Merrick thinks she's delusional."

"What do you think?"

"I don't know," I whispered. "Can a witch be wrong, but also be right?"

Aurora chuckled. "You're asking about every witch when you ask *that* question. We're all wrong, and we're all right, all the time. It's a matter of perspective, and a matter of choice."

I softened. For a moment, it felt like Grandfather returned through her sage wisdom and wry tone. Another reminder he hadn't abandoned me. Noticing my expression, a hint of venom returned to Aurora's stare, as if annoyed I'd caught her caring.

"Some things are wrong, Bianca. Georgette controlling the process of the Sisterhood and destroying opportunities is one of them. Domination, not collaboration, is her end. Whether she's acting in the name of safety or selfishness doesn't matter. Wrong is wrong."

Setting aside her empty tea cup, Aurora stood. She wiped her hands off with a double smack of her palms and called for her coat with a spell. It elevated off a rack near the door and swept over.

"Be wise, Bianca. There aren't many witches I'd enter the forest to warn." Her nose wrinkled, lips puckered, into a sass-filled frown. "Take the compliment."

The fire crackled after her departure. Nursing my coffee, I kept an eye on the clock and let her warnings swirl through my mind. Tyrant attempted to speak, but busy machinations and plans allayed it. No room for regret or guilt today. The remaining minutes passed slowly.

Once the long hand snapped to twelve, I moved into action.

Chapter Twenty-Seven

The rally gathered under torches, rafters, and beams along Chatham City storefronts. Hundreds of witches filled the cobblestone roads, slowing foot traffic to single lanes on either side of a standing crowd. An elevated platform stood in a circle where five streets knotted together. Stupid, really, to host a rally in the middle of a busy morning, but no one involved in Chatham City paid attention to grid structure and efficiency.

It wasn't a rally, but a conflagration.

Transformed to a grubby teenager who lived on the street, no one paid me any attention. Soot marred my face. My hair appeared short and red beneath a shoddy hat. My tattered dress, too short at the ankles, gave way to ratted boots. As a final precaution, I altered my eyes to palest blue.

Murmurs whispered. Papers circulated. Newsboys handed information out by fistfuls to anyone who would hold it. I crouched behind a barrel and peeled a parchment from a frozen puddle top.

Protect Our Lives From Internal Dangers

Shouts prevented me from reading more. I folded the paper, shoved it into a pocket, plucked another from the snow that said **The Sisterhood Failed** across the top.

A familiar voice rang down the road, carried by a spell, requesting silence. Witches faced toward the circle, muttering. The crowd thickened, elbows bonking, witches exclaiming. There must be witches standing at planned locations, propagating Georgette's voice with spells as far as Chatham Road.

Georgette's voice crashed over the silencing crowd. "Thank you for gathering, witches of the Central Network and Chatham City. We are here to discuss many things, including your protection."

An approving cry.

"Your lives!"

Louder.

"And the witches who would threaten both!"

Her choppy sentences provided space for livid audience reactions. With her absolute drivel in my ear, I ducked into an alley, slipped around cast off *Chatham Chatterer* scrolls and a heap of discarded potato peels. Broken wagon wheels stacked high behind a store. Bracing my foot on the sturdiest, I began to climb.

"Do all of you know the witch named Bianca Monroe?"

Georgette stating my name sent a shock through me that I ignored. Jeers replied. I rolled my eyes as I perched on the rickety edge of a wheel. Smattering applause covered my bobbling attempts to climb higher.

"Miss Monroe has a long and storied history with the Central Network. She entered the castle at a young and impressionable age, with a father who has been as dramatic and problematic as the witch herself."

All five wagon wheels swayed. Abandoning that spot, I switched to invisibility, transported to the roof next door. A milliner's shop. I crept along the roof edge where seams would hold, each step intentionally planted. Snowflakes drifted from a slate cloud, pirouetting in livid circles. Wind aggravated them in bursts, brushing my cheeks.

Careful now, Tyrant crooned. *You must keep your own life safe, though you hold little regard for innocent others.*

From this vantage, the crowd swelled to breathtaking proportions, spilling from the inner circle and down every visible street. Georgette stood on the platform, surrounded by a circle of torches. Her gown glowed like liquid gold, mimicking standing fire. As the material ascended, it shifted to burnt orange, crimson, scarlet. Slight movement created a sheen. With her coiffed hair and brilliant dress, she was as mesmerizing as she was poisonous.

She didn't capture my attention, but every witch that stopped their lives to listen to what she had to say. Did they truly join her? Many witches gathered here, but they were a minimalistic representation of the Central Network.

And yet . . .

Merrick's firm voice asked, *Where are you, B?*

I'm safe.

Where? he demanded.

At the rally.

I know, he snapped. *But where?*

Above the milliners near Georgette's platform.

A cheer exploded from the congregation, bursting in a raucous crescendo. Georgette beamed, eyes fluttering, her wide smile taken aback by the energetic response. Basking in the attention, she took her time elevating a hand and requesting calm. Quiet uncurled as quickly as chaos roared.

"Thank you, witches." She laughed softly. "I am so honored we join together in our beliefs, our desires, and our concerns for the future. Thank you for your presence." A hint of sternness sharpened her tone. "Tonight, we are not here to attack Miss Monroe, and I forbid any physical or emotional violence." After a prolonged reluctance, she admitted, "We must acknowledge that she *has* served the Network—however modestly."

An invisible hand touched my shoulder. *I'm here,* Merrick murmured. Grateful, I collapsed against him. Until he crossed an arm around my chest and anchored me, I hadn't realized that I'd been trembling.

"She made trouble!" shouted a nearby witch.

Another cried, "She brought god magic to Alkarra!"

"Then she got rid of it!"

Whoever defended me, their voice was indistinguishable from this vantage. Merrick tightened his arm. He didn't try to convince me to leave. Like always, he stood at my side, his hand in mine. Tyrant grumbled away.

"Gentlewitches," Georgette crooned, "we're here to discuss a government that would allow a witch with preferential treatment to potentially take office. Had Miss Monroe not withdrawn the Sisterhood herself, would her nascent idea have continued? Not with me in charge! Not with me in power!"

"The gods," Merrick muttered.

I couldn't summon the energy to giggle from astonishment. This was the delusional result of Georgette's work laid bare.

"You deserve safety, and you deserve it from the right witches!"

Cries rippled through the crowd. Deafening; so loud I almost didn't hear Leda.

You're there, aren't you?

Yes.

Me too.

Where?

My mother has a friend that lives in downtown Chatham City. I'm standing at her window. I can hear everything. How are you?

I'm with Merrick.

Relief weakened her reply. *Thank you for telling me.* Leda's thinking tone followed, reassuring me that whatever happened between her and Hiddleston, all was not lost. *As expected, Georgette's making a whipping post out of you.*

I didn't know what to say, so I let my silence do the work.

Georgette's words ranged to her plans for Central Network security. To ensure witches were safe from enemies within and without. I winced when she mentioned Greyson. Fragile ground. Scarlett kept Greyson on the Council while High Priestess, but she hadn't appointed him. Georgette's condemnation could point a finger at a High Priestess she shouldn't make an enemy out of.

Would Scarlett truly retaliate? Scarlett wasn't afraid of naysayers, and Georgette knew it, but Scarlett never amplified problems.

Minutes of more rambling, cheers, and brilliant smiles followed. The success of Georgette's gathering appeared to expand by the minute. All of Chatham City turned out to hear. The shouts strengthened.

"How long will you stay?" Merrick asked. "She's closing her statements now, I think. See the torches around her dimming?"

"We can go, but I want to hear what witches are saying as they leave."

"I'll follow you."

Merrick knew my magic signature the way he knew breathing. Trailing me in a busy, disheveled marketplace while invisible would be no hardship. While Georgette spoke her closing words, I slipped down the ladder. Merrick held my hand as we crossed the alley, trodding through slushy puddles. We stalled ten paces from standing witches gawping, wide-eyed, brows knitted. Georgette's echoing refrains sent chills under my skin.

"Together, we'll ensure that the Central Network is protected from within and from without. My office is open to you, witches. Come to me for any of your needs."

Bold, Leda muttered. *She's speaking for the Central Network, not Chatham City. She has no—*

Leda broke off. When she didn't resume, I inquired, *Leda?*

Later, she hastily squeaked. *Later! I just had a thought—*

She didn't speak again.

The torches around Georgette extinguished at once, leaving a vacuum of silence. Chatter filled it within moments. Witches shoved with elbows, lours, muttered threats. Pickpockets scampered between legs, vanishing like smoke. Movement, but not progress, became the crowd.

It's a miracle it hasn't been violent yet, I said to Merrick.

He squeezed my fingers.

Not here.

Somewhere else?

Yes.

Oh, I said, contrite. *That's why you sought me?*

The Brothers are dealing with it.

I'm sorry, Merrick. I should have told you where I landed sooner.

His invisible, searching hand found mine. *We're here together. That's what matters.*

As witches scattered, gaps created space. Carts rolled and animals bellowed. Activity resumed. We invisibly slid into the chaos with our ears opened and my pained heart closed.

Chapter Twenty-Eight

Sand blasted the back of my calves as I stood outside of the third Thabit camp, studying the interior. In the last two days, absolutely nothing had changed except for children scampering around at different hours.

I slunk along the outer ring, where shadows swayed, searching for clannish witches. They could be difficult to locate. My eyes became deft at spotting their sable hair, low eyes. They never left camp, unless they buried waste in the sand.

Before Gregary and I swept through the living areas, tribal witches didn't bother watching the menial tasks. To where would the clannish witch escape? Today, they still watched like desert hawks. Three warriors had been patrolling each camp at night, up from their previous one warrior, but they had now scaled back to two in the night. Heightened paranoia continued around clannish witches, though it waned. The environment wasn't quite ready.

Second counting confirms your number, I said to Merrick. *Fifteen clannish witches at camp three.*

I counted twelve at camp two.

Smiling, I said, *Me, too.*

With two warriors guarding camp two.

Confirmed.

They're lowering protection a little, but not much, he murmured. His tone elevated. *We're a good team, you and I, Miss Monroe. Think we should get handfasted?*

I snorted. *Fat chance.*

If we'd been together, he would have laughed. Rather serious, he said, *Transporting to camp one for next confirmation.*

I'll go to four.

Understood.

We swapped camps to confirm the number of clannish witches just in case something kicked off our plan early, for which we still had no firm date. The waiting game might kill me first.

Tysen and Gregary executed the same counting task earlier today. It allowed each mission member a more intimate knowledge of each camp, though one Protector would handle one camp. In case events lurched sideways, we'd be prepared to assist.

Details, details, abounded. The Sisterhood wouldn't plow into this problem, as it had the Eastern Network insurrection. Complexity had entered the fighting ring. I grappled with it, willing to learn. Eager to tangle into details and forget Georgette, ignore Tyrant, put off grieving Grandfather.

Less than an hour later, I finalized camp four.

Eight at camp four. Our lowest clannish witch count, I said.

Confirmed, Merrick replied. *I counted ten at camp one. Same.*

We started at camp five, with nine clannish witches.

Fifty-four, I said to all in the group, my teeth pinching my lower lip. *Merrick and I confirmed fifty four clannish witches against five camps.*

Gregary said, *Confirmed.*

Us, too, Tysen replied. *They're in agreement with Rognvald's earlier report.*

As Head of the Brotherhood, Rognvald spied on his own in the predawn hours. His work on our mission, despite the weight of Brotherhood leadership he carried, hadn't suffered. His numbers matched mine and Merrick's. He reported the location of each clannish witch in every camp without fail. He had the memory of an ironclad vault, as well as a real fear of being left out of something fun and dangerous.

We're one short. Digging my fingers into a pocket, I touched Alina's latest letter, as if my fingers could draw the details to my mind. *Alina said fifty-five have been reported on their last count.*

The plan relied wholly on stealth and speed at the same time, and we couldn't afford mishaps, nor leaving a single witch behind. After we acted with total and holistic force, the Thabit tribe might take drastic measures against any clannish witches that remained.

I'm surprised it matches, Merrick said. *Considering the clans hadn't been reporting all of them until more recently. Could be a clerical error, B.*

I won't bank on it. Besides, the clans are *reporting witches now that we've saved a few,* I countered. *They're more willing to come forward when there's hope and action.*

We'll keep an eye out, Tysen said. A suggestion not to worry about it.

Days ago, Haruto, Alfea, and another camp leader— camp number five, I later learned—had spoken about *the right clannish witch,* frustrated that they had only *one.* One witch, which matched our miscount.

I noticed a lessening paranoia in general, Tysen said. *If we wait too long, we run the risk of something happening, and then ramping security again.*

My nose wrinkled at the thought. Tysen had a point. Haruto could unexpectedly move all the camps, requiring us to re-memorize and locate the clannish witches to optimize.

There's no moon in two nights, Merrick said.

If they have two warriors on guard tonight and tomorrow, then I vote we act with the moonless night, Chi replied. *Tysen is correct. The longer we wait, the worse our chances.*

Rognvald followed with the final detail needed. *We also have three Brothers that returned early from successful missions, which provides us with available backup. They'll be reassigned in three days. I say we move in two nights, first dark, at Chi's recommendation. We can take advantage of their help.*

The chatter calmed, waiting for my final permission. Only Gregary didn't input his thoughts, but he rarely did. Thinking through it, I couldn't help but agree. My instincts leaned into the idea, particularly the additional Brothers for assistance. There was a relief in making the decision. I let that carry me into confirmation.

Agreed, I said. *We act at first dark in two nights. I'll speak with Alina tomorrow night and confirm. I'm worried they're hiding a witch. I'm going to look into it.*

No one disputed my assertion.

* * *

A yard lurked through the trees ahead. From it issued a scream, panting breaths, silence. From the middle of the forest, I peered around a tree trunk and onto an open meadow. A familiar old school, composed of stones, frozen trellises, and time, loomed in the background. Miss Priscilla's School for Girls.

A young girl stood in the middle of the snowy field, arm up, elbow bent, snowy projectile in hand. Her tight black curls, filled with flurries, bounced as she spun on the spot. Breaths curled out of her full, parted lips. A scarf hung from her right shoulder, dragging the snowy ground.

"Cheater!" she shouted, whirling in a circle. "You're a cheater! You can't use god magic during a snowball fight."

I smiled.

A ha.

As expected, Baxter *was* nearby, and losing a snowball fight to his niece, Ava. He loathed snow, and he hated the cold. Despite growing up on a tropical island, exterior conditions rarely bothered Ava. She had a definite advantage against the prissy demigod.

Snow shifted behind her, just subtle enough she'd miss it. *Gotcha,* I thought, and transported into sight behind the moving snow. Witchy magic couldn't sense god magic, and vice versa. Often, however, sensing wasn't needed.

Catching my unexpected appearance, Ava whirled around to face me. I held a finger to my lips before blinking out of sight with an invisibility spell. With her excellent instincts, Ava prowled as if she hadn't seen me. Her low crouch, wrinkled brow, bespoke predatory intent. She moved with all the finesse of a forest lion, and twice the ferocity.

"You're a coward," she called, quietly, stalking her uncle. "You taunt me with snowballs, but hide at the first sign of competition."

If I guessed correctly, Baxter should be ahead of me. I took a chance and leaped. My unseen body collided with an invisible shoulder. Both of us toppled to the ground in a spray of snow and exclamations.

Laughing, I removed my spell and shouted, "I've got him, Ava!" but she'd already cut to my side. Baxter materialized with a grunt, snow smearing his face and packing his ears. Weapon at the ready, Ava smashed the slushy ball into his nose and rubbed it across his brow.

"Coward!" she cried, laughing. "You'll never win against Bianca Monroe!"

Baxter shouted his protests, flinging me off his side and into a snowbank with a powerful sweep of his arm. Snowy fractals billowed around me. I laughed as the two of them descended into rabid warfare. Minutes later, they collapsed several paces apart. Arms sprawled, legs thrown wide. Their breathy laughs surged into the sky, dissipating like smoke.

"Surrender," Baxter gasped. He rolled onto his side, shards of ice in his eyebrows. "I . . . surrender."

His reddened cheeks, askew coat, and sodden hair was a sight to behold. Orderly, organized, fashionable Baxter had become an absolute mess. His snowy curls danced across his forehead as I stepped up to his side.

"You really need better strategies. You realize that, demigod?"

He glared at me, squinting. "I was attacked from behind!"

Nudging him with a booted foot, I said, "*Remember* that. I'll always have Ava's back against cheating wimps, and you're not as subtle as you think."

Too seriously, he said, "I'm glad to hear it," and leaped to his feet.

Baxter, a demigod, had far superior physical skills and

strength. His act was just that—a facade. While he didn't enjoy snow, he could have easily defeated Ava and myself within moments of the snowball fight commencing. But Ava glowed with pleasure and windy breaths, and being a mortal in a witchy world gave her so few wins. Baxter created as many as he could.

Ava pushed out of the snow and rammed into me with a hug, arms squeezing tight. Breathless, I patted her shoulder.

"Good to see you, too, Ava. Good job walloping him. Demigods aren't easy to defeat, but you found his weakness and went for it. Just like I taught you."

Baxter winked at me.

From a window high above, Priscilla called out. "Bianca, send my student inside, please! Her lunch break is over."

With Priscilla's lovely cream shirt, a high collar, and minty eyes set against porcelain skin, she was the picture of a strict, but loving, school marm. Ava waved a hand with a bright smile, but turned to me with a frosty glare.

Ava muttered, "She's a fun killer."

I rolled my lips to suppress a laugh. Reassuring Ava with a pat on the arm, I said, "It's not forever. School will end eventually, and then your agreement with Baxter will be over and you can sail the seas all you want."

Mumbling under her breath, she trudged through the snow. Baxter and I waved to Priscilla before she slid the window shut and retreated. Baxter eyed me with an appraising stare as Ava closed a back door.

"You look absolutely no worse for wear, B. You're not even sweating. Did you fight, or simply invoke chaos?"

Scoffing, I said, "Invoked chaos! I grew up in this forest. Some of us are smart about our snowball fights. There's no need for such energy expenditure. It's about packing the snowball just right, and keeping a cache of them."

Irritated, he grumped a response. I pointed to the forest with a gloved hand. "Follow me? I want to talk. I couldn't find you in the Eastern Network and took a chance you'd be here."

His nose wrinkled. "You want to meet with me in the woods?"

"Yes!"

"There's no path." He elevated a foot. "And these boots are not winter worthy. Can't we find somewhere to take tea together?"

I elevated a sympathy-free eyebrow. Rolling his eyes, he muttered, "Fine," and replaced the poor choice of low boots with another pair through the ease of god magic. I grinned.

"Ah ha! God magic *is* an option for your creature comforts. You act like you have to pay a devil before you can use it."

"Gelas is a devil," he mumbled.

I laughed.

"Don't tell Ava," he added. "I'm not supposed to use it for small things. But, in the grand scheme of life and winter in Alkarra, a solid pair of boots will serve me well. Gelas certainly doesn't ask for accountings, anyway."

"A good pair of winter boots would help you visit Tipa in the Southern Network more often, eh?"

He glared at me.

I dismissed the subterranean question. Baxter still hadn't admitted to having feelings for Tipa, but I felt relatively certain something simmered beneath the surface.

We trod into the forest. Once well clear of Miss Priscilla's School for Girls, I found a footpath worn by mortegas and other creatures where we could easily walk side by side. The trees crooned as we entered the quiet woods, hushed with snowfall.

"I need some help, if you're willing," I admitted.

He stuck his hands in his greatcoat pockets. "With what?"

"A mission of mercy for the South."

Baxter stared ahead, lips twitching. "For Alina?"

Surprised, I turned to him. "How'd you know?"

"Tipa mentioned something might come up."

"Tipa isn't supposed to know about it."

He laughed. "Sure."

Annoyed, I let that slide. It didn't surprise me that Tipa tracked more than she let on, but it did irritate me that I hadn't considered it. Alina hiring me was an attempt at independence. Something Tipa, and the Gelas, god of ice, should appreciate. One never knew with gods, however.

Baxter waved a mittened hand. "Proceed."

I rolled my eyes at the inherent command, but caught him up on the problem, the mission, and his part in it. Before I could make the official ask, he said, "I'm in."

"Really?"

"Yes. I see why you'd want a demigod to help."

"Would Gelas approve this use of magic?"

His thoughts seemed to darken. "Whether he approves or not, I'm helping. He would, anyway. On a different topic, I've been tracking your mess with Georgette and what's happening. Why aren't you fighting back?"

Lightly, I replied, "Who says I'm not?"

He blinked, then frowned, then smiled. "Bianca Monroe," he muttered, shaking his head. "I can't fathom how Derek hasn't had a heart paroxysm over you already."

"You're not the first to say it."

"You heard about the rally?"

"I was there."

"No." He shook his head. "Not that one. Certainly, that was interesting. I'm talking about the one tomorrow morning."

Tipping my head to the side, I cried, "There's *another* one?"

Grim-faced, he nodded. "Mentioned in the *Chatterer* this morning. At the square in Ashleigh. Georgette discovered excitement and unexpected momentum in her last one, so she's not going to stop while she's ahead. Not sure what time it starts, but it's bound to get interesting."

Chapter Twenty-Nine

Dawn hinted at a far sky, staining the dome with a first blush of light amongst lessening night.

By this time in the summer, I would have been awake for hours, cleaned up from a long run, eaten breakfast, and been on my way to my next task. Light touched everything those days. In these deep winter doldrums, glimpsing daytime at all felt like a cherished gift. Sleep and rest ruled these hours.

While Merrick finished his breakfast and checked in with Rognvald, I set out with a promise to meet up with them in an hour. We'd conduct a final review before saving the clannish witches tonight. Thus far, the Thabit tribe gave us no reason not to take advantage of the moonless evening.

Short of the city square, I stopped. The beginnings of something familiar and equally ridiculous began to piece together in Ashleigh.

A team of ten witches worked in the burgeoning morning light, breath billowing like mini fires from cold lips. Most of them were unrecognizable because of thick coats, scarves dusted with frost, and heavy hats. They moved slowly and steadily, setting up barriers, stands, and another pulpit-like structure.

Four or five hours from now, Georgette would stand there and address Ashleigh City. Merrick hadn't understood why I insisted on laying my eyes on it. While Georgette spouted words against me and the Sisterhood and vague leadership she didn't name, I would be elsewhere, trying to solve the problems of other Networks. But she would be here, using my name, and disgracing my reputation.

And I would let her.

Because . . . what else? When she found me at Papa's, we hit an impasse. Georgette wouldn't back down, and neither would I. My choices narrowed to the impossibility of nothing. And, perhaps, the temporary solace that came from ignoring her to focus on what really mattered: helping witches.

Angered responses had begun to fill the *Chatterer* now that Georgette moved her affectations to a wider stage. Frustration against her and the wasted time. Against me for not sticking up for myself. They were kind in their caring, but I had bigger plans.

Something eased in my chest, having seen the place. Removing the ethereal, and making her vague threats as solid as possible. Like throwing open the closet to reveal the monsters. This was my metaphorical equivalent to swinging a broomstick under the bed.

Smoke. Shadows. That's all Georgette gave. She waged a war no one saw, no one fought. Like control seekers and anarchists before, she'd fade away. When she did, I'd be in the exact position I desired.

Invisible.

I turned to go, but a familiar figure strode toward me.

Aurora? She almost strode past me. Instead, she reached blindly for my sleeve and commanded, "With me, you fool."

We strode down the road side-by-side until we cleared the rally square. Ashleigh City and her wealthy streets, lined with cobblestone and charming townhouses and flower boxes that looked adorable even under winter's grip, slipped by. Aurora led us to a darker part of town that, compared to Chatham City, was practically a newborn.

Cleared from the rally by sheer distance, I removed my spell.

"You're a fool, Bianca Monroe," she muttered.

"I've heard."

"Why are you here?"

"Why are *you* here?"

"To prevent you from making a stupid mistake." She eyed me, speaking low. "Were you sabotaging the rally?"

Laughing, I said, "No! I just wanted to see it. She's going to spend half the day throwing my name into the mud, I figured I might as well see the spot where my reputation withers and dies."

Aurora pressed her lips together, then pushed on my arm, shoving me through an alley. Finger pressed to her lips, we headed through without speaking, then spilled out the other side.

It took us to the edge of a frozen pond ringed with wooden benches. A rock skittered away from my foot, bouncing over the sleek top which was cut through with lines from sharp skates. Ashleigh pond. A community gathering place known for ice skating in the winter and singing performances in the summer. During the solstice, witches gathered here in hoards to celebrate.

With her elbow, Aurora nudged me to a trail that

ringed the sides and took us away from the city. The snow pressed into a firmer texture. It didn't give way as we crunched over the top, almost skating in our boots. Halfway around, Aurora stopped. Her eyes bore into mine.

"I have it on good authority that Georgette has evidence you're acting as the Sisterhood and plans to call you out. She wants you to attend a rally and answer to her and the witches in a public way."

I rolled my eyes. "How is she *escalating* this?"

Aurora waved a hand.

"She has to know I won't have anything to do with it."

"How are you suddenly so dumb?"

"What?"

"Don't you see it?" Aurora hissed. Her eyes glided to the sides, and then back. There was nothing hostile in her bearing, only intensity. "She *knows* you're out there working. She knows you're keeping the Sisterhood alive."

"What proof?" I retorted.

Aurora sucked in a breath. "That information I couldn't get. Sleuthing," she sniped, "is *not* my job. Nor is hunting around for information that helps you, Bianca Monroe. All I know is she has information on a potential Sisterhood mission that you're engaging in despite *dissolving the Sisterhood*. She's trying to humiliate you, or somehow bring the law against you. The more publicly she can do it, the better."

"She's been trying to humiliate me for weeks."

"That's not all that she's doing," Aurora snapped, "and if you'd take your head out of your arse, you'd see it. She made it *very* clear with the first rally. Georgette is using you to create insecurity around Scarlett."

That stopped me in my tracks.

I breathed, "What?"

"You are one of Scarlett's biggest weaknesses. Don't you see that? Georgette has created drama around you in the public eye, and thereby weakened Scarlett's position because she hired you. Scarlett stood behind *you*."

"But—"

"Georgette is the hungriest witch I've ever met, Bianca Monroe, and don't you forget it. If she can create doubt around Scarlett, she can exploit it. She's doing a fine job of building a foundation to discredit our leader, if you ask me."

Breathing hard, I took in her declaration with new eyes. Jikes, but how *hadn't* I seen it? All this time, floundering about Georgette's deeper motivation, unable to see her true aim. While I thought Georgette was skirting careful lines, she was setting me *and* Scarlett up to fail.

Aurora folded her arms over her chest and glowered uneasily at the pond.

"Last night, Georgette finalized one thousand signatures on a petition that, if she receives five hundred more, will give three citizens an opportunity to stand before the Council and discuss a law that would prevent the Sisterhood from forming in the future. If the Council were to pass it, it puts Scarlett in an untenable position."

Understanding felt like breaking ice inside my blood. If the entire Council voted to pass a law, but Scarlett disagreed, it would create tension and awkwardness. Normally, that would be fine. One law? Who cared? But *this* law had so much drama and attention that it would matter. Georgette could cite Scarlett's favoritism for me, blindness for the true needs of the Network. If Scarlett voted with them, the Sisterhood would never have a chance.

"Jikes," I whispered.

"Exactly," she hissed. "The gods! And you're over here looking at the rally, you idiot! Don't you have better things to be doing?"

"Like what?" I shot back.

"Like helping Alina in open defiance of that fool! The only power you have is to annoy Georgette into making a mistake. It's good she knows you're out there. It's good you're making her stressed. Go do *that* instead of giving her ammunition here! She needs to think you don't care."

Blinking, I reared back. Half of the time, Aurora's initial delivery didn't make sense. After a few hours, sometimes days, I could parse out a message behind her cryptic musings. Most of the time, she had valid points, even if I didn't always find them. Today, it rang crystal clear.

"You *have* to keep pressing against Georgette in utter silence. Do what you're doing. Defy Georgette. Ignore her. Your rebelliousness in light of her social flailing is going to undermine her confidence. The only thing that's giving her any insecurity at this point is that *you don't care.*"

I hid a smile. "So . . ." I drawled. "You're telling me I've been correct all this time? Any chance you could casually mention it to Leda?"

"Goddess help us again." Aurora tipped her eyes heavenward. "With arrogance like that, I should *let* Georgette have you."

"You just said—"

"Keep working, and you'll distract Georgette. If she calls for you to answer in a rally, you ignore her. Make it so she'll have to find you. You can put her into a position where she hangs herself, so to speak."

The scuff of shoes sounded from a nearby trail, so I cloaked us in a spell. Two Guardians strolled by, one of them yawning, and moved on. After they left, I took

Aurora's arm and led us deeper on the trail, spiriting us into a small grove. The trees here whispered unintelligibly. A vine lowered over my head. Two saplings leaned closer.

"What if she becomes out of control?" I asked.

"I'll handle Georgette."

"How?"

"Don't worry about it," she added, "Leda had a brilliant idea. I'm helping her execute it so her name is kept out of it. And no, Leda hasn't told you because you're planning this mission and need to focus on it."

Sighing, I said, "Sounds great to me. What about Scarlett?"

"Of course Scarlett knows," she cried under her breath. "You think I'm an idiot like you? There are ducks, Bianca, and they're in a line behind me. You are, of course, the last in that line and the only one flailing around, trying to be a goose instead. Just do as I say, will you? Solve Alina's problems and let us handle Georgette. Stop wasting your time at rallies and get to . . . wherever you're going."

The cloaking spell bled away, and we stared hard at each other. Aurora was mean, played a little dirty, and rarely had anything nice to say. I couldn't fathom another witch that I'd want more on my side.

"Thank you," I said.

"Get out of here," she muttered, shoving my shoulder. "I'm tired of you."

* * *

An hour later, winds trailed my hair off my shoulder, dancing the tendrils in the desert breeze. Heat sliced through my chilled skin like a hot knife, whipping the wintry remnants of the Central Network away.

I burrowed my bare toes deeper into heated sand, relishing the anchoring sensation. The conversation with Aurora slid off my back. I left Georgette, the rally, and thoughts of anything else firmly behind me. Leda, Aurora, and Scarlett could deal with Georgette.

I had a mission to focus on.

Witches bustled through the Thabit oasis. Their daily ministrations sounded much like the music of Chatham Castle. Clearing throats, distant cries, shuffling fabrics, clinking pots filled with water sent directly from the warehouse at the oasis. Only the bellows of desert camals entered the area here, different from the castle.

Chi watched camp four. *Nothing changed here,* he said.

First camp clear, Merrick chimed in. Tysen cleared camp two, Gregary camp three, and Rognvald camp five. Papa and Regina had their own assignment elsewhere, and they would work with Baxter.

There aren't as many people in camp this morning, Rognvald said. *The rush of ice availability pushed many of them back to the oasis. Good call, Sisterhood, to have Alina ramp up ice production in wake of our mission.*

I smiled.

Perfect.

The rest of the team awaited my word.

Confirming our descent tonight at full dark. I'm meeting with High Priestess Alina to confirm that all's ready from the clan. You'll hear from me within the hour. I paused. *See you this evening, gentlemen.*

An hour before the expected sunset in the Western Network, I strode through Zamok Castle in the Southern

Network. Unescorted, because I'd snuck in. Despite demigods lurking around, it wasn't that hard.

We need to tell Baxter that security in the Southern Network is abhorrent.

I'll let you do that, Leda replied.

I snorted.

While navigating down a familiar hallway, jogging to make sure I arrived on time and didn't miss my narrow window of opportunity to speak with busy Alina, my thoughts remained in the Western Network. The mission, Aurora's warning against Georgette, and Tyrant's ramp up in the wake of my nervousness, created a sense of foreboding that followed me, despite my anticipation for a new mission. Eagerness to return these captive witches to their families hadn't aided the reality that something was missing.

Why didn't the count match? The camp leader's vague statement still haunted me. *We need more of the right clannish witches. Thus far, there's only one.*

Anxiety was a terrible bedfellow. I'd had enough emotionally draining events the last several days that I couldn't be certain I wasn't just . . . tired. Stressed. An overwrought leader.

Pick the poison.

At Alina's door, I rapped my knuckles three times, then twice, then one. After ten seconds, I rapped one final time. The door opened, allowing me inside. Alina's maid closed it behind me. Recognizing her, I removed my magic. She gave a low smile, curtsied, and swung an arm toward her High Priestess. Alina stood near a fire. She was one of the only Alkarran leaders I rarely saw sitting down, even in her own chambers.

"You're the only High Priestess who never invites me to her work office."

Blandly, she gestured around us with a sweep of her arm.

An obvious lack of paperwork, ink, or scrolls made me doubt the notion that this *was* her office. If anyone would work out of her chambers, Alina would be the witch. Less space to control, fewer security cracks to protect. Her maids must squirrel away all signs of paperwork in between meetings. She did have a small desk she'd written at before. Orderly, blank paper awaited near a blotter, a quill, and ink pot.

"Then I rescind my observation."

Her lip twitched with a slight smile. Glancing to her maid, and nodding once, Alina motioned to a chair.

"I'd rather stand," I admitted.

Inclining her head, she said, "Me too."

Hands folded behind my back, I joined her near the fire. "Our plan to remove the clannish witches tonight continues. We've confirmed the camps, the warriors, everything. The clannish witches match up to the number you provided . . . except for one. We're missing one witch. The Brothers have suggested it's a clerical error, or that a clannish witch may have died."

"None of the rescued witches have reported a clannish death. They would have known."

"I agree, which means we have a missing witch."

Her expression hooded, like a cloud over the moon. "I may know who it is. I sent an emissary to the silk clan, and they returned last night."

"Oh?"

"There is a missing silk witch named Lev. He's a clannish witch, like all the others, but not *only* a clannish witch. He grew up in the silk clan, so we call them silk witches instead of clannish witches. But he left his home clan to experience the world."

My eyebrows rose in surprise. She'd never mentioned this distinguishing feature before. "Is that a bad thing?"

She scoffed without humor. "If you're a silk witch, yes. Some would call it a betrayal and cut him off. There are silk witches that look down on clannish witches because they don't serve the silk trade, but partake in the hereditary culture. To be a clannish witch at all implies ties to the silk trade. If they aren't in the silk village, they —or their ancestors—are in violation of clan law. They aren't punished," she said quickly, anticipating my question. "When a witch leaves the silk clan, the clan creates an . . . emotional disassociation . . . as well as a physical one."

"Complicated," I murmured.

She sighed. "Very. I'm attempting to sort through the layers now. All the same," she concluded. "Lev's disappearance has stirred up the leader of the silk clan, who happens to be Lev's father."

"Ah . . . interesting. Even though Lev isn't claimed anymore?"

"That," she murmured, "is why it's interesting."

"Will the silk clan be a problem?"

"Not for you."

The easy cadence in her tone was a lie. Exhaustion appeared in her eyes. I had so many questions to ask, but they were outside my bounds as a hired help. Not outside the bounds of a friend, however. Were we friends? Yes, as much as Alina had friends. Yet, in this situation, I sensed it wasn't my place to inquire.

"None of the witches you have returned reported seeing a clannish witch with his description, nor a clannish witch named Lev. While in the West, they seemed to do their best to keep track of each other. Thus, I believe Lev is our missing witch."

"Assuming Lev *is* the missing witch, would they have a reason to keep him separate?"

She frowned. "I have theories, but nothing firm. Their motivation appeared to be currency, at first. Your recent revelations make me think there are ulterior motives greater than a successful oasis with fresh, cold water."

Instinct nagged me to Lev and his position in the silk clan. To Alfea, Haruto, and the camps. The clannish witches, and all the details to keep in line. *We need more of the right clannish witches. Thus far, there's only one.*

"Alina, are there any *other* silk witches taken?"

"Not that we know of."

"Can you tell a silk witch from a clannish witch by sight?"

Slowly, she said, "No."

"And do silk witches leave their clan to go into the other clans?"

Weakly, she said, "Often enough."

My heart sped up as I considered what a silk witch could know, or do, that other clannish witches could not. Every answer returned to the silk trade. Swallowing a gathering lump in my throat, I asked, "And if you wanted to exploit the silk trade by finding a silk witch that knew its secrets . . ."

Alina's expression lost pallor. "The silk magic," she whispered. A hand rose to her lips, as if she wanted to remove the suggestion. I watched her closely, letting the deductions rumble and settle until I could make sense of the details.

"They want the silk magic," she continued, hastily. "They want the *silk magic.* That's why they've taken Lev. That's why they're taking clannish witches." Alina reached out, snatched my arm. She squeezed tight. "That's what they meant by the *right clannish witch.* Not only are they using our witches as slaves, but they want *the silk magic*."

The silk magic, a guarded secret available only to witches born in the silk clan, was highly protected and utterly unavailable. Across history, multiple attempts to steal the grimoire that housed all the secrets had failed. No one outside the silk clan had access to its secrets. Only the witches *in* the silk clan.

Despite Mikhail's betrayal, and Southern Network witches everywhere losing magic, rumor existed saying that the Mansfeld Pact hadn't harmed the silk workers. No one knew for certain. Silk continued to pump from the clans, creating ever-greater mysteries. Articles in the *Chatterer* and Eastern newsbooks speculated that the silk clan, who never considered themselves part of any Network, had no place in the magical repercussions. They had always operated outside normal bounds.

"This isn't only about water."

"They want our silk trade," she hissed. Her fingers released me to pace. Silk trailed behind her in a restless drape as she moved swiftly from spot to spot. She padded barefoot despite the chilly stone floor. "That's why they're taking witches. Moving from lake to lake. They're attempting to find witches like Lev, because they likely can't find the silk clans. No one can. They're too protected."

"The Thabit tribe is hoping to take a clannish witch that also happens to know the silk trade? If they aren't from the silk clan, they use them as willing workers."

"Yes!"

The potential upset had catastrophic repercussions on the Southern Network. Losing their grip on the silk trade could overturn their whole society, which continued because of the silk export trade. The Thabit tribe were troublemakers, and there was no other way to look at it.

"Bianca," Alina said with guarded passion, "you *must* find Lev. You must do whatever you can to locate him and learn what he's said, done. What they *know*. There should be protections, but . . ."

She trailed off, and I knew exactly where to look. There was one spot in the Thabit camps that we hadn't checked. One spot I hadn't questioned as much as the others.

"I think I know where he is," I stated. I held out a hand, stopping her movement utterly. With a promise I had no reason to impart, I said, "I'll find him."

Alina's shoulders relaxed.

"I'll speak with my silk clan representative," she whispered. "I'll warn them. See if they've noticed anything missing, anything wrong with the magic. I don't know how it works . . ."

Nodding, I stepped back. "Keep me updated through Leda. Send any correspondence to her, and she'll notify me through our communication magic. Any detail, Alina. Anything."

Her heart filled her frightened eyes.

"I trust you, Bianca Monroe."

Chapter Thirty

The Brotherhood descended silently, without trace or detection, an hour after the sun vanished beneath sultry sands. Our adventure began with starlight and camal cries. A steady stream of updates chugged through my mind as I skimmed around the outside of the oasis in a final check.

Calm skies.

Cooling sand.

Awakening witches.

No visible clannish witches worked in the oasis—only tribe workers and warriors, but I monitored every witch for transformation magic, in case they change any clannish witch to look tribal, and detected none. Lev wasn't out here.

Most activity in the oasis clumped around twilight and sunrise, when campers left and new ones arrived at the end of a dusty night trek. Caravans resumed their trek across sweltering sands, stars as their guide across a sea of granules instead of droplets.

Reassured by the balking camals as they departed for

farther places, and the lack of anything out of place, I skirted along the edge of the oasis and listened to the Brotherhood updates.

Present, Rognvald said. *All is as expected in camp five. Backups available at first requirement.* Merrick, Chi, and Tysen had already reported affirmatively, with Papa closing them out.

In place, both Regina and myself.

Ready from Chatham Castle, Leda added.

She sat in her apartment, with details, maps, and a list of clannish witches' locations sprawled on her table. I imagined her murmuring updates to herself, making notes, sipping tea, tracking changes. The comfort of her table and a crackling fire was the closest she wanted to be to any mission. She still hadn't spoken about Hiddleston since he accepted the position as the High Priest's Assistant, and I hadn't seen her, either. Retreating from my sight to lick her wounds guaranteed something *else* floated beneath the surface with them.

Gregary spoke last. *In position. No changes observed.*

Thank you, team. Hold.

The initial spike of anxiety faded. All Brothers in position and ready. Nothing massively unexpected thus far, which put us well underway.

Action was much less stressful than waiting. Our simple plan had plenty of opportunity to go awry, but so did every mission. Each Brother would find the clannish witches, transport them to a waypoint manned by an invisible Papa and Regina, and return to find the next clannish witch. Speed was our most important factor.

At the waypoint, not far from the oasis, our backup Brothers held in position to provide security. Baxter, using untraceable god magic, would take the clannish witches to Alina. God magic didn't create discomfort for the magicless witches, and guaranteed that tribal warriors couldn't follow.

After deducing who the missing witch might be, I planned to investigate the ice shed at the oasis. Instead of staying at a camp, Haruto and Alfea made a fire not far from the shed, which might be ideal. If they received news or updates from one of the five camps about disappearing clannish witches, I'd waylay them to prevent an attack. Any Brother that finished before others would help the camp with the most clannish witches remaining.

Leda said to me alone, *Remember that no Brotherhood member can be seen tonight.*

I know.

We've already discussed it, I know. I could picture her rolling her eyes. *And all are aware of the political ramifications of a Protector staging a mission against a tribe at the behest of the Southern Network High Priestess. I repeat again—none of you can be seen.*

Thank you, Leda. To the rest of the group, I said, *Do your final review of each camp and confirm that the clannish witches are in the correct general area. Please report any barriers we haven't anticipated or changes to everyone, including our backups, before we begin.*

While the Protectors set to the final checks and updates, I slunk along the edge of the oasis and toward the ice shed. Powerful magic always emanated from within, which made sense. One would need robust spells to keep ice from melting in this torrid environment. But maybe it was something else. My curiosity over Lev and the magical ice shed propelled me closer.

Honing in on the rickety, slipshod warehouse they'd taken the donkeys inside, I crept close. Magic radiated from the ice shed, conveniently disguising my invisibility spell. Beyond it lay Alfea and Haruto's shared tent. Their fire climbed high, casting light and shadow into distant reaches, like a beacon. They sat close to each other, while the leader for camp five sat across from them, listening while Haruto spoke. Haruto drew in the sand with a stick, gesturing to it. Every so often, the camp leader regarded it, nodded, and returned his attention to Haruto. The conversation moved steadily.

Nothing to be concerned about yet. I took a risk and cast a spell to listen in. Their expressions didn't stir. They didn't seem to notice the magical use, so I stretched it closer. Their voices and general noises from the camp grew in my ear, obscuring Haruto's words.

Confirmed for camp one, Merrick said. *Clannish witches are where expected* .

Chi, Tysen, Rognvald, and Gregary followed with similar statements. Leda brought up the end of the confirmation.

We're ready to go, Bianca.

Her words gave me a shot of courage. Drawing a breath, letting the heat swill at the bottom of my lungs, I said, *Thank you. We're set to wait. First removal will begin closer to midnight, when your camp settles down. Work to your own advantage, but let's try to coordinate around the same time to avoid tipping off other camps.*

Thinking of Leda's earlier warning, I added, *Be advised that capture is not an option. If anyone knows that the Brotherhood staged an attack on the Western Network while working for the Sisterhood, Council Member Georgette will happily fry all of us.*

Their grim responses, though distant, were felt.

We settled in.

* * *

The hours ticked away with steady but relentless movement. No one spoke. Haruto and Alfea entered their tent around ten thirty and settled on the ground, feet visible from outside. The oasis eased into waiting for the next wave of travelers to arrive in the early hours, when the first watch from each camp would transport in. We'd be long gone.

The final clannish witch has retired to his bed in camp two, Tysen said. *Two guards are awake, drinking. They're inebriated and making a lot of noise. I'm removing the first clannish witch while they draw attention.*

Where is the camp leader? I asked.

Sleeping.

My nose wrinkled. This felt like an egregious oversight on their part, but one we could lean on. We'd hoped for this, but planned for alternatives. Tysen already knew what to do next, and he executed it flawlessly.

Good for camp one to go, also, Merrick said.

Administering a sleeping spell, Tysen said.

The other Brothers reported a similar state of readiness, closing with Papa's quick declaration of, *We're ready for your witches.*

I replied, *Good luck, gentleman. Haruto and Alfea appear to be asleep. I'll be in the ice shed.*

With the slumbering, and the other Brothers moving into place, I crept around the side. Magic infused the two entry doors, big enough for donkeys and wagons to pass through, but nothing else. A swinging lock held them together. Enchantments infused the whole shed, hiding the true interior.

Pocket magic, Leda once called it. Few understood how a large interior could hide in a small exterior, but the West often conjured strange magicks thanks to their willingness to take grimoires.

Protective spells along the walls and entryway were surprisingly basic. Two of the spells were common in the West. If the witch who cast the spell wasn't well-versed in protective magic, they would have set the spell and left. If they *were* used to protective magic, they would have added an additional phrase at the end of the incantation. A lock to ensure no one but them could remove it. With rotating workers, I doubted the latter and hoped for the former.

As I silently pressed my fingers to the doors and issued a spell, keeping a wary eye on Haruto and Alfea's fire, the magic dissolved starting at my fingertips. Like retreating light swirls, the protective signature wrapping the ice shed ebbed into nothing. Each known protective spell bled away and left one—maybe two?—unfamiliar magic systems.

The previous pulsing tamed, not quite as colorful or garish. Whatever spells remained, they had an inherent weakness. I could overpower them, but it may not be quiet. I stepped away, gazing around the corner. Alfea and Haruto's feet hadn't moved. Another scan of the oasis confirmed I remained alone.

Whispering an incantation to create a sound barrier around the lock, I placed both hands near it. A shimmering circle should have evolved around my wrists, but nothing revealed.

I tried again.

A half-hearted circle appeared. I frowned. This incantation wasn't one I used often, so a lackluster performance wasn't a huge surprise. Or someone placed a spell to prevent this kind of overpowering. There wasn't time to attempt a third time, so I overpowered the lock. When nothing happened, I repeated it again, opening my magical reserves. A *bang* broke the night, exploding the shield, which absorbed only half the sound.

Instead of waiting to see who investigated, I pried open the doors, slunk inside, and closed them. A deception spell recreated the lock, just in case. While my eyes adjusted, the Brotherhood chattered in the background.

Two clannish witches obtained, Merrick said. *Moving to the third.*

Received, Derek said.

One obtained, Tysen replied.

Baxter is taking the first five. He's . . . gone.

On my way, Rognvald said. *Two in tow.* He had the camp with the most clannish witches. As Head of the Brotherhood, I wasn't overly surprised that he'd transport two other witches with him. A herculean feat that I'd only managed once, and out of sheer necessity. Rognvald had the mother-child pair that I'd specifically made certain he was in charge of, and removed first.

The Brotherhood's low chatter, spoken quick and without hesitation, was a reassurance that the mission moved as we planned. They should be done within the next fifteen minutes if all went accordingly. Exhaling, I returned my attention to the shed.

Darkness and space awaited. The damp, heavy air expanded, giving way to a shed interior three or four times wider than the structure outside. I anticipated that, but not the chill. Scuttling away from the door, I ventured in. Five steps later, my shin hit something hard and fuzzy. Suppressing a curse word, I hopped around, clutching the offended spot.

Once the pulsing pain subsided, I reached out. My tentative explorations with hands and feet led to a hard wall on the right and left. A hallway. A physical vibration changed the air, setting the hair on my arms on edge.

Merrick said, *I sense gathering magic around the*

outside of camp one. There are five points, I believe invisible witches. I'm holding in place, near target four.

Five points here, said Chi.

Tysen, a moment later replied, *None here. I'll keep going. Three obtained. Working toward the fourth.*

The tension in Merrick's voice amplified my rush. A swipe of my hand roved over wet, crumbly material. Sawdust? It formed the wall to my left and right. I couldn't burrow deeper, so it must be solidified with magic. But that wasn't the source of the uncomfortable, buzzing sensation.

Straight ahead was a . . . barrier? A layer? The pressure and sensation burrowed under my skin like knives, uncomfortable, halting. It stopped me in my tracks.

What *was* it?

Leda?

Yes?

There's an active magic ahead of me, in the ice shed. It . . . seems like it's . . . attached to a wall? There's something odd about it. I've never felt it before. It's physically painful to stand near it.

Can you see anything?

Too dark.

No glowing lights?

None.

You're sure it's magic?

Yes. I haven't tried sensing *it, it's just . . . that big. If I opened my senses to magic, I can't imagine how much it would hurt. It would be brutal.*

Until I knew better what awaited inside, I didn't want to conjure a light. So I edged forward while she searched her prodigious historical or magical annals. My fingers trailed the walkway, too far apart for me to reach with both arms wide. Foreboding increased until I couldn't tell between instinct and magic.

The closer I move to it, the more painful it feels.

Hold, please.

The feeling of standing before a blasting sun emanated from the black barrier, though nothing moved. Whatever it might be, it was a magical signature I didn't know existed in Alkarra. Breathing hard, I asked, *Anything?*

I . . . can't believe I'm even suggesting this but . . . have you ever felt . . . a portal?

A portal?

Yes.

Does that magic exist?

She spoke quickly, the way she did whenever she found a scholarly hole. *Rumors of portal magic exist. But it's not an active magic, or known to be active, for at least a millennia. The grimoire that hosted the portal spells was destroyed. Supposedly,* she tacked on.

My discomfort increased ten fold.

A portal?

Why is a portal any different than transporting? I asked, inching closer. The magical force lurked ahead, beckoning and repulsing at the same time. The urge to touch it was profound, but fear over the other side held me back. Who knew what secrets ruled ancient magic like portals? My fingers trembled, held in front of me.

A portal would be very different from transporting, she said. *It has a location at the end, and strict rules. They're unforgiving, reportedly used for suppression.*

What kind of suppression?

Flustered, she replied, *Ah . . . life, I suppose? Many witches would be taken hostage, stuffed into a one-way portal, and abandoned. Their abandonment wasn't always the extent of the abuse, and often could be worse.*

My throat tightened. By the goddess, what had these witches done?

Don't touch it, Bianca, she growled. *We don't know what we're talking about. Portals only require physical touch to enter them. Some of their rules are difficult to ascertain, and you can't break a portal without significant work on the spell itself. There's an unwinding, I think? Not sure. Some portals allowed only one witch through at a time. Some of them, based on ancient and uncertain stories, took witches to places* outside *of Alkarra.*

I registered her words, the risk.

There has to be a reason they have a portal.

I'm sure there is, she said tartly, *and you don't need to chase it into the portal until we know more! Ideally, we would find the witch who cast this magic.*

But what if Lev is inside?

Bianca—

Her chastisement cut off at the sound of a whisper behind me.

"She's not here."

My heart stuttered. I knew that voice. That voice shouldn't be *here*, but in camp three. Not in this strange, magical building that should have only housed ice, but could be the beginning to something horrendous.

I froze.

Another voice followed, equally as familiar.

"She's here," Georgette hissed. "I know she's here."

Chapter Thirty-One

Darkness surrounded me, and three walls. Georgette and Gregary's voice barreled down the only open space—the walkway I'd just wandered down. They cut off my escape route. Georgette must have known, because she continued toward me, and not all that quietly. Their whispers practically shouted through the icehouse.

"You said the Brotherhood mission was underway," she snapped.

Irritation framed Gregary's reply.

"It is underway."

"You said Bianca is assigned to the oasis."

"She is," he ground out.

I closed my eyes.

Betrayed by a Brother.

"I sensed something over here at the ice shed, so we find her in here and then you're done."

Gregary replied, "No. This is the end of our agreement. I said I'd bring you to the oasis, and that's it. I did it."

"No! You said you'd help me find her."

"You thought she was at the ice shed, and I brought you, so our bargain is fulfilled. If you want to find her in this mess, you do it yourself."

"You can't leave!"

"Watch me."

"We have a deal! I will not speak to your *former* wife on your behalf if you don't help me prove Bianca is here. You will never see your children again. Do you hear me? I can so easily convince one of my best childhood friends that you're a monster. She's fragile and broken enough, thanks to you, it won't be that hard."

Fury slid through me like white hot lines of light. Georgette had been conniving and vicious before, but never like this. To blackmail a desperate father into helping her with the hope he could see his children again?

And he'd *accepted.*

I'd known Georgette would descend to deep places to be rid of me, but this? Shock trickled into regret and loathing so intense it nearly took my breath away. Had Gregary told her where to find Papa's house, too? Brought her to the oasis the first time? He'd been surprisingly irritated and growly with me the day he beckoned me here, particularly when I didn't talk to Georgette.

Remembering anew, I straightened. Gregary *brought* me to Georgette at the oasis. He . . . wanted me to know? The good gods, this became more complicated by the second.

"There's more to our situation than a failed handfasting," he insisted, "and you know it."

"See this through," she growled, "and you'll at least have access to your children. If you don't, you'll lose your position in the Brotherhood *and* your children. You will lose everything." Her voice elevated. "Bianca? I know you're here, and I know you can hear us! Let's make this easy, shall we? I put a sealing spell on the door. You won't be able to leave that way. If you transport, I'll follow."

The insanity of her command was laughable. If she couldn't find me, how would she follow my transportation magic? With the blasting power from the supposed-portal, she'd never stand a chance? She hadn't sensed me eavesdropping outside her office.

Tyrant sent a disconcerting thought in immediate response. *Or did she, you vile bag of putrescence, and didn't let on? She's probably far smarter than you realize.*

Ignoring Tyrant wasn't easy. The last person I wanted to underestimate was Georgette, but then, I already had. Gregary scoffed, as if he shared my assessment of her capability. He bit out, "Sense Bianca yourself. I have a job to do."

The quiet answered as he departed. Ramifications of Gregary's betrayal interrupted my frantic search for safety. What would Rognvald say? I should message him immediately. And yet . . . the fear in Gregary's voice. His wife, taking his children, and Georgette . . .

Leda's sharp tone jolted me. *Bianca? What's happening?*

Though tempted to tell Leda to remove Gregary from the communication magic immediately, I paused. He said he had a mission to do, right? We couldn't afford to lose him now.

Ask Gregary for an update on his position, please.
What?
Please?
Fine.

To Rognvald, I readied myself to say, *Gregary betrayed us,* but Georgette advanced from the other end of the ice hall. The brush of her skirt and low footsteps gave her away. I pressed my shoulder to the wall on my right and shrank. She'd have to search for me, and I felt confident she wouldn't know my invisibility spell, which would force her to feel.

Tysen shouted, *Attack at camp two. Ten warriors surround the camp. They have weapons drawn, but haven't shot.*

My blood ran cold.

Same in camp four, Chi said calmly.

As usual, Merrick gave more detail. *Warriors transported around the edge of camp one from elsewhere. I recognize one of them—he was supposed to be working at the oasis. I'm hovering above the trees and looking down. They don't appear to be searching higher, just on the sand.*

Where are they coming from? Rognvald asked. *Does anyone notice a lower population in their camps?*

Merrick said, *No idea.*

To my surprise, Gregary spoke. *Camp three is calm. Removing two witches while it stays this way.*

Dare I trust him?

There's your update, Leda said.

My eyes remained trained on the spot where Georgette advanced. Best I could tell, she'd stalled in the middle of the walkway. Sensing magic, perhaps? I doubted she had much experience, which would force her to stop and think. Most witches didn't bother, leaving the skill for others, like Guardians. With so much power blasting from every ice block, the walls, and the distant wall, she might not notice me.

Confirm from my father that Gregary shows up, please, I asked of Leda.

What's going on?

Gregary has been working with Georgette. Georgette is in the ice shed with me. Gregary brought her here.

Oh. I see.

Do not tell anyone. I don't . . . I think . . . it's compli-cated. Georgette is threatening to tell his former wife not to give him access to his children. She's holding it over him. I don't know the whole situation.

Leda hissed, *Just wait until Aurora and I get our bureaucratic hands on Georgette! With what we have planned . . .*

Later, I insisted.

Rustling sounded from Georgette's location. The slow trod of a boot. I cursed myself for not searching for a spell that allowed me to see in the dark—not that I'd ever heard of one. The benefit would be novel.

Right. Leda's voice tilted to her professional control. *There's chaos in the Brotherhood.* A pause, then, *Derek just confirmed Gregary's retrieval. He says he's already heading back for more clannish witches.*

Well, that meant something.

Steeling myself, I said, *I'll deal with Georgette.*

Don't do anything stupid, Bianca.

I made no promises.

The Brotherhood remained calm under unraveling pressure, so I shut their voices out. They faded, leaving Leda alone in my head. She'd help them deal with the situation. I trusted them.

Georgette approached with another hesitating foot-fall. I felt, more than saw, her approach. Shuffling fabric and light, quick respirations. At this rate, she'd walk right into me. A frustrated hiss of breath led me to believe she couldn't sense me. Too much alternate magic occluding the careful art.

Good.

Tyrant revitalized with a drawling, *Do you think Geor-*

gette knows you're a murderer? Don't you think it's in her purview to rid the Central Network of filth?

Georgette crept closer. If I hovered over her with a spell, she'd be able sense the magic for certain. How much space did I have overhead, anyway? I might need to hover horizontally to glide by, and I wasn't certain how to do that. The incantation supported vertical hovering, not horizontal. Which left a less obvious option.

The portal.

But, no. *Not* an option. Definitely not.

My third option was better, but not by much. Gently, I withdrew the Volare from its case. It slid free with a soundless loosening of pressure and scooped me up, hoisting me higher. I held a hand up to protect my head from unexpected objects as the Volare elevated.

It rose moments before Georgette leaped into the corner where I once stood with an, "I've got you!" and then a frustrated breath.

"Bianca Monroe!" she shouted, hands balled at her side. "We need to talk. I've caught you mid-mission. I *know* you're lying about the Sisterhood, and I'll make sure the entire Network knows it, too!"

My skin prickled as I waited in the rafters. Here, less intensity emanated from the wall by a small margin. Georgette wouldn't be able to recognize the Volare magic, but perhaps my invisibility. I removed it.

Georgette exclaimed quietly, "Oh! Something left."

She silenced as quickly, as if she hadn't meant to speak out loud. Her dress rustled. Something—maybe an elbow—scraped sawdust with a low *thud*. She muttered.

What's happening? Leda asked.

I evaded Georgette with the Volare. I'm . . . waiting to see what she'll do. I don't want to use the Volare in case it calls to Alfea. She was sleeping not far from the ice shed when I came inside, but I had no option.

The Brotherhood needs help. Rognvald called in their extras, but it doesn't sound good. All the camps are surrounded by warriors, and no one is certain where they're all coming from. They must have enlisted help from an outside tribe.

"Bianca," Georgette called. "Give up this hiding game. It's time for us to meet as women. Where are you? Tell me where you are, and I'll let you finish this mission successfully. *Then* we can talk about my contract."

Get out of there, Leda continued. *Chi finished his extractions and is at the oasis. He reports twenty tribal warriors converging on the ice shed.*

"Warriors are coming," she continued in a singsong. "They will find you in this . . . strange place . . ."

A shudder skimmed her voice.

"If you won't present yourself, then we're at an impasse. Fortunately, I planned for that, as well. Haruto and I only have a few questions."

Haruto's name brought a fresh wave of rage. Haruto? She'd worked *with* the Thabit tribe to locate me? Of course. Why else would she speak with Stef, whom I had a feeling Georgette must have personally known. Georgette knew I owned the Volare. If she put out inquiries to her friends in the Western tribes about me, and learned of a young woman with a Volare . . .

"Answer our questions," she continued, "and Haruto has promised to let the clannish witches return to the Southern Network. Now that, Miss Monroe, is how you bargain. Subterfuge is unnecessary! Our bureaucratic, political process is far superior to brute force."

Tyrant cackled and cackled.

Georgette's angle stoked my burning rage. How bold.

How fastidious. How absolutely ruthless. She'd engineered every bit of this. Such brutality would not go unanswered. Besides, she didn't have all the pieces. The only way Haruto would allow the other clannish witches to leave is if he found what he wanted.

Lev.

"And," she continued, downright melodic with glee, "if you come now, I'll conveniently forget that you roped the Brotherhood into helping. The Council would not be pleased with that information."

Her plan lay manifest. Georgette had gone over me, engineered control of the situation, and executed it so I'd be livid at her butting in. She'd physically and metaphorically cornered me into a situation from which I couldn't unwind without losing what I wanted.

If I ignored her, she'd sabotage the mission—already had, in some ways. If I spoke with her, that would admit my presence. My guilt was assured. She had already worked witches in the Central Network to utter outrage over me already. Either way, she tainted my career, proved her point.

If I did *anything*, Georgette won.

Rage thundered through me, then quieted. No. That wasn't entirely true. I had one other option.

"Bianca?" Georgette sang.

I can't explain now, I said to Leda, *but I'm going through the portal.*

No!

I have to.

If that is a portal, she snapped, *you will be far from fine!*

Shouts came from outside. Hands on doors, squeaking hinges. The door glided open just enough to admit a body. A hint of starlight appeared with a singular twirl of heat. Voices chattered as witches rushed inside.

Confident, Georgette called, "I know you're here, Bianca, and you're cornered." Her tone lowered, as if she spoke to the incoming witches. "Hello, yes. Greetings. Where is Haruto? Tell him to come inside and speak with me so we can finalize our exchange." She spun, calling for me again. "Oh, Bianca? It's best for the Central Network, really, for you to stop this foolishness. You're caught."

The Volare slipped to the far wall, invisible with a fresh spell. Her voice faded into many others while I lay back, wrapped my fingers around the edges, and pulled the rug around me. If traveling through a portal was anything like transportation magic, this would not be fun.

You and me, I thought to the Volare. It momentarily tightened around me in agreement, then halted. My fingers reached overhead, reaching for the blazing, magical center. Pain prickled through my fingertips, shooting down my wrist, arms, into my ribs. Ugh. This would hurt.

The shed doors burst all the way open. The silhouette of a tall witch, backlit by the bouncing light from dozens of torches, filled the doorway.

"Where is it?" Haruto shouted. "I sense the Weaver's spell. Where is she?"

Georgette scuttled, her shoes moving rapidly along the hall, seeking the main doors. She called above the melee.

"Haruto!" she called. "I'm here."

A slap, then a cry, silenced her. The thud of a body hitting the floor reverberated through the night.

"Shut up," Haruto snapped. "You're finished."

Georgette cried out.

"Take her to my tent," he commanded. "We'll hang her this evening and leave her body outside the oasis. A warning to those willing to exploit the Thabit tribe." He added in a purr, "We have what we want."

As he advanced, his leg kicked to the side. Georgette moaned in pain.

Well, Tyrant crooned, *isn't that a lovely twist of fate? You have yet another opportunity to see your enemies die. And you proved you are smarter than her. Well done.*

No, I wanted to say. *No, that isn't what I wanted either.* The words stalled. What was Georgette's fate to me? She'd brought herself into it, with willingness to see me destroyed. Another part of me—petite, ever-so-fragile, burgeoning from ashes—spoke between Tyrant's words.

She deserves it.

The profound truth stuck in a loop, preventing other thoughts.

She deserves it.

She deserves it.

Did she? Did we earn our ends? Did fate truly hand us inevitability? Georgette would shortly die a very violent death. She'd be lucky if they didn't rape her before she hung, her body bloated by the Western Network sun. Not even Lana would interfere for a Central Network Council Member who inserted herself into the Thabit oasis, for the tribes had their own law.

Georgette gambled with the devils, and lost.

What a dream, Tyrant continued, surly and vexed at my stroke of luck. *Naturally, the world bends to Bianca Monroe. It gives her the opportunity to dole out death time and time again!*

"Find the witch!" Haruto commanded. "Bring me the one with the Reigning Volare. She can die with this one."

Go, Tyrant hissed. *Go to your freedom. Touch the portal. Transport away. You have what you want, don't you? Georgette will die. Your troubles are gone. Like before, you'll have no pain on your conscience.*

Screwing my eyes shut, I attempted to think through the dissonance. The tiny voice, begging to be rid of Georgette's presence. Tyrant, insisting this wouldn't be my fault. Amidst their confusing chatter lurked another voice. I couldn't find it. Couldn't find *myself.* Not with the livid haze Georgette's betrayal inspired.

She engineered her own death at a time when I had little doubt she would have left me to my own.

This is who you are, Tyrant insisted. *This woman who doles out life and death, this woman fated to destroy her enemies. None will step in your way now. Can you imagine your return? Georgette defies you, and she dies?*

He scoffed.

I attempted to swallow past my dry throat as Haruto and others raced for me. Georgette betrayed more than me, but Gregary. The Brotherhood. The entire Central Network. The clannish witches, and Alina. The list of her own body count would be far longer than mine.

What do I do? I pleaded.

Warriors shouted, drawing closer. Chaos filled the ice shed, as loud as my own mind. *Depart!* Tyrant thundered. *Let her die.*

Amidst these, I found what I sought. The steady, quiet solace of my inner voice. The guide. The one I knew without question.

Grandfather.

There are bad witches in the world, Bianca, he had said before he died. *You are not one of them.*

You would save her, I thought.

As if he stood next to me, his voice flowed, steady and filled with love. *As would* you. *Tyrant is only fear. He is normal. He is a* choice. *Release Tyrant and those deaths he represents. You cannot take responsibility for everything. Embrace your own wisdom, and be who Bianca Monroe would be. Then, my dear, you are always strong enough.*

Haruto advanced, a stream of warriors following him. Georgette screamed again, but it was cut short after another firm smack.

Tears clouded my eyes.

I don't know if I can do this, Grandfather. To give her another chance she may not have given me.

His voice replied in a resonant echo of his final words to me. *Everything you need is right here, my dear. It is within you.*

Resolve solidified. I knew the path. The *right* path. Tears trickled out of my eyes and into my hairline.

I know who I am, I said. Tyrant's maniacal chatter stopped. *I know who I am, Tyrant, and I am not fear. I am not guilt. I do not dole out life and death. I save when I can save. The deaths in the Eastern Network were not my fault. They aren't mine to claim, nor yours to torture me with. I will not bear them. I will not.*

Tyrant sputtered, the voice incomplete. Dying. It curled into itself like churning, chuffing waves.

Nor will Georgette's death be mine.

My fingers curled into a fist, away from the beckoning portal magic. I gritted my teeth. Instead of shoving through the portal, I resolved a new, though foolhardy, plan. The irony.

To the Volare, I said, *Like the forest, I belong to you. You belong to me. Together, we'll save each other.*

A languid wave rippled through it, piercing my mind. I felt it, the Volare. The power. The loyalty. We raced away from grasping warrior hands, groping toward the Reigning Volare they sensed, but didn't see. It dumped me on the ground. I landed like a cat on my feet, crouching. It rolled up, slid into the case as I padded to the left, slinking along an ice wall. Haruto's steps banged closer.

"Where is she?"

"It's gone, Master!" a warrior cried. "The magic is gone."

"Did she enter the portal?" he hissed.

"No!"

Haruto barked commands. Bodies flooded the ice room with torches, light. Blessed light, I could *see*. I snaked around a corner along the edge, vanishing in a break that led to more blocks. Somewhere, *somewhere*, I had to find the entrance. Georgette would likely be there, or near to it.

Invisible again, I worked through the maze. Perfectly square ice blocks, stacked between a thumbs length layer of sawdust, stacked thirty paces high. They emanated cold. An open area above the shelves bled light as I searched for the door. Too many warriors raced around, seeking me. I couldn't stay down here.

My eyes rose higher.

Ah.

Over the top, it was.

Spells that made my hands and feet sticky were ideal for climbing, but they'd be useless here. If I transported, Haruto would sense it. Warriors must surround Georgette, making it unlikely I could transport to her, grab her, and go. Had they moved it?

"Where are you?" Haruto thundered.

Sucking on my teeth, I shook my head. Hovering spell it was. I'd have to vault over the top and lower to the ground quickly. *Very* quickly. After locating her, I'd transport both of us away. Surprise was my only hope. Haruto would sense my magic, even if he couldn't see me. Invisibility, hovering, and transportation at the same time? I should have practiced.

Warriors slid into view at my back, torches held aloft. I commanded the spell. My anxiety propelled the hovering magic to excessive speed. I vaulted so high, so fast, my spine slammed into the roof with a grunt. Dust shivered in a rainfall that drew Haruto's attention.

"There!" he shrieked.

Breathless, I dropped onto the top of an ice wall near the door. Cold emanated as I shoved to my feet, raced over the top, and leaped. Haruto's scream followed me.

"I sense her! At the door! At the door!"

Warriors scrambled in a panic, unable to see me as I plummeted down. Thank the good gods, Georgette was crumpled in a heap on the ground near the door, surrounded by two warriors and gasping for breath. Blood trickled from her face. She wept into her hands.

With a finesse I'd never managed before, l stopped just short of crashing on top of her. Planting my feet on either side of her body, I blasted one warrior with a violent stomach cramps curse. He doubled over, vomiting in seconds. The second received a simple, but effective, tripping curse. When he turned to help the other warrior, he face-planted on the sawdust floor.

My hands landed on Georgette's shaking shoulders the exact second I issued the transportation spell.

I gritted my teeth and threw us into the magic without a word of warning.

* * *

We landed in dust.

Empty, lonely sand.

The only sign of life under the explosive stars was a set

of footprints here and there. Baxter must be in between trips to Alina, or he also remained invisible while waiting. Georgette collapsed, sobbing half breaths. Blood trickled from a split lip, one nostril. She doubled in half, wailing. I released her the moment she landed, hovering above her to avoid footprints. Transportation, hovering, and invisibility completed—at the same time.

Again, Grandfather's memory asserted, *Everything you need is right here, my dear. It is within you.*

I see, I thought.

On my silent wish, the Volare withdrew from its container on my back. Extending my invisibility spell so Georgette didn't see it, I commanded the Volare beneath me.

Papa barked in my head, *What is this?*

A present. She betrayed us by aligning with Haruto and attempting to sabotage the mission so I could fail. Haruto was going to hang her. Don't mention that I saved her; I didn't reveal myself. Contact Leda and let her decide what to do. I surrender Georgette to her hands. I have a clannish witch to save.

The gods, he muttered.

That taken care of, I returned.

* * *

A roar welcomed me fifteen seconds after I left. Some witches claimed that transporting into mid air was possible, but it didn't work tonight. Perhaps I was too tired from navigating this confounded shed, or maybe it *wasn't* possible.

I'd returned to the same spot they'd swarmed Georgette, which wasn't what I wanted. Other witches congregated there now. The original warrior continued to vomit, the other to fall. The Volare, on the other hand, did *exactly* what I wanted.

It arrived on the other side of the shed, far from me. Gliding overhead, though invisible above the ice stacks, it toyed with the warriors in lazy, swooping curls. Recognizing the reappearance, warriors shouted not far away.

"I feel it!" Haruto called. "She has returned!"

All warriors scrambled to chase the Volare while I slipped away. I wound toward the portal, given almost free reign. Haruto's voice became more distant. Someone shouted from a more distant spot, "She's heading for the door." Warriors converged, chasing my rug.

A little longer, I promised the Volare. *Just a little longer.*

Torchlight brightened the space behind an approaching wall, where the blazing portal awaited. No one impeded my path this time. I sprinted through the ice stacks until the wall came into view again.

The equally terrible and powerful magic curled me closer, even as it repelled me. Sticky and painful, like drawing claws down my skin, it whispered. Wincing, I pressed closer. The sensation increased.

To Leda, I said, *I'm going through the portal.*

Fine. I know I'll never convince you this is madness. Good luck. Let me know if you can hear me whenever you get to . . . where you're going.

I will.

I commanded the Volare to my side again. Despite tribal witches leaping for it, their fingertips grazing the underside, the Volare leaped out of reach and zipped to my side in mere seconds. It paused at my feet.

"Bring me that Volare!" Haruto shouted.

Stepping off the sawdust, the bottom of my feet touched the Volare. I dropped, snatched one side, yanked it over me, and rolled. At the same time, I commanded the Volare forward, and it shot quickly.

I lurched to a stop.

Two hands grasped the Volare from behind. Haruto, I could *feel* his determination to have it. "Volare!" Haruto shouted. "You are loyal to your blood! Do not obey this imposter!"

For a breathless moment, I wondered: what would the Volare choose?

The rug—*my* rug— shook. The shivering movement bucked the grasping hands free and spirited me to the wall at impossible speeds. My hand slammed into the portal. It turned to jelly, then warmth, then air, and then . . .

. . . darkness pulled me all the way through.

Chapter Thirty-Two

The Volare and I dropped off an edge, plummeting into wind and tempest and pandemonium. I gripped my rug, felt the threads wrap and tighten around me as we hurried through the complete unknown.

Seconds later, my shoulder slammed into something hard. I bounced, thudding downhill. My hip bounced off another edge, throwing me through the air and onto a hard floor. The Volare attempted to counter the wild movements, removing some of the pressure, but pain ricocheted across my body regardless.

I rolled to a stop. Breath continued. My slowing heart. Pain meant I hadn't died, at least. *Leda?* I queried.

I can hear you!

Relief flowed through me. Access to Leda was a surprising boon. I must have stayed in Alkarra. *I'm through the portal. In the portal? How do these work?*

Doesn't matter. Where are you?

No idea.

Summon your map! Describe your surroundings. Give me something to work with.

Groaning, I rolled onto my back. *Give me a moment.*

The absence of aggravating magic was the next thing I noticed, and then a smell. Mold and moisture and time and rock and earth. My eyes fluttered carefully open. The Volare, cradling half of my back, gently lifted me.

Eyes peered at me.

I jolted.

A young man, poised across the way, sat with his hands on skinny knees. His wide, blank stare regarded me in pale shock. He had the slender features of a clannish witch; thin eyes, black hair, fine as spiderwebs strings. I guessed him to be no older than twenty-five.

Candles illuminated him in a circle, casting buttery lines on a cave floor. His left leg lifted, canting to the side, as if he prepared to move quickly. Dust coated his feet and ankles. Boxes stacked five or six high filled one wall. Candles spilled out of one, silk pooled on the ground from another. The others were hidden mysteries. Nothing else existed in this rock warren.

I slowly straightened to my knees, hands held out. "Common language?"

He swallowed hard, nodding.

"Yazikan?"

Another nod. He stood so smoothly the flames barely quivered.

"Bianca." I set a hand on my chest. "My name is Bianca." I repeated it in Yazikan. Based on his tilting lips, I butchered the attempt.

He mimicked my gesture.

"Lev."

Lev stood in a chamber as wide as my treehouse. Rock undulated, folding in rills and ripples that cast shadow.

Striations of darkest slate flowed with pale yellow and sepia. Boulders as long as I was tall, and tall as my hip, filled the corridor. Their odd coloring—grays and yellows and browns—made it impossible to decipher where in Alkarra we must be. Beyond Lev, I spied the blackest tunnels and corridors.

He followed my studious gaze. When our eyes met again, his clenched jaw hung loose. Curiosity filled his eyes.

I said, "Alina sent me."

Astonishment lightened his query.

"My High Priestess?"

"Yes."

I sketched the fastest briefing I'd managed thus far. From Alina's request for help, to our understanding of what the Thabit tribe did with the clannish witches they abducted. His elbows pulled into his ribs. He coiled inward like a tightening snake, ready to strike. Lev exhaled, running a hand through his loose, unwashed hair. The gesture did nothing to ease his tension.

"It's . . . much," he struggled to say.

"Yes. A lot of details."

I silenced, giving him a moment to absorb. His arms crossed his chest as he chewed on his bottom lip, considering the ground with intense focus. An attempt to summon Papa's map met with failure. I queued up the transportation spell, but nothing happened. No rise of magic, no response. Not entirely surprising. Portal magic might negate the spell. Some witches claimed that deep rock could prevent transportation as well, though I'd never been far enough underground to test it.

What's happening? Leda asked.

I found Lev.

Alina will be pleased. Can you get out?

Not sure, yet. I can't transport, nor summon.

For a portal, that makes sense. It's such powerful magic, it might override everything.

Not everything. We're speaking.

This is minimal magic in comparison, but worth noting. More likely, though, Haruto put spells up to prevent the transportation and summoning, just in case.

Good point.

Lev cleared his throat. "Thank you for coming," he said with a new resolution. "You have endangered your life to search for me, I can see."

"Thank me when I get you home," I replied wryly. "First, can anyone else come through that portal?"

His hand dismissed my fears with a careless swish.

"No. You stopped the magic."

"What?"

"It's a one-way, one-witch portal. You can only come in through that entrance." He pointed to a blank wall behind me, set above a hill of collapsed rocks I'd tumbled down. "No one else can follow until you leave the cave."

How awful for Lev, never knowing when stone would birth a stranger. *One-way, one-witch portal,* I said to Leda. *We'll have to find another way out.*

Fascinating. And good news, I suppose.

Haruto can't follow.

Through that portal. Can you tell where you are?

A definite coolness filled the room, but nothing extraordinary for a stone surrounding. The Southern Network would be far colder at this time of year. Unless Lev somehow heated it? No signs of a fire existed. Could a cave lay deep enough to avoid the cold? Would it be even colder?

Western Network, most likely. Along the western edge of the desert, there were known red-rock cliffs. The same that sprinted north, along the sea, and eventually became the Arck Castle. Witches millennia ago had chiseled the castle from their stone behemoths. I'd wager Haruto had stuffed Lev there. It made far more sense to keep Lev under tribal influence, and might also explain the yellowish-orange rock striations.

I assume the Western Network, I finally said. *It's not abundantly clear.*

Send me any details you find.

"How do we exit?" I asked Lev.

He hooked a thumb the opposite way, near the collection of shadows. "He leaves that way."

"That's good news," I murmured. "At least we have an exit. You're certain no one will come behind me?"

"I'm certain."

"Great! Let's go."

His upheld hand prevented me. "If it were that simple, don't you think I would have done it?"

The slow way he spoke arrested my haste. There was no mocking, only a simple question. Lev's smooth cheeks and rounded features had a bit of boy left in them, as if they were the last to go. Yet, an unchecked wisdom filled his eyes and prominent worry lines. An old man in a young body.

Lev looked over his shoulder with a grating, frustrated breath. "There is an obstacle I cannot face without magic. I've tried. Many times."

"What is it?"

"Enchanted sand."

"Quicksand?"

He shrugged. "In Yazikan, the word is *buchye pesti.* The sand that pulls."

Nothing the Volare couldn't easily handle. Jerking my chin to the rug, I said, "We can easily get over it."

Lev stared uneasily at the Volare and drummed his fingers along his arms with restless energy. "Alina truly sent you?"

"Yes. Me and my team are freeing all of the clannish witches taken from the Southern Network tonight."

He closed his eyes, tilted his head back, and sighed. "Thank you."

Something in his gratitude, and the obvious weight that was unburdened with it, caught me by surprise. It didn't match what I expected.

"What do you mean?" I asked slowly.

With a solemn brevity I'd never seen in someone so young, he said, "It's my fault all of them are here."

"You?"

"Me."

His assertion kicked up clouds of senseless dust. That made no sense at all. What could a young, twenty-something witch have to do with Haruto's plans for currency and overcoming the silk trade?

A twitch of Lev's hand drew my gaze to the boxes stacked along the walls. He gestured to debris along the ground. Fluffy, wispy sort of things, thin as moth wings. Shells, were they? No, not quite. Round, tubular cylinders. Shavings, I'd wager. Like a discarded caterpillar cocoon. They littered the ground. Nature's rubbish.

Understanding coalesced, gliding closer.

"Lev," I said carefully, "you're a silk witch, right?"

"Yes."

"Are those . . . is that . . ."

He met my stare. "You're trying to ask the right questions, Miss Bianca, but you don't know enough."

"Bianca," I whispered. "Please, call me Bianca."

He nodded. "Bianca." A hand swept to the fluffy chaos. "Do you see this?"

"Bug remnants?"

A chuckle followed. "Close, but not quite." He crouched. Reverently, the tips of his fingers graced the discarded husks. He murmured, "These are silk worm remnants. The creatures died."

My breath caught.

Silk worm remnants.

"Haruto and Alfea seek silk witches, like myself. But they don't know where to find the silk clans, so they sweep up clannish witches as they're able and test if they know about the silk worms. They caught me weeks ago." His nose wrinkled. "What month is it?"

"The second month of winter."

His eyes widened. "Two and a half months."

"Which is when their abductions slowed," I said, recalling what Alina told me when we first came together. *Two months ago, the abductions stopped. Thinking the problem resolved, the clans went silent.*

"Yes. They found me, a former worker in the silk clan. They brought me here, told me to make the silk worms grow, and spin, and toil. They want me to make the silk for them. Once they found me, they stopped abducting other witches, hoping I would be enough. Alas," he sighed, "I am not. They began again. They attempt to find other silk witches. In the meantime, their oasis gives them stability, and somewhere to hide their true motivations."

"Jikes."

Sorrow filled his voice, elongating his words. "I cannot do what they ask. The silk magic wouldn't allow it, even if I desired to betray my clan. There are many layers to the magic. Witches, time, conditions . . ." A spike of something like amusement laced his words, as if he were quite pleased with himself. "But they don't know that."

Gesturing to the silk worm shells, I asked, "How did

you do this?" Without magic, he couldn't have summoned them.

"I always had them with me," he whispered, and something caught in his voice. "I was the fool that left my clan. Withdrew from the protection the magic offered. Now, I've lost my magic, and perhaps my life."

My breath caught. "Have the silk witches *not* lost their magic?"

"No. We," he murmured, as if repeating an oft-recited refrain, "are not *they*."

Lev harbored an entire story behind all of this. Why did he leave the silk clan? When? Clearly, he departed before Mikhail broke the Mansfeld and doomed his witches to a magicless life.

With a nod to the littered remnants, I murmured, "You've been pretending to make it work, haven't you?"

"Attempting to, but they're catching on. I've found rocks, rolls of dirt. I make it look like I'm caring for them." He jerked his chin toward the boxes. "They bring the twigs I ask, the type of soil. I pretend that I carried silk worms with me, just in case . . ."

"You're wasting Haruto's time."

Lev spoke quietly. "I hoped they would stop searching. That they would grow discouraged with the idea when it never works. They'll stop if I can prove it's not possible."

"They'll kill you."

He pressed a fist to his breastbone. "I have accepted this fate for my clan. That is all I can do. Otherwise, Haruto desires to sell silk in the Western Network tribes, then expand. With their magic, they can overpower our market. How could we stop them? The silk witches have magic, but they won't leave to use it. The other witches in the Southern Network are slower, without the benefit of spells."

"You have demigods."

He scoffed bitterly. "The demigods cannot sense witch magic, and I believe Haruto and Alfea's plans to keep the source of the silk hidden."

"You mean that Haruto and Alfea would act as if it were from the clans?"

Lev nodded. If the magical witches in the Western tribes could take over silk routes without the buyers being aware of it, there'd be no real trail. As a diabolical idea, Haruto and Alfea had it locked down.

"They ask me many, many questions."

"Let me guess?" I said with an attempt at some lightness. "Your answers are a lie?"

Lev's smile grew. "Every word." He sobered. "Which is why they must again seek other silk witches from the clans. They assume I'm lying. I believe they think that I can't make it work and must find someone else. My life has days left, at most. When they find another silk witch, and that witch tells them something different and exposes my lies, I will be slain."

He uncurled his fingers toward me. "You came to save me, but I'm sorry, Bianca. You fell into their trap. Now we are both here, and no one can save you from Haruto and Alfea."

Blowing a raspberry, I said, "Ah, don't worry about that. I'll get us out of here."

"But . . . how?"

"Not sure, but we'll get there. It's not enough to return you and the clannish witches. We have to stop Haruto and Alfea."

Lev made a noise in his throat. I began to pace. The Volare stayed in the same spot, hovering near my waist.

"You said there is an exit?"

"Yes, but challenges." He eyed the Volare. "Haruto says there's not just one, but many. Magic is required to survive. I doubt your rug would pass through all of them."

I'd figure that conundrum out later.

"Give me a moment?" I asked. Lev nodded, gesturing around, as if to offer the entire cave to my service. He returned to his candlelit circle, moving with such easy grace that the flames barely flickered, yet again.

I resumed pacing.

Leda?

I'll have you know, she immediately sniped, *that it's been one of the most difficult trials of my life to not demand more information from you. What are you* doing? *What's happening? You haven't spoken in minutes, and it's chaos at the tribes. Well, sort of. The Brothers have it well enough in hand. They're banding together, distracting the warriors while others get the clannish witches.*

Long story, will tell you later. Have you discovered anything else about portals?

One of my Underassistants has been trying to research them, but is unsuccessful with local resources in the castle library. At least, that's what he says. Though, maybe . . .

Her responding silence rattled me. After five seconds passed without a sound, I asked, *Leda?*

I've been waiting ten minutes for you, you can wait ten seconds! she snapped. *I'm in the middle of a brilliant thought.*

Reassured, I settled in. A glance confirmed that Lev remained in the same spot, eyes closed, hands resting with open palms on his knees. Did he spend much of his life here in this position?

Was it a silk witch thing?

Leda rejoined my swirl. *Caroline refuses to leave her office to answer my questions, even at Scarlett's behest, and the Librarians and Underlibrarins still awake are searching, but don't know of any active titles. One of my Underassistants is attempting to bribe a Librarian at the Great Library of Burke. I'll let you know if he lets us into the Room of Ancient Tribal Myths and Folklore, but I'm warning you that there's not much there.*

Your Underassistants are awake?

They are now!

I grimaced. When I couldn't figure out a magical puzzle, that meant one thing. When Leda and her minions couldn't either? Something else altogether. My gaze darted overhead. *Lev has been kept in a cave, pretending he can make silk to distract Haruto and Alfea, whom Lev confirms wants to take over the silk clans.*

That . . . oddly makes sense.

Lev says there's a series of obstacles preventing his escape.

There may not be another portal to exit. It may have taken you to a cave system that you can walk out of.

I thought of that.

While I know next to nothing about portals, they're associated in my mind with chaos and tribes. I'm sorry, Bianca.

We'd have to proceed without a plan. A particular specialty of mine. Instinct compelled me forward. The longer we waited here, the greater the chance of Haruto, Alfea, or both of them cornering us, somehow.

I'm going to leave with Lev and find the exit.

Keep me updated.

How's Merrick?

Fine. He promised me not to bother you. I'm giving him updates.

Thank you.

Spinning to Lev, I asked, "Are you ready to go?"

Lev's fingers tightened around his knees.

"Now?"

"You have any other appointments?"

"N-no."

"Do you know where this exits?"

He shook his head. "Haruto or Alfea come through the wall, and leave through there." He pointed to the dark tunnel, wafting chilly darkness.

"You said there's quicksand?"

"Yes, and other challenges as well. At least, that's what Alfea once said. I didn't get far enough to see any others after trying to cross the sand. And almost dying," he added with a sour twist of his lips.

Breathing out, I nodded one. "Right. We'll take this one hurdle at a time." While I summoned a few candles from the floor—*that* spell worked, at least—and stuffed the unburnt ones into my pockets, I asked Leda a nagging question.

Any thoughts on destroying a portal?

Don't be stupid, she said coldly. *You'll be lucky to survive exiting one.*

A noise caught my ear. Lev tensed. His eyes snapped to mine. A low voice called from the twisting tunnels.

"Oh, Bianca," Haruto sang. "Where are you?"

Lev's eyes widened. We were perched birds. Not only did Haruto have all the advantage of knowing exactly where we stood, but our dead end. This cave had no way out. No transportation, no exit portal.

Unless . . .

I put a finger over my lips and mouthed, "I have a plan."

Lev nodded.

"Bianca?" Haruto crooned, closer now. We had ten seconds, at most.

Pointing to the ground, I mouthed, "Pretend you're asleep."

Lev nodded again.

I cast one hasty spell as Haruto's foot scraped the ground. Lev altered, his hair elongating, shoulders lessening, clothes morphing. Another spell altered me when Haruto trilled, "Reigning Volare, you fiend. I can *sense* your power."

I shoved Lev on top of the Volare. The transformation hadn't completed over his face, so I shoved hair over it to hide his masculine features. Dropping into the haphazard circle of candles, I slammed my eyes shut.

Haruto emerged from the dark.

"Well, well," he called. "What have we here?"

Chapter Thirty-Three

Haruto studied me, the huddled figure on the Volare, and me again. I tried not to study my curled-up double on the Volare, tucked into a ball, hair wild. Meanwhile, I resembled a skinny clannish witch with a head of messy hair and a frightened expression. At least, I hoped that's what Lev looked like whenever Haruto arrived.

I needed one chance to knock Haruto unconscious—physically, not magically, because he had all the markers of a witch that could easily overcome the spell. This situation required something with more brute force than constantly casting the same spell to subdue a witch, as I did in the Eastern Network. Haruto studied my likeness laying on the Volare.

Lev, goddess bless him, breathed in and out regularly.

Bianca? Leda inquired.

Haruto is here, I said hastily. *Can't talk!*

Haruto turned to me. "What happened?" he demanded in the common language. I strove to hear beyond him, but couldn't. Unless a witch hid or crept up, he came alone. Transformation magic didn't alter my voice to resemble Lev's, so I shrugged.

Haruto asked, "She's not dead?"

The question made no sense. Of course not. Lev breathed in and out. Frowning, I shook my head. Clearly rattled, but untrusting, Haruto rooted to the spot. His eyes narrowed, as if he suspected something off. He filled up the narrow doorway, our only exit, with his hands braced on his hips. A plethora of weapons hung from his belt. Two daggers of varying sizes, a sword.

My eyes almost bugged out.

The sword!

I hadn't transformed a replica of Viveet! She was still attached to my hip, hidden from sight by the transformation magic. If I moved, she would swing around. I had to play this oh-so-carefully.

Haruto crept forward a step, peering at Lev—but my —still form, and I assessed my chances. If he came any closer, I could ram him into the wall. There was a convenient overhang just above his left ear, perfect to bash into his head for a little nap . . .

Haruto paused.

His eyes snapped to mine, and I saw his understanding. The chance had passed. Haruto sensed the magic. His eyes dilated. He dropped into a snarling crouch. Grabbing a lit candle, I shoved to my feet as he pounced. Swinging my arm around, I slammed hot wax into his cheek. The molten stuff sprayed, splatting my arm, my neck. He screamed.

I shouted, "Up!" to the Volare.

Haruto stumbled as he attempted to scrape the wax off his burning skin. I leaned on my left leg and slammed my right into his chest. My heel connected with the bottom of his sternum, sending him crashing into the wall. His head hit stone with a loud *thud* and he fell to the ground, occupying too much space for us to sprint past.

The Volare and Lev dashed for me. Haruto, reeling, staggered to his feet with a useless cry. I sent a spell that turned the top layer of rock into water—typically used by gardeners—that Grandmother swore by for watercress. Haruto plummeted into the sloshy water with a murderous shout.

The Volare whisked us out of sight.

I clung to the back edges. Lev, pasted to the rug, closed his eyes and gripped tight. The Volare had been a strange and uncomfortable experience when I first rode, and it hadn't been in defense of my life through dark, winding passages. Haruto howled, in fast pursuit.

Removing the transformation magic from both of us bought me a little power and lessened Lev's discomfort. Away from the candles, the darkness became opaque and overwhelming, yet the Volare navigated with graceful speed.

I sent one barrier spell, attaching it near a narrow gap the Volare swept us through sideways. I hoped it stuck. A *thud* and an answering roar brought an affirming smile. It worked.

Our short time advantage dissolved seconds later. The smell of wet sand hit me like a slap. The Volare plunged down, then curled to the side, probably dodging unseen stone structures. My stomach swooped with it. Sickly air swept across my face when the Volare skidded to a fast stop, rumpling in the middle. My left eye collided with Lev's elbow.

For several seconds, I heard only rustling granules.

"What is it?" I whispered.

"Buchye pesti."

"The quicksand?"

Lev gulped in response.

The *bang, bang, bang* of Haruto attempting to overcome the barrier spell thudded closer. Using a spell, I conjured a ball of light. For caution's sake, I cast a second barrier spell behind us, where I could see the walls and reinforce it. Magic worked away from Lev's cave, at least, which confirmed Leda's suspicion.

A needed boon.

Ten paces away, a wall of sand poured in shimmering curtains. Mesmerizing and terrible, as wide as I was tall, and twice as long. A teeming pit that looked like water swirled along the bottom of the sandy drape.

Liquid sand?

Was that . . . real?

Lev's voice trembled. "Don't get too close," he whispered. "It can pull you in. Take you under."

Any idea how to get through a curtain of quicksand? I asked Leda.

Quicksand? she shrieked. *Are you mad?*

I guess that's a no.

The distant barrier cracked once, then twice. Licking my lips, I closed my eyes, reached for awareness. The sand screen in front of us was magic, which meant it could be overpowered, but . . . no. It couldn't. Too mighty for me to overcome without knowing the original grimoire or spell. With no familiarity, that plan had no hope.

Recalibrate.

I opened my eyes, clearing the senses. Another transportation test failed. Haruto must have come through the quicksand, though there had been no sign of sand on his clothes. He might have removed the sandfall and replaced it? I doubted it. This magic had complicated notes.

There had to be a simpler way. My eyes dropped. The

liquid pool was the problem, not the falling sand. That was a mere curtain. A thick one, with ample weight.

"I'll kill you!" Haruto screamed, fists thudding the second barrier. He tossed spell after spell. The clear magic wavered, forming cracks. Fury raged in his wide-eyed stare, bloodshot.

Lev cried, "We're going to die!"

"Nah." I gripped the Volare. "Just hang on tight."

I tossed the light ball into the quicksand, and it vanished. Darkness quenched the sight of Haruto's mad hammering. Lev shrieked, filled with panic, as I used a spell to adhere him to the Volare. He clung to it, sticky from the chest to the legs against the textile.

I gave the Volare my command with a thought.

I trust you.

As Haruto busted through my barrier incantation, the Volare shot upward and forward. We flipped upside down as the Volare darted directly through the sand curtain, the underside scraping the ceiling. Falling sand thudded the top, shoving us down. We lost instant height, but the Volare battled through. Sand surged to either side, filling the air. Lev screamed. I coughed. We belched out the other side.

The Volare spun, righting us, and gained momentum. I removed the sticky spell as Lev hacked, his chest pressed to the rug fibers.

"Hang on!" I shouted.

Go fast, I commanded the Volare silently. *As fast as you can manage.*

Unrestrained by lacking sight, the Volare pelted through the labyrinthine maze. Smells, air textures, noises assaulted each second. We passed a roaring waterfall, slid through thickening air, wound beyond tight, confined, thin spaces.

Movement, constant movement, became our savior.

Lev buried his head in his arms. A different spell adhered him to the rug, just in case, but there wasn't room for both of us to stick. Exhaustion crept through my mind as I attempted to hold tight, countering the Volare's rapid-fire speed.

Scuttling bugs clacked and clattered. The image of scorpions swirled through my mind. They populated the Western Network caves with abandon. If stung, their lashing poison would kill us before we saw daylight again. The Volare blazed through the creatures, unimpeded. Popping sounds crescendoed. Had the scorpions been deception spells? Another obstacle?

The exit, I thought. *Where's the exit?*

The Volare didn't change pace or speed when a blast of light appeared from behind. "You're mine!" Haruto shouted. "You'll never escape."

He closed in on us, but how? Another transportation spell faded. How far underground *were* we? Did he have his own carpet? Did he use a spell? A blighter zipped past my head, which explained the blast of light he sent. I considered what would happen if we turned off course, dropped, or Haruto overcame us. My magic wasn't entirely crippled, but I couldn't do the most important spells.

I trust you, I said to the Volare. *I know you'll get us out of here.*

Steady and quick, the Volare never altered. No speeding up, no slowing. It blazed through what might have been other obstacles—the clicking of a scorpion nest, another rush of air, fetid and foul, like a boiling underground bog. Lev quieted, gripping with steely hands, while Haruto closed in.

A speck of light appeared ahead.

My heart caught.

Sunlight beckoned, drawing Lev's eyes higher. We soared, locked in a speed game with Haruto. The Volare flew so fast tears streamed out of my eyes. Light clarified the tunnel we barreled down. It closed in, only as wide as twice my height. Pale, brown rocks littered the bottom, revealing a slight footpath. Frigid air swept toward us, glacial and blistering.

Was that snow?

The Volare slowed.

Lev cried, "What's happening?"

"I don't know!"

"We can't stop!"

Heart in my throat, I called, "I trust the Volare! Everything will be all right."

"But why are we stopping?" Lev screeched.

Haruto shouted from behind, closer than ever. The Volare lessened again. Did Haruto have control of it? No. The Volare was loyal to me. Something about this situation didn't feel right. Snow? This cave couldn't be the Southern Network. All details pointed to the West. It didn't make sense.

I closed my eyes, sensing ahead. A spell blazed at the intersection of light, frost, and air. I knew that spell. Not a portal, but a diversion. A mirage, possibly like the scorpions. We barreled closer to a false exit, thinking it was our escape. I had little doubt a solid wall existed there instead of a hole to freedom. We'd slam into it at top speed, crunched to dust. Haruto correctly assumed I'd ride the Volare to freedom from Lev's room, and conjured this genius little maze.

The Volare knew, too.

"You know," I murmured, stroking the fibers. "You are a wise and loyal friend."

We had seconds to act. Magic responded to my quick test, full and powerful and brimming. Wrapping my arms around Lev, hooking my knees around the edge of the Volare, I called. "Hang on! This will hurt."

I commanded the transportation spell. Magic surged. Haruto screamed, hand outstretched for my ankle, soaring on a rug of his own. I finalized the spell.

The illusion was a mere touch away when we zipped into magic. A scream, and a hard *thud*, escorted us from the cave.

Chapter Thirty-Four

The Volare burst out of the transportation pressure and awfulness and into sky.

So.

I *could* transport into air. On the Volare, at least. We paused midair at my mental caution. Haruto wouldn't follow. The sickening thud of his last moments resounded in my mind.

Still . . .

Satisfied, I called over the blizzard, "Take us to Alina!"

Lev cried out from the pain on his magicless body, then gasped from torrents of snow. Frozen fractals assaulted us, swirling from all sides. Wind buffeted from the left, the right. It surged under the Volare, which elongated and lifted its sides overhead in a protective cocoon.

Sobbing, Lev curled into a weak ball. I crouched over him as the Volare carefully descended. The spires of Zamok Castle appeared in the swirling blizzard, the icy front glazed with snow.

I'm out of the portal, I said to Leda. *Haruto is dead. I have Lev. I'm taking him to Alina.*

After a minute, Leda quietly said, *I've updated the others.*

The Volare descended on Alina's porch, where flurries collected as deep as my knee. We unfolded. I kept a hand on Lev's shaking shoulders as I shifted into the freezing snow and pounded on her door. Two maids popped into sight, eyes wide. They scrambled to admit us.

Return to your father's house, Leda said. *We'll debrief you there. All is fine, and the clannish witches delivered.*

The maids opened the doors.

Lev and I spilled inside.

* * *

Clannish witches huddled in Zamok Castle's main hall, shivering. Maids and butlers wound between them, delivering hot drinks, blankets, messages. Lev, ensconced in a thick blanket, spoke with a man with gray dusting his dark, short hair. The uncanny resemblance between them hinted at a relative. I hoped it was his father. He summoned a drink and offered it to Lev, whose trembling hands accepted it.

Alina's eyes flickered toward the alcove where I hid behind an invisibility spell, watching the rescued clannish witches reunite with their families. For the second time, I counted each. All accounted for.

Relief and exhaustion crept up.

The Southern Network High Priestess strolled by my hiding spot. Without changing gait, she commanded, "Come with me," so quietly I barely heard.

I trailed behind.

We entered a turret stairwell. Once in the safety of the close staircase, Alina began to speak.

"You've done it, Miss Monroe. Your team has

returned all of my clannish witches, as well as Lev, and helped me bolster a tenuous relationship with the silk witches. Not to mention many lives, and the future security of my witches. My appreciation knows no bounds. Oh, and thank you for involving Baxter instead of Tipa."

Amused, I asked, "Have you told Tipa?"

"She's aware."

Her lofty response left something to be desired, but I was too exhausted to read into it. The blizzard unleashed a particularly high-pitched screech that unnerved me, and I wanted to go home.

Alina opened a wooden door with a point at the top. She ushered me inside a room filled with burgundy and copper tones. Window panes dusted with snow looked out on the rampaging sky, stories overhead. The whirling storm made it impossible to see the ground. Alina motioned to the sconces.

"If you please?"

I cast a spell. Light bounded to life on each candle in a breathy wind, illuminating wooden bookshelves filled with trinkets, a wide desk of darkest mahogany, and stacks of parchment and quills.

I spun in the middle of it. "Your office, I presume?"

She gifted me with a rare smile.

"I thought—"

"You think a lot, Miss Monroe." More soberly, she asked, "Is there anything I need to know? Lev gave me a very hasty story while getting patched up. "

I was tempted to sink into a chair, although she hadn't invited me. But I didn't because I knew that the moment I let my body relax, I wouldn't rise. Alina and I might have a sort of friendship, but that didn't make an overnight stay wise. Besides, the Brotherhood awaited.

I rubbed a hand over my face, sketching through most of the details. "I'm happy to answer more in-depth questions later, particularly after you question all the clannish witches and Lev."

"You're satisfied that Haruto is dead?"

"Yes. I can confirm it tomorrow by transporting to the spot, if you like."

"No. Your assurance is all I require. We can consider this matter settled, thanks to the Sisterhood."

Other factors lingered. What of Alfea, Haruto's partner? The tribe leaders? Was this really an end to the raids? I didn't know the state of the Thabit tribe after the Brotherhood finished the mission, so I kept my mouth shut.

Deductions later.

Alina laughed, a breathy thing. "Go home, Bianca. I have it under control here. You've earned your rest. My payment will not be many days behind you."

* * *

Seeing the team gathered at Papa's, ragged, a little bloody, and hungry though they were, soothed my rattled nerves.

All my struggling energy regained itself when Merrick shot to his feet, yanked me into his arms, and held me for a full minute. Maybe two. As our hearts synced in the same beat again, my knees turned to water. I leaned on him.

He pulled away.

"You're all right?"

"Fine."

Smiling, he said, "You smell like a bog."

I huffed a laugh, sank into the chair, and smiled at Papa. Merrick stood at my back, hands protectively on my shoulders. Papa nudged me as he slipped by, his heart in his eyes. Leda, across the table, gave a tired smile.

You made it, she said.

I met her eyes. *Thank you.*

A nod was a sufficient reply.

Grandfather's missing presence loomed in the room like a forgotten heartbeat. He would have advanced on me at this point, arms outstretched, tea tray at his side and sustenance in the wings. I missed him, but soaked up the comfort from Papa, Merrick, and the other Brothers. They waited with undisguised curiosity.

Gregary didn't join us.

Rognvald captured my stare. *Gregary came to me with a full confession after we finished with the clannish witches. I'll deal with him later.* His nose twitched, hiding a pained expression.

Is there mercy to give? Georgette put him in a very difficult situation, and he tried to alert me. He went to the clannish witches as soon as he could.

To my surprise, Rognvald said, *I hope so, but I don't know yet.*

I nodded.

Finally, I could relax. The tendrils of worry that connected me to the mission expired. Like birds in flight, responsibility vanished. The weightless feeling left me giddy, like I'd drunk too much wine.

Sighing, I said, "There's explaining to do."

Regina cried, "But first, hot food and drinks will do you some good. The Brothers can update you on their side while you eat. These louts have already demolished three loaves of fresh bread and butter and are still ravenous." She shot me a private smile. "I know you don't care for tea, but Marten would have recommended this particular blend. It's the last of his stash."

The smell of blended lavender and chamomile, Grandfather's favorite, reached my nose. Tears collected in my eyes. Merrick's warm hands squeezed my shoulders.

"Thanks Regina," I whispered. "Hot tea sounds just right."

Chapter Thirty-Five

Leda and I stood outside the old Thabit oasis, staring into the ruined husk of what used to be. Days after Haruto's death, the entire expanse had been abandoned. No more magical trees, cluttered tents, protesting camals. The fountain lacked a magical source, thus diminished to sand. Only a handful of trinkets and thousands of footsteps scoured by the desert wind testified that anyone once lived here.

"It seems strange to see such . . . emptiness," Leda murmured.

"Like bones."

"Forgotten bones. What will the Thabit tribe do next, you think?"

"No idea."

The haunting words carried in the wind, whisked from our lips. The desert had her beauty, scrubbed free and wide-open to sky, but I longed for my forest. A slow ride on the Volare through the boughs would restore my tipping imbalance. I pointed to where the ice shed once stood. Mere sand piles now, it held nothing of its former magical strength.

"That was the shed." My arm swung to the left. "That was Haruto and Alfea's campfire. I entered the shed here." Farther out, I gestured. "The portal was there."

Leda followed each movement with pert lips and cutting eyes, studying the contours and hollows of the sand. She wanted to put the mission together in her head.

"It's interesting coming in after the fact."

"Confusing?"

"No. It . . . it helps. I can't see what it was really like here, with all the structures gone, but . . . I get it. Next time, if we can, I'd like to see the mission site before I need to navigate from afar."

"Good idea. When we can, we shall."

Peering around, she asked, "Where did your father and Regina wait?"

I waved to the east. "Over there."

She nodded, spun a circle, and came to rest with her skirts swirling her knees. Snow fell lazily back at home in direct opposition to this brutal heat, where high pink color rose on her cheeks, experienced without the benefit of shady leaves. Her lunch break would end soon.

"We can return," she said. "Thank you."

Before she could leave, I asked, "Do you have news on Georgette?"

The uncomfortable topic sat on hot coals in my stomach. After telling the full story during the mission debrief at Papa's, I'd avoided speaking about her. What purpose did it serve? The betrayal still cut deep. Leda had immediately turned Georgette over to Scarlett when Papa contacted her. The High Priestess had been *dealing with the situation* for the last several days.

Best I could tell, Georgette retreated to her personal estate and hadn't left. Armed Guardians guaranteed she didn't. Apparently, Aurora built up an extensive array of evidence proving that Georgette overstepped her bounds by speaking on behalf of the *Central Network* instead of just Chatham City, even as she extended her rallies outside her covens and into Ashleigh Coven. An egregious overstep of her power.

Many legal ramifications would follow.

The situation Georgette created was far from simple, nor was Aurora's response. She'd been working through the intimate details of Georgette's plans, the different articles and statements that could be taken as open rebellion against Scarlett, and the nefarious blackmail against a Protector. Her extensive work built a picture that no witch could unwind from.

Whatever Georgette unleashed on me would soon return to fall upon her own head.

Fourfold.

Leda suggested giving the truth to the Central Network: holding a rally, during which Georgette's actions would be laid bare. Neither Scarlett nor myself felt comfortable with the ramifications. It threw attention onto Alina and the plight of the Southern Network and brought the Sisterhood out of hiding. Not to mention highlighting yet another corrupt Council Member that went too far. The Brotherhood also felt the effects, since Gregary had been part of her devious plan.

Yet, Scarlett wasn't satisfied with Georgette not bearing the full weight of her responsibility. I didn't envy Scarlett's difficult position. Whatever she decided, Georgette would lose her position as Council Member.

Leda pinched her lips together as she considered my question. Determination filled her expression. "Yes, I do have news about Georgette. She's standing before the

Council in two hours with a full confession of her guilt, which is something she offered. *After* Aurora had a chat with her," Leda added, smiling slyly.

My mouth dropped.

"A full confession?"

A decisive nod replied. "After she confesses in full, Scarlett is allowing the Council to discuss what they feel should happen with Georgette before she makes a decision. The Council advocated for greater involvement with Network ruling, so they can help deal with their fellows. Two birds, one stone."

Blinking, I murmured, "But . . . that could mean anything. Many of them followed Georgette."

Leda's lips twitched with a smile. "Oh, I'm not worried about them. Considering that Council Member Clare has just been instituted as the new Voice of the Council in Georgette's place, I think the odds are in our favor."

Clare would be happy, and perhaps she'd earned an opportunity to wield her own power. Far from comforted, I said, "I see."

"I've listened to almost every interaction Scarlett and Georgette have had since Georgette's betrayal. Georgette suspects, but has no proof, that you were in the ice shed. Beyond Gregary speaking about you, of course, but he has discredited his own testimony by his removal from the Brotherhood."

I winced. Rognvald removed Gregary a few days after our debriefing, and said nothing more about it to me. I hadn't asked for details, and Merrick proffered only, *Gregory is leaving the Brotherhood and receiving a chance to patch up his family as a result. His wife is . . . open to discussion. It's for the best, even if shrouded in betrayal.*

Returning to Leda's former point, I clarified the most important part.

"Georgette doesn't know I saved her?"

Leda snorted. "She knows. She won't admit it. In my opinion? It's killing her, knowing you silently saved her and still haven't crowed about it. It's . . . sublime." She laughed, an airy thing. "The whole debacle has left Georgette looking like an unstable shrew seeking vengeance. In the end, you were right. Staying completely out of it was the right path."

"I didn't know," I retorted. "I didn't *know* it would be the right path at the time. I was . . . surviving. Just trying to get through each day."

"Your instincts," she added with persuasive force, "are top notch, Bianca. That's all I'm trying to say."

After a few moments to think through all she revealed, I chortled. "Clare as Voice of the Council. How bold the irony."

"Indeed."

Leda brushed her hair over her shoulder. "Well, Georgette is not your problem anymore, and that's that. Nothing has surfaced in the *Chatterer* about the Brotherhood in the West, nor the Sisterhood. We managed to slide under general awareness, as desired."

"Wonderful."

The first moment of true relief followed her report. These handful of days, I'd been gripping my breath. Now, I could accept that the mission was well and truly over. Not just Alina's request, but Georgette, life after Grandfather. All the questions came together in something like a neat little knot. I settled into peace, grateful for an end.

"Where's Merrick?" she asked. "Wasn't he going to come with us today?"

"Rognvald tasked him with something in Custos City.

Said he wanted eyes on some of the escalating issues Lana is having with the tribes. Something about protests in a marketplace near the Arck Castle."

She frowned. "That's not our business."

"The protesting tribe lives along the Borderlands when they aren't trying to destroy Custoas, and has been known in the black market. He wants to keep an eye on them in case they return to the Borderlands."

"Fair. We never found Alfea, either. The Brotherhood searched, in case she tries to subvert the silk clan again."

The Thabit tribe left with little trace. I had no desire to see them again, nor seek them out, so I let them dissipate into gauzy smoke in my memory. If I never heard Alfea's voice again, it would be too soon.

Eager to turn the subject, I asked, "How is Hiddleston?"

She pointedly ignored me. "I'm not sure."

"You're not?"

"No."

"Can we—"

"No." Her firm insistence, tinged with desperation, shocked me. "No, I don't want to talk about it."

"Have you broken up?"

Leda sucked in a breath. "I . . . I don't know. There's more to this story than you think, and I'm not ready to say it." More quietly, she asked, "Please."

Nodding, I said, "Of course. Whenever you're ready." To take mercy on her, I turned topics again. "Remember that list of letters we received after Georgette's first swing at me? The ones requesting help?"

"Why yes," she drawled, stuffing all signs of pain aside. "I know that list quite well."

"Where is it?"

"In my apartment."

"Oh?"

Her smile brightened. "They're safe, stacked in a drawer, listed in order of when I think you should contact the originator. There are a few jobs in there that I think you'll find very interesting." More seriously, she added, "Whatever Georgette, the Council, or the Network thinks, the Sisterhood is far from dead."

Energy infused me again. The Sisterhood was very much alive and ready to do good in the world.

"Let's go home," I said, grateful to leave this behind.

The mission was done.

Epilogue

The shieldmaker was a wizened old woman with a habitual smile, crinkled eyes, and a giggly nervous habit. She stood as tall as my elbow, as round as she was short. Her gray skirt danced over her quick feet as she whirled a circle around me. When she tapped on my elbow, I elevated Viveet, whose brilliant blaze danced high and happy.

The witch cooed, small eyes alight with the sapphire flame.

She stated something I couldn't understand. With a wave of her hands in my face, she brought both arms to her side. Understanding the silent command, I sheathed Viveet. The shieldmaker touched Viveet's handle, withdrew her slightly, and studied the warbling leaf design.

With another babbling comment I couldn't hope to understand, she toddled away. Lips curled to hold in my giggle, I watched her slide behind a counter as tall as her. Crashing sounds followed.

I didn't dare move from my spot. After following Alina's directions, I hadn't seen the shieldmaker's cottage at first, as it was perched in a low area on the tundra. Only after I had arrived at the edge of the drop, saw the stairs cut into the snow, did I notice the piping chimney and cozy arrangement.

Standing here, looking at glimmering shields every bit as elaborate and magical as Viveet, I had so many questions. No rumors of a shieldmaker existed in Alkarra. No one spoke of her shields or her work. There was no name attached to her, like Andrei. Simply a woman, in her cottage, in the vast tundra.

An interesting antithesis to Andrei, the swordmaker.

While she hummed and bobbed and tossed and sang, I sent Merrick a message through the magic. He didn't reply right away. After I finished inspecting a shield with a lovely, warbling filigree that reminded me of Camille, Rognvald spoke to me.

Have you heard from Merrick?

No. Have you?

He didn't reply.

The shieldmaker tripped to my side, catching herself before she fell, and held up an elegant shield. My breath caught. The piece of work was beyond what I could have dreamed. In it, I finally saw what I'd been attempting to articulate to other shield makers, but didn't have the words for.

My eyes widened. The design along the edges exactly mimicked the vines along Viveet's length. Letum ivy. A hint of sapphire wound through when the shield hit the light just right. I reached for it; the shieldmaker released it.

The moment my fingers touched the metal, the blue seams sparked to life. I sucked in a low breath. The shield seemed to reach out for me, curl me closer, as if it had been waiting. Like Viveet, I heard no words, but I felt a connection.

A grasp.

"You," the shieldmaker breathed, a finger pointed at my chest. She motioned to the shield. "Veyrin."

"Veyrin," I murmured.

Color blazed off the shield when I said its name. In her sheath, Viveet rattled, When I pulled her free, fire blazed. Veyrin slid onto my arm, light as a feather. It peaked in the middle of the top, then tapered to a point on the bottom. Covering me shoulder to waist, it felt as if I held nothing at all.

I met the shieldmaker's stare. "Mine?"

She smiled, gave a nervous chuckle, and stepped back. Both arms waved up and down, encompassing me, Veyrin, and Viveet. My old shield, which I had loved because it taught me how to step into swordwork and learn, had never touched me like this magic-born shield.

So many questions flooded me, but I couldn't ask. Perhaps that was for a reason, because whatever the woman said, it was no known language in Alkarra. She babbled, and perhaps the babbling itself protected her, and this cottage.

This special, hallowed place.

Gripping Veyrin tight, I whispered, "Thank you."

The shieldmaker bowed, hands steepled in front of her.

And then I was gone.

The house, the shields, the crackling fire, the tundra disappeared around me, as if someone had taken a boot to my back and shoved me out. Blinking, I stood on the Wall at Chatham Castle, where I'd been before I went to visit Alina. Where Merrick had kissed me goodbye, promised to see me for dinner, and departed for his mission as Rognvald ordered.

Rognvald? I inquired.

In the Gatehouse, he growled. *There's a . . . situation.*

Plowing inside, I stumbled on Papa, Rognvald, Chi, and Tysen grouped together. Lines crossed their forehead. Papa started toward me, then paused. He blinked, staring at the shield.

"What is—"

"What's wrong?" I demanded. Their halting expressions told me more than Merrick's enduring silence. He still hadn't responded.

Rognvald motioned to Papa, who cast him a wary, questioning look. "Go ahead," Rognvald muttered.

"Papa?"

Thank the goddess for Papa, who didn't mince words or soften anything. "Merrick is missing."

"What?"

"He went to the West—"

"I know. He only left a few hours ago."

"He should have been back," Rognvald said, "It was a quick hour trip, at most. Intelligence gathering. He stumbled into a problem, he said, and was observing, right before we stopped hearing from him. I asked him what came of it half an hour ago, and he hasn't responded."

Chi drew my attention when he whispered, "I went to Custos City, and he's not there. There's no sign of him, but . . . there was a fight. A bloody one. Many witches lay slaughtered in the sand."

My heart hammered. "He's not one of them, right?" I demanded, stepping closer to Chi. "He's not—"

"No. I've confirmed twice. Tysen also confirmed it. We've found no familiar magical signature nor trace of him."

Rognvald's nose twitched. "We're making a plan to return with a team and. . ." But his words drawled off when a letter appeared in the air above me and drifted lower. The Gatehouse seemed to hold its breath as the letter descended, hovering before my eyes. My name scrawled on the front in a handwriting I didn't recognize.

I snatched the letter, tore through the wax, and began to read.

Bianca,

You took mine, I take yours.

Alfea

A cold chill swept me from head to foot, prickling my veins in an ice bath. I read it twice, breathing fast, while Papa read over my shoulder. He put his arm around me, passed the letter to Rognvald. Words passed through Papa's lips, but I didn't hear them. Rognvald replied, and a storm of ideas and plans barreled into the Gatehouse.

My mind couldn't ungrasp the words.

You took mine, I take yours.

No.

This couldn't be happening. This couldn't—

It could.

Alfea escaped, like many tribal witches, during the removal of the clannish witches and the subsequent rising of tribal warriors. The Brothers reported that most women and children left when the warriors arose, as was their usual way when fighting in the desert.

Before I could possibly fathom what to do next, could wade through the disbelief and panic, another letter descended.

The Gatehouse fell quiet as I ripped it open.

Bianca,

Meet me in my office immediately. I have informa-tion on your husband. Do nothing *else and speak to no one. The opportunity to do so will come after we have discussed this volatile situation.*
Come alone.

Lana

I handed the letter to Papa and calmly whispered, "Don't follow me."

About the Author

Katie Cross is ALL ABOUT writing epic magic and wild places. Creating new fantasy worlds is her jam.

When she's not hiking or chasing her two littles through the Montana mountains, you can find her curled up reading a book or arguing with her husband over the best kind of sushi.

Visit her at www.katiecrossbooks.com for free short stories, extra savings on all her books (and some you can't buy on the retailers), and so much more.

9 781946 508997